LOVE BY THE BOOK

OTHER NOVELS BY
CARA LYNN JAMES INCLUDE

Love on Assignment
Love on a Dime

LOVE BY THE BOOK

A
Ladies of Summerhill
NOVEL

CARA LYNN JAMES

THOMAS NELSON
Since 1798

NASHVILLE   DALLAS   MEXICO CITY   RIO DE JANEIRO

Published in Nashville, Tennessee, by Thomas Nelson. Thomas Nelson is a registered trademark of Thomas Nelson, Inc.

Thomas Nelson, Inc., titles may be purchased in bulk for educational, business, fund-raising, or sales promotional use. For information, please e-mail SpecialMarkets@ ThomasNelson.com.

Scripture quotations taken from the Holy Bible, King James Version.

Publisher's Note: This novel is a work of fiction. Names, characters, places, and incidents are either products of the author's imagination or used fictitiously. All characters are fictional, and any similarity to people living or dead is purely coincidental.

Library of Congress Cataloging-in-Publication Data

James, Cara Lynn, 1949–
  Love by the book : a ladies of Summerhill novel / Cara Lynn James.
    p. cm. — (Ladies of Summerhill ; 3)
  ISBN 978-1-59554-681-4 (trade paper)
  1. Guardian and ward—Fiction. 2. Newport (R.I.)—Fiction. I. Title.
  PS3610.A4284L64 2011
  813'.6—dc22   2011010637

Printed in the United States of America

11 12 13 14 15 16 RRD 6 5 4 3 2 1

To my young grandson, Damian Lott,
who always brings a smile to my heart.

PROLOGUE

NEW YORK CITY, JANUARY 1901

M elinda's sharp intake of breath shattered the silence.
All eyes turned toward her, but Melinda could do nothing but stare at the attorney. Had she misheard her sister's
will? Or had he misread it? How could Cora leave her daughter to
Melinda's care—as well as Nick's? She couldn't imagine.

Cora had never mentioned such an odd arrangement, but then
again her sister normally avoided unpleasant subjects. A wave of
panic swept through Melinda. No one loved Nell more than she.
No one. But being a mother was far different from being the doting
aunt . . .

Attention shifted from her to Nick. Seated at the other end of
the semicircle of family members, Nick's blue-gray eyes were still
wide with shock.

The minutes dragged by until finally, mercifully, Mr. Ricker
concluded the reading and dismissed the others. Nick immediately
rose and walked over to join them.

Mr. Ricker cleared his throat and spoke in a hushed tone. "You
both seem surprised by the custody situation. But let me assure
you, Mrs. Parker Bryson insisted you two share guardianship—for

reasons of her own." He looked from Melinda to Nick, frowning. "I understand that arrangement might be somewhat unconventional, but she knew you two would see it through. It is what Cora and Parker desired for Nell."

"Of course," Melinda answered politely, though she feared their unconventional arrangement would cause innumerable problems. Nick appraised her with a cool, sweeping glance. Taken aback by his attitude, she twitched a small smile, but it did precious little to soften his austere demeanor. Where was the gentleman who usually hid his feelings behind a chilly, but always courteous, smile?

"First we'll need to make living arrangements for the child," Mr. Ricker said.

Melinda nodded. "My mother and I are happy to care for Nell. I couldn't bear to be apart from her. Of course Mr. Bryson can visit her as often as he wishes."

Nick shook his head. His dark brown eyebrows drew together in a frown and she recoiled at the fierceness in his eyes, as gray and stormy as the north Atlantic. "My brother told me he wanted me to bring up Nell," he grumbled, "with my family's help." He raised a hand to silence the attorney when Mr. Ricker opened his mouth to speak. "I know, I know. Since Parker passed away first, Cora's wishes supersede his. Still, I'm shocked and disappointed that Cora didn't leave me sole guardian. Melinda, I hope you see Parker's wisdom, and relinquish full custody to me."

She swallowed a gasp, then paused for a moment to regain her composure. "I'm sorry, Nick, but that's out of the question. I'd also prefer sole custody of Nell."

"Think about it for a moment, Melinda. Do you truly see yourself as a mother?"

"Do you truly see yourself as a father?" she returned. Of all the nerve—the man was pushing her to be most crass and disagreeable!

Mr. Ricker said, "It's certainly understandable that both of you want to bring up the child by yourself, but I'm afraid that's impossible. You must compromise in order to abide by Mrs. Bryson's wishes."

Nick sighed and raised his palms in reluctant surrender. "All right. I propose we split Nell's time between our two households, six months in each."

Melinda nodded, though her hands moistened with perspiration inside her black gloves. "I suppose that's a fair solution, but it's like dividing her in half. I really believe she'd be better off residing with just my mother and me. She needs one stable, permanent home."

Nick's full lips thinned. "I refuse to argue under these sad circumstances."

Melinda blushed and then nodded. "You're right. Somehow we'll make this all work out—for Nell's sake."

His icy stare finally broke. "I have business in England, so I'll be gone for some time. You can take the first six months. You're still very young, so if you find the task too difficult, my sister Florrie can help you."

Still very young. Heavens, could he *be* more condescending? She was almost twenty-three! "Thank you for the kind offer, but I'm sure I'll be perfectly capable of caring for a three-year-old." Heat spread from Melinda's tightly collared neck into her cheeks. He never failed to bring out her worst qualities and most childish behavior. And now she had to deal with him far more often than before.

His half bow suggested acquiescence, but it was still laced with condescension. "Yes, if you're sure you're ready for the task. When I return from Europe in the summer, I'll contact you to arrange for Nell's transition to my own care for a time. Is that all right with you? Are we in agreement?"

"Yes, of course." Yet every nerve ending quivered with apprehension. What if he tried to take Nell away through some legal manipulation? Melinda knew the Brysons never hesitated to use their financial and social powers to impose their will. But surely he wasn't that cruel, just obligated. Obligated to raise his brother's child and keep her safely tucked within the Bryson fold.

And sweet little Nell deserved far more than chilly relatives raising her out of some sense of duty.

Mr. Ricker strode to his desk and returned with a sealed envelope. He handed it to Melinda. "This is from your sister. She asked me to give it to you in the event of her death."

"Thank you." Melinda hurriedly stuffed the letter in her reticule. "I shall read it when I get home." She'd gotten this far; she wasn't ready to do anything that might reduce her to tears in front of the stalwart Nick.

HOURS LATER, WHEN she and her mother were alone in their Fifth Avenue mansion, Melinda pulled out the note with a trembling hand. Certainly Cora's letter would offer an explanation for her strange decision to split guardianship. Mama sat on a wing chair near the drawing room fireplace, her face nearly as white as the newly fallen snow. She'd been too distraught to attend the reading of Cora's will and had stayed home to rest.

Melinda cleared the emotion clogging her voice and read aloud.

My dearest sister, please share this note with Mama. I do hope and pray you will never have to read a word of this. I am in perfect health and expect I shall remain that way. But if the Lord takes me while my sweet Nell is still a child, and Parker as well, I want you to understand why I designated you her coguardian.

Parker believes that Nick should raise Nell by himself since he's a wealthy and responsible man.

Melinda winced. She'd overheard enough gossips' cutting comments to know many considered her flighty. She suspected the

Brysons might be among her detractors, especially old Mr. Bryson, Parker and Nick's formidable father.

"Go on, Melinda," her mother urged.

But I believe you are the right person to provide a happy home for my darling little girl. With your joyful, carefree ways, you'll bring her the same delight and pleasure you've given me since our childhood. I trust you to instill in Nell proper values, and a love for the Lord.

Parker insists you share guardianship because he believes Nick will be a steadying force. If you give him half a chance, dear sister, I believe you'll find Nick to be a shrewd and yet thoughtful man. Please don't allow his serious and sober attitude to dampen Nell's joy of life—or your own. Help him as he will help you.

Melinda wiped away tears with a linen handkerchief trimmed in black and stared over to her mother. "She knew that Nick might be a problem. And yet she did it anyway."

"Yes, she did," Mama said. She looked to the window, eyes glassy with tears. "But if she had not . . ." Her voice broke. "Then we'd have none of our Cora left, would we?"

ONE

❦

JULY 1902

Melinda Hollister burst through the front doorway into the foyer of her New York mansion. "Do be careful with those packages," she cautioned her maid. Cecile stumbled right behind, laden with boxes and parcels precariously balanced and piled almost as high as her head. Before an oval hatbox thudded to the marble floor, Mr. Harders, the butler, grabbed it and placed it carefully at the foot of the wide stone staircase.

"Thank you so much. There's a splendid porcelain figurine in that box, so I'm most grateful you caught it in time." Melinda nodded toward the middle-aged servant. "If you'd bring all these things to my sitting room, Cecile can take over from there."

As Melinda unpinned her straw hat trimmed with silk violets and matching tulle, the double doors to the drawing room opened wide and her mother gracefully stepped across the threshold. Still in black crepe, Mrs. Hollister glided across the waxed floor, her face appropriately solemn. A twinge of conscience unsettled Melinda. Perhaps she should have continued wearing black a few weeks longer, though it wasn't necessary to extend mourning for a deceased sister beyond the sixth month. Melinda liked feeling young and alive and nonfuneral once again.

Her mother's eyebrows knit in a frown when she glanced at the dozen boxes and packages on their way upstairs. "Will you join me for tea, my dear?"

Melinda nodded. "Of course, Mama. I'll tell you all about my shopping trip. Wait until you see the angel figurine I bought and the lovely hats. They're the latest fashion directly from—"

"I'm sure they are," Mama interrupted, gesturing forward.

Melinda frowned and followed the older woman into the drawing room. The day's splendid purchases had lifted her spirits. But she regretted her insensitivity. Perhaps Mama was not yet ready to rise from her grief—Melinda understood that too.

Mama rang for their refreshments before she settled onto the stiff settee covered in jade green brocade. It was several shades lighter than the curtains that flanked the tall, multipaned and partially raised windows. Golden sunlight flooded the spacious room along with a warm, summer breeze. Melinda dropped down beside her mother, happy to sit after hours of scouring her favorite shops. She wished she could kick off her new boots that pinched her feet.

After the tea and small cakes arrived, Mama poured from a silver pot and handed her daughter a delicate china cup. Melinda declined any sweets, afraid her tight corset might split open.

"I'm so anxious to show little Nell the beautiful dress and bonnet I found for her. She'll look adorable." Melinda loved to pick out frilly clothing for her niece. Who cared how impractical ruffles and lace might be for a youngster?

Mama nodded without her usual enthusiasm. She sipped the steaming tea and then placed her cup on the marble-topped table. "We must talk."

Melinda laughed. "Of course. That's why I'm here." She really ought to control her effervescence; Mama seemed even more distressed than usual.

"Mr. Morton, my attorney, paid me a visit this afternoon."

Mama took a deep, unsteady breath. "He gave me some disturbing news." She paused and her lower lip quivered. For the first time Melinda noticed the lines around her mother's perfectly shaped lips seemed deep. "He insists we economize immediately."

Melinda let her teacup clatter to the saucer. No one she knew *economized*, unless . . . She swallowed hard. "Are you quite certain that Mr. Morton used that term? Or was he merely expressing some caution?"

"No, Melinda," Mama said, staring over at her. "He was most clear."

Agitated, Melinda rose to her feet and a few drops of tea splashed on her pearl gray walking suit. She quickly set her cup on the table. "But, Mama, that doesn't sound right. Papa left us a fortune when he passed."

"That was five years ago. We've spent most of it."

"Surely not. Mr. Morton must be mistaken. Or perhaps you misunderstood."

But Mama's silent response told her she disagreed.

Melinda paced in front of the mantle, trying hard to think of a solution, in case one was truly necessary. But disjointed thoughts slammed into the corners of her mind and broke apart. "There must be something else we can do instead of, of . . . economizing. Did he offer any other suggestions?"

"Yes, a few. He said we must sell this mansion and move into a smaller home. And let most of the servants go. We need to sell all but one of the carriages."

"Oh my. Oh my! We really are poor." Suddenly drained of energy, Melinda dropped onto the settee again.

"Yes, I'm afraid so, but we must not let anyone know." Mama took a bite of cake and then continued. "This is all my fault. Mr. Morton warned me your father left less money than we expected. And he strongly encouraged me to invest what we had in safe stocks and bonds. But I chose to spend it instead."

Melinda felt nausea roil her stomach. "If I'd known, I'd have been more careful with our money."

"If we hadn't bought our costumes from Paris and kept up appearances," Mama said, "society would've dropped us long ago. I couldn't allow that to happen."

Melinda nodded. "There's truth to that." Their fall would've come a few years earlier and ruined her chances for a good marriage. Melinda drew out a sigh. "I suppose I must return most of my purchases, except for Nell's new frock. I can't bear to send it back."

"I don't suppose one child's dress would hurt. But starting now we must be frugal."

Melinda nodded. She'd keep the cunning hat, but return the exquisite figurine. Since she had no other choice, she'd comply. And without complaint. Poor Mama didn't need a whiny daughter to add to her troubles.

"Do you think I should sell my blue diamond necklace for some extra money?" Melinda held her breath, hoping her mother would discourage her from taking such a drastic step.

"No, you're not to sell your jewelry. You'll need to wear all of it this summer."

Melinda smiled with relief. "Thank you, Mama."

They sat silently for several seconds. The answer to their problem hovered in the air between them, sparking like an electric current. "I assume I must marry someone rich," Melinda murmured, "without delay."

Then her mother could buy a modest, less fashionable residence and not lose her social status. She could claim their Fifth Avenue mansion was much too large for just one person and most would accept her reasoning without too many questions. Neither one wanted their friends to gossip. Or pity them. Or even worse, ignore them.

Melinda said, "I don't object to marriage in principle. But I'm not quite ready for such an important step."

"You're twenty-three, my dear." Her mother spoke softly. "You're not a debutante any longer. I've never pressed you to settle down because you so enjoyed all the dances and parties. But you must accept your duty to marry well."

Melinda's wince quickly vanished. "I understand. So if the Lord sees fit, I shall find a husband." She'd hoped for a few more years of fun and frivolity, but perhaps she'd wished for too much now that she was Nell's coguardian. Melinda cocked her head. "I don't expect we can afford to summer in Bar Harbor or the Berkshires. Certainly not Newport. They'd be the best resorts to find a spouse."

Mama sighed. "I'm afraid they're all too expensive."

"Then I must visit a friend."

A hot and humid summer in New York City held no appeal for anyone with even a little money, while a season spent at a resort sounded delightful. She'd hoped for an invitation from one of her friends, but so far none had come. Everyone, no doubt, thought she'd choose to mourn awhile longer. *Or perhaps "Out of sight, out of mind" and all that.*

"I shall write Louisa Davenport and Clarice Carter today and pray they'll send an invitation."

"Perhaps that won't be necessary." Mama drew a letter out of a hidden pocket and handed it to Melinda. "The return address says Summerhill, Newport, Rhode Island. I believe that's where Nicholas Bryson is staying with his sister and brother-in-law."

Melinda sucked in her breath. They'd been awaiting word from Nick for weeks now—half hoping he'd forgotten about Nell, half wishing they could just get it over with. The pain of letting the little girl go would be horrifying; anticipating it coming any day was excruciating. Without waiting for a letter opener, Melinda tore open the envelope with her finger. "It's from Florrie Van Tassel."

Flora Bryson Van Tassel was Nick's sister, who had to be about thirty-five but appeared ten years older. Melinda scanned the page of heavy cream stationery and squinted at the spidery writing. "It's an invitation. Her father has rented a cottage for the season. They're inviting Nell and me to Summerhill for July and August. Of course you're welcome as well, Mama, but she says she understands if you're still in mourning and unable to accept. She also mentions how much she misses Nell."

"You must go. This is the best news we've had in ages." Mama smiled faintly but with satisfaction. "Not only do you get a few more precious weeks with Nell, but you'll also be in the summer capitol of the nation, a prize to be eagerly accepted. At once."

Melinda nodded as she returned the letter to its envelope. "I suppose it's excellent news, but I'm not anxious to see Nick again. I doubt he'll be thrilled to see me either." She sighed. "Well, Nell and I shall enjoy our summer by the sea regardless of whether Nick Bryson wants me there or not. I've been invited and I shall gladly go." She flicked a smile, but she wasn't anywhere near as optimistic as she sounded.

"Good, then that's settled. Mr. Morton insists we put the house up for sale by September at the latest. Then I'm afraid everyone will know of our reduced circumstances. And your chances of finding a suitable husband will diminish considerably."

Melinda nodded. Her opportunities would trickle away by Thanksgiving and vanish by Christmas.

Mama tipped her head and pursed her lips. "This might sound peculiar, but why not set out to change Nicholas's mind about you? I know you don't particularly like him, but he's a reliable man, hardworking and well set financially. Perhaps you two simply got off on the wrong foot and with a turn—"

Melinda waved her hand in dismissal. "My goodness, Mama. Nick may have all the qualities of a good, Christian husband, but he's dreadfully serious. Life is difficult enough without marrying a man with a gloomy attitude. I want someone who's lighthearted and makes me laugh." Not that a simple "turn" in their relationship would make him like her. She didn't know why, but she suspected he thought her too superficial.

Ever since she'd met him at the tender age of thirteen, she'd found him captivatingly handsome, but too reserved, distant, and sometimes brusque. She'd often tried to charm him, but to no avail. Even when she'd blossomed into young womanhood, he'd never noticed. He was one of the few gentlemen who ignored her.

Mama nodded. "I'll admit he's somber at times, but don't disregard him. He'll wear well and that's important in a marriage."

Melinda shrugged. "I'm certain I'll meet a man who'll suit me far better than Nick." She rose. "If you'll excuse me, I'll go upstairs and show Nell the dress I bought her. And then I shall write to Florrie."

As she climbed the stairs to the second floor, her heart thudded with a fast and uncomfortable beat. Mama's news upset her far more than she wanted to admit. She clearly recalled how dreadful life had become when Papa lost his fortune for a short time right around her fourteenth birthday. Everyone they knew stopped calling and extending invitations. The Hollisters found themselves cut off from society. Hardly anyone at Miss Gibbons Female Academy spoke to her anymore.

The same thing would happen all over again. Only this time, no one but her future husband could rescue Mama and her from the horror of poverty and social obscurity. Rivulets of sweat snaked down her back.

If only she had someone to depend upon. And she wouldn't settle for someone she couldn't charm. She needed a man who loved her with a grand passion and a devoted heart. Two months wasn't very long to find him, but with the Lord's help all would be well. It had to be.

Once upstairs in her bedroom she tossed her reticule, parasol, and hat on her bed. Cecile arrived to unpack the purchases.

"I've changed my mind. Don't open the boxes from Tiffany's

or from Schuyler's. Just return them, please." Melinda bit her lip hard to distract herself. How could she be so attached to material possessions? These were trinkets she didn't need, a pretty porcelain piece and an exquisite triple-strand choker of pearls with a purple amethyst in the center. A tear escaped and she brushed it away with the back of her hand.

Oh, Lord, please forgive me for loving beautiful things. I should set my mind upon You, not on my earthly treasures. But I must admit it is hard for me . . .

She sighed and then searched for Nell's new dress made of thin, summery lawn. She fingered the delicate lace. From this point on she'd have to give up these extravagances for herself and even for Nell. But she wouldn't slip into the doldrums over her sudden change in circumstances.

Life was too short to waste it wallowing in self-pity. Melinda lifted her chin and then headed for the nursery with the frock and a new bisque doll tucked under her arm. She refused to send back this delightful gift for Nell either.

Melinda found her niece in the nursery—a sunny room overlooking Central Park—rocking back and forth on her wooden horse. Her nanny gathered toys and tossed them in a chest. As soon as Nell spotted Melinda coming through the doorway, she jumped off the rocking horse and ran into her arms.

Melinda bent down and gave her a big hug. "I've just returned from shopping and I have something new and pretty for you to wear."

"What is it?" Nell lifted the cover of the box and peeked inside.

"It's a lovely dress with your favorite color ribbons." Melinda retrieved the garment before Nell dragged it over the carpet. Holding it up, she saw Nell smile.

"Purple! I love purple!"

"That's one reason I bought it. And I have one more gift, so close your eyes."

Nell squeezed her fingers over her eyes, then opened them a little. "What is it?"

Melinda chuckled. "No fair; you're peeking."

As Nell's fingers quickly closed the gap, Melinda lifted the doll from its box. "You may look now."

Nell's eyes widened. "A dolly! Thank you." She threw her arms around Nell's legs. "I love you."

"I love you too, sweetheart. Look, she has blond hair and blue eyes just like you."

Nell patted the doll's hair. "I think I'll name her Melinda." She cradled her baby doll to her chest and warbled an off-key lullaby.

Tears welled as Melinda glanced at Nell's blissful face. The poor little girl didn't smile often anymore, but perhaps she would soon. "I have wonderful news. You and I are going to the seashore for the summer. We'll be staying with your cousins, Janet and Julie."

Nell clapped her hands. "They're my very best friends."

"Uncle Nick will be there too."

"Uncle Nick! I want to see him. Now."

"We can't go today, but very soon."

Melinda couldn't imagine how the cold and remote Nick Bryson could engender such excitement in the sweet little girl. Was there something about him that she was missing?

A WEEK LATER Nick batted the tennis ball over the net, careful not to slam it at his sister. Florrie seldom managed to connect ball to racket, though she practiced diligently beneath the warm Newport sun. Tall and fit, she looked athletic, but her lack of coordination betrayed her best efforts and lithe figure.

"You won once again." Florrie grimaced as she gathered the balls that had gone astray.

Nick swallowed a chuckle. He always beat her at tennis, but like all Brysons, Florrie competed regardless of the odds of winning.

The fight mattered as much as the results. She gripped her racket and strode toward the net, perspiration glistening on her lightly tanned face. Grabbing a handkerchief from the pocket of her white tennis dress trimmed in navy blue, she wiped off her high forehead and sunken cheeks.

"Shall we have some lemonade or ginger ale?" she asked.

"Moxie sounds good, if you have some."

"We do, indeed. Just for you. No one else will drink the stuff." She wrinkled her long, straight nose in disgust. "It's much too bitter for my taste."

They left the grass court on the side lawn of Summerhill, the seaside mansion Florrie and her husband, Jasper, were living in for the Newport season. A rambling, white-shingled cottage with twenty-two rooms, Summerhill boasted wide porches and an informal feeling the newer showplaces didn't have. Heading across the grass, they strolled toward the back veranda facing the sea. A cool breeze refreshed.

"I'd like to talk to you, Nick. About Nell and Melinda." Her voice sounded light, but underneath her casual tone he detected a note of tension.

"Oh?" He turned toward his older sister, seven years his senior. "Go ahead. I'm listening."

They climbed the wide, shallow steps leading up to the open veranda that Newporters often called the piazza. After ordering their drinks from a maid who seemed to appear out of nowhere, they settled into the comfortable wicker chairs. A fern dipping in the breeze brushed against his nose. He picked up the pot and exiled it to a far corner of the porch.

He focused his undivided attention on Florrie's narrow face. "Now, what is it you wish to say?"

"Melinda will arrive tomorrow morning with Nell," she said.

He grinned broadly; he couldn't help it. "Yes, I know. I'm looking forward to seeing the little sprite. I've missed her."

During those long days in England he'd often pictured his tiny niece and wondered how she was faring, how much she'd grown, and what she was like now. He'd heard that children changed very quickly. She'd turned four during his absence. On May fifth. He'd asked Florrie to choose a special gift and give it to her. Nell might not remember him too clearly after six months, even though he'd sent a photograph of himself from England. He'd make up for lost time this summer.

Florrie leaned forward, her fingers steepled. "I'll get right to the point. I'm concerned about the child. I fear Melinda isn't the best influence on her. Oh, Melinda is a darling, but she's still very much a spoiled girl." A disapproving frown swept across Florrie's face and vanished into a pained half smile. "She's hardly a woman, despite her appearance."

A very beautiful woman, Nick thought. Blond hair, eyes as blue as morning glories, creamy skin, and rosy cheeks. And full lips that tilted upward in the brightest smile he'd ever seen. He met his sister's steady gaze. "Melinda is . . ." He groped for descriptive words that didn't allude to her physical beauty. "A lot of fun."

Florrie rolled her eyes. "Yes, she's full of gaiety. But certainly not a proper influence on Nell."

Nick's eyebrows lifted. "I wouldn't say that, Florrie. Melinda is kind and . . ." He realized he didn't know her well, except as a relative by marriage and an infrequent dance partner at society balls. In turn, her frolicsome behavior intrigued him, then irked him. He couldn't imagine engaging in a meaningful conversation with her—but then, he'd never tried. Not really. "And intriguing, in a way," he finally finished.

Florrie's chocolate brown eyes narrowed to slits. "You sound enamored."

"Good heavens, Florrie, she's not my type. She's a little too . . ." He reached for a word other than *superficial*. "High-spirited."

He squirmed in his chair. What was he thinking? Melinda

Hollister flitted about like a butterfly—or a mosquito. Sometimes her charm attracted his interest, but more often than not he felt repelled by her shallowness. But Florrie was really addressing her as a mother figure for Nell, not as a woman. "I'm sure she brings joy to the nursery," he said. "But possibly too little discipline."

A maid handed them their drinks. Nick gulped his cold Moxie. It tasted more bitter than he remembered.

"Please watch her carefully, Nick. I'm afraid she won't provide a firm hand with Nell. Melinda Hollister is so scatterbrained and undisciplined, I shudder to think—"

He put up his palm. "Don't worry. If it's necessary I shall take full charge of the child. You can be assured I'll not let Nell run wild. If you'll recall, I never approved of joint custody and I tried to convince Melinda to allow me to bring up Nell by myself." He had to agree that Melinda's high spirits and capricious manner might not set the best example for Nell. But then neither could he imagine hauling the child and a nanny to England for six months; it would've been most . . . cumbersome.

"Actually, I was thinking you might let Jasper and me raise her along with our own. Little Nell needs both a mother and a father."

Florrie had been hinting at the possibility all week, and he'd thought about it. "I appreciate your offer, but no, Nell is my responsibility. It's what Cora and Parker wanted."

"I understand, but you'll find it quite difficult to raise her by yourself, even for just six months of the year."

Perhaps she had a point. A small one. But Florrie herself left most of her girls' care to a nanny. He could certainly do the same.

Nick rose. "Don't worry. I can take care of Nell."

Florrie sighed. "I suppose you must try. But when you realize my plan is for the best, I want you to know our offer still stands."

He nodded. "Thank you."

Time might prove her right. If only he had a wife and was more settled . . . He started at the thought; he hadn't considered married life since Alma Noble had refused his proposal and nearly broken his heart. But for his niece's sake, he'd reconsider, if necessary. He loved her that much.

He watched his sister enter the cottage. She'd probably retreat to her studio where she'd paint still life for the remainder of the day. Since Florrie spent little time with her own two, why would she wish to add to her family? Of course with a nanny in charge, one more little one wouldn't make any difference. Still, generosity wasn't Florrie's strongest suit and certainly not Jasper's. What trick did Jasper have up his sleeve?

Thoughts of his brother-in-law made him frown. Florrie might make a decent sort of mother for Nell. But there was no way Nick would ever hand the child over to Jasper's care.

TWO

❧

Filled with apprehension and a queasy stomach, Melinda boarded the Fall River Line steamship that evening for the overnight journey from New York City to Newport. Her doubts plagued her. What if she couldn't care for Nell by herself? She'd always relied on the little girl's nanny, but in the face of their new *circumstances*, she'd had to let her go. Fortunately, in her letter Florrie mentioned her daughters' nanny and nursemaid could watch over Nell too. *Lord, please help me. I have so much love for Nell, but absolutely no skills.*

Once bedded down in their private stateroom, she read Nell the Noah's ark story and prayed aloud for each of their family members by name.

"And take care of Mama and Papa in heaven," Nell said. "And God bless my friends Gertie and Sally and Francis—and Nanny, who's going to take care of a new little girl."

"Aren't you forgetting a few others?" Melinda encouraged in a whisper.

"Oh, and God bless all the help—Cook and Tillie, Mr. Harders, Cecile, all the maids and footmen, the coachman, and everyone we know. Amen."

"Amen." Melinda forced a gentle smile to her lips—thinking about all those people, soon out of work—and bent to kiss the child's forehead. "Good night, sweetheart."

"G'night, Auntie Mindy."

Melinda turned the light low and tried to sleep curled up with her niece. Not accustomed to retiring early, Melinda stayed awake hour after hour as the luxurious steamer plowed through the waters of Long Island Sound and passed the Connecticut coast heading toward Rhode Island. The hum of the engines should have lulled her to sleep, but anxiety sloshed through her like giant waves.

Normally on a cruise to Newport she'd wile away the hours dancing in the ship's ballroom to the strains of an orchestra. But tonight, with Nell in tow and no companion of her own, she had to pass up the opportunity. She suppressed a sigh and prayed that the Lord would take away all traces of self-pity. She was most definitely made of sterner stuff.

Just as she was drifting off to sleep, Melinda felt Nell stir. Her warm little body nuzzled closer. A muffled sob and small shudder brought Melinda back to wakefulness.

"Nell, are you all right?" Melinda whispered. "Are you crying?"

The little girl sniffed. "I miss my mama and papa." She turned toward Melinda.

Melinda reached for a handkerchief on the nightstand, gently patted Nell's eyes and nose, and then folded her tightly in her arms. Even in the dim light of the brass bedside lamp, she noticed tears trickling down Nell's round cheeks.

"I know you're sad and lonely, sweetie. I wish your mama and papa were still here with us. I miss them too. But they're in heaven with Jesus, so I know they're happy." She'd explained this to Nell again and again since the accident, but of course she still needed reassuring. "You know you have me—and Uncle Nick and the rest of our family. We all love you so much."

A few more tears escaped and rolled down Nell's cheeks. She

wiped her eyes and then slipped her damp hand into Melinda's. "I love you too." A few moments later she asked, "Will you and Uncle Nick be my mama and papa?"

"Yes, sweetie, we will. Always."

A faint smile curved Nell's lips. "Will all of us live together?"

Melinda's breath caught. "Well, no—except for this summer. For two whole months we'll be at Summerhill with Uncle Nick." What could she say to cheer her niece without fibbing about the absurd notion of her and Nick ever being bound in marriage?

Fresh tears streamed from Nell's eyes.

"Of course, no one knows what the future will hold, except for the Lord. So I can't truly say one way or the other if Uncle Nick and I—" She couldn't finish the sentence without giving the child false hope. "We'll always be here for you, and that's the most important thing. Don't you ever fret about that."

Nell nodded and closed her eyes, apparently ready to settle down to sleep again. But the idea of somehow linking herself to Nick kept Melinda awake and restless for the rest of the night.

THEY AROSE BEFORE sunrise for an early morning arrival. Melinda dressed Nell in a pink organdy frock with a rose sash, and brushed and braided her white-blond hair. It took far longer than Melinda expected, and one braid resembled a thick rope and the other a thin cord. Nell started to whimper from all the awkward fussing.

"Ouch! That hurts!"

Melinda stifled a groan as she tossed the silver brush and hair ribbons on the bed. Instead she breathed deeply to lower the tension mounting in her chest. "I'm sorry. I know I'm not good at fixing hair. But when we get to Newport, Janet and Julie's nanny will braid your hair, and I'm quite sure she'll do far better than I."

Nell tilted her head. "Thank you anyway, Auntie. I still love you."

Melinda squeezed her niece and swallowed the lump in her throat. Why was she feeling so emotional? *Probably the lack of sleep.* "There. We're all finished and you look lovely," Melinda said with a small smile.

When the steamship finally docked, they were both more than ready to disembark, though Melinda still had to throw all the things she left lying around into her valise.

Once on deck she quickly spotted the Brysons' landau and carry-all at the pier, and she breathed easier. Nick emerged from the open carriage, which was painted black and royal blue around the wheel rims and sides. The fouled anchor crest of the Bryson family stood out in gold lettering against the blue. But Melinda barely noticed the impressive carriage as her gaze focused upon Nicholas Bryson and his strong-featured, square-jawed face. His eyes lit up when he saw them—so much so that it made her breath catch.

Nick strode forward and waved. Tall and broad shouldered, he wore his clothing to great advantage—a navy blue sack suit, white shirt with turned-down collar, bow tie, and derby. How had he ever managed to escape the society ladies and their mothers for so many years? He must be close to thirty. Maybe his cool manner intimidated them.

But an unusually warm grin illuminated his face as his eyes rested on Nell. He opened his arms so the little girl could leap into his embrace. Swooping her up, he squeezed her in a bear hug. Then his gaze swept down to Melinda, and he nodded with polite indifference. She wasn't accustomed to indifference of any sort. Except from him—always from him. Somehow, she'd hoped that their shared custody of Nell and the invitation from Florrie would thaw his cold demeanor toward her. Irritation pricked at her confidence, but she quickly brushed it away.

"Welcome to Newport. I'm so glad your here, Nell. And you too, Melinda. Of course." He swung Nell down and then half-bowed to Melinda.

She stood as tall as her medium height allowed, but she only reached a few inches above his shoulder. "We're happy we're here. Thank you for the kind invitation."

"You must thank Florrie. She suggested you might enjoy a summer vacation."

She half smiled; so Nick really hadn't had anything to do with it.

He directed the carryall driver to gather their belongings from the steamship and then he assisted Melinda and Nell into the landau. He settled into the leather seat across from them.

The coachman returned several minutes later loaded with far more Louis Vuitton luggage than she remembered having, including two large hampers for her hats. But everything he brought was hers.

The carriage soon lurched ahead and rolled down Thames Street, the narrow road fronting the harbor, and then out into the countryside.

The morning fog swirled around them, veiling the wide lawns and mansions. Melinda saw the vague outlines of tall chimneys rise into the gray sky as she inhaled the salty sea air, strong and dank from low tide. Yet she didn't mind the smell or the chilly temperature. Her forest green travelling suit with a long-sleeved jacket and white, high-necked blouse staved off the bracing breeze. She wore a matching hat with a wide brim and plumes and carried a silk parasol.

As the horses trotted around the winding Ocean Drive, she felt her muscles tighten. Nerves were seldom her struggle, but this summer her entire future was at stake. *Please, Lord, don't let Nick or any of the Brysons discover my secret.*

Nick chatted with Nell for the entire carriage ride while Melinda stared at the rocky coast bathed in fog. How rude to exclude her from the conversation, even if he was overjoyed to see their niece. Actually, she'd never seen Nick so animated. He seemed like another person—one with a few drops of human warmth.

The carriage turned onto a long drive and rumbled over dirt

and pebbles toward an old-fashioned, white-shingled cottage rambling across a wide swath of emerald lawn.

"We're here." Melinda looped her arm around Nell and hugged her small shoulders. "You'll soon see your grandpapa and your aunt and uncle and cousins. Isn't that exciting?"

Nell nodded. Melinda straightened her niece's straw hat and re-tied the pink satin ribbon beneath her chin. "There, that's better."

As they approached Summerhill, the mist thinned. Melinda noticed the wraparound porch and flower boxes resting upon the railings between the posts. Red and white impatiens burst through greenery and spilled over the spindles. All along the veranda, roofline gingerbread trim added a touch of hominess.

Her heart banged against her rib cage. She didn't know what to expect from the Brysons this summer, especially from Nick. She hoped for a summer free from stress so she could focus on finding a spouse. But could she rediscover her carefree side when she so feared exposure, humiliation, loss?

The carriage jerked to a halt in front of the freshly painted mansion. Nick directed the servants to unload the mountains of luggage from the carryall and take it upstairs to the bedrooms. As the men hoisted steamer trunks and suitcases, valises and hampers, Nick led Melinda inside the cottage. It had a spacious, antique-filled foyer with a grand staircase in the middle.

"Let's stop by Florrie's studio and say hello. She's anxious to see you."

Melinda followed Nick down a hallway to the back of Summerhill and his sister's art studio. They found her behind her easel assessing her painting. She glanced up and lowered her brush. Streaks of paint covered her hands and smock. Florrie came forward and gave Melinda a quick hug.

"Welcome, Melinda. We're so happy you and Nell could join us."

"Thank you for inviting us. We're both looking forward to a wonderful summer."

"Please don't mind me or my messy appearance. I spend much of my time painting unless Nick drags me off for an occasional tennis match. Sometimes I get so carried away I forget all about my social obligations. But now that you're here I'll try to be more conscientious."

They spoke for a few minutes until Florrie stole glances toward her canvas, obviously losing interest in their conversation.

Nick took the clue. "If you'll excuse us, I'll have Mrs. Finnegan get Melinda settled."

"Yes, do that. She can fetch you anything you need, Melinda. She's a marvel."

Returning to the foyer, Mrs. Finnegan appeared. The white-haired housekeeper—who was nearly as round as she was tall—waddled in from a hallway, a smile splitting her pasty face.

"Mrs. Finnegan will show you to your room, Melinda," Nick said. "And Nell to the nursery. I'll take Nell and Janet and Julie out on the back lawn after a while. If you'd care to join us once you're settled, we would be glad to have you."

"I'd be delighted." Melinda nodded, though on second glance, his cool, appraising eyes weren't at all welcoming.

"Fine. I'll leave you in Mrs. Finnegan's capable hands."

The housekeeper's toothy grin broadened. "Come with me, miss. Your room is all ready. I hope you'll be likin' a lovely view of the sea. 'Tis a bit damp in the wee hours, but if you keep the window shut tight at night, you're sure to be toasty warm in the morning." Mrs. Finnegan bent down to speak to Nell. "Let's be off to see your cousins. They're quite beside themselves waiting for you. You do like to play, I expect."

Mrs. Finnegan chattered in a lilting brogue as she led the two upstairs. They spent several minutes with the brown-haired Van Tassel girls, Florrie's daughters, aged four and six. They wore identical gingham dresses with immaculate white pinafores. The younger one, Julie, took Nell by the hand and led her to a large dollhouse in the corner of the bright, yellow room filled with toys and books and games.

"I shall be back for you in a few minutes, Nell. Then we'll go outside to visit with your Uncle Nick," Melinda said.

Nell nodded. Friends since babyhood, she obviously felt right at home with her cousins, even after their six-month absence from her life.

Mrs. Finnegan led the way to a pair of uniformed servants. "Nanny Wells, I'd like you to meet Miss Hollister, Nell's aunt. And this is Peggy, the new nursemaid."

The pretty raven-haired girl, probably not yet twenty, curtsied and mumbled, "How do you do, miss?" She wore a black dress, white apron, and doily cap with streamers, identical to Mrs. Finnegan's and Nanny Wells's. Her sweet smile and curvaceous figure undoubtedly made her a favorite among the male staff.

Nanny Wells also curtsied. Around fifty, the eagle-eyed woman looked quite self-assured and competent. Even a little prim. But her high-pitched, girlish voice added an attractive softness to her personality.

"Mrs. Van Tassel said you would watch Nell right along with Janet and Julie."

Nanny Wells nodded. "Yes, miss. Nell will be no trouble at all, I'm sure."

"Please let me know if she misbehaves. I don't expect she will. She's a delightful child," Melinda said.

"And so very beautiful," the nursemaid added. "I'm sure we'll all get along famously."

Melinda followed the housekeeper down the narrow hallway toward the guest bedrooms at the opposite end of the second floor. Just as Mrs. Finnegan had claimed, her bedroom overlooked the wide lawn edged by enormous boulders jutting into the sea. Melinda inhaled the faint smell of seaweed that blew through the screens. Even from across the yard she heard the sound of breakers crashing against the rocks.

"What a wonderful place," Melinda murmured.

She loved her bedroom—the wallpaper patterned with giant pink roses and green leaves, the white wooden mantle, and the twin beds with satin and velvet spreads in complementary shades of pink.

"Summerhill belongs to Professor Wilmont and his new wife Charlotte," Mrs. Finnegan said. "They usually live here year-round, but this summer the family is off to Europe. Lovely people, they are. Now if you need anything a'tall, just ask me, miss. I'm always glad to help." Mrs. Finnegan departed then, leaving behind a mild scent of linseed oil.

The ladies' maid to Summerhill's female guests arrived, introduced herself as Denise, and unpacked several of Melinda's gowns that had been carefully wrapped in tissue paper. For the next hour Melinda supervised the arrangement of her belongings in the wardrobes, chiffoniers, and dressing room. Denise helped her change into a peach-colored frock overlaid with ecru lace and decorated at the neck with a simple cameo. How fortunate her summer wardrobe had been finished and delivered before she'd received news of her financial straits. She searched for her parasol and found it still buried at the bottom of a trunk among her reticules and a satin box filled with two dozen pairs of new white gloves.

She glanced out the window once more, drawn to the fresh ocean breeze. Sprawled beneath the leafy arms of a sugar maple were the three little girls and Nick. So he hadn't waited for Melinda to bring the child—he'd fetched her himself. Apparently he couldn't wait to be with their Nell.

A twinge of apprehension shot through Melinda's chest. What if Nick campaigned to take Nell away from her? And what if their niece wanted to live with him full-time? Worse, what if the summer did not deliver a suitable groom as she hoped? Destitute and single, there would be little chance that she could maintain custody of Nell, even part-time.

She tried to breathe deeply to calm herself, but it did little to help quiet her jangled nerves. *Nothing but ridiculous qualms*, she told herself, as she hurried outside to join the little party.

But the butterflies that tumbled through her stomach wouldn't stop fluttering.

NICK READ THE last line of "Little Red Riding Hood" and lay the book of fairy tales on his lap. "There, that's enough for today." He leaned against the tree trunk and stretched his legs over the grass. Sunshine had broken through the clouds, banished the early morning mist, and dried the dew.

He looked up and spied Melinda gliding across the lawn, a vision of beauty. To his surprise and annoyance, his pulse quickened. A parasol tilted above her blond pompadour, and her wide smile warmed the cool day. A lacy frock set off her slender but shapely figure capable of catching any man's eye. In fact, he knew Melinda Hollister had bewitched many a New York bachelor, but to date, no one had won her heart. At least he hadn't heard of an engagement. When she came closer he started to rise, but she gestured for him to stay seated.

"May I join you?" she asked in a sweet, musical voice. Fortunately a wooden bench was nearby, in the deep shade of the tree. He couldn't imagine her risking her peach frock with a seat upon the grass.

"Please do," he said. "I left their nanny in the nursery. That was brave of me, don't you think?" His mouth curled in a wry smile. *Stop flirting, Nick. You'll give her the wrong impression.* He was hardly the sort of man who lost his reason over a pretty face and sweet smile. *How banal that would be.*

"Indeed, I do. Three girls can be quite overwhelming, though they all seem to be on their best behavior."

She turned toward the trio crowded next to Nick. "Would you like another story?"

They all nodded, and Janet's and Julie's long curls bounced. Nell clapped her hands, then jumped up and nestled beside Melinda on the bench. Obviously the youngster adored her. That was good, he supposed, but he preferred the child didn't get too attached to her aunt.

"'Cinderella' is my favorite story," Julie proclaimed.

Nick handed Melinda the book, and she paged through the text until she found the right tale. Her dramatic reading mesmerized her audience, including himself, much to his surprise. He couldn't tear his gaze from the gleam in her bright blue eyes and the grin that curved her full lips. Her voice brought the story to life. The girls edged closer to her as she drew them into her fairytale world.

How could he ever compete with her charisma? Her love for Nell seemed genuine and the bond of affection they shared so strong. While he'd conducted business in England, Melinda must have eased her way into Nell's heart. He pulled up a blade of grass and tore it in half. Could such a capricious lady also be a dedicated mother? He doubted she'd stand up to even a minor crisis. He'd wager that under pressure she'd melt like sugar.

When Melinda finished reading two more tales, she lowered the book to her lap and leaned closer to the children. "I want to tell you a story about three girls exactly your ages, two with wavy brown hair and one with blond curls." When the trio giggled, she continued, "Something very exciting happens to them. Would you like to hear about it?"

Inwardly, Nick groaned. She could make up stories as well as read them.

They nodded and Melinda dived into her story, weaving the fantasic tale that the girls rewarded with squeals of delight. Her eyes gleamed, her voice changed with her different characters, her arms gestured gracefully. She captivated the girls and when she finished, they begged for another story.

"Let's save that for tomorrow. Look, here comes Nanny Wells."

Their nanny strode across the lawn and took charge. "It's time for a snack, little ones." She whisked the girls inside the cottage.

Nick glanced at Melinda, who looked more than a little self-satisfied. "Would you care to join me for a walk?" he asked, rising from the grass. Standing just a few feet from Melinda, he caught the fresh scent of lavender.

"Yes, that would be delightful. I'd love to see more of Summerhill's beautiful grounds."

He offered his arm and she took it with a light hand. "I expect Nell and I will have a splendid time here. And I'm looking forward to seeing my friends again. I missed them all while I was in mourning for Cora, but I needed every day of that time to recover."

He nodded. "Yes, I understand. I miss Parker very much too. Not just as my partner at Bryson Steamship, but also as my brother and friend." Parker never failed to cheer him or make him laugh. And when Nick was at odds with their father, his brother had acted as a buffer.

A small smile turned up the corners of Melinda's mouth. "Cora and I used to spend most of our summers in Newport. Year after year our parents rented the same cottage on Narragansett Avenue. It wasn't nearly as grand as Summerhill or the Bellevue Avenue mansions. But to Cora and me it was quite magical."

He liked the softness of her voice as it rose and fell much like the swish of the sea over sand. "I'm glad you and Nell could come. I've missed her a great deal."

As they strolled down the pebbled walkway toward the shore, Melinda dropped her hand from his arm but continued to match his stride. Had he said something to offend her? Not that she seemed unfriendly. Just a touch wary, despite her prattle.

"Nell missed you dreadfully," she said, glancing at him sideways. "It's a shame your business had to take you abroad at such a fragile time in her young life."

He bristled. "I regretted leaving, but it couldn't be helped. I have business obligations, as well as my familial obligation to watch over Nell."

Melinda nodded. "I understand you must work. Fortunately, I don't have to divide my attention between Nell and business responsibilities. She's my primary concern."

Nick cocked a brow. He didn't appreciate her none-too-subtle criticism. But then her cheeks burned red and she bit her lip.

"Please pardon me, Nick. I didn't mean to pass judgment on you. Of course you have to help run Bryson Steamship. And I'm just a society woman who has never labored a day in her life. I merely meant that I have a lot of time to devote to Nell."

And you don't hung unspoken in the silence between them.

"True," he admitted.

But she also devoted herself to fun and fashion. At least, she had until Cora and Parker died. Now that she was out of mourning, was she anxious to resume her old life of parties and pleasure? Was that really why she was there? He'd soon find out. An endless round of social activity in Newport would tempt her away from their niece just as much as business stole his attention. He'd find out who she really was beneath her sunny exterior—and if he had to truly worry about her influence on their niece.

"I would've preferred to stay in New York and help you with Nell, but I needed to go abroad. I'm afraid the company took priority." Yet his tone sounded testy, not contrite, even to his own ears. A bad start to their delicate relationship.

By the time of the railway accident that killed his brother and sister-in-law, his once formidable father had faltered in two ill-conceived business ventures. Nick had no option but to take control, at least to the extent his father allowed. Soon he might have to insist the elderly tycoon relinquish all his responsibilities, or there'd be nothing left of Bryson Steamship Company on which to build.

Nick halted and looked her in the eye. "I would love to share our New York home with Nell on a full-time basis." Melinda didn't faint or scream, as he feared. But he didn't like her silence either. "Of course you'd be welcome to visit Nell at any time," he said in a rush.

She nodded slowly. "I see your point. It's a well-known fact that the Brysons have a fortune very few can equal. Certainly I can't compete financially. But Nell requires so much more than just money. She needs love and—"

"I can give her all my love." He felt his jaw jut in protest. "There's nothing I can't provide for her."

Melinda's voice stayed soft and unexpectedly reasonable. "There's nothing I can't give her either, except perhaps more material goods than she needs."

Nick choked back a snort. How could Melinda Hollister sound so mature about worldly riches when she herself craved luxuries and privileges? Parker used to complain that both Cora and Melinda never found a bauble they didn't covet. The Hollister sisters were among society's most notorious spendthrifts, right along with their mother.

"Why don't you think it over? Caring for a young child is a tremendous task for a young woman. I can relieve you of the burden—"

She shook her head so fiercely a hairpin popped out. He reached down to retrieve it from the walkway. She stuck it back behind her ear, but tendrils still curled around her pink face and moved gently in the light breeze.

"Don't you see that Nell is not a burden to me? She's a great joy and a blessing." Her eyes filled with tears. "I adore taking care of her. I shall never replace her own mother, but I'm doing my utmost to ensure she has a happy life. I'll never willingly relinquish custody."

Just as he feared. He'd have to approach this differently.

Her cheeks reddened as she continued. "Are you concerned about her spiritual development, Nick? To me that's more important than anything else."

"I am." Her words shocked him. Since when did Melinda Hollister care so much about her Christian walk?

Melinda strolled toward the gigantic boulders that edged the coastline and protruded into the surf. Stopping at the end of the lawn, she turned back to him. "I've always been close to Nell. Right after she was born I helped Cora care for her. Nell is special to me."

"Yes, I understand," Nick murmured, feeling a pang of guilt. But he couldn't allow her to awaken his sentimental side. He needed to employ reason, not emotion, to solve this dilemma.

"So you see, I feel responsible for her well-being. Cora wanted it that way. Please don't try to take Nell away from me." He could hear the fear in her voice and her unabashed appeal to his better nature.

"All right." What was the point of fighting? Maybe, in time, she'd come to see reason. "But what about later on, Melinda? What happens to Nell if one of us, or both of us, marries? We might move to another section of the country or to Europe. How will that work out?"

"Probably not well," she agreed. "But those are future problems and I'll not fret about them now."

He gave a reluctant nod, suppressing a wince. He truly wished she'd mature for Nell's sake. Their niece needed a mother more than a big sister.

Melinda lifted her chin. "There's no point in worrying about something that may not happen. If problems do arise, the Lord will provide a solution."

He stifled a groan. "Sometimes the Lord encourages us to use our God-given faculties. Especially if we have sound judgment." Truthfully, he seldom consulted the Lord before he acted. Fortunately he normally knew what to do.

Although he wasn't at all sure what to do about Melinda.

THREE

❧

As Melinda approached the piazza she hid her distress behind a smile. Nick vanished inside Summerhill, relieving her of the pretense of being more cheerful than she felt. Nick Bryson was the most annoying man she'd ever encountered. Imagine wishing to raise Nell by himself without a wife—unless he planned to marry. She hadn't heard of him courting any of the young society ladies, though mourning had left her out of touch of late.

If Nick wanted to marry, he'd have little trouble finding a wife. Rich, cultured, and intelligent, he'd have his pick of brides. Some bluestocking debutante who didn't object to his preoccupation with business and frequent absences might find him ideal. And he was certainly attractive, despite his aloof demeanor. But even if he married she'd never allow him to steal Nell. Still, she had to admit he was in a far better position to bring her up than she was—unless she married too. And of course that was her plan. But why didn't she feel her normal confidence?

With a soft breeze at her back, Melinda climbed the steps to the veranda that extended the length of Summerhill and opened to the sea air. A jungle of gently bobbing ferns and palms edged the white wicker chairs cushioned in a floral print. She almost missed the young woman half-hidden among the greenery and engrossed in the Bible. Dressed in a tan frock with only a crocheted lace collar and white buttons to relieve the plainness, the lady had mahogany brown hair scraped back in an unfashionably tight bun. But when she glanced up, her smile illuminated the deep shade of the porch.

"Glynna Farnsworth! I didn't know you were at Summerhill! What a grand surprise." Melinda rushed forward as Glynna rose and opened her arms wide. They hugged tightly and then settled into the soft cushions padding the wicker chairs.

Glynna removed her spectacles, revealing dark, widely spaced eyes. "Cousin Florrie said you'd arrive today and I've been looking forward to your visit. I'm so glad to see you again. It's been at least three or four years."

"I believe the last time I was at Cora and Parker's home for Thanksgiving dinner . . ." Melinda's voice caught. The thought brought back unexpectedly poignant memories.

Glynna said softly, "I'm so sorry for your loss. Cora was a dear. We so miss Parker too."

"Thank you." Melinda paused for several moments. "It's been a terribly difficult time for me and especially for Nell. We're trying to get on with our lives, but it's so hard for a little girl to lose her parents. I'm hoping our visit here will help her recover." Melinda felt the pressure of tears building behind her eyelids. She forced herself to brighten. "Are you and Stephen here for the season?"

Glynna nodded. "Yes, Florrie invited us to stay for July and August. Then in the fall we'll return to Africa where we are planting a new mission school."

"That's wonderful."

Glynna squinted. "Are you feeling all right, Melinda? You look a trifle upset."

"Oh, do I?" Melinda said, unable to completely mask her

feelings. "I guess talking about my sister still upsets me a bit. But something else is bothering me as well."

Glynna's shy smile reached Melinda's heart. "I'm a good listener," she said.

Should she confide in a cousin of the Brysons? Probably not. But they'd been friends since their student days at Miss Gibbons Female Academy. Glynna had been like a big sister to her after Cora had graduated.

Melinda's reservations weakened. She didn't like to keep her emotions bottled up to grow and fester. "Are you certain you want me to bare my soul?" Melinda asked with a wry twist of her mouth.

"Yes, indeed. I wouldn't have asked otherwise."

Melinda believed her. "All right. Thank you." She breathed deeply and then her story spilled out like a waterfall to her sympathetic friend.

"Oh my. No wonder you're distressed, Melinda. But I'm sure Cousin Nick meant well, though obviously he needs to consider your feelings more. And Nell's. I shall pray for understanding between you two."

"Thank you." Melinda leaned back into the cushion and sighed. "Several months ago I thought Nick ought to give me total custody. But now I see how dearly he loves Nell and she loves him. I know he should be her guardian too. But I'm disappointed he doesn't feel the same about me."

Glynna nodded. "Perhaps God will change his mind during the course of the summer."

"I do hope so. Anyhow, thank you so much for listening." Happy to have found someone to confide in, Melinda leaned closer to Glynna. "Enough about me and my troubles. Tell me about your plans in Africa." During more affluent times she and her mother had contributed to a mission school in China. Somehow church workers dedicated to spreading God's Word in foreign lands seemed out of place among the extravagance of Newport. "I trust some of the cottagers will help fund your efforts." She would need to find a way to contribute to the Farnsworths' mission . . . somehow.

Glynna's laugh had the tinkling sound. "That's one reason why Florrie invited us to Summerhill. She had the same idea. Stephen and I are going to open a small school in one of the larger villages, and that takes a lot of money. But Florrie expects her friends will give generously. I do hope so. In fact, Florrie is hosting a fundraising reception for us."

"I'd love to help you and Florrie with the party. If you'd like I can plan the menu and choose—or am I overstepping my bounds? I don't want to intrude . . ."

Glynna leaned over and squeezed Melinda's hand. "Not at all. We can certainly use your assistance. Florrie is so involved with her painting, I'm making many of the arrangements myself." She laughed. "And to tell the truth, I don't know the first thing about throwing parties. Missionaries aren't accustomed to arranging fancy receptions, and my days among our friends in society seem longer and longer ago."

"I'd love to take it on."

"Oh, thank you, Melinda. That's quite a relief. Stephen and I are scheduled to speak at the reception and that nearly overwhelms me."

"Why? You'll have the heart of every person in the room within moments." She reached out to squeeze Glynna's hand.

Glynna gave her a rueful smile. "I feel a bit self-conscious asking the Brysons' friends for funds, even though it's for the Lord's work, not our own. I suppose I shouldn't care that they'll think of us as beggars."

Melinda shook her head. "I wouldn't worry about accepting money from the cottagers. They have much more than they need."

Glynna smiled. "All right. And of course we shall pray for them."

"That shows your appreciation more than anything else possibly could. They have everything, but probably not someone to pray for them."

Glynna leaned closer. "I'm uncomfortable about asking for funds because . . . Well, I'm afraid it's sheer pride that makes me hesitate. And I hate to speak in front of a crowd, but Florrie says we must explain our mission. Stephen is eager and he expects me to add a few remarks. I agree it's important, but I tend to jumble my words."

Melinda nodded. "Well, we all have our weaknesses and failings, don't we? At least you're fighting to overcome yours."

"I pray about overcoming all the time," Glynna said.

"And the Lord hears your prayer. I also pray to conquer my failings, but perhaps not with enough fervor." Melinda felt her cheeks color. Now that she teetered on the brink of poverty, she realized how strongly the bonds of greed entangled her. She'd never resisted the urge to acquire beautiful things nor did she really try or even want to. Her parents had pampered her and even encouraged her to indulge her every whim. But she had little choice now except to start disciplining herself. She felt better that no one—not even a woman dedicated to spreading God's Word or helping others—was perfect.

"If I might ask . . ." Melinda hesitated. "What propels you to risk your life and your health for people you don't even know?" She hoped she wasn't too inquisitive.

"Stephen and I are often asked that question." Glynna's face lit up with enthusiasm. "We live our lives according to the Book. You know, God's Word. I'm afraid we fall short, but we do try. The Bible directs us to spread the Gospel to the ends of the earth. And like everything in Scripture, we take the Lord's commands seriously."

Melinda nodded. She was most definitely a Christian, but she never thought too much about the Bible as a guidebook for daily living. She followed her own desires and sometimes strayed down the wrong path. Her own judgment had occasionally—no, often— been impulsive and foolish.

"No matter what your problem, the Lord provides an answer either directly or through His wisdom." Glynna tilted her head. "I'm not sounding preachy, am I?"

"Not at all. I think what you say makes perfect sense," Melinda said.

She needed to turn her woes over to the Lord and trust Him to guide her. If only she had the strength and focus to follow His precepts instead of grasping for financial security and social position. She should also learn what God said about material prosperity, though she suspected she already knew. Often she skimmed over the parts of the Bible she didn't like. What if He demanded a bit of self-sacrifice? She shuddered to think of the discomfort that might bring. Once she had more time for real Bible study, she'd give it the attention it deserved.

They talked for nearly half an hour before Florrie came to announce she was on her way to the Casino where the Newport crowd gathered for entertainment. Within its shingled walls and open courtyards, the cottagers watched tennis, bowled, played cards, viewed theatricals, and danced. It was the gathering place, a club for both men and women to socialize when they weren't visiting each other's homes.

"Would you two like to come along?" Florrie asked.

"I would, indeed." Melinda rose. The Casino was the perfect place to begin her marriage campaign.

She felt a twinge of disappointment when Glynna declined. But they'd have plenty of opportunities to spend time together during the coming days.

Melinda decided to wear the frock she had on with its lovely lace inserts. Florrie's dress of sage green made her sallow skin look ghastly. Poor Florrie had all the money in the world, but no taste. Yet Melinda suspected she didn't care one bit about the most flattering colors or latest style. As a rich, married woman, she didn't have to.

When they arrived at the Casino, tucked behind a row of exclusive Bellevue Avenue shops, they stopped to chat with at least a dozen friends she'd rarely seen during her mourning period. They hugged and gossiped and promised to catch up on all the news during the coming days.

"It's positively wonderful to see everyone again," Melinda said. She wished she could be as carefree as her old friends, but it seemed her carefree days were behind her.

They wandered over to the tennis match. Two men in white shirts and trousers volleyed the ball over the net as she and Florrie took seats in the second row of wooden chairs. Melinda leaned to the side, but she couldn't quite see around the broad-brimmed hat in front of her. Not that she truly cared about the game. She folded her gloved hands in her lap and hoped someone interesting would come along.

Only a minute or two ticked by before a gentleman in a tan suit with the standard brown bowler asked permission to sit beside her. Phinneas Dalton, a widower with an obscenely large fortune and six rowdy children, bent forward. His breath gusted with peppermint not quite strong enough to conceal the awful cigar stench that still clung to his mouth and clothes. Somewhere around forty, Mr. Dalton looked weathered and well past his prime. A potbelly and a jowly, hound face revealed his age, along with a drooping walrus mustache heavily laced with gray.

"It's good to see you again, Miss Hollister."

She wished she could say the same. His reputation of chasing young ladies both married and single preceded him.

They talked for a few minutes and then he heaved his body closer. "I'm so terribly sorry about your loss, Miss Hollister. Such a tragedy. We missed you in New York these last few months. So glad you're back in circulation."

She twitched a half smile. "Thank you for your condolences. I'm not sure *circulation* is the right word. But I am back in society

once again, even though I'm not truly over my sister's passing."
Did one ever recover from the death of a beloved sister and friend?

He nodded vigorously. "Yes, yes, I understand. My wife died
two years ago, and not a day goes by that I don't mourn her." While
he spoke his gaze travelled down her face and rested on her bosom.
His eyes glinted like green glass.

Heat seared Melinda's face. If only the tight-fitting style didn't
emphasize that part of her anatomy, she'd be less self-conscious.
She whipped out her fan to block his view. His momentary scowl
brought a bubble of laughter to her throat. But she coughed it back
down.

"It must be difficult for you and your little ones with your wife
gone," she said, feeling like a hypocrite since she didn't mean a
word of it.

"Oh yes, it gets lonely at Pinehurst, I assure you. So many
empty rooms begging for a woman's touch to brighten them up."
He tilted his head and lifted an eyebrow as if appraising her as he
would a prize filly.

He had the cash, and she had the personality to bring life back
to the Elizabethan cottage that overwhelmed a prime Bellevue
Avenue lot. She tried to picture herself as stepmother to a flock of
unruly children—at least they were reputed to be full of sass—
but she couldn't envision such a dreadful situation. And the idea of
kissing Mr. Dalton sent a wave of repulsion spiraling through her
chest.

But was she being too quick to eliminate a marriageable candi-
date? Maybe. Or maybe not. She'd consider him later, if absolutely
necessary. For now, and she hoped forever, she'd drop him to the
bottom of her list.

"So tell me about your children. How old are they now?" she
asked.

He rambled on and her mind wandered. As the conversation
lagged, Florrie leaned over Melinda and thankfully took up the

slack. Melinda's attention strayed to the tennis players, especially the tall, athletic blond. His white clothing accentuated tanned skin and thick muscles. She recognized him instantly. Her heart tapped a faster beat, though she wished it hadn't. It was Clayton Underwood, one of the few bachelors who'd escaped the clutches of unmarried girls and their eager mothers.

Clayton had courted her two years before, but she'd quickly rebuffed his marriage proposal. At the time she wasn't ready to consider a serious relationship, especially with a man from Texas, way out in the Wild West. The Underwoods usually spent several months in New York and Newport, and often returned to their home state for extended periods. At the time, Melinda couldn't conceive of being so far from everyone and everything she loved. But now she felt a twinge of remorse for dropping him without even a thought for his feelings. Perhaps he'd be attending the Johnsons' ball tomorrow night and she could apologize to him for her callous behavior. And maybe they might start up where they'd left off— even if that did seem rather manipulative and self-serving.

She continued to search the crowd for suitable prospects and found many of the young men she'd once flirted with were now either spoken for or married. While she'd spent the last four years whirling around gilded ballrooms, other young ladies had skimmed off the cream. How had she let this happen? She'd ignored her mother's gentle warnings to enjoy her carefree days but to not put off marriage for too long. Instead she'd dismissed her advice with a laugh and waltzed away, confident she'd snag the right man when the time came. Now she was wondering if she'd delayed too long.

She spent the rest of the afternoon at the Casino, preoccupied with her own thoughts and feeling lonely for little Nell. She finally gave up on her fruitless socializing and returned to Summerhill, electing to go in search of her niece as soon as she arrived. Melinda found the child spinning tops with Julie and Nanny Wells while Janet glanced through a picture book.

Nell reached up and threw her arms around Melinda. She scooped her up and hugged her tight before depositing her back on the carpet. How warm and soft the little child was! And oh, how she would miss her when she had to leave her behind with Nick . . .

"Will you play with us for a while?" Nell pleaded.

Melinda grinned. "Of course. But first let me speak to Nanny for a few minutes."

Nell ran back to Julie while Melinda led Nanny Wells to the window seat in the opposite corner of the spacious room.

After they settled on the soft cushion, Melinda asked softly, "How is Nell adjusting to Summerhill?"

"Why, she's doing fine, Miss Hollister. She and her cousins get along so well. Nell is such a happy child, I don't believe you have to worry about her. She's taken quite a liking to Peggy."

The dark-haired girl looked up from putting dolls in their cradles. "We're getting to be good friends." She giggled and blushed. "We both like to play with dolls."

"Splendid. I'm so relieved things are working out so well."

But would her own life progress as smoothly? If the gentlemen at the Casino were any indication of this season's bachelors, then she might run into trouble finding a suitable match. And that was terrifying.

FOUR

❧

Later that afternoon Nick met his father and brother-in-law, Jasper, in the library. Nick's vision soon adjusted to the dimness of the long, cavernous room paneled in rich, dark wood. He joined the pair seated on leather chairs by the screened windows. Rays of sunlight slanted through the back veranda and into the library. Nick liked this masculine room lined with floor-to-ceiling bookshelves, comfortable chairs and sofas, and an unlit fireplace. The aroma of Jasper's pipe tobacco clung to the air. As Nick dropped into the empty chair facing the men, he felt the heat of the afternoon sun warming his hair and neck.

"Good day," he said to the man across from him.

The great steamship magnate, Frederick Bryson, sat in a dark brown wing chair, swallowing it with his presence, though he was a small, scrawny man, shrunken by sixty-five years of toil and scheming. Thin white hair was combed to the side over a shiny pate.

"Have you talked to Melinda about guardianship of the child?" he asked brusquely, eying Nick with a confrontational stare.

"I have and she declined my offer." Nick shifted and crossed his leg, unwilling to discuss such a sensitive subject in front of Jasper. But his brother-in-law leaned forward, looking far more curious than he had any right to be. With a square face splattered with an embarrassment of freckles, he had reddish-brown hair, the color of paprika, and amber eyes wide-set like a salamander's.

"Now can we get down to business?" Nick asked. "I just received a letter from the Blue Star Line. They've decided to sell the company. If we're still interested, they'd like to negotiate a sale." He kept his voice even, although he found it difficult to contain his enthusiasm.

His father sat up even straighter, easily distracted by talk of business. Excitement softened the muscles in his drawn face. He had sought to acquire the British passenger ships for several years, but success had eluded him. But when they'd heard rumors Blue Star might want to sell their fleet, he'd sent Nick to England to negotiate. Unfortunately, the owners vacillated between selling or continuing to limp along in their operations.

"So they've agreed to put the line up for sale. Excellent news. Good job, my boy. I knew they'd come to their senses eventually and agree to sell." He reached for the letter, squeezed the bridge of his nose to secure his pince-nez spectacles, and skimmed the print. "But the price they're demanding! Good gracious, they're pirates. You'll have to make them see reason."

Frederick passed the letter to Jasper, and he shook his head and frowned as he read. "Outrageous. I think we ought to consider this purchase more carefully. We haven't the need—"

"We do have the need," Nick interrupted, knowing Jasper's arguments all too well. "Our fleet is aging rapidly, and Blue Star would immediately bring us up-to-date. If we're too cautious, we'll lose the sale to someone else." And repeat the mistake they'd made before by relying on Jasper's advice to take their time and dither.

"Blue Star vessels are excellent. They're known for safety, comfort, and luxury. Even the third-class facilities have dining rooms with good linens and silverware. And the menu cards have postcards on the back—"

"What earthly good does that do?" Jasper rolled his eyes.

"The passengers can write to relatives in their home countries and urge them to travel on Blue Star."

Frederick held up his hand. "I shall consider all the pros and cons. In the meantime, Nicholas, try to negotiate them down. Far down. Set up a meeting in New York. But we can't seem too anxious to jump at their offer."

Nick nodded slowly. "Remember, Father, their asking price is merely a starting point." Why must his father be so belligerent? He'd always been difficult, but never so angry.

"I'm depending upon you."

Nick saw Jasper wince. As the accountant for Bryson Steamship Company, Jasper expected a stronger say in decision making. But Frederick wouldn't give either his son or son-in-law much authority. He pitted them against each other as they jockeyed for power, and he seemed to enjoy every minute of their struggle.

MELINDA SPIED NICK in his office behind the half-open door. On impulse she stopped to say hello. "May I come in?" she asked, poking her head into the small study equipped with only a desk and telephone, bookcases, and two chairs.

"Yes, of course," he said with more good manners than enthusiasm. He put down his fountain pen and straightened his papers. "Do sit down."

Melinda lowered to the chair on the opposite side of the desk from Nick. "I see you're working. I really shouldn't disturb you."

"That's quite all right. I'm finished for now."

His eyes appeared tired and, if she wasn't mistaken, a bit worried. "It's summer, so perhaps you ought to work a little less and have a bit of fun."

He shook his head. "I can't. Work continues whether I'm here or in New York. We're hoping to purchase several ocean liners from a British company, and I'm going over all the facts and figures before we begin to haggle over the price."

"Tell me about it . . . unless it's a secret."

He chuckled. "Nothing but the deal itself is a secret." He folded his hands on the desktop and leaned forward across a neat stack of papers and file folders. "You're not really interested in business, are you?"

She shrugged. "Probably not, but I'd like to hear about the ships anyway."

"Alright, if you're sure. The Blue Star Line wishes to sell its fleet; we'd like to buy it since our liners are aging and we need to expand. They'd like to sell because they've lost two ships recently due to storms in the north Atlantic, which has crippled them. They're in debt and need ready cash."

"Are these the kind of ships immigrants sail on?" Melinda asked. Large influxes of Irish and Scandinavians from Norway and Sweden arrived in New York daily and spread out all across the nation, though many remained in the city.

"Yes. The Blue Star's six newest vessels carry up to four hundred passengers in first and second class and two thousand passengers in third class. They can also transport up to 17,000 tons of general cargo."

"They sound impressive. Mama and I have traveled on Cunard and North German Lloyd ships. And last year we crossed the Atlantic on the White Star line. We sailed on the *Celtic*," Melinda said. "It was quite luxurious, though of course I only saw first class."

"Blue Star ships are somewhat slower than some of the others, but cruising at around sixteen knots keeps the fuel consumption low and, in turn, the price of a ticket reasonable for the immigrants."

"That seems like a splendid purchase for your company. Do

you have any photographs of the ships? I'd love to see what the interiors look like."

"As a matter of fact, I have several." He rifled through a folder and removed pictures of the staterooms and saloons. "Here you go."

She studied the images. "They're quite elegant. The décor is Louis XV, just the style people like these days. The saloons are spacious and the furniture looks comfortable. But do you know what first-class passengers appreciate more than anything else?"

He grinned and shrugged. "Speed? Or price? Maybe good food?"

"No, those are important, but I believe travelers value service the most. If you want to continue to attract the crème of society, then provide the best service possible, even if you have to hire more stewards."

His head tilted in apparent surprise as he leaned across the desk. "Do you really think so?"

"I do, indeed. Your passengers expect to be pampered and you have several days to please them. If you succeed, then you'll earn their loyalty and they'll book passage on your ships the next time they sail."

His eyes focused on her—*with admiration*, she thought. Melinda felt the heat of satisfaction and even pleasure blast through her cheeks. For the first time in her memory Nick Bryson gazed at her with genuine interest.

"And if you want to appeal to more immigrants in third class, then improve their lot. You could feed them decently, and provide better sanitation and medical care."

Nick stayed quiet. Was she posing good possibilities or just betraying her ignorance?

"Excellent ideas, Melinda. The Bryson Steamship Company doesn't cater to the wealthiest class like many of the European lines. But when we buy Blue Star we'll assume their reputation and hopefully their passengers. They'll expect a lot from us. If we don't deliver, they'll travel on White Star or Cunard—or one of the German, French, or Italian lines. So I'm interested in your impressions."

"Thank you. Would you like me to write down what I think of each line? Not the details like speed and safety, of course, but the other things like the cuisine, activities, and amenities. I'd be delighted to give you my two cents worth."

"Yes, if you don't mind."

"Not at all." Gratitude rushed through her. Men seldom listened to her ideas about anything significant. It was almost beyond her comprehension that Nick Bryson, of all people, took her seriously.

Nick's smile vanished as his father entered the office. "I heard you two talking about our ships. Really, Melinda, what do you know about ocean liners except as a passenger? Why are you spouting your opinions as if you're some kind of authority?"

"Please stop it, Father. You're being rude." Nick's face flushed, but he kept control of his voice.

Old Frederick *harrumphed* as he drew closer and then leaned over Nick's shoulder. "What's that letter you're working on?"

"It's our response to the Blue Star line."

The tycoon curled his lip in a sneer. "What response? What are you talking about?"

Nick paled. "I'm setting up a meeting to discuss the sale."

Old Mr. Bryson reared back. "What sale? I don't recall authorizing a meeting or a sale. You're taking things in your own hands again and I won't stand for it."

Melinda winced. Her gaze riveted on Nick's stony countenance. But beneath his controlled expression she detected a hint of dismay.

In a deathly calm voice, he replied, "We spoke about it earlier, Father. You want me to offer a lower price and attempt to purchase the line."

Confusion followed by anger flickered in Mr. Bryson's eyes. "Yes, of course I remember." Abruptly he turned and stormed out of the office, leaving behind a frowning Nick.

"Please excuse him, Melinda. He hasn't been himself lately."

She nodded. "Is it serious?" Old age must be overtaking him.

"Probably."

"Is there anything I can do to help?"

Nick shook his head. "Pray for him."

"Indeed, I shall."

NICK INHALED THE lingering fragrance of her lavender perfume long after Melinda left. Her scent reminded him of Alma and stirred his memory of good times they'd had so long ago. But since their relationship had ended sadly, he wouldn't think about it. He couldn't imagine Melinda dwelling on the past. Perhaps in this one respect he should follow her example. She'd certainly impressed him with her enthusiasm. Now he'd wait and see if she'd follow through with her assessments.

He tried to work, but his father's troubling behavior nagged at his mind. Nick leaned back in the hard wooden chair. If he didn't gain control soon, his father might drive Bryson Steamship Company into bankruptcy. They couldn't afford any more of his mistakes in judgment or failure to remember critical facts.

Two hours later Glynna's husband, Stephen, knocked on his door and stuck his head inside. "We're all going on a drive. Would you like to come along? You look like you need a break."

"Indeed, I do. But I probably should stay right here and work some more."

"Nonsense. Your nieces will be most disappointed if you don't join us."

Nick hesitated. "All right, I'll come." Now that Nell was here he wanted to spend more time with her. He shouldn't let business responsibilities deter him from his duty to his niece. Parker would want him to take his place in Nell's life. A familiar feeling of melancholy settled over him. How he missed his brother's high spirits and constant banter, a wonderful antidote to his own more serious nature.

Somehow he found himself driving the carriage with Nell wedged between him and Melinda. The Farnsworths and the Van Tassel girls followed in another rig. The late afternoon air felt warm and pleasant as it penetrated his navy blue jacket and brushed against his face. The sun sent golden rays to settle over the surging ocean waves and the jagged rocks and the emerald lawns rolling to the shoreline.

Out of the corner of his eye he saw Melinda smile. Her face was shaded by a straw hat decorated with fake roses and a mesh veil, but he could still see that bright grin of hers.

"Nick, I'd like to show Nell the cottage where her mother and I used to stay every summer as children. It's on Narragansett Avenue. And I think I'll have my mother send all the photographs she and Papa took in Newport so Nell and I can put together an album."

"I'd like that." Nell clapped her hands with delight. "Would you take photographs of Janet and Julie and me at Summerhill?"

"Yes, I certainly will. I brought my Brownie camera from New York so I can take dozens of pictures."

"That's a grand idea," Nick said, a bit surprised at Melinda's thoughtfulness. But pleasantly so.

"Are you having fun with your cousins?" Nick asked as Nell snuggled into the side of his jacket.

"Yes. But I like being with you. I wish you and me and Auntie Mindy could be together. Always. Just the three of us, like Mama and Papa and me."

Nick's attempt at a light laugh sounded hollow. "But they were married. And your aunt and I aren't."

"You could get married."

Melinda looked over and chuckled at his embarrassment. "God chooses who we'll marry, Nell. If we're praying and listening to Him, we'll find the right person."

Nell cocked her head. "Do you pray a lot?"

"More and more, all the time," Melinda said softly.

"Does God talk to you?"

Melinda rubbed Nell's hand. "Sometimes."

"What does He say?"

"He tells me He'll let me know when the time is right for me to marry. He didn't actually say the words out loud, but I understood in my heart." Melinda thumped the ruffled bodice of her silk blouse.

Nick clamped his lips together, astounded by Melinda's simple, transparent declaration and the intimacy of the moment. It was almost as if she'd forgotten he was there.

"Oh." Apparently Nell also understood. "Do you pray too, Uncle Nick, about who you should marry?"

Nick hesitated. "From time to time, I ask the Lord to help me make sound business decisions, but I've never thought to get Him involved in my personal life." He saw from Nell's puzzled frown she didn't quite understand. "So I suppose my answer is no."

"Perhaps you should." Melinda looked sideways through her short veil and twitched an amused smile that gave her an impish look. "You ought to ask the Lord for guidance in every area of your life. You never know what habits He might wish for you to correct. For example, He'd like me to shop judiciously and be a wise steward of the money He gives me."

Nick couldn't keep from rolling his eyes. "And have you obeyed His wishes on that account?"

She chuckled and shrugged. "I try, but sometimes I fall short. Very short." That playful grin broadened. "And what about you? Do you think the Lord might like you to curtail your work so you can spend more time with your family?"

He bristled at her criticism. "I hardly think so, Melinda. I don't work so many hours because I enjoy doing so. I work hard because Bryson Steamship Company needs someone to run it smoothly." He stopped. If he were honest with himself, he'd admit he *did* love his work. But certainly there was nothing wrong with that.

She leaned across Nell and lightly tapped his arm with her folded fan. "Well, no matter what your reason, you must take more time out for yourself and for Nell."

"I'll try to." He had to admit, these were the best moments of his day. "As soon as I complete the purchase of Blue Star, I'll give more attention to the most important member of my family." How could a pampered young woman like Melinda really understand?

"I don't mean to scold," Melinda said, looking contrite. "I'm sorry, Nick."

"No, don't be. You're merely speaking honestly. I can't fault you for that."

Nell touched both their hands. "I'm glad we're here together."

They continued around the Ocean Drive, all three in companionable silence until they came to Bellevue Avenue. As they headed north they passed several secluded cottages tucked behind gates and shrubbery and turned right on Narragansett Avenue.

"There's Oakwood." Melinda gestured toward a driveway up ahead.

Nick reigned in the horses and halted before a closed wrought-iron gate. Stephen pulled up behind them. Above the circular drive stood a weathered, shingled cottage sprawled across an acre of smooth grass and shaded by towering oaks.

"Let's peek through the gate," Melinda said.

They all piled out of the carriages and gazed at the mansion. Melinda pointed at the wide lawn studded with trees. "Cora and I used to climb those trees, though we had to escape our nanny first. Nell, one summer your mama fell right out of that apple tree over in the corner and broke her arm."

"Did she get into trouble?" Julie asked.

"Yes, she most definitely did. And so did I. I ripped my white stockings to shreds and tore the lace on my dress. There was no supper for me that night."

Delighted, the girls asked a dozen more questions until they reluctantly returned to the carriages.

"Now I'd like to stop and show you where I'm going to build a cottage some day." Nick hadn't expected to share his future plans, but for some reason he felt inclined.

He drove back down Bellevue Avenue, turned onto a dirt path, and drove toward the sea. The wind blew in gentle gusts and hummed in his ears. Birds sang from the branches of maples scattered across the grassy lot. To the right he spotted the chimneys of a French chateau rising above a row of tall hedges and to the left, a mansard roof and another set of massive chimneys. He halted the carriage, secured the brake, and helped Melinda and Nell to disembark.

"What a perfect place for a summer home," Melinda said, her eyes brimming with admiration. "You choose well."

"Thank you. I think so too."

The girls skipped ahead toward the shore as the four adults strolled behind. "Will you build a grand French chateau or an Italianate villa like the Breakers?" Melinda asked.

"I haven't given the architecture much thought."

"To do this lot justice, you must build a palace or a castle. Something splendid to take your breath away." Melinda's eyes lit with enthusiasm as she surveyed the grounds bathed in mellow light and deep shadow. "How about a marble—"

Glynna interrupted with a laugh. "My cousin doesn't like ostentation. He's practical to a fault and perhaps a bit frugal." Glynna and her husband, Stephen, walked arm in arm a few steps behind Melinda and Nick.

Nick nodded. "You're quite right. I have no interest in a

showplace—just a comfortable home. Maybe a clapboard or shingle style."

Melinda's eyebrows drew together in a slight frown. "Then I think you're missing a splendid opportunity. Now if I had the chance to plan a cottage from scratch, I'd design the most beautiful mansion on Bellevue Avenue."

"So all your friends would be jealous?" Nick asked with a wry twist to his smile.

Melinda shrugged. "Perhaps, though that sounds rather petty, I'll admit. I'm afraid I enjoy lovely things. Is there anything wrong with that?"

"That's for you to decide," Nick answered.

Obviously feeling chastised, Melinda turned toward the hissing sea. "I think I'll join the girls."

Once she was out of earshot, Stephen said, "Now you've hurt her feelings." Medium height and thin, Stephen matched his wife in appearance. His dark hair was straight, his eyes soft and chocolate brown.

Glynna gently squeezed Nick's arm. "She's sensitive about her spending. But she was raised like most in your set to value possessions. You seem to be immune to conspicuous consumption, yet you're the exception, I think."

Nick kept his voice low. "Melinda has several wonderful qualities. But I find her desire for station and possessions distasteful."

"Come on, Nick. Don't be so harsh in your judgment. No one is perfect," Stephen chided. "Aren't you out to acquire Blue Star, yourself, at the moment? Do you not reside, this very summer, in a home with the finest of furnishings? Is Melinda so very different?"

The breeze increased as they approached the coast and sent a chill down Nick's spine. "True," he admitted.

He looked toward the girls scampering over the rocks that bordered the ocean. "Shall we keep them away from the edge?" He strode ahead, glad to move away from the topic of Melinda. And himself.

THE FOLLOWING AFTERNOON at two minutes past two Melinda rushed down the wide staircase, late for luncheon. Squeezed into a tight corset, she panted audibly as she burst through the archway into the dining room. Six pairs of eyes focused on her as she hurried across the parquet floor and took her place beside Glynna at the only place setting left empty.

"So glad you could join us," old Mr. Bryson snapped as a footman pushed her heavy chair into place.

"Please excuse me for being late," she murmured, her eyes cast down on the gold-rimmed plate and soup bowl. "I was just—well, never mind." She felt like a ten-year-old schoolgirl reprimanded by the headmistress. Embarrassment burned through her cheeks. Mama always pointed out she flustered too easily and ought to cultivate at least a small measure of poise. "I shall be more prompt in the future."

"See that you are," Mr. Bryson added before he returned to his soup.

The footman ladled some consommé into her bowl. She swallowed the tepid liquid and felt it drizzle down her throat toward her empty stomach. Melinda glanced around the long table with Mr. Bryson at the head and his daughter, Florrie, at the foot.

Everyone concentrated on finishing their course in silence while Frederick surveyed the group and grunted. "We're all abnormally quiet today. Anything wrong?"

Heads shook and tongues murmured, "No." Then back to the soup.

"Well, I'd like to welcome Melinda to Summerhill. It isn't often we get a fresh young face in our home. No offence to Florrie or Glynna. Perhaps I should say a fresh, young, unmarried face."

So apparently my tardiness has been forgiven, she thought.

"Mark my words, Melinda," the old man went on, "you won't stay single for long with all the eager swains in Newport." Frederick guffawed until Florrie interrupted.

"Please, Father, let's not tease Melinda. We all know she'll be the belle of every ball. It's unnecessary to comment on it." Florrie sent a sympathetic smile across the table.

Glynna reached over unobtrusively and squeezed Melinda's hand.

Jasper put down his soupspoon. "I heard you've already captured the heart of Phinneas Dalton. Any truth to that rumor, Melinda?" he asked with a smirk.

She shook her head, afraid if she tried to speak she'd let out a sob instead. Why was he taking such pleasure in ridiculing her?

"Phinneas is boasting all around town you'll be his wife before the end of the summer," Jasper added.

Nick glared at his brother-in-law. "Stop it, Jasper. Melinda will find her own husband, I'm sure, when she's good and ready. So don't speculate about things that are none of our business."

"Now that's where you're wrong," Old Mr. Bryson said. "She is our business because she's indirectly part of the family, thanks to Cora's . . . *decision* to declare her coguardian." He directed a hostile stare at Melinda and she flinched. "Your actions reflect on all of us, young lady, and don't you forget it, even for a moment."

Melinda's lower lip trembled, but she refused to defend herself or even speak. One moment the old man was welcoming her, the next threatening her? Was this a part of his senility?

Glynna piped up. "Really, Uncle Frederick, she's done absolutely nothing to disgrace us, and I'm positive she never will. Her behavior is above reproach. Please don't imply otherwise."

Old Mr. Bryson's pale face reddened. "You always see the best in people, Glynna Farnsworth, even when it's not warranted. But I suppose I should expect that from a missionary."

Glynna smiled sweetly. "Indeed, you should."

Melinda stifled a giggle.

Florrie leaned over her bowl. "My dear Melinda, I know you can do far better than Phinneas Dalton. A man with a large family needs an older woman, preferably a widow, to care for himself and his children. You'll want a dashing young man from a fine family and a great fortune." Her eyes swept to her brother for a second, but from his sudden frown, he'd apparently caught her meaning and didn't like it.

Jasper chimed in, "You wouldn't want a whole passel of ruffians when you already have Nell to watch over. That's quite a task for one who's so inexperienced."

"I'm doing quite well with it, thankfully." Melinda forced a smile. She wouldn't let this bunch get the better of her, though she couldn't imagine why she was the object of so much negative attention.

"Let's leave Melinda alone to finish her meal in peace," Nick said without looking her way. "I for one don't like people talking about me in my presence as if I weren't there."

After that the conversation veered away from Melinda, and she relaxed somewhat, though her stomach didn't settle. She dutifully sat, uncharacteristically silent, but she didn't dare enter into a discussion of passenger liners or business dealings. Relieved when the meal finally ended, she quickly exited and headed for her bedroom where she'd change her outfit for afternoon calls. But first she'd stop by the nursery for a quick visit with Nell.

Nick stopped her in the foyer. "I apologize for my family's rude behavior. Please forgive all of us."

Melinda felt a surge of warmth for the normally aloof Nick. "Thank you, but it's all right. I don't hold grudges."

"Good." She felt his hand lightly touch her sleeve. Nick lowered his voice and leaned closer. "My father's health is deteriorating and it's frustrating him. And the rest of us as well. He's always had a difficult personality, but it's worse lately, as you've of course noticed. He seems to have lost all his manners and tactfulness. Don't pay any attention to him."

She nodded. "All right, I won't. Thank you for telling me."

Maybe Nick really had a few drops of sympathy coursing through his veins. "By the way, I've finished a memorandum about various ships' amenities," she said. "Let me fetch it for you."

When she saw surprise in his eyes, she could barely contain a chuckle. Apparently he never expected her to follow through on her promise.

THAT EVENING MELINDA stared at her reflection in the oval mirror above her dressing table as Denise, the ladies' maid, fastened her blue diamond necklace, a gift from Grandmother Kendall on her eighteenth birthday. In the family for generations, Grandmother's necklace had been reset to suit the latest fashion. It was by far the most beautiful and ostentatious piece Melinda owned. Every time she gazed at it, her heart fluttered at her good fortune. Denise fitted a feather into her thick, upswept hair, stood back to take a better look, and nodded with satisfaction.

"Thank you. I do believe I'm ready for the ball."

Melinda rose, examined the silver lace overlaying the blue satin of her gown, and then accepted her reticule, fan, and wrap. It was too warm for a wrap right now, but the air would turn damp in the small hours of the morning when they returned to Summerhill.

A few minutes late as usual, she joined Nick and the Van Tassels in the foyer. Nick glanced at his pocket watch and frowned, but she ignored his silent rebuke. They soon boarded the waiting carriage and headed to Fairview, one of Newport's showplaces.

Melinda chatted with Florrie all the way around Ocean Drive to Bellevue Avenue where they found the Johnsons' cottage ablaze with lights. An Italian Renaissance villa, it dominated its prime lot with its sheer size. Elm and maple trees barely reached above the tile roof that topped the third floor. The leaves swayed in the light breeze blowing in from the water as the Van Tassel coach pulled up in front of the portico. With a swish of satin and taffeta skirts, the ladies piled out and picked their way across the gravel driveway to the cottage sparkling with light.

Escorted by Nick, Melinda followed the Van Tassels inside Fairview. They were greeted by the Johnsons, a young couple from Philadelphia, newly included into the upper ranks of society. By the large crowd assembled in the ballroom, it appeared they were already a popular pair. Melinda left her shawl in the cloakroom and then strolled through the foyer and into the ballroom. She accepted a dance card at the door. Immediately swarmed by gentlemen eager to request dances, her spirits soared. This was what she had been waiting for. She knew most of her admirers, at least by name, though a few were new to society. As her escort, Nick asked for the first waltz and the last dance before supper.

Again and again she heard the same question, "Will you honor me with your hand for a quadrille or a waltz?" Each time she thanked the gentleman and wrote his name on her ball card, a small, decorative booklet that listed the order of the evenings' dances. Soon all twenty-four dances—waltzes, polkas, schottisches, lanciers, and Virginia reel—were filled. She'd keep this card as a souvenir to add to her large collection.

If all went well, perhaps she'd meet her future husband tonight. Maybe she'd already met him. Her heart quickened with hope as Nick tied the card to her wrist with the attached blue ribbon.

"Thank you," she said.

He bowed and then appraised her with a gaze that seemed to penetrate right through her. What did he see? Probably a harebrained young thing without enough sense to carry an umbrella on a rainy day. Or perhaps what she was—a lady in search of a husband.

His full lips—so often pressed in a grimace—curved in a tentative smile. "I believe this is our dance."

The orchestra at the far end of the ballroom struck up a Strauss waltz. They threaded their way through the crowd to the dance floor. Nick drew her closer and she placed her hand on his shoulder. Her heart surged with hope. This proved they could be friends and enjoy each other's company from time to time. In fact, it would certainly be better for Nell if her guardians were cordial. When the dance ended, Nick bowed and another gentleman claimed her for a polka.

"I shall find you later," Nick said with a flash of very white, even teeth. He wove his way through the assembly to locate his next dance partner.

Melinda watched him disappear into a sea of pastel gowns and black evening wear, thinking he was being uncommonly social this night. But her attention was soon captured by the gentleman who'd claimed her for the next dance. With his smooth pink face and no trace of whiskers, he couldn't be any older than a boy, much too young for her. Before arriving in Newport she hadn't thought about age. But it was all too true—she was inching toward spinsterhood—or even worse, galloping toward it full speed. She had to find someone of a more suitable age. Quickly.

She danced several more times before glancing through the crowd. Melinda found herself face-to-face with Nan Holloway, an acquaintance since childhood, though never a friend. Close to Cora at least in years, the birdlike woman greeted her with a high-pitched voice and the phoniest smile in the ballroom.

"How delightful to see you again after what must have been a most painful time. Oh how I miss your dear sister. We were so close." She squeezed Melinda's gloved hands. "And how are you doing?"

"I'm recovering, thank you." With the murmur of conversations and the sounds of the orchestra, Melinda could barely hear Nan—which wasn't altogether a bad thing.

Nan wore a lemon yellow gown with a feather sticking above her head, and she looked every inch like an exquisitely turned out porcelain doll. Melinda doubted anything had ever marred her life, except perhaps the roving eye of her husband.

Melinda remembered how Nan had treated her and Cora many years before when their father squandered his fortune on worthless land in Canada. How could a social cut hurt as much as the slice of a knife? But it had.

All the pain of those awful days came flooding back. When Nan had learned of their reduced circumstances, she'd informed them they needn't come to her skating party since they'd feel awkward and out of place. And even worse, their presence would make the other guests uncomfortable. So she and Cora remained at home on a sunny winter's day, perfect for skating in Central Park. Soon all invitations stopped coming, and friends ignored the Hollisters when they met on the sidewalk or in the shops. Several months later her clever father earned most of his fortune back. But the humiliation she'd suffered during those dreadful days once more stirred in her heart. *Oh, Lord, please don't let that happen to me again.*

She'd do everything in her power to marry the gentleman the Lord chose for her. And she couldn't imagine He'd pick anyone who couldn't provide the wealth and security she needed.

As Nan chattered on, Melinda spotted her next partner, Clayton Underwood. He looked just as attractive in his evening attire as he did in tennis whites. He had the golden tan of an athlete and ice blue eyes that resembled a Siberian husky's.

Clayton bowed. His once-over, almost hungry gaze made her squirm. "You're a sight for sore eyes, Melinda. I'm sorry all those months of grieving had to keep you away from society. Mourning is such a barbaric custom, don't you think?" he asked as he led her out on the dance floor. His slow western drawl was modified by his time spent in New York City.

"Actually, I needed the time alone." She could see from the skepticism in his face he didn't agree. "But I'm happy summer is here and my mourning period is completed."

"I'm sure glad you're back. I missed your pretty face and lively ways. New York was so dull without you, I headed home for a time."

"Thank you, Clayton. You're quite the flatterer." She blushed at his exaggeration and awkward attempt to charm.

And then the polka music blared and Clayton grasped her tightly and whipped her around the dance floor. When it stopped, he led her to the side.

"It's stifling in here. Shall we stand by the terrace door?"

She fanned herself to cool off. "Yes, that's a good idea." Maybe this was just the opportunity she needed to tell him how sorry she was for her cavalier attitude toward their courtship.

They took glasses of punch from the refreshment table and strolled down the wide hallway past the card room. A few young couples were outside on the moonlit terrace, holding hands and standing closer than propriety permitted. She recognized two of the couples, newly engaged. Perhaps she shouldn't stay out here with Clayton, a man who wasn't courting her. He looped his arm around her waist, making her so uncomfortable she tried to ease away. But he held tight as he talked about his sailboat and his father's two-hundred-foot steam yacht. He loved the outdoors and detested slaving away at a desk in his father's bank.

"I understand why you'd rather be sailing than confined to a stuffy New York office." Though she didn't like boats much either.

"Maybe I'll spend next winter in Italy or Greece. My father won't like it one bit, but I have my great uncle's inheritance so I'm free to do as I please. He'll take me back next summer." Clayton grinned. "I'm his only son, so he has to."

Melinda nodded, not quite liking his cavalier attitude.

"Or maybe I'll head back to Texas. We have a branch bank in

San Antonio—not that I've ever liked banking. But the West is a grand place to live. The East is too tame for my blood."

The other couples wandered back inside the cottage, leaving her alone with Clayton.

She nodded.

"Clayton, I'd like to apologize for my behavior when I turned down your proposal. I merely wished to remain unmarried for a few more years. I'm sorry if I was tactless or unkind." As soon as the words left her lips, she felt better.

"Apology accepted. But maybe we could take up where we left off . . ."

Her tension eased. "Perhaps. We'll have to see how . . . our friendship . . . progresses."

Apparently Clayton took her words an as invitation. He spun her around on the heels of her satin slippers and pressed her close. She tried to ease away, but he held her in a tight grip. Her gaze darted toward the French doors open to the cottage. If she wrenched free, she could rush inside and find Florrie or even Nick. She wanted to extricate herself without making a scene.

"If you'll excuse me, Clayton, I must—"

Without answering he leaned down and smashed his mouth into hers. Shock immobilized her for only a second. She struggled to free herself, but the man, almost as tall and muscular as Nick, held her in place with an iron grasp. Dropping her head, his lips found only the top of her head. She hoped he got a feather in his mouth and choked on it.

Then suddenly he let go and she lost her balance and fell backward into something firm, but not as hard as the stone urn to her side. Arms wrapped around her. She caught the scent of Nick's familiar bay rum aftershave. He helped steady her as she regained her balance.

"Get out of here, Clayton, and leave Miss Hollister alone." Nick's menacing tone sent a surge of gratitude through Melinda. She need not fear Clayton with Nick by her side.

Clayton strutted toward the door. "It was just a misunderstanding. I didn't mean any harm. My apologies, Miss Hollister." He disappeared.

"Thank you, Nick," she whispered. Her legs shook so fiercely she feared she might collapse. "I never should have come out here with Mr. Underwood. But I needed fresh air—"

Nick gave a curt nod. "What would've happened if I hadn't been nearby? You should think before you act. Clayton Underwood might be wealthy and available, but he's no gentleman."

Nick's hard, almost disdainful gaze startled her. But on second glance she detected fear for her safety as much as anger. "Yes, it seems you're right. I'll not be so careless again."

She squeezed his hand and headed for the ballroom. She'd scratch Clayton off her list of eligible suitors or at least drop him down to the bottom next to Phinneas Dalton. He looked so handsome, but obviously she'd been greatly mistaken about his character. Usually her mother alerted her to possible fortune hunters and disreputable men. Mama could spot a potential rogue a mile away and had been wary of Clayton. Melinda thought he might have matured during the last few years. But apparently not.

This summer she stood alone without guidance or protection and burdened with a formidable task.

Thank You, Lord, for sending Nick to rescue me. And please give me the discernment to tell the good from the bad.

FIVE

❧

As he watched Melinda vanish, Nick wondered if she assumed his sudden appearance was coincidental. The truth was simple—he'd followed her around all evening. He couldn't take his eyes off her even though she seemed to take pleasure in chatting with the most boring and some of the shallowest of men. She certainly lacked the qualities he admired. Sincerity, a quiet spirit, depth. Still, her golden beauty enchanted him. She exuded charm and grace and high spirits—and the fragrance of lavender, his favorite scent.

If she weren't Nell's coguardian, he wouldn't care who she flirted with. But everyone and everything that concerned Nell concerned him.

Nick strolled back to the ballroom, found his partner for the next dance, and scanned the crowd for Melinda. Safely seated beside Florrie on one of the gilt chairs that lined the ornate room, Melinda looked drained of her normally rosy coloring. She stared down at her hands folded in her lap and even frowned a little. He hoped she was contemplating her recklessness. She looked chastened for the moment, but he knew she'd soon bounce back.

He'd have to keep an eye out for her this summer since she obviously couldn't discern a good man from a bad one. He didn't wish to chase after her when he'd rather concentrate his energies on business. But obviously Melinda's quest to have fun, or maybe find a husband, needed monitoring and he was the most obvious person to do so.

Yet trailing after her sounded tedious. He didn't enjoy the dinners and balls and sporting events she loved. Socializing brought out the worst in him—a tendency to harden like a lifeless statue. He had trouble with banter and small talk. Melinda was like a bubbling fountain while he was a dry creek bed. And he truly didn't care—at least not too much—because he shied away from most social situations. But her craving for society would drag him along in her wake. This might well prove to be the most irritating summer on record.

Melinda certainly wasn't anything like Alma Noble. She had understood his dislike of fancy entertainment designed to display one's wealth in the most ostentatious and often vulgar way possible. He still missed her.

If he ever married—and he assumed he would eventually—he'd choose a solid, God-fearing woman like Alma. It wouldn't matter if she were tall or short, pretty or plain, as long as they understood each other. Such a lady would be difficult to find in his set, but the Lord would provide when He saw fit. And until then, he wouldn't worry.

Although, much to his chagrin, he did worry. Little Nell had tugged at his heart. She wanted him and Melinda to marry. Of course, to a four-year-old child who only felt her own needs, marriage between her two guardians made perfect sense. She couldn't understand that adults didn't marry just to please a child, no matter how deeply they loved her. But he didn't know the right words to explain it.

He danced with his next partner—a young lady who tripped

all over his feet—then returned her to her mother seated in a gaggle of females lining the wall. He headed for the refreshment table. Accepting a glass of punch from the uniformed footman, he took a sip and noticed Melinda laughing with Simon Preston in front of the palms near the orchestra.

Tall, broad shouldered, and unfailingly polite, Simon was one of the bachelors targeted by society mothers and their daughters. He lived in Pittsburgh and owned more steel mills than anyone except Andrew Carnegie. If Preston pursued Melinda during the summer, Nick knew he'd have to scrutinize his background. Not his financial credentials, which were impeccable, but his social reputation. Melinda might be fooled by charm and money, but he certainly wasn't. He had a responsibility to safeguard Nell's happiness and her future.

MELINDA ENJOYED EVERY moment as Simon whirled her around the polished dance floor. An old acquaintance from her debutante days, she recalled he liked dancing as much as she did. But as soon as the orchestra stopped for a short break and they started to chat, she suspected the spark that had once flared between them had flickered out. *There'd never be a flame of passion to sustain this relationship.*

But given her circumstances she couldn't dismiss him out of hand. His good looks—towering height, raven black hair that waved more than curled, and olive skin—appealed to her.

They wandered over to a quiet corner. "It's a wonderful surprise to meet you again, Miss Hollister. Are you enjoying Newport this season?"

"Yes, indeed." They ducked behind a bank of potted palms, not quite out of sight of the crowd, but away from the roar of too many conversations.

"Do you enjoy chess, Miss Hollister? It's my favorite game. I thought perhaps we might play a game or two." His voice was a trifle hesitant for a man of such physical stature.

She accepted a glass of champagne from a footman carrying a silver tray of drinks. "No, I'm afraid it's too complicated for me. And I can't sit still for very long." She smiled, but his face dropped at her admission. "But I do enjoy sailing and tennis."

"How about stamp collecting?" He smiled hopefully.

She almost laughed until she noted the earnest look in his beautiful, deep blue eyes, the color of an autumn sky. What a shame she had so little in common with this handsome man with one of the largest fortunes in the country. She had to try harder to find similar interests.

But ten minutes later she gave up, even though Simon seemed more than ready to pursue her. Well, she wouldn't eject him from her list of possible husbands; after all, he did have many important attributes to recommend him. And he was a fine dancer and that had to count for something—though she knew she couldn't credit it with too much importance.

Her next partner, an older attorney with some money and little grace, whisked her away for a schottische. So far no one had truly caught her fancy. But if she were to make a match this summer, she'd have to settle for someone with wealth and character—though possibly without that indefinable quality she yearned for.

Love. She wanted love. Truth be told, she wanted love as much as money. Possibly even more so.

But was her wish too impractical? Mama would never condone such immaturity when their future was at stake. "Love will come in time," she often said. "Find a dependable, wealthy man, and build a life together. The love will come."

While Mama's words mollified Melinda, she wondered if they were true. Or simply a way toward security over substance.

STANDING AGAINST A Palladian window in the ballroom, Jasper watched Nick waltz by with a dark-haired beauty and disappear into the crush of dancers. The sounds of strings whined in his ears. The shuffle of shoes against polished wood, and the murmur of voices rising higher and louder as they vied to be heard all made his head ache. To aggravate matters, Florrie, not usually a magpie, chattered without pause. He couldn't hear her, so he nodded and smiled until his jaw hurt.

His eyes surveyed the crowd and stopped at a gigantic man, his head rising high above the dancers. Albert Underwood, financier and banker. Jasper wished he could vanish into the green damask wall behind him, evading the big man. But when Underwood's mouth tightened to a thin, grim line, Jasper knew he'd been seen. The man began a slow walk toward him around the rim of the ballroom, halting to speak to friends, but never taking his eyes off Jasper for more than a second.

"Florrie, would you care for a glass of punch or perhaps champagne?" he asked. She looked like a carrot in that dreadful orange gown.

"Why, thank you, Jasper. I should like some of that delicious punch."

He'd prefer a whiskey. "I shall return in no time." Escaping his wife, he skirted the perimeter, tucking his head to his chin so he need not greet anyone. Glancing sideways, he saw Underwood had lost sight of him and was scanning the room.

Jasper's heart thumped so hard he thought it might crack his rib cage. He slipped through the open doorway and came to the foyer, nearly deserted except for waiters carrying trays of champagne. *It must be ten degrees cooler here*, he thought with relief. Breathing easier, he headed to the terrace, hoping to disappear into the starry night. He'd send a message to Florrie via a servant that he'd gone home with a headache. He crossed the stone patio, ran down the steps and onto the darkened lawn. The night seemed to swallow him after the blur of light and color inside. He stood still while his eyes adjusted to the faint shadows of trees, their leaves stirring in the breeze. He padded over to a wide-skirted maple. Leaning against the rough bark and out of sight, he felt his heart rate gradually return to normal.

A twig cracked behind him. Jasper gasped and whirled.

"Hiding from me, Van Tassel?" Albert Underwood gave a nasty laugh. "You can't avoid me, you know. Not unless you hightail it abroad, and even there I have my connections."

Jasper didn't doubt it. "I'm not trying to avoid you. I merely stepped outside for some air. Beautiful night, isn't it?" Jasper's voice trembled, betraying his lie.

Why had he ever allowed this crooked moneylender into his life? All he'd wanted was a loan to cover his expenditures, but he hadn't thought it necessary to read the fine print. And Underwood hadn't mentioned that the interest was exorbitant. Highway robbery, in fact.

"Actually, the wind is picking up and making it chilly. But even in the dark I can see you're sweating." Underwood laughed with malice. "I won't take up much of your time, Jasper. You seem to forget you owe me quite a substantial sum. I'm not a patient man. I'll expect your repayment by August. I'll be in touch." Underwood turned on his heel and strutted back to Fairview.

Those business investments Parker praised so highly turned out to be ill-advised, risky ventures. Jasper knew he should've checked them out more thoroughly before snatching them up. If only he'd listened to Nick instead of Parker, who talked a good story but was far from the astute businessman Frederick thought he was. Now he had to pay the shyster back with exorbitant interest. And then there were those gambling debts he'd accumulated in New York over the winter and spring. Tens of thousands of dollars lost at the baccarat table still owed to several friends who weren't acting like friends of late.

Jasper mopped his brow with a handkerchief. Where would he find the cash? And lots of it? Without it he might as well run off to South America, though he'd heard Pinkerton's men could track anyone anywhere. He had no choice but to get the money.

Returning to the foyer he stopped a footman with a tray of drinks in hand. "Would you tell my wife, Mrs. Van Tassel, I'm indisposed and going home early? She's the lady in the orange gown over in the corner."

"Yes, sir." The footman nodded and disappeared into the ballroom.

Jasper soon rode off in his carriage. The coachman would return to Fairview and bring Florrie and the rest of them home during the early morning hours when the orchestra finally put away their instruments. He'd have a chance to ponder his situation and, hopefully, work out a solution before Albert Underwood came calling.

AFTER THE BALL Melinda decided to check on Nell, though she expected to find her snuggled in her bed and fast asleep at two in the morning. As she walked the hallway, the Oriental runner muffled her steps. A few gaslights cast a dim glow, washing the corridor in deep shadows.

The tall, surly-looking footman she recognized from luncheon stepped out of the nursery and padded off in the opposite direction. Alarmed, Melinda hastened to the playroom and found Peggy, her curly black hair a mess and her doily cap askew. When she spotted Melinda, she flushed and stammered.

"Beggin' your pardon, miss, I didn't know you were there."

Melinda entered the dark playroom and led the nursery maid over to the window seat and out of earshot of the children's bedrooms. Moonlight filtered through the screens and hushed space.

"What was that man doing in here?" Melinda asked in a quiet tone. No point in reprimanding the girl until she received an explanation, though she was quite sure what happened.

"I was speaking to Eddie, the footman, miss. I know that's

against the rules, but you see, he's my sweetheart and he wanted to say good night, so I invited him into the playroom so we could have a moment of privacy. We're both off duty so I didn't see the harm of saying just a word or two. I hope you don't mind—too much—miss. I promise I'll never break the rules again, if you'll just give me another chance to prove myself."

Even in the dimness, Melinda saw the fear in her eyes and heard the desperation in her soft voice.

"Yes, Peggy, I shall give you another chance. I'm not unreasonable. But please wait until your evening off to see your young man. Nanny Wells could have caught you and then you'd surely be in a world of trouble."

"Yes, miss. I do thank you from the bottom of my heart."

For a moment Melinda was afraid the poor, grateful nursemaid might embrace her in a hug, but the girl quickly regained her dignity. "May I go now, Miss Hollister?"

"Yes, certainly." How could she reprimand the girl who only wanted a bit of fun and maybe a kiss or two? She worked hard all day with little opportunity for socializing.

Melinda shuddered to think how she'd manage to live under such austere restrictions.

THE NEXT AFTERNOON Melinda poked her head into Florrie's art studio. "The three little girls are having a tea party in just a few minutes. They hope you can come."

Paintbrush in hand, Florrie stepped away from her easel. Smudges of yellow paint soiled the apron that covered a worn cotton dress.

She sighed. "I'd love to, of course, but as you can see, I can't leave right now. Perhaps I'll pop in when I'm done, though I'm afraid I might not finish for hours. And I do lose track of time when I paint."

"They'll be disappointed."

"Tell the children I'll come to their next tea party and to have a splendid time," Florrie said as dismissively as if she were speaking to the children themselves. She returned to her easel before Melinda had a chance to say good-bye.

Melinda climbed the stairs to the nursery playroom and entered.

"Well, what do we have here?"

Melinda glanced over her shoulder and saw Nick filling the doorway. Her heart flip-flopped, a most unwelcome reaction. "The girls are having a tea party. Do come in and join us. Nanny and I are pouring, Nell and Julie are putting lumps of sugar in the cups, and Janet is serving cakes."

"Stay, Uncle Nick," the trio begged. Apparently he couldn't resist their pleas and hopeful smiles because he strode across the carpet to the table. He gingerly lowered himself to one of the miniature chairs. A grin split his face as he accepted a china cup hand-painted with violets.

"This looks delicious," he said to the delight of the girls.

Melinda suppressed a laugh at the sight of the long-limbed man attempting to tuck his legs beneath the low table. His knees smashed into the wood and he let out a groan. He turned the tiny chair sideways and stretched his legs. "There. That's better. Now may I have a tea cake? Please."

He looked ludicrous, but also endearing. He wore white flannel trousers, a starched shirt with a bow tie, and a navy blue jacket, the standard outfit for the Casino. Very jaunty.

Melinda rose to help Janet put three tea cakes with a swirl of vanilla frosting on a china plate, and then Janet handed it to Nick. He took a bite and said, "We must compliment the chef. He outdid himself, as usual. Or did you girls make these yourselves?"

They giggled at the very idea of baking.

"I'm too little," Nell explained. "I can't reach the baking table."

"Maybe not yet. But you're four now and soon you'll be big

enough to try baking with the chef's help." Nick took a bite and declared the cake delicious.

When they'd all eaten their fill, Nanny and the girls cleared the table and placed the dishes on the dumbwaiter. Melinda and Nick said their good-byes and headed downstairs to the drawing room. It was two o'clock and Florrie's "at home" day, the time each week when the women in the family were available for visitors. Although, technically, she wasn't.

Melinda paused at the French doors leading into the drawing room. "Florrie asked me to take her place earlier. She's busy painting."

"She always painting," he mumbled.

"That's rather critical, isn't it, Nick?"

"I'm sorry. She is a talented artist."

"What does she paint?" Melinda asked as they descended the stairs.

A small smile played at the corner of Nick's mouth. "Nudes— in addition to other things like scenery and still life."

"Oh my," Melinda murmured. She felt her cheeks heating. "Does she use live models?"

He let out a chuckle. "Not that I know of."

Melinda entered the sunny drawing room, anxious to change the subject. "If you'll excuse me, I'll wait for Florrie's visitors."

"And I shall wait with you."

Surprised, she lifted her eyebrows. "I would have thought you'd have more important things to do than keep me company." She descended to the white and gold brocaded settee and spread her fine muslin skirt over her legs.

The grandfather clock in the foyer chimed two. "I have a lot of work to do, but it can wait for a while."

"Well, I appreciate your thoughtfulness."

A few minutes later, when the butler announced the arrival of two young gentlemen who'd obviously come to call on her, she understood Nick's motives. His eyes narrowed at the sight of Reggie Parmenter and his sister, Camy, and their houseguest, Simon Preston.

Reggie was a bit too short and lumpy—with a shock of unruly honey brown hair and a ruddy complexion—to make him truly eligible among their set. But he was sweet enough.

"It's so nice to see you back in society, Miss Hollister," he said in a high-pitched voice. Then he flashed a grin, as if he'd said his piece and now could sit back and listen to the rest of the conversation without having to contribute anything more. She'd forgotten how shy he was, especially compared to his effervescent sister Camy who never struggled for something to say, appropriate or otherwise. But Melinda liked both Parmenters, in small doses.

Simon Preston bowed and handed her a bouquet of red roses. *Despite his interests in stamp collecting and chess, he might be worthy of a second look,* she mused.

"They're beautiful," she said and chose to ignore Nick's arched brow. She rang for a parlor maid to place the flowers in a vase on the marble-topped side table.

"You will be joining us at the picnic tomorrow, won't you?" Camy later asked, looking from Melinda to Nick. He nodded without comment. "Good. Mrs. Van Tassel accepted for everyone last week. We'll have a splendid time, I'm sure."

"We'll be delighted to come," Melinda said.

She needed to attend every social function she could, though she noticed Florrie got so involved with her art she sometimes forgot her obligations. Not appearing that afternoon was a dreadful faux pas that might prompt insulted hostesses to scratch her from their guest lists. But Melinda suspected Florrie's eccentricities were quickly forgiven because she belonged to a prosperous and well-respected family who'd been in society for generations.

After they set down their cups, the Parmenters excused themselves and headed for the double doors while Simon lingered.

"I'm delighted you're going to the picnic. If I may be so bold, I look forward to spending time with you." He gazed at her with a quiet warmth she found a bit disconcerting, but rather exciting.

"We'll both be in attendance," Nick interjected abruptly, in a proprietary manner she found irksome.

"We're all going," she said, trying to smooth over his odd manner. "The entire household. A picnic is such a nice change of pace from all the formal entertainment." As she watched Nick frown at Simon, she chattered on without pausing for breath. Anything to ease the unspoken tension.

She didn't let Simon get a word in edgewise, but he didn't seem to tire of her monologue.

Finally Camy called from the door, "Do come, Simon. We have more calls to make."

"Of course." He dragged his feet across the Aubusson carpet.

When only Nick remained, Melinda relaxed. She smiled at Nick's glowering face.

"What charming people. I had a most enjoyable afternoon. How about you?" When his countenance darkened, she knew she shouldn't have asked such a silly question. Obviously he'd endured the small talk for her sake—unless something else was bothering him.

"I'd better get back to work. If you'll excuse me." He rose and started for the door.

"Is anything the matter, Nick? Was it something I said?"

"No, not at all. I'm annoyed with myself. I shouldn't have wasted two hours chit-chatting about inconsequential things when I have a business to run. Or help run." He left in a huff.

Melinda wasn't sure which bothered him more: time frittered away or listening to trivial banter. Or perhaps her potential suitors parading into Summerhill annoyed him most. Now that she and Nick were bound together by Nell, he seemed determined to watch her every move. She felt sure he was judging her behavior and finding it wanting. That didn't seem at all fair.

It came to her then: he was evaluating each potential suitor as a stepfather for Nell. Well, who she married really wasn't any of his concern. She'd never dream of suggesting who he ought to court, though she couldn't imagine anyone at all wishing to marry such a disagreeable, irritable, noncharitable man.

HER DEPLORABLE TASTE in men caused Nick to shudder. He wouldn't allow her to choose a fortune hunter, an oaf, or a sportsman for Nell's stepfather. No spoiled or lazy mama's boy would do. He couldn't help but worry about her future and Nell's since Melinda seemed so determined to catch a husband. But surely she'd never consider someone as bland as Simon Preston. Somehow he had to ensure she chose wisely. He brooded for the remainder of the day and into the evening, until finally, blessedly, sleep overtook him.

THE NEXT MORNING Nick didn't feel one bit better. Wandering out to the veranda he found his father reading the *Wall Street Journal*.

A warm breeze rattled the sheets of newsprint clutched in his blue-veined hand. "Have a seat, Nicholas."

Everything Frederick Bryson suggested was a command. Nick dropped into a wicker chair in front of the potted palms and waited for his father to speak his mind.

The old man raised one white brow. "Why so glum? Surely you're not panting after that giddy Hollister girl. She's just like her sister, may God rest her soul. Neither one ever had an ounce of common sense."

Nick felt his neck stiffen. "Certainly she's lighthearted, but I'm sure she's sensible." He wasn't sure of any such thing, but he always defended those his father criticized, usually unjustly.

The elderly man peered through his pince-nez. "Make sure you don't marry her yourself. You two have nothing in common."

Except for Nell. "I'm not planning to marry anyone, least of all Melinda." Nick felt like bolting, but no one dared leave Frederick until he dismissed them. "Why are you linking me with Melinda? I've never shown any interest in her—since I don't have any."

His father grunted. "I've noticed you follow her around."

Nick shrugged. "That's just your imagination, Father."

"I don't think so. But it's about time you took a wife. If you're unsure who would suit you, ask your mother when she comes to Newport. Although in her last letter she hinted she might stay with her sister in the mountains for the rest of the season."

"She wants to mourn Parker without a houseful of people disturbing her solitude." A woman who lost her child remained in mourning far longer than her husband, an odd custom that his mother strictly observed. She seemed more affected by the deaths than his father, though Frederick's crusty manner might be covering up a grieving heart. If his father even had a heart. "And Mother is staying in Bar Harbor with her brother and sister-in-law, not in the mountains."

Frederick dismissed the comment with a wave of his hand. "It doesn't matter. I merely got confused for a second. I'll give her a few more weeks and then insist she come to Summerhill." Frederick leaned forward and lowered his voice. "Marrying someone suitable would allow you to sue for sole custody of Nell. No judge would deny you and your wife. But you won't be in any stronger position than Melinda unless you marry. She's only a girl from a nouveau riche family, but she very well might charm a susceptible judge. We can't take that chance. Nell belongs with us. She's a Bryson."

"Why don't you like Melinda?" Nick had often wondered why Frederick made so many disparaging remarks about Cora and Melinda. Neither one deserved such strong disapproval.

Frederick snorted through his long, prominent nose. "She's all right, I suppose, just immature and a bit flighty. Caught up in society and far too concerned with clothes and such. Remember, I saw her often when she visited Cora. Couldn't help but notice a pretty young thing dressed in ruffles and lace."

"I assure you, Melinda is an adult now." At least her devotion to Nell showed she was starting to grow into a caring young woman. Nick agreed she might still be materialistic and shallow, but he would no longer disparage her. After all, she had many redeeming qualities . . . kindness, a brilliant smile, love for their little niece—

"It's more than just the girl herself." Frederick cocked a brow. "I never approved of her parents. Her mother's a great beauty, but a blatant social climber. And her grandfather sold boots with cardboard soles to the Union Army." He shook his head with disdain. "I never respected the man. Did I ever tell you that story?"

"No, Father, you didn't."

"Well, I should have." His testy voice choked. "My brother Garth died during the War from influenza. He most likely caught it from getting his feet soaking wet from wearing Carson Hollister's shoddy boots."

"Surely you can't know that, Father," Nick protested.

"I do know that. Selling cheaply made goods was worse in the Confederate Army than in the Union, but there were some unscrupulous contractors in the north as well. And Hollister was one of them." Frederick's mouth pressed in a tight line. "The army sent me Garth's personal effects, and right there among his uniforms was a pair of worn-out boots with holes the size of playing cards. And they were Hollister's brand."

"You can't blame Melinda for her grandfather's sins."

Frederick shrugged his squared shoulders. "Perhaps not, but nobody can force me to like her. And I don't want another one of Hollister's granddaughters in my family."

"Well, don't worry, Father, I have no intention of marrying Melinda."

"See that you don't. I credited you with some sense and I'm gratified to see I was right. Now if you've got some time to talk, I'd like to discuss my retirement."

"Your retirement?" The words nearly hitched in Nick's throat. That would be a godsend.

"I'm giving the idea serious thought. I'd like to take your mother on a cruise around the world and I can't do that if I'm worried about my steamship line. So obviously I'll have to step down and turn over the presidency to someone." He narrowed his eyes at Nick.

His pulse quickened. He'd been waiting patiently, though sometimes impatiently, to gain control. And if all went well with the purchase of Blue Star, he'd run the largest line of passenger ships in America. Well prepared to take over, he'd build the family business into an empire.

Frederick would be proud of him—for once. The old man had invested all his time, hopes, and energy into grooming Parker for leadership, but after his death, Nick had assumed his brother's position.

"Don't look so gleeful, Nicholas. I haven't decided when, or even if, I'll retire. I'm still mulling it over. But if I do, I'll decide who'll succeed me—either you or Jasper."

Jasper? If his father had pounded his face to a pulp, it wouldn't have hurt any more. How could the old man even consider a syco-phant like Jasper? Nick felt his internal temperature rise. The very idea of Jasper taking over was irresponsible and downright treacherous.

"He's an accountant, so he might make a capable president." Frederick's eyes glowed with so much malicious glee Nick recoiled. "What do you say about him?"

Nick fought to keep his frustration under control. "I say he's too conservative. He's afraid to take risks. But that's not prudence, it's cowardice." His father had baited him and he'd snapped at it. But he wouldn't apologize for telling the truth.

Frederick gave a nasty laugh. "Those are strong words, Nicholas. Can you back them up?"

"Not yet, but I shall. As soon as I purchase the Blue Star, I'll convince you I'm right," Nick said with more bravado than he felt.

"See that you do, son," he said, sticking an unlit cigar in his mouth. "See that you do." Frederick leaned forward and raised an eyebrow. "This is your opportunity to prove yourself. If you can close the deal and satisfy me, I'll be inclined to favor you over Jasper. But if you can't, well, you know how it is, don't you? I must think of the company first and foremost."

Nick nodded. He'd always known that.

SIX

❧

The Van Tassels' carriages halted in front of the Middletown farmhouse the Parmenters had rented for their picnic. With the coachman's help Melinda climbed down along with the Farnsworths. The Van Tassels and Nick emerged from the other rig.

"Picnics certainly excite the cottagers." Nick flashed a sardonic grin as he led the group across the lawn to the picnic area by the edge of the woods. All around them friends jabbered as if this outing to a rented farm was a special treat.

Melinda nodded. "Everyone says it's fun to pretend to be common folk, at least once in a while. But actually living like them would be altogether different." If she didn't catch a husband, she'd find out all too soon.

They stopped beneath the deep shade of an oak tree, and Melinda spread her quilt over the freshly cut grass. She breathed of the sweet scent. "My, what a lovely day." She lowered onto the brightly colored blanket and fanned her mauve skirt over her legs. Only her cream-colored boots showed beneath the hem. Beyond the lawn, low, rolling hills, green meadows, and a fieldstone farmhouse made for the perfect setting for an afternoon's picnic, peaceful, bucolic.

While the cottagers lounged, footmen and maids busily un-packed baskets and hampers and set up the luncheon buffet brought by the Parmenters' staff. Most of the servants would soon disap-pear and then the gentlemen would take over and wait upon the ladies who always found this change of role quite amusing.

The Farnsworths settled beside her on a quilt while Florrie and Jasper sat nearby in the sunshine. Several yards away footmen stuck croquet wickets into the lawn, and some of the picnickers reached for wooden balls and mallets. Farther out another footman set up a tennis net for the more athletic.

"Do you mind if I join you?" Nick asked, dropping his quilt next to hers.

How could she possibly attract suitors with Nick hovering around? "Of course, if you'd like," she answered with a half smile.

Obviously tone deaf, Nick sat on his lone star quilt and stretched out his long legs. "Quite a crowd today."

"Yes. I believe I know most everyone here," Melinda replied.

That wasn't too remarkable since most of the cottagers came from New York. Fewer hailed from Boston, Philadelphia, and the Midwest. Every summer they converged on Newport and formed an elite summer colony envied by those less privileged. She'd grown up in the New York Knickerbocker set and socialized with them since her debut. Had it actually been five years come this fall? Time had flown by in a whirl of fun.

Melinda surveyed the guests as they strolled past. Many of her friends and some of her mother's stopped to chat. Camy and Reggie Parmenter strode over with Simon Preston at their heels.

"May we join you?" Camy asked Melinda. Camy looked lovely in a blue-green outfit with a pleated bodice and ruffled skirt. Her straw hat had a flat crown with a turquoise band and streamers.

"Yes, please sit beside us."

They tossed their blanket onto the only available patch of grass right next to Melinda. Simon edged his quilt even closer.

Exchanging small talk, she eyed him. With the exception of Nick, Simon boasted the most striking appearance among all the young gentlemen—not that looks were the most important asset to a suitor. She glimpsed other ladies gazing his way, and she felt a small glow of self-confidence, happy she hadn't lost her appeal. They talked about friends and family and the season's entertainment before Simon leaned closer.

"Do you enjoy coaching, Miss Hollister? If you do, perhaps you'd join the Parmenters and me for a race Tuesday afternoon."

"I'd be delighted. Of course I must check my calendar first, but I believe I'm free."

From the corner of her eye she spotted Nick's tight-lipped scowl as he straightened up. Was he just a little jealous? How absurd. He probably didn't want her to marry. But if she remained single, she'd no doubt have to rely more on him for support than she wanted.

Simon's round blue eyes sparkled. "I hope we can get better acquainted this summer."

"Yes, I'd like that."

From the gleam in Nick's eye, he fought back a derisive snort. She ought not feel so embarrassed. Every unmarried lady her age searched for a husband, though most gentlemen pretended not to notice. She certainly didn't wish to be the season's laughingstock by blatantly running after every available man. But without powerful family backing, she was less desirable than wealthier ladies with less beauty. What a shame she had to rely upon her reputed charm and appearance.

"Would you like something to eat, Melinda?" Nick asked as he rose. He held out a hand to help her up. Amusement still tugged at the corner of his mouth.

"Yes, I would. Thank you." She chose to ignore the fact that he found her situation amusing. Perhaps being on his arm would alert other suitable bachelors that they ought to step up or they might very well lose out.

They strolled toward the trestle tables laden with trays of lobster tails with mayonnaise, baked Virginia ham, roast beef, cold poached salmon with cream sauce, all kinds of salads, and a trifle for dessert. Chilled champagne, raspberry lemonade, and hot tea were also served. Baskets of wildflowers added bursts of bright color to the white linen tablecloth. Even though she had no appetite, Melinda placed a piece of crusty French bread and a bit of chicken on a china plate. Thanking Nick for a goblet of lemonade, she glanced around the picnic grove. Surely there must be many more unattached gentlemen, but it seemed the pickings were distressingly slim.

Then she sighted Clayton Underwood climbing down from a coach emblazoned with a gold crest. He lifted a hand in greeting, and her heart squeezed with annoyance at the liberties he'd taken at the ball. He spotted her, smiled with apparent pleasure, and bowed.

"Clayton Underwood acts as if he's still a friend of yours. Is he?" Nick asked with disapproval in his voice.

"No, definitely not after the other evening. But I'll admit he was—once. We courted for a time. But I haven't seen Mr. Underwood in quite a long while."

Probably Nick had never heard the story of how she'd rebuffed Clayton's proposal when most of society expected their engagement to be announced. Several matrons openly criticized her decision and declared her a fool. But she knew she did the right thing for both of them. Even Mama defended her decision to wait awhile before marrying. She hoped Nick hadn't heard the gossip because she didn't want him to judge her as flighty and self-centered as others had. Perhaps she'd deserved the label, though she didn't think postponing marriage was wrong for a young lady.

"Are you acquainted with Mr. Underwood?" Melinda asked.

"Only by sight and reputation."

Melinda swallowed hard. "Would you care to elaborate?"

"No, I've said more than I should."

Clayton didn't hurry over to join her and Nick, but that was just as well. Perhaps Clayton thought they were a couple and he didn't wish to intrude, especially after Nick had interceded. She might approach him later when the time was right. They needed to reconcile after the incident at the ball. At least find their way to civility. If he held a grudge or spread lies about her, he could ruin her chances for a good match.

"Shall we sit down and eat our supper?" Nick asked, eyeing her with curiosity.

She nodded. They strolled back to their spot, and she settled onto her wedding ring quilt shaded by the leafy elm tree. Against her better judgment, Clayton still sparked her interest—until she saw him arm in arm with Louisa Davenport, one of her closest friends.

But later, while Nick was returning the luncheon plates, Clayton appeared at her side. Tall and broad shouldered, a blond curl fell over his eye. He wore a tan sack suit and patterned silk vest. His black string tie and tall Stetson hat gave him a western look that distinguished him from everyone else.

"It's good to see you again, Miss Hollister. Beautiful day, isn't it?"

She nodded. "It is, indeed."

"I was wondering if maybe you'd care to take a boat ride. The pond is calm, so there's no danger of tipping over. And I'd like to apologize for my unforgivable behavior at the ball. I'm truly sorry." He tucked his chin to his chest and looked at her with boyish charm lighting his eyes.

"I should say no."

"But you won't, will you?" he asked.

"No, I shall give you another chance." Especially since she spotted Phinneas Dalton strutting her way. She didn't want him to monopolize even one second of her time.

She and Clayton crossed the lawn together until they came to a duck pond edged with water lilies blooming near the reeds. He scrambled onto the rowboat and with a flourish of his handkerchief wiped off the already clean wooden seats. Steadying the boat, he helped Melinda on board. Once they were both settled, he grasped the oars and smoothly sliced through the glassy blue-green water. She opened her ruffled parasol, made from the same silk as her frock, and tilted it for a clearer view of Clayton. They talked of insignificant things, and Melinda began to enjoy herself.

"I've decided to return to Texas and settle down. We have a bank in San Antonio so I might work there for a while. I really want to buy a ranch—a large spread with the biggest herd of cattle in the state."

"That sounds exciting." Melinda watched his face warm up. But she knew he never settled on one project for long.

He nodded vigorously and his hair shone like gold in the sun. "You'd love Texas. Maybe you'd consider coming with me and—"

She cut him off. "Oh my, Clayton, you know I'm an Easterner. I could never adapt to sage brush and cactus, although I'm sure it's all quite beautiful." She tossed him a nervous laugh. "I'm also a city girl. You understand, don't you? I came out here with you so that we might find our way . . . to friendship."

Clayton's frown deepened. "You've changed, Melinda. I thought you craved excitement and maybe a little adventure. Just like me."

She laughed. "Well, I most certainly do like fun, but I prefer it confined to a ballroom here on the East Coast."

"It's the girl, isn't it?" he muttered, cocking a brow her way. "A child can get in the way of a person's plans."

Melinda frowned. "My niece adds something very special to my life. She doesn't take anything from it." A little time perhaps, yet the child had a nanny to care for most of her needs. Melinda had never found her an inconvenience, even while they travelled alone on the steamship from New York. A challenge because of her own inexperience, but not an encumbrance.

But Clayton's scowl unnerved her. A cloud skittered across the sun and the breeze freshened.

"No, Melinda, you are changing, only you don't realize it." And his tone added he wasn't one bit pleased about it. "You've lost your high spirits."

And appeal, apparently. His face was as cold now as if she'd thrown water on him.

A short time later, when they returned to shore, Melinda wondered if other gentlemen would find her less pleasing once they realized she had a duty to her niece. She hoped not. *Lord, please remove such discouraging thoughts from my mind. I'm sure You have plans for me. I'll try to be patient. Please let me discern Your will. Sometimes I'm easily misled. Oh, Lord, don't let me make a mistake and marry the wrong man because I'm too anxious. And desperate. But please don't let me pass by the right one.*

"Why are you so quiet?" Clayton asked.

He'd laugh at her if she admitted she was praying. "I was thinking."

"You're more amusing when you laugh. You have the most joyful laugh I've ever heard."

"Thank you." But life wasn't all happiness and cheer. She also had moments of serious reflection. She suspected Clayton wouldn't like those thoughtful times nearly as well.

As they strode toward her friends, Melinda spotted Nick, scowling at them. Clayton greeted him and the Farnsworths and then hastily excused himself. He ambled toward the tennis game at the far end of the lawn.

Nick yanked up a blade of grass. "Clayton Underwood is quite the ladies' man."

Melinda's eyes widened. "What do you mean?"

Nick quirked an eyebrow as if she ought to know exactly what he meant. "Perhaps I needed to be clearer with you earlier. I thought you had more sense than to take off with him again, alone."

She bit her lip. "He was a perfect gentleman. And you know as well as I that crossing someone in society could destroy the entire season."

"Melinda," Nick said tiredly, "he always has a lady on his arm. He spends most of his time on his yacht or playing polo."

She put her hands on her hips. "There's nothing wrong with sports. Or having the funds to . . . *enjoy* life's pleasures." Why couldn't Nick be more pleasant and less critical?

"But all play and no work makes a man restless. It's not a satisfying life. He's bound to wander."

"I'm not about to marry him, Nick," she whispered fiercely, "if that's what you're insinuating. I merely sought a measure of civility."

And besides, how could he know whether Clayton would continue to be a pleasure-seeker as a married man? Every man needed to find his balance, Nick included. He worked hard, but from what she'd seen, he seldom played. Even in Newport he usually holed up in his tiny study by the telephone conducting business with the company's New York office. Drudgery seemed to be his only real enjoyment.

"A life of uninterrupted leisure wouldn't be good for Nell."

"And a life of unmitigated work would leave her a tired, boring girl too," she retorted.

He stared down at her for a long moment.

"Nick, you have no say about whom I marry," she said softly. "I don't need your approval."

"You're right. But every decision you make affects Nell. And therefore, they then affect me. I'm looking out for all of us."

It was Melinda's turn to stare up into his eyes. *How could he possibly—In what way did he believe—*

Finally, she simply shook her head. "There's nothing further to say."

"There's a great deal—"

"No, Nick. You've overstepped your bounds. I'd appreciate it if you would kindly find somewhere else to sit for the rest of our time here."

"I'm afraid I cannot abide by those wishes," he said, folding his arms in front of his chest.

She tucked her chin, surprised at his poor etiquette. "Very well, then," she said, finding that she was folding her own arms.

"Very well," he returned.

DURING THE REST of the afternoon, Nick watched the young swells swarm around Melinda as if he wasn't there. Tyler Brooks, his friend's younger brother, practically tripped over Nick's outstretched legs as he brought her a glass of iced tea. Someone else presented a plate of petit fours and dainty cookies from the dessert table. She accepted all of it, nibbled and sipped, but ate almost nothing. Her laughter resounded like music against the hum of nearby chatter and the chirp of birds nesting in the trees. She flirted with every admirer who stopped to talk and beamed from the attention.

Sitting beside her and totally ignored, his mood gradually soured. He admitted to himself that he would've liked to talk to her alone, quietly, about some consequential topic that interested both of them—if they could find one. Maybe Nell.

Then Simon Preston rose from his quilt. His besotted gaze still rested on Melinda as it had throughout the afternoon. It probably gave her great satisfaction to attract the attention of such a sought-after gentleman.

"Miss Hollister, would you care to accompany me on a short walk?" Simon asked.

Her lips curved upward and her head tilted coquettishly. "I'd like that."

Simon helped her up and off they strolled, with not one glance back in his direction. At least she wasn't off with the despicable Clayton again. Simon was careful to stay within sight of the picnickers. He seemed affable enough, if perhaps on the dull side—a gentleman who'd soon bore Melinda to distraction.

Nick squirmed on the quilt, tired and sore from sitting on the ground for too long. He rose and poured himself another cup of tea at the trestle table and chatted with old friends for a time. When he returned to his spot beneath the trees, Melinda was back and still flirting with Simon. But soon one of the other young ladies slid her arm into the crook of Simon's arm and led him toward the croquet area. He looked back to Melinda longingly, but headed away.

"Mr. Preston seems like a nice man," Nick said as he dropped onto the quilt beside her.

"Really, Nick," she said with a sigh. "I thought I'd made myself clear."

He shrugged. "I'm merely paying the man a compliment. Is that not allowed?"

"Yes," she said tiredly. "He's quite . . . nice."

Her lukewarm endorsement lifted his spirits like a helium balloon. She'd probably not marry a man who didn't fascinate her. And from the look on her face, she was far from enthralled. Yet if she were set on marrying before she fell into spinsterhood, she might very well consider Simon.

By four o'clock rain clouds formed overhead, the sky darkened, and in the distance thunder rumbled above the merriment of the picnickers. "Shall we leave?" he asked, rising.

He was glad for an excuse to return to Summerhill; he'd neglected his work long enough.

Melinda nodded. "It looks like we're in for a downpour."

All the guests gathered their belongings and retreated to their equipages for the trip back home, which would leave ample time to prepare for the night's entertainment. But he'd skip the ball this evening and catch up on the work he'd neglected all afternoon.

After they piled into the enclosed carriage, Florrie leaned across the aisle toward Melinda. "My dear, you're positively glowing. You have every one of those young gentlemen wrapped around your little finger." She smiled her approval.

Nick scowled. Florrie never delved beneath the surface of relationships because she might hear something unpleasant. As long as she had her art studio and a nanny to watch her children, she was happy. And she liked to assume others were equally content with their lives.

"Yes, I had a grand time," Melinda said, wiggling closer to the door and away from Nick.

He fought off the glower that tightened his face. Melinda did look satisfied, even a bit smug. She could command any man she wished. Well, nearly. He was more immune to her charms than the younger crowd, a naive bunch easily enthralled by a pretty face and dazzling smile. Still, he understood why they were captivated.

Florrie cupped her hands and whispered to Melinda, "I heard a rumor; Louisa Davenport has an understanding with Clayton Underwood."

Obviously surprised, Melinda leaned closer. "I don't believe so. I'd never have gone boating if she were interested in him— although I haven't seen much of her since last fall. Oh dear me, I hope I didn't do something awful." She pushed back into the plush seat, her shoulders slumping. "I shall speak to Louisa just as soon as I can."

The rain held off until they reached Summerhill. Heading their separate ways, Nick started toward the library, then stopped and turned back to Melinda. His annoyance steadily mounted while his good sense weakened.

"I want to warn you there's something unsavory about Clayton. I can't pinpoint it, but I'm sure he's not someone you should . . . encourage."

She rolled her eyes, not bothering to answer. Which was just as well since he'd only alienate her more with his unwanted but worthwhile advice. If she only had the logical mind and sound judgment of his lost love. Alma provided an example of strong Christian womanhood he used to measure every other lady. Unfortunately he'd never found anyone her equal. Certainly not Melinda, despite her other rather obvious charms.

But then Melinda raised a teasing smile. "I understand your concerns about Clayton. But what about Simon Preston? Do you find anything improper about him?"

Nick's lips thinned. "No, as far as I know, his reputation is impeccable."

"Just as I thought." She smiled, swept around, and ascended the stairs.

Nick glared. Stephen Farnsworth, Glynna's husband, followed him into the library. "Can we talk, Nick?"

Nick nodded as he started a roaring fire and took a seat near the hearth. The crackling flames added cheer to the dark and cavernous room while the roar of thunder shot through the closed windows. Rain splattered against the glass.

"I'm going to intrude into your personal life," Stephen said, sitting on another leather chair on the opposite side of the fireplace. "Do you mind?"

Nick chuckled. "You've been giving me advice since we were freshman at St. Luke's. Why should you stop now, and why should I begin to listen?"

Stephen groaned. "I'm usually right, aren't I?"

Nick shrugged. "I don't know. I've never heeded your advice."

Stephen picked up a rolled newspaper and threw it at him. "Well, you certainly should."

They both laughed and ordered cups of strong coffee from a footman. When he returned with the fresh steaming brew, they settled down to talk.

"What is it you wish to tell me?" Nick asked.

Stephen leaned back in the leather chair and eyed Nick. "You're not going to like this. Glynna and I were talking and we agree you

ought to marry"—he paused to glance toward the empty doorway—"Melinda Hollister."

Nick's eyes widened and he coughed up a laugh. "You are jok-
ing, I hope."

"Do you have anyone else in mind?"

"No, I don't. Not yet, any way. But I'm sure I will in the future.
You know I'm not a confirmed bachelor, but the notion of marrying Melinda is absurd."

Stephen nodded and then sipped his coffee. "The reason I suggest you marry soon is because I believe Melinda is on the hunt for
a husband and unless you're the one, you won't see Nell very often
in the future."

"Isn't that cynical reasoning for a missionary?" Nick asked,
surprised by his friend's practicality.

"Yes, it probably is, but you're a logical man, so I shouldn't
have to point this out to you."

Nick nodded. He didn't make decisions based on sentiment or
impulse. "Actually, I've considered marrying her purely for Nell's
sake. But I decided against the idea because, even though it would
offer a solution to the custody situation, it would create an even
bigger problem. Melinda for a wife." He winced at the idea of the
flirtatious little vixen tugging at his heartstrings and playing him
for a fool. "It would make both of us miserable. We're completely
incompatible, or haven't you noticed?"

"Actually, I haven't." Stephen chuckled. "Most men would be
delighted to win Melinda's hand."

Nick grumbled, "Well, I'm not one of them." He rose and took
a long time stirring the fire until it once again flared. He threw
another log on the pile, even though it didn't need it.

"Any chance you'll reconsider?" Stephen asked.

"None whatsoever," Nick replied, wondering if maybe he
spoke more forcefully than he ought. You could never quite guar-
antee the future would go in the direction you expected or hoped

for. But he couldn't envision wedding a social butterfly and living happily ever after. And he'd bore her to death with his serious, hard working ways. He was afraid he'd bore most women.

"All right," Stephen said with a sigh, raising his hands in surrender. "Think what you like. But Glynna and I will continue to pray about this. And we both like Melinda very much. She always looks on the positive side of life."

"And of course, I don't," Nick mumbled.

Stephen laughed. "Well, do you?"

Nick grunted. He found himself glowering too much lately, and knowing the cause of his bad temper just made it worse.

"Remember, Nick, love is more than just an emotion. It's a commitment too. Marrying Melinda would please Nell and give her a family. And who knows, maybe you'd even grow fond of Melinda after a while."

Stephen soon left, and Nick settled down with his work. But he found it impossible to concentrate. If only everyone would leave him and Melinda alone to live their lives, go their separate ways . . .

Or . . . He held his breath.

They couldn't possibly be right, could they?

SEVEN

❦

L ate the next morning Melinda attended church services with
Nick and the Farnsworths and later escaped her frowning,
silent, self-appointed guardian and spent a leisurely afternoon
with Nell and her cousins down at the small Summerhill beach.
They frolicked in the water, collected clamshells, and built lopsided
sand castles that soon washed away. She snapped photographs of
them at the water's edge with her new Brownie box camera and
later helped Glynna plan the simple menu for Florrie's outdoor
reception. As she settled into bed that night, she figured she'd need
to remain that busy every day, if she didn't wish to quarrel further
with Nick.

So in the morning Melinda decided to pay her friend Louisa
an informal visit and learn if she had feelings for Clayton. Not that
she herself was interested any longer. But if Clayton was the poor
potential mate that Nick made him out to be, perhaps she'd find a
way to caution her friend.

Melinda donned a flowery hat and left the cottage. At this time
of the morning Louisa could be swimming at Bailey's Beach, the
exclusive enclave of the rich, or she might possibly still be home.

She'd take a short walk to find out. Honeysuckle Lodge, the Davenport's rambling Queen Anne, edged the Summerhill property. As Melinda crossed the lawn, she saw Honeysuckle's many rooflines rise into the clear blue sky from behind a tall row of box hedges. Brilliant sunshine had burned off the morning mist and promised a beautiful day.

She passed the stables and continued toward the gated space in the hedge that created a small opening between the two estates. Squinting against the sunshine, Melinda spotted Louisa leaning over her veranda railing and gazing at the sea. A rare moment of contemplation from her friend who normally ignored lovely scenery in favor of amusing people. Louisa adored parties and beaux as much as she did. As soon as Louisa saw her, she brightened. Then she flew down the porch steps and across the lawn, holding up the hem of her fine dimity gown so it wouldn't drag on the grass or trip her up. Her chestnut hair dislodged from its pompadour, and silky strands fell down her back and swirled around her heart-shaped face.

"You've come to visit. I'm so delighted." Louisa folded her long arms around Melinda in a delicate hug. "I've wanted to speak to you, but we were both so busy at the picnic I didn't get the chance." She caught her breath and gave Melinda the once-over. "What a lovely frock. Teal blue is most definitely your color."

"Thank you. I'm happy to be out of black."

Louisa's small features instantly sobered. "Yes, mourning is a difficult time." Her own brother had died a few years before of consumption.

"Have you heard I've custody of Cora's daughter? Coguardianship, that is." With great effort she kept a grimace from scrunching up her face. Louisa nodded as she pushed a few stray curls behind her ears. "I've heard. But naturally she has a nanny to help you out."

Melinda nodded.

"Splendid. Then you'll have some time for fun."

"Yes, of course." The flatness in her own voice alarmed Melinda; she couldn't even drop a small hint about her financial affairs or Louisa might innocently let a word or two slip to her mother who'd spread the gossip all over town.

They strolled toward the piazza. "Whatever made Cora give Nick Bryson coguardianship?" Louisa paused for a moment. "I suppose she assumed he'd help you with financial matters and such. But still, Nicholas Bryson is so solemn. Whenever I speak to him I get the feeling he's thinks I'm a silly little girl."

Melinda giggled. "I know just what you mean. But I do believe he'll assist me if I need it, though I don't expect to. And as much as Cora might have wished for Nell to be with me, perhaps Parker felt equally as strong about his brother."

"That's true. I see Mama and Mrs. Carstairs sitting at the end of the piazza. Even if we whispered they'd hear our every word. So let's sit in the gazebo."

They wandered away from the Lodge and avoided Louisa's younger brothers playing ball with their tutor on the lawn. When they came to the gazebo, they dropped onto a wooden bench. Close to the cottage garden, Melinda inhaled the fragrances of lavender and honeysuckle and glanced at the riot of colorful blooms—sweet William, primroses, violets, pink carnations, and hollyhocks. A couple of hummingbirds took an interest in the honeysuckle and hovered around the small white flowers.

"Louisa, I'd like to ask you a question of a personal nature," Melinda said, her voice hesitant.

"Go ahead."

"All right. At the picnic I saw you talking to Clayton Underwood. I was wondering if you had any interest in him—romantically."

Louisa tossed back her head and laughed. "Oh my, no."

Melinda scrutinized Louisa's face to see if her expression matched her words. It did. "That's good, because if you did I'd owe you an apology for taking a boat ride with him during the picnic."

Louisa's eyes widened. "I know you'd never try to steal a suitor from me. But Clayton Underwood isn't even a possibility. He's quite self-centered. Isn't that why you broke off with him a few years back?"

Melinda nodded reluctantly. "Yes, I suppose so—at least in part. He was chasing after Clarice Carter while he courted me." She'd forgotten that unpleasant fact until just now. "And also I wasn't interested in marriage at the time."

"I remember. You're not thinking of renewing your courtship, are you?" Louisa grabbed her hand. "Promise me you won't let him back into your life. He'd make a dreadful husband. Oh, I know we both should marry soon or we'll be considered old maids, but don't compromise your principles. Clayton is rich, but he has little else to recommend him."

Louisa's warning solidified Melinda's resolve. "You're right. But I want to find a husband this summer and from the bachelors I've seen so far, no one is very charming."

"What about Simon Preston? I saw you walking with him at the picnic. He's certainly worth cultivating. And I believe he's unattached." The gleam in Louisa's eye made Melinda blush.

Melinda shrugged. "He's pleasant enough . . . I'll get to know him better—just in case."

"Do. It's much too soon to strike him off your list."

"But what about you, Louisa? Aren't you interested in him?"

Her friend shook her head. "No. Mama will only allow me to marry a New Yorker. She wants me to stay close to home. And I want to as well. I've been to Pittsburgh and, believe me, I'd rather stay in New York." Louisa laughed. A gust of wind ruffled the pink ribbons on her dress.

She wasn't in a position to be as choosey as Louisa when financial disaster loomed over her head like the blade of the guillotine.

"What if . . . what if we waffle for too long, Louisa? Lose our chance to find a suitable mate?"

Her friend groaned. "It's a troubling situation, I'll admit. But we're far from old maids yet! Let me mull over this for a while. Perhaps I can think of someone else for you. In the meantime, we have a few hours left before luncheon. So why don't we go shopping? I spotted a lovely pearl ring in Tiffany's the other morning and my mother agreed I might have it."

"Of course." Maybe shopping would cheer her up. Even if she could only window shop.

They rode in the Davenport's open Victoria toward the shops in town. The carriage rolled down the shady Bellevue Avenue, address of the most fashionable summer homes in the nation. Replicas of Italian villas, French chateaux, and English Tudor manors nested one after the other on small lots, partially hidden by stonewalls, iron fences, or hedges. Massive gates kept the public from trespassing. The cottagers valued their privacy and exclusivity, just like those who owned more acreage around the windswept Ocean Drive.

"I've been thinking about possible suitors for you, Melinda. But how about Nicholas Bryson? Now don't eliminate him out of hand," Louisa warned.

"You yourself said he was too solemn. And I quite agree."

"Perhaps you can liven him up. But think beyond his reserved personality. He's solid, industrious, rich, and—"

"You make him sound so boring. I want to marry a gentleman who's cheerful and full of sparkle."

"I'll concede he's not that. But my mother insists those are the qualities to look for in a dance partner, not in a husband. A husband has to wear well over the long run. Do you think she's right?"

Melinda shrugged. "Possibly. I don't really know, but my mother says the same thing." Mama had married the love of her life, and Melinda remembered how unhappy they'd become over the years. Papa's love of coaching and yachting had gradually worn thin. "But perhaps she has a point. I just don't know."

The liveried coachman, resplendent in black top hat and a burgundy coat, halted the carriage in front of the shops fronting the Casino. During the next hour they met several friends they only saw during the summer. Anxious to catch up on news and gossip, they stopped at a café for a frosty glass of lemonade. Later, after Louisa purchased the pearl ring, they wandered into a milliner's shop, drawn by a window display of fashionable hats.

Melinda found a ribbon hat for Nell that would compliment her new lawn dress with the violet sash.

Louisa picked up a white straw creation with ribbons, pink tulle, and big silk roses on the wide brim. "This one is perfect for you. Do try it on."

Melinda knew she should exit the shop before her willpower failed her. But she removed her own hat, donned the captivating one, tilted to a fashionable angle, and saw in the glass oval that Louisa was right.

"You must have it," Louisa said as Melinda preened.

"I'm sure it's too expensive," she whispered.

"Nonsense. I'm sure it's quite reasonable. And since when did you worry about cost?" Louisa's eyes sharpened and demanded an explanation.

"I don't," Melinda muttered, ashamed of the sad truth. But the hat was too splendid to pass up. "I shall buy it."

When she learned the price, she choked back a gasp. "Send the bill to me at Summerhill," she said in a ragged voice. At least she had awhile to figure out how to pay for her purchase.

As they left the shop, Melinda slowed her pace, knowing she ought to return the hat immediately. But her feet took her out to the sidewalk instead. Disgust with herself banished her high spirits. She felt like a little girl who'd eaten too much cake and ice cream and felt it heaving upward.

I shall never do this again, she vowed, hoping she could stick to her promise.

CARRYING THE TWO hat boxes, the coachman followed Melinda into the foyer where Nick was passing through. Lavender scent permeated the space with its floral fragrance.

"Gone shopping, I see." He couldn't hide his amusement. "It looks like you found what you were looking for."

Melinda blushed up to her hairline. "I purchased hats for myself and for Nell. Nothing much. That's all." But then she smiled. "Would you like to see them? I'm afraid I couldn't resist."

"I'll wait until you're both wearing them."

"Suit yourself," she said with a smile.

Despite her playful manner, he got the impression she was embarrassed by her shopping trip, though that made little sense. All women seemed to shop, all the time, except for Florrie, who'd rather paint. And Alma. Although well dressed, Alma had buried herself in her books and refused to haunt the fashionable shops in search of new clothing she didn't need. But how many women were as sensible as Alma Noble?

He watched Melinda climb the stairs with an inborn grace most others would spend years acquiring. Without a doubt she was fetching; he'd never met a prettier lady or one more cheerful. Not even Alma, who also possessed a sweet manner and sharp mind. But no one had Melinda's cheer and optimism; she'd turn away an insult with a laugh or a smile. Even after the sharp words they'd exchanged at the picnic, she'd found a way to be at ease with him again. Her good nature was truly a gift from God.

Nick went to his room to supervise his valet's packing for his trip to New York that evening. The Blue Star representatives, in the States for a short time, had written to arrange for a meeting.

Hopefully he'd return in a week or two with the purchase of the steamship line completed.

Lord, if I can't buy the ships and my father makes any more ill-conceived deals, our business will be ruined. I ask for Your guidance in all things, especially now in this venture.

When things were going well it was easy to think success was all his own doing. *Lord, please don't allow me to turn to You only when I need Your help. I should remember to always seek Your guidance. Amen.*

AFTER MELINDA RETURNED from paying afternoon calls with Florrie and Glynna, she found her niece in the nursery watching her cousins play with the figures in the giant dollhouse. The room seemed dim since the sky had darkened to gray and threatened rain. Melinda could feel the moisture in the hot, humid air penetrate the thin sleeves of her batiste dress. Peggy, the young nursemaid, carried freshly ironed frocks to the girls' bedrooms while Nanny pulled a rocking horse out of the way of the play area and into a corner.

Melinda joined the girls crowded around the dollhouse set on the middle of the carpet. She scrunched down among the children while they rearranged the miniature furniture intricately carved from wood and upholstered in fabric remnants.

"Nell, are you feeling well?" The little girl's face appeared flushed. She sat with her head tucked to her chin.

Nell shook her head. "My throat hurts. And I ache all over."

Melinda placed her hand on Nell's forehead. "Oh dear. You're quite warm." She glanced toward Nanny, who was selecting books from the shelves on the opposite side of the playroom. "I believe Nell should be put to bed until she's feeling better and her fever subsides. And we should send for the doctor."

"Yes, miss. I'll have Mrs. Finnegan telephone Dr. Dean right away." Nanny hurried out the door.

Melinda nodded. "Come, Nell. After you get into bed, I shall read you a story."

When the girl didn't object, Melinda knew she must feel dreadful. She led her by the hand, but the little tyke dragged her feet across the carpet and hardwood floor. Melinda scooped her up and propped her on her hip. Although petite for the age of four, Nell's weight still twisted pain into Melinda's back and arms, but there was no other way to get her there.

Once in the small bedroom, she helped Nell change into a white cotton nightgown with a pale pink ribbon tied at the neck. She helped her into the high bed and then tucked her in. Through the screen she glimpsed lightning split a charcoal-colored sky.

"Oh dear. I think we're in for a big storm."

The first drops of rain grazed the partially open windows, then slapped them hard and streaked the glass. Melinda closed and locked them before the downpour soaked the sill and sprayed into the room. She turned up the gaslight, found a book of nursery rhymes, and squeezed onto the single bed with a polished brass headboard and footboard. She helped Nell prop herself against a fluffy pillow, then pulled up the sampler quilt made of pastel calicoes.

Nanny Wells hovered in the doorway. "Excuse me, miss. I sent for the doctor. He'll arrive shortly. Is there anything I can fetch for you or Nell in the meantime?" Nanny asked.

Melinda looked to Nell, who barely shook her head. Her eyes looked dull and her eyelids droopy.

"Try to rest," Melinda said as she touched Nell's hot forehead. The knot in Melinda's stomach twisted. Cora had entrusted her precious daughter into her care and she'd do everything in her power to warrant her sister's confidence.

When Nell couldn't sleep and drifted into moans, Melinda read rhymes, fairy tales, and Bible stories to try and distract her from her own misery.

"Nell, I know you feel dreadful, but Jesus will make you well, just as He healed so many people when He lived on earth." She flipped through her Bible to Matthew 8 and read. "'When he was come down from the mountain, great multitudes followed him. And, behold, there came to him a leper and worshipped him, saying, Lord, if thou wilt, thou canst make me clean. And Jesus put forth his hand, and touched him, saying, I will; be thou clean. And immediately his leprosy was cleansed.'"

Melinda assumed the little girl wouldn't understand, but she might find the words soothing.

"What's that mean, Auntie Mindy?" Nell asked.

"It means Jesus healed the sick man. And, sweetheart, He'll heal you too. I'll be praying Jesus will make you feel better very soon."

Nell lifted a small smile. Thankfully she at last dozed off. She looked so much like Cora with her pale skin, white-blond hair, and rosebud mouth. Melinda sniffed back tears.

Quietly she slipped down off the bed and settled into a chintz-covered chair by the window. Her heart filled with love for Nell just like Jesus' love for all. Of course her feelings were imperfect, tempered by her mood and fatigue and even selfishness, while the Lord's love was pure and powerful and unwavering. Yet Nell meant more to her than anyone else on the face of the earth, with the possible exception of Mama. *Dear Lord, please heal Nell quickly.*

She read her favorite psalms until the doctor arrived, damp from the rain. At the sound of his deep voice, Nell awoke and whimpered. Dr. Dean, a tall, hunched man with white, mutton chop whiskers and an ominous manner, examined her gently. Melinda sat on the chair beside the bed, holding her breath and praying she'd over-reacted to a mild illness.

"Shall we step out into the hall?" the doctor asked, frowning. Or maybe he merely looked grave, as physicians often did.

Once out of Nell's hearing, Dr. Dean bent toward Melinda and spoke in a low, sober voice. "It's possible your niece has diphtheria.

It appears she has a thick, gray, fuzzy membrane in her throat, a sure sign of the disease. She's also fatigued, and her lymph nodes are slightly swollen."

"Oh no." People called diphtheria "the strangling angel of childhood" because it often struck the young. She knew the possible effects—heart muscle damage and nerve damage resulting in paralysis. And sometimes death.

"I believe she's in the early stages of the infection, but I'm not quite sure just yet. Let's pray if she does indeed have diphtheria she has a mild case."

"Do you think she'll be all right?" Melinda's voice cracked.

"We'll have to wait and see. I'll come tomorrow and hopefully I can make a more definitive diagnosis. Keep the other children away from her. And be careful yourself. Diphtheria is highly contagious."

Melinda's hands shook. "We shall all be very careful."

The doctor continued, "She may have difficulty breathing or rapid breathing and chills and fever."

Melinda nodded. "What can we do to make Nell more comfortable?" She couldn't just sit still and watch her niece suffer.

"Give her plenty of soup, beef tea, and every form of light nourishment. I'll send a nurse over as soon as I can. She'll put up a sheet sprayed with carbolic acid in the doorway of the little girl's bedroom. She'll also spray her bedding."

Melinda nodded. "Anything else, Doctor?"

"As soon as the rain stops, open her windows to let in fresh air. And make sure to enforce strict bed rest."

"I shall. Thank you, Doctor." Melinda followed him to the playroom door. As Nanny Wells led him to the stairs, Nick appeared from another wing of the cottage. He glanced toward the doctor and frowned.

"Is someone ill?" he asked Melinda as the doctor and nanny disappeared down the stairs.

"Yes, Nell has a bad sore throat."

Nick paled. "Is it serious?"

Melinda stepped into the hallway and closed the door. "Dr. Dean thinks she might have diphtheria." All the energy drained from her body and apprehension bubbled to the surface, making her tear up. "I'm frightened she won't get well. Oh, Nick, I couldn't bear to lose her. Except for my mother, Nell is all I have." Tears escaped and rolled down her face. She tried to blink back more, but instead she burst into quiet sobbing. She accepted the handkerchief Nick offered and dabbed at her eyes. "I'm sorry for being so emotional, but I can't help it."

Her shoulders heaved as Nick encircled her with his strong arms and drew her close. She pressed her head into his jacket, not caring if he thought she was weak and overwrought.

"It's all right to cry, Melinda. Go ahead and let all your tears out," Nick said softly as he awkwardly patted her back. "I feel the same way about Nell. From the time she was a tiny baby, she's given me so much joy."

Melinda glanced up at him, surprised.

Nick let out a chuckle. "Don't look so shocked. I'm reserved, but I'm not coldhearted. I feel a responsibility to take good care of Nell, and I truly love her." His voice cracked. "And right now I feel quite helpless."

Melinda nodded. "So do I, but we can't forget the Lord is in control."

He sighed. "Yes, I know. But little children often pass away despite excellent medical care and frantic prayers on their behalf."

Another small sob escaped her lips. She couldn't refute that, and it strangled most of her optimism.

"I'm sorry, Melinda. I didn't mean to upset you even more." He pulled her closer and she felt a little tension ease from her shoulders.

"All we can do is cling to the Lord and ask for His grace and His mercy," she said.

"You're right, of course. I run to God when things go wrong and I can't handle them myself. But the rest of the time I forget about praying for guidance." He smiled a rueful, half smile.

Melinda nodded. "But that's not what He wants."

"No, I suppose not. I prefer being in charge of my life—until it falls apart." He laughed self-consciously. "I dislike people like that. The Lord probably does too."

Melinda squeezed his hand. "I'll pray for you *and* for Nell."

"Thank you." Nick cleared his throat, but his voice emerged ragged and raspy. "This brings back memories of my sister Alice. She died of diphtheria when she was only five." Nick glanced at Melinda with a sad expression.

"I didn't know that. I'm so sorry." She wished she could erase his melancholy with a kind word.

He gave a quick nod. "She was only a year older than I, so we played together all the time. I missed her terribly."

Melinda nodded, not knowing what to say, as they stood in the hallway silent and locked in their own thoughts.

Nick hesitated. "I hate to desert Nell when she's so ill, but I'm afraid I must leave for New York on the night train."

Melinda's eyes widened. "Leave? Now? She needs you here. And I need you here too." As her courage melted away her anger flared.

His lips pressed hard. "It's business. I don't have a choice. Believe me, I'd stay if I could."

Leaning back against the wall, Melinda shook her head. "I don't understand how business can be more important than your own niece."

He bristled. "Of course it's not. But I also have a duty to the company. And I know you'll take good care of her." He paused and shook his head. "Melinda, please don't stare at me as if I'm the devil. I love that child just as much as you do."

"Well, you have an odd way of showing it," Melinda snapped back, then immediately regretted her harsh words. She really didn't question his affection for Nell. But when her needs interfered with his business obligations, Nell automatically took second place. Obviously the family company took priority over everything else. Melinda sighed. She hated to face this crisis alone.

"I'm sorry. I know you love her, Nick. Please forgive me for questioning your devotion." Her energy gone, she dropped into a hall chair placed next to a marble-topped side table with a vase of yellow carnations.

He nodded but still looked offended. "Excuse me. I'd better see to packing my things. I'll be gone for a week, possibly less, and I'll telephone daily." He turned on his heel and strode down the hallway.

So it was up to her, alone, to care for Nell—and to find a forgiving spirit toward Nick.

On her way back to Nell's room Melinda glimpsed Peggy, the nursery maid, and the children in the playroom. Peggy joined her by Nell's bedroom door.

"Excuse me, miss, but how is the little one doing? Please forgive Nanny and me for not noticing her bad throat earlier, but she was fine just a short time ago. But I'm so very sorry we didn't catch it quicker." Peggy's lips curved downward.

"I think you noticed soon enough."

Peggy nodded so vigorously a few dark curls escaped by the side of her round face. "And we'll be praying for her too, Miss Hollister. If there's anything you want, I'll be glad to fetch it. It's hard watching a sick child day and night. I remember my little brothers when they got the measles. Beggin' your pardon, miss, I shouldn't go on about my family."

"That's quite all right, Peggy." Maids were usually seen but not heard, much like children and sometimes even women. Employers forgot their servants were human beings just as they were with personal lives and families. "Tell me about your brothers and sisters." Melinda dropped into a rocking chair by the playroom window.

"Really, Miss Hollister?" Peggy eyes opened wide.

"Yes." Melinda nodded. "It'd be a welcome distraction from fretting over Nell."

"All right then. There's seven of us; three more passed on as children. My mother nursed them until I thought she'd die from exhaustion, but she survived. In fact, my younger brothers and sister still live with her and Dad right here in Newport."

"That must be nice for you," Melinda said as she rocked on the hardwood floor, envious of the girl's large family.

"Yes, indeed, it's grand. But of course someday I might have to leave them. If I marry, that is." She blushed rose red right up to her wavy bangs.

Melinda smiled. "That's right. You have a young man."

Peggy averted Melinda's gaze. "I know we're not supposed to have admirers when we're in service, but I do like him ever so much." Probably the footman.

She envied her even more, especially now with the responsibility of Nell weighing so heavily upon her shoulders. And without Nick to help her through this ordeal.

"I understand why you're eager to marry. To have a man to love and rely upon through all life's difficulties would be such a blessing. It's hard to cope alone. But choose wisely because marriage is a very serious undertaking. Who you marry will affect your entire future. You don't want to make a hasty decision you'll regret."

"No, miss, picking the right husband is ever so important." Peggy paused for a moment. "Others have warned me about that. I take their advice seriously."

Melinda nodded. "Yes, indeed. You should."

"Miss, if you don't mind my asking—do you believe a woman should follow her heart or her head?"

Melinda blew out a long sigh. "That a difficult choice, but I'm afraid a woman must follow her head. If she's fortunate, her heart will follow."

At least, she hoped it would.

EIGHT

❧

Their conversation carried out to the hallway where Nick was passing by on his way to find his valet. He paused at the mention of marriage. He refused to eavesdrop, but he couldn't help but hear Melinda's last few remarks.

He wondered if Melinda would settle for a man with a fortune, family credentials, and a congenial personality. Simon perhaps. Or would she wait for the man who stirred the passionate embers in her heart? Someone like . . . certainly not Clayton.

Then whom did she love? Perhaps no one. Yet a beautiful young woman like Melinda wouldn't stay unattached forever. From all her flirting she must have plans to catch a husband this summer. And provide a family for Nell. And that would exclude him.

Nick shook all these crazy thoughts from his brain. He couldn't possibly figure out the workings of Melinda's mind. She, like most women, was a total mystery.

Nick found his father and Jasper in the dimly lit library. On the sunniest of days the library was dark and peaceful, but with a storm raging, it felt quite gloomy. He took a seat with the pair and explained Nell's illness, trying to keep anxiety out of his voice. Jasper's pipe smoke spiraled up toward the coffered ceiling.

"Nell is ill and the doctor believes it could be diphtheria. I was wondering, Father, if perhaps I might postpone my meeting with Blue Line's representative, at least for a few days. I'd like to stay with Nell and support Melinda." It rankled to have to beg Frederick for every favor, just like a child.

"I understand your concern. I'm sure the doctor will send over a nurse if that's necessary. We have an entire staff to assist Melinda. The child will have the best of care. Now go to New York as planned."

Nick gave a curt nod and strode from the room. It was futile to argue. His father had no compassion; he never had. He'd often tried to soften the old man's heart through kindness, but nothing had chipped at the stone. What was the use? In the foyer he met the Farnsworths heading for the staircase.

"Anything wrong, Nick?" Stephen asked.

"Actually, yes."

"We're good listeners. Or would you prefer to speak to Stephen alone?" Glynna asked.

"No, please stay." They ducked into the drawing room and sat by the unlit fireplace. Nick explained about Nell's sudden illness and his father's reaction. There was no point in mentioning his spat with Melinda; anything between them seemed too personal to repeat.

Glynna, seated on the settee beside her husband, leaned forward. "I shall help Melinda all I can while you're away."

"Thank you. She'll appreciate that. She seems vulnerable and very frightened. Melinda's world is usually sunshine and light. So I don't know how well she'll handle this. She's so fond of Nell."

"She may be more resilient than you think," Glynna said.

Nick doubted Melinda's strength. She was about as substantial as a bubble.

"We'll watch over her," Glynna promised.

Nick stood. "Thank you. No matter how much I'd prefer to stay, I can't. I'm sorry I couldn't make Melinda understand that."

God would just have to take care of Melinda and Nell. And deep down at the bottom of his anxious heart, Nick knew He would.

A FEW HOURS later Mrs. Finnegan brought Melinda tea, dinner, and a few words of comfort.

"Nell looks like a sleeping angel," the housekeeper whispered as she smiled at the child. "You'll be needing your rest too, Miss Hollister. I can watch the little one for part of the night right along with you and Mrs. Farnsworth and Nanny Wells. When Nell wakes up, you just ring for some broth and we'll send it up quick as can be."

"Thank you."

"Would you like something else, miss?"

Melinda shook her head. "No, I'm fine."

"She'll be all right, dearie," the housekeeper said, patting Melinda's arm. "I'll be praying for her night and day. You can be sure of that."

"Thank you. And would you please send word to Mr. Preston that my niece is ill and I can't go coaching tomorrow?"

"That I will, right away."

AFTER MRS. FINNEGAN ambled off, Melinda tried a few bites of baked chicken, but she could hardly swallow. Unshed tears stung her eyes as she watched Nell's every twist and turn. She prayed for the poor child's rapid recovery, read several psalms, and then paged through the latest issue of *Ladies Home Journal*. When Nell awoke a few hours later, Melinda told her a funny story from her childhood and read another fairy tale. Although Nell seemed to appreciate someone staying with her, Melinda could tell that she felt too awful to really listen.

Glynna relieved Melinda at two in the morning. Glynna took

her place on the easy chair as Melinda stood by Nell's bed and listened to her niece's labored breathing.

"You look exhausted. Get some sleep," Glynna urged in a low tone.

"I'm more emotionally spent than physically tired."

"Turn to Jesus in prayer and read the Word. One of my favorite verses is from Psalm 119, 'My soul melteth for heaviness: strengthen thou me according unto thy word.'"

Melinda smiled. "I've been praying and praying for Nell's recovery, but I've read enough Scripture to understand I have to accept God's will no matter what it is." Her voice caught. "I'm trying to be like you and live according to the Book."

One corner of Glynna's mouth turned up. "It's not always easy, is it?"

Melinda shook her head. "Sometimes it quite difficult, but with the Lord's help I'll continue to try. I've always read the Bible, yet I often skip verses that pinch my conscience. I'll not ignore them any longer."

"And I'll pray you won't forget after Nell recovers. It's natural to draw close to God in times of trial; it's also natural to become lax when the crisis is over. But we shouldn't forget the importance of the Lord's guidance even when we think we're doing well on our own."

Melinda nodded. "Thank you for the reminder. Now I believe I'll go to bed."

Grateful for Glynna, she stumbled off to her room, her neck stiff from sitting upright in a chair for so many hours. She slept fitfully until the gray light of morning woke her with a start. Glancing out the window, she noted the rain had ended. But a thick fog crept from the sea to the lawn, shrouding everything in its path and ushering in a chilly dampness.

Melinda quickly dressed without the aid of the maid. She brushed her own hair and piled it onto her head in a simple psyche knot. She hurried to Nell's room where she found her propped up and whimpering while the newly arrived nurse tried to feed her some broth. Nell's glazed look indicated she still suffered from fever, but at least she was taking some nourishment.

"I'm afraid she doesn't really want more than a few spoonfuls of soup or tea. She can't swallow without pain, poor little thing." The uniformed nurse looked around thirty-five, plain-faced with a compassionate smile. She'd already hung up the sprayed sheet in the doorway. "I'm Miss Leonard."

"How do you do? I'm Nell's aunt, Miss Hollister." Melinda gently touched Nell's forehead. "Still feverish. Do you still ache too, Nell?" she asked.

"Yes," the little girl mumbled.

The nurse turned to Melinda. "I've already painted the membrane in her throat with silver nitrate. Let's hope her sore throat improves quickly."

Dr. Dean came by at nine o'clock and examined Nell. "Her fever has gone down some, but her throat isn't any better." He shook his head. "I'm sorry to have to tell you this, but Nell definitely has diphtheria. Right now it looks like a mild case, but we'll still have to quarantine the house for at least a week, possibly much longer. And hope for the best."

Melinda sunk into the chair by the window. "Well, at least it's mild. So far." She couldn't imagine what the more serious version would be like; this was awful enough.

After she showed the doctor out, she had Mr. Grimes and Mrs. Finnegan spread the word among the staff. Melinda told Florrie, who promised to convey the news to the rest of the family. Fortunately neither Janet nor Julie showed any signs of the disease. By early afternoon Melinda dozed off.

A short while later Mrs. Finnegan woke her up. "Dearie, Mr. Bryson would like to speak to you on the telephone. Should I explain you're resting?"

"Oh no, I'd like to talk to him."

On her way down the stairs Melinda fixed her messy hair and smoothed the wrinkles of her navy blue skirt. Once in the office she picked up the telephone receiver.

"Melinda?"

"It's so good to hear your voice, Nick. Nell has diphtheria just as Dr. Dean suspected, but it appears to be a mild case. We're quarantined. I'll be sure to let you know when it's all right for you to return to Summerhill."

Several seconds of silence passed before Nick spoke. "I'm sorry she's so ill."

Hearing him all choked up made her want to cry herself. *If only he were here, we could support and encourage each other. There was a reason parenting was designed to be shared between two.*

"Give her all my love, please. And, Melinda, how are you holding up?"

"I'm fine." She tried to sound cheerful, but she faltered. "Actually, I'm tired and worried, but the Lord gives me the strength to keep going. I couldn't manage on my own. Nick, if you start feeling the least bit ill, please see a doctor immediately."

"Of course. But I didn't see Nell the day I left, so I'm sure I'll be fine."

"Yes, no need to worry." But she did worry.

"How are the rest of you doing?" he asked.

"Thank the Lord, no one else has any symptoms." She paused for a moment. "How are the negotiations progressing? Has Blue Star accepted your offer?"

He drew out a long, dispirited sigh. "No, they haven't. They think we're not willing to pay enough. I'll keep trying, but things aren't going as well as I'd hoped."

"Oh dear. I'm sorry." Poor Nick. Everything was going wrong for him.

"Melinda, I miss you and Nell. Give her a hug and kiss for me."

He missed her? He sounded sincere. She was a bit taken aback by such a confession from Nick, of all people, but her heart warmed a degree or two. It'd be nice to have a comforting hug about now. "We both miss you. Telephone tomorrow, please. Your call truly cheered me up."

"I'm glad. You'll hear from me soon."

The days passed in a slow blur. Each morning and afternoon she fed Nell tea and beef broth. And she read stories from Nell's favorite book of rhymes and fairy tales, and a few from the Bible. Daniel in the lions' den, Moses and the Ten Commandments, and David and Goliath.

Nell especially liked the story of the nativity since she remembered all the presents she received last Christmas. This year she'd make sure to impress upon her niece the significance of the birth of Jesus, not merely the presents. Jesus was God's gift to us. Melinda thought she should at least hear about the true meaning of Christmas even if it was more than a four-year-old child could fully understand.

Nell smiled faintly as Melinda droned on. Every day she read until her voice grew hoarse and she had to quit. Then they played with Nell's dolls and dressed them in their splendid wardrobes fit for princesses. When Nell fell asleep, Melinda sat by her bedside and read the Bible and then prayed for her girl's healing. Melinda also skimmed a few of her favorite dime novels by Fannie Cole and Mrs. Southworth.

Focused on Nell's recovery, Melinda forgot about the missed balls and the missed marriage opportunities. Nothing mattered beyond her niece's health. Miss Leonard shouldered the greatest responsibility, checking Nell's temperature and throat and summoning the doctor when she feared Nell had taken a turn for the worse. But the little girl's body fought the disease. Gradually she improved.

Nick telephoned every evening just as he'd promised. Talking to him lifted Melinda's spirits in a way she never could've imagined. Hearing his calm, reassuring voice lessened her fears. And she liked hearing about his negotiations even though they hadn't come to an agreement. His confiding in her had to be good for their relationship. Struggling against each other would only upset Nell.

"And how are you doing, Melinda? You sound exhausted."

"I am. But Nell likes me at her bedside, so that's where I stay. It's what Cora would've done." So tired she felt sick, Melinda realized tears were streaming down her cheeks. "Thank you for caring about both of us. I must be going now," she said before she started sobbing into the telephone receiver.

Things had definitely improved between them, but there was no way on earth that Melinda wanted Nick to think she was little more than a hysterical female.

TEN DAYS AFTER the quarantine began, Dr. Dean declared it over.

"I'm happy to say your little Nell will be fine. The worst is over. We're fortunate her case wasn't more serious." Weak-kneed, Melinda sank into the overstuffed chair by her niece's bed.

"Thank You, Lord," she prayed.

Dr. Dean left, followed by Miss Leonard a few hours later. Nell still felt sick, but her throat was much less sore. It would take at least another week or two for her to regain her strength.

Later that afternoon a soft voice woke her up from her nap on the chair in Nell's bedroom. "Miss Hollister, you have a visitor in the foyer. A Mr. Preston. Are you receiving today?" Peggy asked from the doorway.

"Oh my, is it that time already?" Glancing at her pocket watch she noticed it was past three. She sighed. "I suppose I could go downstairs for a few minutes. Can you watch Nell for a short while?"

"Of course, miss."

When Peggy took her place by the bed, Melinda returned to her own room to freshen up. She hurried to the drawing room where Florrie was entertaining Mr. Preston and serving him a cup of tea.

He rose when she entered the room and bowed with exaggerated politeness. He wore an expensively tailored gray suit, charcoal silk vest, and starched white shirt. His eyes swept over her and then registered shock. No doubt she looked too worn-out and disheveled to receive company.

"Good afternoon, Mr. Preston. My niece Nell is making a slow recovery, and I was up with her for part of the night. Please excuse my appearance."

Of course there was no acceptable excuse for untidiness, but she truly didn't care what he or anyone else thought.

Simon scrutinized her as if she were a strange creature from another universe. But he recovered quickly and managed to turn his scrutiny into concern. "That's a shame about your niece. But you shouldn't put yourself out so. You must have servants who could help."

Perhaps she was merely weary and stressed, but his cavalier manner irked her.

"At any rate," he said, "I'm here to invite you and Mrs. Van Tassel to a spur-of-the-moment get-together at the Casino later today. Some of us are putting on a talent show. It's sure to be hilarious. And what are your hidden talents, Mrs. Van Tassel?"

Florrie hooted. "I'm sure I don't have any talent except for my painting. I can't sing or dance or recite poetry. Dear me, I do sound like such a bore."

"Not in the least. And you, Miss Hollister?" he asked.

She forced a courteous smile. "I'm afraid I have no particular talent. I'd like to thank you for your kind invitation, but I'm afraid I can't leave Summerhill." And she was much too drained to return to society just yet.

He tried to dismiss her fears with a wave of his hand. "I'm sure if you're needed someone can telephone the Casino. You must take a reprieve from the sick room. Something fun to lift your spirits. I think you're overly concerned," he said with a shake of his head.

"Actually I'm not. As soon as Nell is better, I shall be more than ready for a bit of fun. But not while she's ailing." She could barely force herself to be civil. To think, she recently considered him a grand catch! Yet, without other serious suitors, she couldn't dismiss him out of hand, even if, at the moment, she certainly wished to.

Simon persisted. "Are you certain you're not making too much of this? Children bounce back rapidly."

And they also die from disease. No one was safe from sickness and death.

"I'm afraid I wouldn't enjoy myself if I attended." She flashed her brightest social smile, sure to halt his objections. "I'm sorry to miss your delightful theatrical. Have a wonderful time."

She rose and Simon stood up in turn and shrugged. "All right then. Good day. I shall see you soon, I trust," he said.

His childish pout made her wonder if he'd lost interest in her because of her refusal. There were so many debutantes willing to amuse him he might very well not wait for her.

But within the hour he sent a bouquet of red roses and a note.

Miss Hollister, I apologize profusely if I acted a bit peevish this afternoon. I was merely disappointed you were unable to accept my invitation. Best wishes for your niece's full recovery. I hope to see you soon. Simon Preston

She set down the card and stared out the window. So Simon wasn't as self-centered as she feared . . . though from what she'd seen, he didn't have a natural affinity toward children. And that was troubling.

The butler waylaid her near the staircase. "Miss, you have a telephone call from Mr. Nicholas Bryson."

A frisson of joy lifted her spirit. "Thank you. I'll take it."

She hurried to the office and closed the door. She needed to talk to him, to share her good news. She spoke into the telephone and listened to Nick's voice crack over the wires. "Hello, Melinda. How are you and Nell?"

Just hearing him brought a surge of relief. Without resorting to small talk, she relayed the doctor's prognosis. "Nell is quite weak but far better than she was a week ago. Dr. Dean has lifted the quarantine, so you can return and we can move about as we please."

"The Lord heard our prayers."

"Indeed," she returned. "Janet and Julie never even came down with a scratchy throat. We have so much to be thankful for."

"That's wonderful news, Melinda. I'm leaving New York tonight and I'll arrive at Summerhill in the morning."

"Oh, Nick, I'm so glad. Nell will be thrilled to see you. She asked for you again this morning."

"Did she?" he said, obviously pleased. "I've missed her. And I've missed you as well."

Her voice caught. "I'm looking forward to seeing you too, Nick. It seems as if you've been gone forever. By the way, did you finally purchase Blue Star?"

He sighed. "No. We've continued to negotiate, but we can't come to an agreement. If and when they decide to lower their price, I'll return to New York. Right now we're at a standstill. I could wait for them, but I might be stuck in the city indefinitely. I need to be at Summerhill."

Relief at his imminent return drained some of her weariness. "I'm sorry you weren't successful, but perhaps they'll change their minds soon."

"I certainly haven't given up hope. I can't. Their ships are too important to Bryson Steamship Company."

After she hung up the telephone and returned to Nell, she smiled at the girl snuggled beneath the covers.

"Uncle Nick just telephoned. He'll be home tomorrow. And he can't wait to see you again."

Nell's lips curved in a wan but happy smile. It still hurt for her to speak or swallow, but every day she seemed a bit better.

Glynna, standing by the window, grinned. "That's splendid."

She motioned for Melinda to join her in the hallway. She lowered her voice even though the corridor was empty except for a chambermaid at the far end. "I'm going to be a busybody, but please let me have my say." She paused for a second or two. "Try not to be too hard on Nick when he returns. He truly wanted to stay at Summerhill, but his father insisted he go to New York. Uncle Frederick is very demanding, and Nick has no choice but to follow his orders."

Melinda nodded slowly, unconvinced. "But Nick always puts business before family and he does it as a matter of course. I don't understand that. People are so much more important than business. Even my father thought so." She smiled ruefully. "I certainly value money and security, but my loved ones come first."

"I believe they do for Nick too, but I suspect this is more than just a routine business trip."

Melinda's eyebrows lifted. "Do you really think so?" That would make sense.

"From rumors I've heard, Jasper would like to step in as president when Uncle Frederick retires. And my uncle just might favor him. That would leave Nick out in the cold. This was his chance to prove himself and secure his place within the company. I'm sure he's disappointed he couldn't make the purchase."

"Do you think Mr. Bryson would be so cruel to his own son?"

Glynna nodded. "I'm afraid so."

"Hmm." Nick had never mentioned this, but it could be true.

"You see, Uncle Frederick isn't himself lately. I spoke to Dr. Dean about his change in behavior, and he suspects my uncle is in the early stages of dementia. Nick is quite worried about his father's health too; he probably was adverse to upsetting him."

Melinda nodded. Perhaps she'd judged Nick's decision to go too harshly. But what good was a successful business if you didn't have time to enjoy your blessings with your family?

NINE

❧

With the possibility of taking over the number one position at Bryson Steamship Company, Jasper worked diligently all morning and into the afternoon. He spread his paperwork across the library desk instead of in the office so Mr. Bryson would be sure to notice him. And the crusty old Frederick did.

"I'm glad to see you toiling so hard," the man said, staring at Jasper with a sharp, eagle eye. "A bit of competition certainly lit a fire under you."

Jasper felt his cheeks scorch under the mocking glare of his father-in-law's scrutiny.

"I enjoy my work," Jasper muttered. And he'd enjoy it more once he had complete control of the company's finances without Mr. Bryson's oversight.

The tycoon read his New York newspapers for an hour or so and then wandered off. As soon as he left, Jasper gathered his papers and slipped away too. After a promising trip to the yacht Club to locate a buyer for his beloved schooner, Jasper stopped off at the Reading Room, a private men's club on Bellevue Avenue.

He downed a few whiskeys. Two hours later and feeling more cheerful, he drove home in his gig. He arrived right before sunset hoping he wasn't late for some formal dinner or dance. Lately Florrie had been so immersed in her art she hadn't accepted too many invitations. *I should be fine.*

He returned the horse and carriage to the stables and headed back toward the cottage. To the west, the sky blazed with streaks of rose and orange as the sun slipped toward the ocean. A warm, lovely evening. With any luck, he'd sell the *Sea Spray* within a few weeks—perhaps even within a few days—and pay off Underwood. That still left thousands in gambling debts to dispose of, but he'd deal with one problem at a time as long as the other creditors didn't press too hard for their money. He hoped he could hold them off for a while longer until he achieved the presidency of Bryson Steamship.

As he crossed the smooth lawn, he noticed a shadow move behind a giant elm.

"Come away from there," he commanded. Brazen servants occasionally misused the grounds for evening trysts where they could hide behind trees and shrubs and not easily be seen.

A couple poked their heads out from behind a thick trunk and then reluctantly stepped forward. He stifled a laugh. His daughters' nursemaid and a footman. Florrie, like most society matrons, hired tall, strapping men for the job. *"They look impressive in livery while serving dinner,"* she'd said. This one was no different.

But the fetching maid glanced longingly toward the servants' entrance at the back of the cottage as she straightened her doily cap. She guiltily looked down toward the ground, her eyes brimming with tears and a healthy dose of fear. "I'm sorry, sir. Please forgive me. May I be excused?"

"Yes, by all means. Don't let me catch you again, or I'll have to report you to my wife. She has little tolerance for loose women." Jasper dismissed her with a wave. "Go before I change my mind."

She scurried away without even protesting her innocence. He doubted the little thing was guilty of anything more than a stolen kiss and encouraging a follower.

He turned his attention to the footman who looked properly repentant, though his eyes were as hard as gravel. And there was a touch of surliness around the mouth. "Spriggs, isn't it?"

"Yes. Eddie Spriggs. Sir."

"If I ever catch you toying with a maid again, I'll fire you on the spot without a reference. Is that understood?"

"Yes, sir." He glared at Jasper through a thick fan of black lashes too long and lush for a man. But from the look of his arm muscles and the hard set of his face, Spriggs was probably masculine enough to attract any woman he wanted.

Then Jasper noticed a small piece of white porcelain bulging out of the footman's pocket. Jasper reached inside and pulled out a tiny figurine he'd seen in the curio cabinet by the drawing room door.

"Explain this," he said.

The footman didn't say a word, but his face paled and his barely concealed insolence faded. Jasper had to give him credit for his steadiness under pressure. Perhaps he could employ that talent in the future.

"Tell you what, Spriggs. I'm going to dock a week's pay instead of turning you over to the police. But if I hear of anything else missing, I'll assume you pilfered it and I'll send you to jail so fast your head will spin right off your body. Do I make myself clear?" He enjoyed watching the footman squirm.

"Yes, sir. I understand."

"Good. Consider yourself lucky to have this second chance. Now go and don't forget how much you owe me because, believe me, I shall not." Jasper smirked as the man scurried away even faster than his sweetheart had.

Jasper threw back his head and chuckled. Things were looking up.

THE NEXT MORNING Nick stepped off the Fall River Line steamship the moment it docked in Newport. He strode from the pier to the waiting carriage, jumped on board, and urged the coachman to race back to Summerhill. Impatient to check on Nell, Nick climbed the stairs two at a time and only paused when he arrived at her partially open door. He knocked softly and then peered inside.

Propped up in bed, Nell leaned into Melinda as they glanced through a photograph album together. The pair looked so content and so beautiful. He noted their strong resemblance. They both had creamy skin and thick blond hair—though Melinda's was a few shades darker and piled up in a rather messy topknot. Both had blue eyes that slanted slightly upward, making them appear like they were always smiling a little. But today Nell's were half-closed. And while her face was no longer so sickly, she was still drawn and pale.

Even Melinda had dark rings under eyes. She wore a plain plum-colored dress that suggested she planned to stay at home this morning. When she glanced up, she brightened with relief and maybe even a hint of joy. For a moment he thought she might open her arms wide to him, but she merely smiled.

"Do come in," she said. "I'm so glad you're back." Melinda gestured to the flowery chair by the window.

Before he took a step, Nell held out her arms. He rushed forward across the hardwood floor and patterned rug and gently squeezed her. She was so thin he could feel her bones through her nightgown.

"How are you feeling, little one?" His throat choked with a lump of emotion so large he could hardly swallow. To see a child suffer was nearly unbearable; he felt the guilt over his absence anew. "I'm so glad you're getting well. Is there anything either of you need? I'd be glad to fetch it."

"I don't need anything, thank you." Nell's voice sounded weak but happy. "Look at these pictures. Grandmother sent them to Auntie Mindy."

"Yes, they arrived yesterday. I arranged them in this album so Nell could see what her mother and I were like when we were young." Melinda pointed to a grainy photograph of two little girls at the beach.

"Do you have any photographs of you and Papa, Uncle Nick?" Nell asked.

"I'm sure I have a few somewhere. I shall write your Grandmother Bryson and ask."

Melinda nodded, her eyes aglow. "Wonderful. Maybe the three of us can put together another album. Wouldn't that be fun, Nell?"

"Yes, I'd like that."

Soon Nell's energy waned. When she closed her eyes a few minutes later, Melinda laid the photograph album on the nightstand and carefully slid off the bed. Nick followed her out to the hallway.

"I'll send Peggy in to watch over her while I take a walk. I need some exercise." She rubbed her neck and groaned softly.

He struggled to keep his hands by his sides. He wanted to rub the smooth satin skin of her neck and help alleviate her ache. But of course he couldn't overstep his bounds. Only a husband or perhaps a fiancé could take such liberties. He wouldn't pretend to be a suitor when he most certainly was not. To lead a woman on when his intentions weren't serious was despicable, though he knew several men who thought differently. Yet he'd never thought he'd be so glad to see Melinda. And he had to admit her dedication to Nell impressed him.

"So you've been Nell's nurse," he said, watching her closely.

"Actually, I only assisted Miss Leonard. When Nell began to improve, I entertained her with stories. And we played dolls and talked. Well, mostly I jabbered and she listened. She seemed grateful for the company."

He'd never expected Melinda to assume the role of nurse's helper, even for their beloved niece. He thought she'd flee from the sick bed and anything distasteful or demanding so much of her time or effort. But he'd apparently underestimated her fortitude.

"Miss Leonard and I had lots of help from Glynna and Peggy. I never pictured myself as a caregiver, but I must confess I loved watching over Nell—especially after we were through the worst. At first I feared for her life and I was so distraught I could scarcely be of service to her. But the Lord sustained me."

They descended the stairs, strolled down the corridor, and met up with Peggy, who gladly went upstairs to watch over Nell. Except for other servants, the house was quiet. Most of the adults were probably still asleep or only beginning to stir. Nick opened the back door and they stepped onto the veranda. A wave of cool, salty air flowed around him. "Do you mind if I join you for your walk or would you prefer to be alone?"

Her smile lit the early morning. "I'd be delighted. I've felt quite alone these last several days." Stress carved shallow lines into her face. "It's so good to have you here, Nick." She reached over and squeezed his hand, but for only a moment.

Her spontaneous gesture surprised him. Just the touch of her hand sent waves of heat through his heart. They headed down the path toward the rocks and the sea. A breeze freshened the damp air and began to dry the crystal beads of dew filming the grass.

She glanced sideways as they strolled. "I've always adored Nell, but I didn't realize I could get quite so attached. Her illness made everything else seem insignificant. For the first time, I felt more like a mother than an aunt."

He nodded. "You are her mother now." Nick paused. "Have you forgiven me my absence?" His voice held an edge, though he didn't want to provoke a disagreement or, even worse, an argument.

Melinda drew out a long sigh. "I'll admit I didn't at first. But Nell took all my attention and energy, and I soon forgot my annoyance." She flashed a mischievous grin and he relaxed. "I can never stay angry at anyone for long. I enjoy being happy. Holding grudges isn't in my nature."

"You're fortunate. I'm afraid I tend to brood. It's not a very admirable quality."

She shrugged. "I suppose someone has to think serious thoughts while the rest of us waste our time with frivolities." She smiled again, and he took her remark as a compliment.

"Nell's sickness reminded me how important family is and just how fragile we are. Losing my sister was a horrible blow . . . I cannot imagine losing my mother or Nell." Her voice faltered. She shuddered and then pulled in a steadying breath.

"I'll not try to take Nell away from you, Melinda—in case you thought I still might try."

He saw the taut lines of her face smooth out and her mouth curve in a wide smile. "I confess I was more than a bit worried. Your family is so powerful—"

"I'm not heartless." He hoped he didn't sound too defensive, but her words stung.

"Oh no, of course you're not. But if you believed Nell would be better off without me, I thought you'd want me to bow out. And I could never do that."

"I can see how much you and Nell love each other. She needs both of us." She'd never consider him as a spouse, nor should she. They were too different. But happily they were reaching an understanding about Nell.

"Thank you, Nick. I trust your good will. I'm most grateful. We can be friends, can't we?" she asked, glancing sideways. Her smile teased and he couldn't help grinning back.

Somehow Melinda didn't quite fit his criteria as a chum. But she was waiting for an answer. "Of course."

"Nick, I hope we'll never fight over Nell. She needs consistency and a stable life."

"I agree." But they couldn't give her a real sense of home, sending her back and forth between them. Somehow they'd have to work through this dilemma. Together.

They lowered onto the wooden bench facing the ocean and silently watched the waves crash against the boulders. Fear for Melinda tightened his heart. She was naive enough to believe anyone with a smooth line and gentlemanly manners. She'd fallen prey to someone like Clayton Underwood, for example. Even the mild-mannered Simon Preston might not be all he seemed. Someday some man would snatch her in his arms and ride into the sunset with her—and Nell. They both needed protection against such predators. Sheltered by her parents, Melinda had never faced the world, or even society, on her own before. He worried where her instincts would lead her. Perhaps to fortune hunters and bounders and rogues of every kind.

Yet maybe it was her kindness and love of life that drew her toward other people—not her naivety. She *was* more sensible than he'd ever thought.

She gently slid her hand to her lap.

"I can sit with Nell this afternoon so you can rest, if you wish," he said. He'd postpone his work until evening and skip the ball at Ocean View, something he'd rather not attend anyway.

"Why thank you. She'll love that. And I would appreciate some time to myself."

Nick nodded. She'd probably head off on a shopping spree to buoy her spirits. But he guessed there were worse diversions than shopping, if one stayed within their budget. After the difficult week she'd had perhaps she ought to indulge herself.

Then she looked at him, her head cocked and her eyes glistening with humor. "You probably think I'll run off to the Bellevue Avenue shops and buy everything in sight."

Heat rushed to his face. "Now why would I think that?" he asked. He couldn't help the twist at the corner of his mouth.

"Because normally I would shop. But with Nell just beginning to recover, I've lost interest."

He almost laughed, but he didn't want to offend her.

She cocked her head. "I've been wondering if Blue Star came around at the last minute."

He groaned. He'd tried hard, but nothing had fallen into place. "No. But we're getting somewhat closer. I expect they'll reconsider and contact us again. Soon, I hope."

But if he didn't gain firm control of Bryson Steamship soon, his father would undoubtedly jump at some harebrained scheme that would jeopardize the company. Or he might hand over the reins to Jasper, which would be equally as bad. As they watched the surf roll toward shore, Nick felt a powerful urge to explain this to Melinda, but he wasn't sure she'd really be interested. He assumed she already considered him a drudge and a bore. According to his sister, he was too standoffish for the ladies to flirt with and far too involved in business matters. Melinda undoubtedly felt the same way.

TEN

Melinda went back to Nell's bedroom and dropped into the soft easy chair by the window. Nick followed on her heels. She gestured toward the rocker she'd dragged in from the playroom a few days before. "Do come in and have a seat," she said softly. "It looks like Nell's still asleep. I'll feed her some soup in an hour or two when she wakes up hungry."

He pulled his chair nearer to hers and sat down. Their legs were practically touching.

"Do you mind if I ask you a question?" he asked.

"No, go right ahead."

"Melinda, did you always trust the Lord to heal Nell? Did you ever doubt?"

His personal, probing question surprised her. "No, I never doubted He heard my prayers. God is with us and He gives us the grace to accept whatever we must face. He doesn't promise us a life free from pain, but He does promise to be with us. That's enough. It has to be."

"I wish I had your trust. When I was in New York, I worried about Nell constantly. I felt so frustrated and even angry because

I wanted to control the situation, but I couldn't. The impasse with Blue Star didn't help any either."

"I'm just beginning to understand that control of our destiny is an illusion."

He sighed. "You're so right, but it's difficult to accept. I'm used to relying on myself."

"But there are so many things we can't control—like Nell's health. My helplessness forced me toward God." She glanced at Nell, then back to Nick. "Well, I'll just say that I think this has brought me closer to Him than ever before. So even though it has been a horrible situation and I never want to endure such times of fear again, I'm grateful for it. Does that make any sense?"

He nodded and smiled at her. "More than you know." He rose and looked out the window. He was terribly handsome in profile. With a start, Melinda realized she was staring and hurriedly looked back to Nell.

"Melinda, while I was in New York, on the last day—when I realized I couldn't finish the deal with Blue Star and get back to you and Nell—I went for a long walk. I walked three, maybe four miles before I realized where I was, the end of the road, staring at the Hudson."

He was silent for a long time. "And?" she asked softly.

"I stared out at that water, that river moving by, on and on, and I thought it was a lot like God. Moving, constant. Moreover, I was more like one of the boats upon it, pushing, chugging, striving, thinking I could get where I wanted. But if the engine went out, I'd just have to go with the river. And in that moment, for a time, I was all right with it." He shook his head. "I keep trying to get back to that moment of surrender. The idea of it. Giving my life to God—not just asking for wisdom for a business deal."

She stared back up at him, taken aback by the intimacy of the moment. "I know exactly what you mean," she said. "Perhaps we can encourage each other to continue to do so. I think it is there, in that place you've described, we'll each find the peace we seek."

Never had Melinda had such an intimate conversation with a man. And it had been over God! Clearly He was drawing them together, which was such a good thing for Nell. If they could be good friends, surely they could find a way to raise her together, even when they were in separate households.

Joy buoyed her until that afternoon when Mr. Grimes, the butler, delivered her mail before she dressed for paying calls with Florrie and Glynna. A letter from her mother. She'd written Mama nearly every day, but this was only the third one she'd received. Melinda slit open the envelope and scanned the contents of the note.

It contained lots of gossip followed by news that gripped her. She had to read it twice before Mama's words sunk in.

Our attorney located a buyer for the house, and the sale should be finalized within a few weeks. An interested buyer came along much faster than we had anticipated. I'm delighted by the fair offer, though it isn't as generous as I'd hoped for. Unfortunately, most of our profit will disappear when I pay our outstanding bills. Our creditors refuse to wait, so I'm forced to comply before they institute legal proceedings against us. Yes, my dear, our financial situation is far worse than I'd thought.

This morning I informed the staff of the sale, so I'm quite sure they'll spread the word, along with the fact the house I'm purchasing is quite small, though cozy, and doesn't require more than a few servants. Our future, while not exactly bleak, doesn't look promising. Invitations will dwindle once news of our difficulties finds its way around the city. I fear we'll be forced into a situation where we'll have to make all new acquaintances and friends. Naturally this isn't to my liking, but I see no way to avoid it.

So I'm hoping and praying you're having success in making a brilliant matrimonial match. I do so regret placing you in this precarious position, but what is done is done.

I am planning to move to our new home on Sutton Place near Washington Square Park sometime during the beginning of August. Please keep me informed of your progress, my dear daughter. It's vital you make a suitable marriage right away.

Melinda groaned. It wouldn't take long for the dreadful news to spread to Newport and damage her prospects. While Sutton Place was a perfectly respectable address, it was a fast slide down from their mansion on Fifth Avenue.

Unfortunately, none of the eligible bachelors appealed to her. Perhaps if she turned her attention toward widowers the field would widen. She hoped Phinneas Dalton wasn't a typical example. Surely spinsterhood would be more attractive than marriage to such an unsuitable man. Yet if things were as dire as Mama suggested, even spinsterhood was no longer an option; in a few years, perhaps even a home on Sutton Place would become too much for them to finance.

Simon. Simon Preston. Had she been too rash the last time he'd come calling? She'd not even bothered in responding to his kind note.

With the assistance of Denise, she pinned on her new hat that set off her shell pink and white frock. She pulled on kid gloves, gripped her scalloped parasol, and accepted her reticule from the maid. "I'll also need my card case."

With everything in hand, Melinda hurried downstairs to join the other ladies for afternoon calls. Late as usual, she jumped into the waiting carriage. Glynna and Florrie were discussing the upcoming reception for the Farnsworths, so they didn't notice her tardiness.

"Melinda has been a tremendous help. We chose the loveliest floral arrangements for the table centerpieces," Glynna said.

Melinda settled into the plush seat beside her friend. "It was one of the few respites I had from sitting by Nell's bed. And now we're ready for the party to begin."

"Thank you. I'm grateful for all your assistance," Florrie said. The open landau lurched forward down the long driveway. "We'll be stopping by two or three of the cottages this afternoon. In meeting these ladies," Florrie advised, "we'll pave the way—prepare them to donate to your mission at the party."

Glynna barely nodded. "Do you think this might seem a bit manipulative?" She twisted the silk skirt Melinda recognized as Florrie's. An afternoon loan, apparently.

Florrie shook her head. "Not in the least. It is how things are done."

While they chattered Melinda prayed the Lord would again hear the cry of her heart and provide a husband. A congenial one with integrity and a little money, if possible. Perhaps she'd even meet someone today, someone new. Someone perfect. She sighed and stared out at the edge of the road, thinking of Nick's analogy. *I give my life and future to You, Lord. You know what I need. Please give me peace and a trusting spirit. Amen.* For a moment, she felt a measure of quietude. But as they drew closer to town, Mama's ominous words echoed in her mind and she felt the tension build in her shoulders again.

Society women in their loveliest costumes paraded up and down Ocean Drive and Bellevue Avenue in their open carriages drawn by matching horses. They rode through iron gated entrances and sent their coachman to the mansion doors with engraved calling cards. Few of the ladies were ever at home for they, like their neighbors, took afternoon drives and dropped off their own cards. But they found Mrs. Beatrice Carstairs at home at Grassy Knoll, receiving visitors.

A slight woman of fifty or so years, she had a broad forehead and pointed chin just like her daughter, the spiteful Nan Holloway, who sat beside her, smirking. The Van Tassel party, along with Dolly Santerre—whose son had married Nan's sister last summer—gathered in the drawing room. Mrs. Santerre peered at

Melinda through her pince-nez. Melinda smiled back, hoping to crack the ice freezing the older woman's face. She inclined her head slightly in response.

While the ladies chatted about their friends and relations, Melinda gazed around the high ceilinged room. Every square inch boasted of gilding, rare Italian marble, and curlicues on the legs and arms of antique French furniture. No doubt the décor had come straight from some French chateau in disrepair and sold by an impoverished aristocrat to a rich American. Melinda's attention wandered as they all listened to Florrie and Glynna describe the African mission school. But it wasn't long until their host skillfully returned the subject at hand to Newport gossip. When Melinda heard the name of Clayton Underwood, she looked up, careful to maintain a bland expression.

Mrs. Carstairs leaned forward. "I heard the Longs are almost ready to announce the engagement of their daughter, Jeannette, to Clayton Underwood. Now that's a perfect match."

Mrs. Santerre tapped her cane against the floor. "No, my dear Beatrice, I believe that's premature gossip. No one truly knows whom young Mr. Underwood will marry. Everyone wants him for their daughter, but he hasn't rested his eyes upon anyone just yet."

Her glance swept Melinda, but she didn't say a word. Melinda blushed and took a sip of tea. Everyone in society knew Clayton had once courted her. If he were practically engaged, then he'd been trifling with her this summer, while keeping Jeannette on the line. What a cad! How fortunate to have escaped his clutches.

Mrs. Carstairs shrugged, apparently unwilling to argue with her friend about it. "Well, he's quite the prize. And between their fortunes, he'll never have to work another day in his life."

Not that Clayton ever has. She didn't want such a man as her own husband—the thought of it tied her stomach in knots. But the news of yet another former suitor switching his affections made her jaw clench in fear. What if every potential suitor did the same? What if she was left with no one but the likes of Phinneas Dalton? *Lord? Please, help me. Calm me. Help me to trust.*

But fifteen minutes later, as they left the cottage and strolled toward their carriage, her fears continued to descend like a hailstorm. Unless the Lord provided someone quickly, she'd have to lower her standards or retain her independence and be dropped from the only society she'd ever known. A dreadful choice. If she only had more time, she knew she'd find someone more compatible, but time had run out.

Seeing them off, Nan strolled beside her and leaned close, her voice low. "I understand you must be distressed that Clayton Underwood is about to pop the question to Jeannette Long."

"On the contrary. I'm thrilled for Jeannette, not one bit envious. I wish them both the very best."

Nan raised one skeptical eyebrow. "If you say so, then I suppose I must believe you. I've heard Mr. Preston is quite taken with you. He's everything a lady might want—as long as she loves rare stamps." Nan's cackle irritated.

Suppressing a wince, Melinda tossed her a polite smile. "We're becoming good friends."

"What's this? Surely you're not considering . . . He's completely wrong for you, Melinda. Anyone could see that." She stared at her in surprise. "Simon Preston would bore you to death before the honeymoon even got started. He's rich and handsome and a superb dancer, but oh so tiring in manner. At any rate, since you're staying at Summerhill, why not charm Mr. Bryson? He's on the sober side, but he has many commendable qualities." Her eyes gleamed. "Of course everyone says he's never recovered from Alma Noble's defection, but I'm sure you can make him forget all about her. You do know Alma, don't you?"

Melinda said evenly, "No, we've never met." She stepped toward the Van Tassel landau. Nan lightly touched her arm with her tiny, gloved hand.

"You're much prettier than Alma. And she's such a tedious bluestocking. All she can talk about is Shakespeare and Milton. She married a terribly dull intellectual and now they teach somewhere in the hinterlands. They dropped out of society years ago." A twist to her mouth accentuated her smirk. "No, you wouldn't have any problem distracting Mr. Bryson. From what I've seen, you already have." Nan's laugh sounded so tinny and insincere. "Of course Mr. Bryson appears immune to charm. He doesn't seem to admire society women. So he probably, deep down, is just like every other man. Idly interested in every pretty thing that crosses his path."

Melinda couldn't wait to get away from her but forced herself to share parting niceties. Even as the carriages finally lurched off one after the other, Nan's remarks echoed in Melinda's mind. Nick's true love, Alma, had obviously been better suited to him than she could ever be. She shouldn't mind he had a romantic past—after all, she did as well—but she did mind, very much. A twinge of ridiculous envy pinched at her heart. She and Nick were merely Nell's coguardians, and new friends, but definitely nothing more.

DURING THE EARLY evening before sunset, Melinda walked along the coast and then down the rickety wooden steps to a curve of beach sandwiched into a small cove. Mama's bad news had thrown her way off course. A few minutes alone to gather her wits and pray might restore some peace. She watched frothy water slide over smooth, silver sand, then wash out to sea. Its gentle swish soothed her a little. Yet the crashing of surf against rock just beyond the beach seemed calmer than the turmoil still tumbling through her head and heart.

At the creak of footsteps on the stairs, Melinda glanced over her shoulder. Glynna waved as she trudged through the sand.

"Were you looking for me or just out for a walk? Is Nell all right?" Melinda asked. A gust of wind whipped a few strands of hair from her carefully coifed pompadour. She pushed the stray pieces behind her ear.

"Fine—sleeping again, according to Peggy."

Melinda took a full breath, relieved. How long would it be until she stopped fearing for her niece?

"I wanted to speak to you before you're off to the musicale." After paying afternoon calls, Glynna had changed back into a blue and white striped frock, devoid of lace and ruffles, but most becoming just the same.

"Aren't you going too?"

Glynna laughed. "Oh my, no. While I can go calling with you, missionaries really do not belong at such functions. Especially missionaries about to plead for funds. It's a delicate balance—maintaining relationships and yet not presenting oneself as anything but frugal."

Melinda grinned. "You do a brilliant job of it."

"Melinda, I saw how you paled when Mrs. Carstairs announced Mr. Underwood's engagement. I wondered if perhaps you still had feelings for him."

"I did once, but not in a few years. This summer when I met him again I thought perhaps I'd made a mistake in turning him down. But after a few . . . *conversations*, I'm relieved we didn't marry. I've lost all interest in him."

Glynna nodded as if she didn't need a detailed explanation. She seemed to see right through people. Pursing her lips, Glynna hesitated. "Becoming Nell's guardian has most likely changed your plans. You're seeking a husband?"

Melinda laughed, hoping her desperation wasn't too obvious. "Indeed, I am. My mother insists. I've probably waited too long already."

"Nonsense." Glynna tilted her head. "Have you ever considered marrying Nick?"

Melinda's eyes flew open and her gaze fastened on Glynna's face. "Are you serious?"

"Indeed, I am." Her earnest gaze made Melinda look down at the soft sand and half-buried shells before she responded.

"I hardly think he's interested in me. And besides, we're completely opposite. We'd be at each other's throats right from the beginning." She did like Nick, but she wouldn't waste her time chasing after him and possibly making a fool of herself. Worse yet, she might destroy their new, fragile friendship.

Glynna stared back at her. "I believe you're most suitable."

"Ha! I doubt that very much. And I hear he still carries a torch for Alma Noble." The words slipped out. She wished she could stuff them back in her mouth.

When Glynna paused, Melinda knew she'd guessed right. He still cared for Alma.

"I believe he's over her. Their romance ended years ago, before she married her professor."

"Has he said so?" Melinda asked, kicking the sand with the toe of her shoe.

"No, Nick seldom tells me anything personal. But I have eyes and I can see how he looks at you. I'm sure he has romantic feelings for you."

Melinda faced her friend with her hands on her hips. "Usually I trust your judgment, but this time you're most definitely mistaken. You're misinterpreting his interest in Nell for interest in me." Still, her heart squeezed at just the thought Nick might care for her.

Glynna shook her head. "I don't think I'm wrong, Melinda. Please take my advice seriously. Promise me you'll at least consider him. Pray about it."

Nodding, Melinda turned back toward the rickety stairs. "I will."

AT DUSK JASPER finally found Nick in the library. Panting from hurrying around Summerhill in search of his brother-in-law, he leaned against the doorframe until he breathed normally. He ran his finger around his tight collar to relieve the pressure on his neck. Scarcely an hour before he'd heard good news at the Reading Room and then rushed home as fast his horse could pull the gig. Nick glanced up when Jasper strode across the room.

"I have some surprising news you'll want to know."

"What is it, Jasper?" Nick pinched an unwelcoming smile as he lowered a stack of papers to his lap.

Nick's tone of exaggerated patience irked him. Jasper dropped into the soft leather chair. "I just heard Mrs. Hollister sold her home on Fifth Avenue and dismissed most of her staff. They say she's lost all the money. Probably overspent, if she's anything like her daughters. Anyway, she and Melinda are financially ruined." He could barely keep the laughter and relief out of his voice. He felt a twinge of pity for her, but undoubtedly they caused their own downfall.

"I'm sorry to hear that. It's very unfortunate for Melinda." Nick pulled a frown and laid his papers aside on the sofa.

Jasper nodded vigorously. "Indeed, it is. But it's not so unfortunate for you."

"Oh? I don't understand." Nick's frown deepened.

Why couldn't the man add one and one and get two? "Can't you see your opportunity? Now you can give Melinda a sizable amount of money in exchange for full custody of Nell. I suspect she'd even accept a small sum. They're in dire straits. In fact, they owe all the funds from the sale of their home to creditors."

Try as he might, Jasper couldn't keep a satisfied grin off his face. But Nick peered at him with shock and disdain just as if he'd suggested something illegal. What on earth was unethical about helping out the young lady? With a large chunk of cash she'd be able to stay in society and catch herself a rich husband. They'd all win.

"I can't believe you'd even suggest such a thing." Nick shook his head slowly. "Taking advantage of Melinda's situation would be despicable. I'd never do that."

"But," he said slowly, "you wanted sole custody. Frederick wants this. Nell's a Bryson, and now, more than ever, her association with the Hollisters is only bound to harm her. And us." The man was as thick as a brick. How could he ever expect to run a major business like Bryson Steamship Company if he couldn't see opportunity and seize it?

"Nell's *association* with the Hollisters is that she is blood kin. And I'm positive Melinda would never agree to such a plan—nor do I believe she should. The benefit of having Melinda and her mother in Nell's life, whether it be on Fifth Avenue or at a far less desirable address, outweighs the negatives."

Jasper's eyes narrowed. Why was his brother-in-law so self-righteous and stubborn? "She's charmed you—gotten under your skin."

"I don't know what you're talking about. Melinda and I have become friends."

"Then be a friend to her, Nick." Jasper shook his head and leaned forward. "Melinda's future is dire, indeed, without money to help her secure a good marriage. Give her a sum to see her through, and all this will be over with. She doesn't have a choice."

Nick reared back. "Of course she does. They can live quiet, respectable lives outside of society." From the sad look on Nick's face, he obviously pitied Melinda's fate. "At least she'd still have Nell."

Jasper stood and began to pace. "Being snubbed by society might not bother you, Nick, but it would destroy Melinda and put Nell in a precarious position. If it seems too much, I repeat my offer—Florrie and I would be delighted to help. We'll even adopt the child, if you're willing."

Nick scowled and rose, papers in hand. "That's completely out of the question. I shall never let Nell go and I'm positive Melinda wouldn't either. Please don't bring up the subject again. I'm tired of you and Father harping about it."

Jasper shrugged, pretending nonchalance. "All right. There's no need to get angry. I'm merely trying to help you." He felt sure Nick would come around once he had a chance to think it over. He was offering the perfect solution.

Nick's eyes squinted. "But why do you and Florrie want Nell? You have two children of your own. You don't need another."

"It's not a matter of need, at least not for us. We're only thinking of Nell. She'd have two sisters close to her own age. As well as anything else she desires."

Skepticism blanketed Nick's face. In fact for a moment Jasper wondered if he was going to laugh with derision. "Don't you dare suggest this to Melinda. She'd be terribly offended."

Jasper threw up his hands. "All right, I won't." Nick was probably correct. Melinda was a most stubborn and uncooperative woman. "But when you discover it's very difficult for a bachelor to bring up a child on your own, remember my offer."

He stifled a frustrated sigh. He'd counted on Nick jumping on this opportunity and sending him a monthly stipend in exchange for raising Nell. That would at least make a dent in his repayment to Underwood and his other creditors who were beginning to make trouble. Jasper shook his head in disgust.

He'd have to take other measures to secure the funds.

ELEVEN

❧

As much as he despised it, Jasper was right about Melinda's slide down the social ladder and its impact on Nell. Nick mulled it over and prayed, but by midevening he knew he had to make a decision. He walked the coastline and scrambled over the rocks to watch the fading sunset, a glorious blend of pink and crimson. An idea came to mind and he felt the Lord was giving him an answer. He wasn't at all sure he liked the solution, but he knew beyond a doubt God was nudging him to take action. He'd vowed he'd trust the Lord with his decisions—personal and professional—and now was his opportunity to follow up.

Nick returned to the cottage as darkness slowly swallowed the evening light. But a full moon rose in the blue satin sky and cast a pale path across the lawn. Nick found the gaslights in the back hallway turned low, indicating most of the family had gone out.

"Have you seen Miss Hollister?" he asked the butler who was sifting through calling cards in the silver tray by the front door.

"Yes, sir. Miss Hollister went out for the evening with Mr. and Mrs. Van Tassel."

Nick nodded his thanks. They'd all be having dinner at some cottage and then attending the musicale at Hartsfield.

Once upstairs he bade the girls good night and ordered his meal. He ate a light supper of consommé and broiled trout in his room since he didn't wish to eat alone in the cavernous dining room with a table large enough to seat thirty. After, he dressed in his evening clothes and left for the musicale.

MELINDA FOLLOWED FLORRIE and Jasper through the foyer of Hartsfield, quickly glancing at her reflection as she passed the enormous, gilded mirror. She looked fine in her beaded, ice blue gown, and the plume in her hair dipped slightly as she moved. Her heirloom blue diamond necklace and matching earrings sparkled beneath the crystal chandelier. A crush of cottagers wove their way around the little groups who stopped to talk before heading out to the back lawn. Once outside Melinda drew a breath of cool, fresh air.

Instead of holding the event in their music room, the Normans had built a stage for the orchestra and singers on the back lawn between two giant elm trees. Torches lit the area with a warm glow. She surveyed the crowd milling around the yard. They were strolling toward rows of gilded ballroom chairs set in front of the makeshift stage. The ladies, dressed in their finery, had feathers in their hair and jewels glittering around their necks and wrists. They chattered and laughed with the gentlemen who all wore formal black tailcoats, silk waistcoats, and white ties.

Strolling down the aisle between the rows, she heard a familiar voice.

"Miss Hollister, may I speak to you for a moment?"

She turned around. "Oh, Simon. Good evening." She'd prefer to take her seat before the music began, but she couldn't be rude. It was sad how her heart refused to flutter when she saw him. *Kindle my feelings for this man, Lord.*

"Let's walk by the refreshment table," he suggested.

They strolled by the long table covered with white linen and a tempting array of sweets. She accepted a glass of punch and followed Simon over to a stone bench several yards away, but in direct sight of the crowd. She wouldn't slip into the deep shade and cause people to gossip. She could ill afford any further hits to her reputation. Especially now.

"It's a beautiful night, is it not?"

"Yes, indeed." Stars twinkled in a clear, dark sky, and the moon shone bright like a Japanese lantern. "How was your talent show at the Casino? I'm sorry I couldn't attend."

"Oh, it was grand. You missed out on a lot of fun." His voice sounded so petulant she assumed he was still annoyed she hadn't attended, despite his lovely bouquet of flowers and note.

"I'm sure I missed a delightful event, but it couldn't be helped." How could he possibly expect her to put his whims ahead of her sick niece?

Simon shrugged and then dropped to the stone bench where they sat side by side, but not too close. Bright torches bathed the area in soft light.

He gave a wave of dismissal. "But never mind the talent show. I have a question for you, my dear."

My dear? Her throat went dry.

He slipped her hand into his, and she resisted the urge to slide it out. "May I call you dear, or am I too forward?"

"I suppose you may, if you'd like," she murmured. "Now what is your question, Simon?" She hoped he wouldn't get too personal, but she suspected what was coming.

"This may shock you, but I've been thinking hard about us and how we'd make a splendid match."

She wouldn't characterize their match as anywhere near splendid, but she nodded, anxious for him to continue. She needed a husband more than ever, but she wasn't ready for a proposal from

Simon. At least not yet. What was wrong with her? Melinda whipped open her hand-painted fan and waved it through the warm air to cool off her flaming cheeks.

"I'm hoping your feelings for me have grown over these last weeks—or at least may I hope you believe they shall, in time?"

After a sharp intake of breath, she stared but didn't say a word. Her heart wavered for only a few moments before common sense prevailed. She didn't love him; she didn't even like him very much. How could she answer without hurting his feelings? He was self-centered and proud, but he still deserved a gentle response. She didn't know what to answer, but that didn't deter him from continuing.

"Miss Hollister," he said, taking her hand in his and twisting toward her. "Now I know this is awfully sudden, but I've grown so fond of you . . . Would you do me the honor of becoming Mrs. Simon Preston?"

When he paused, Melinda shook her head. "I appreciate your proposal, but—"

"You can even bring that little niece of yours to Pittsburgh for six months of the year," he said hurriedly, "if that's what your heart desires. Yes, I've heard you have coguardianship and a duty toward her. Children are a nuisance, and that's a fact, yet I'm affectionate toward them in my own way. So don't hesitate because you think she'd be an imposition on me." He cocked his head and grinned in a way she knew was meant to disarm her. "What do you say, Melinda? Will you accept my proposal?"

This was her chance to change her future. Her mother's future too. Yet she didn't like what it promised. A man with a fortune but no love for children. A marriage with no love. "You've honored me, Simon. And I thank you so very much. But you must give me time to consider my answer. Marriage is such an important decision."

"Yes, indeed." He removed a small velvet box from his pocket and opened the lid. A square-cut diamond sparkled in the descending light. "May I slip it on your finger, my dear?"

He hadn't listened to a word she'd said. "It's beautiful, Simon, but I can't wear it—at least not yet. I want to make certain this marriage is right for both Nell and me. She plays a major part in my life, and she'd need to become important to your life as well. We must both consider that."

His eyes flickered with annoyance, followed by a tight smile. "As you wish. I can wait." But obviously he wasn't used to waiting. "As I said, the little girl won't cause me a moment's concern. I'll send her off to school when she's ready so she won't be a burden to you."

"Simon, Nell is a blessing. She will never be a burden to me."

"I didn't quite realize her importance." He tucked the box back in his pocket and shifted away from her ever so slightly.

Melinda nodded. "So you see we both have much thinking and praying to do before we commit to a future together."

"Of course. But, Melinda, I do want you for my wife. Nell must never become an obstacle between us."

She smiled gamely. "Thank you. You have done me a great honor." She believed his sincerity, but she wasn't convinced he understood how a child would affect his life. And in the end he might very well resent her for bringing Nell into their marriage.

WHEN NICK SPOTTED Melinda, his heart jolted. Standing beside a stone urn that frothed with flowers, she looked up at Simon Preston. His mouth was turned up in a blissful smile. Nick expected to rescue her from that cowboy who liked to hover about her, Clayton Underwood. But instead Nick spotted Clayton leaning over Miss Jeannette Long, one of his own distant cousins from Philadelphia. Tension drained from Nick.

As he drew closer to Simon he noted the man's eyes were gleaming with hope and barely concealed desire. Nick grimaced. Why was he imagining such terrible things? If she cared for him, and he for her, Simon's wealth would resolve many problems for Melinda. He ought to be happy for her, not resentful.

Nick noticed the pair was engaged in serious conversation. He knew he should leave them alone, but his footsteps took him closer. They turned his way. Simon's face scrunched with irritation, but Melinda just looked startled. Her face seemed ghost-white. When his pulse quickened in fear, he told himself to calm down.

"Bryson, good to see you," Simon said, suddenly beaming an ear-to-ear grin. "Beautiful night, isn't it? I must tell you my good news. Our good news."

"And what's that?" He stared at Melinda, his eyes demanding an explanation, disbelieving she'd have anything to share with Simon, especially good news. They'd only recently become acquainted, he thought. *Just this summer, right?*

She glanced at her clutched hands, then looked up and flashed a nervous smile. "Mr. Preston has proposed to me."

Her crazy announcement took Nick several seconds to process. "And did you accept?" He didn't recognize his own ragged voice filled with dread. He couldn't manage even a shallow breath while he waited for her answer.

She wore a brittle smile. "No, not yet. I need some time to consider Simon's most gracious offer. It's such a serious step, and it affects Nell."

She looked so miserable Nick thought she might bolt or at the very least cry. At least she hadn't accepted the proposal. And if he had anything to say about it, she wouldn't sacrifice herself. Not for what he knew must be driving her.

Simon's long arm wrapped around Melinda's back and gripped her tiny waist. She seemed to ease away from his touch, but Nick couldn't be sure. He clenched his fists to his sides to keep from pushing Preston into the rose bushes—just like a jealous suitor might do.

Simon puffed out his chest and narrowed his eyes at Nick, clearly recognizing his unspoken challenge. "I can offer Miss

Hollister everything she could possibly want, and I'd be thrilled to do so."

Nick grunted. Put that way, the proposal sounded logical, even desirable, at least in theory. But Melinda's gaze darted from Preston to him, and her bottom lip quivered.

But Simon wasn't even looking at her. Satisfaction oozed from him. "I trust I'll convince her this very night to accept my proposal." He leaned forward to add in a conspiratorial whisper, "Women must not appear too eager, you know."

Nick knew he couldn't wait a moment longer or Melinda might feel she had no alternative. He cleared his throat and met Melinda's gaze. "Before Miss Hollister answers you, she must know that your offer is not the only one she must consider." He stood up tall, his stare riveted on Melinda's beautiful, but puzzled, face. "I also wish to marry her."

Her eyes widened in utter surprise. For a moment Nick thought she might burst into tears. "I—I don't know what to say to either one of you. I'm overwhelmed, but truly honored. Thank you both. Now, if you'll excuse me . . ." She swirled around and strode away, the heels of her blue satin shoes clicking against the flagstone path. The silver embroidery and glass beads in her blue gown shimmered as she walked away.

"Poor form, Bryson, poor form," Simon complained, crossing his arms. "If you had intentions toward her, why did you not make them known before now?"

"I didn't know before now that I did," he muttered.

"She's lived under your own roof this past month! There hasn't been anything untoward—"

Nick swallowed a retort and strode across the lawn in pursuit of Melinda. He caught a glimpse of her disappearing into Hartsfield through a crowd of guests. He followed, but once in the deserted foyer, he realized she'd probably gone home. As he neared the front door, the butler silently opened it for him. Nick spotted the

Van Tassels' carriage rolling down the driveway toward Bellevue Avenue, its wheels crunching against crushed stone. Then it vanished into the night. Without Melinda, he had no reason to stay at the musicale. They needed to talk. And the sooner, the better.

Jumping in his gig parked at the end of the circular drive, he grabbed the reins and spurred on his filly. In the distance he sighted Melinda's brougham. The dark, twisting roads of Bellevue Avenue and Ocean Drive forced him to decrease his pace, even when he longed to whip his filly into a gallop and overtake Melinda's carriage.

He hadn't meant to blurt out his proposal. His offer shocked her, and he understood why. Out of nowhere he'd asked for her hand and in a truly crude manner. He'd given her precious few signs of his hidden but growing affection. He still worried that they had little in common except for Nell. He felt sure they could make their marriage work for the child's sake alone—if they both wished to. But he wasn't at all sure Melinda would accept, regardless of her financial woes.

Her carriage was just ahead now. *So close . . .*

When they slowed down around a turn, Nick spurred his horse for one final burst, galloped past the carriage, and forced it to a halt by the side of the road. He braked the gig, jumped out, and flung open Melinda's door. Before she could object, he stepped inside and sat across from her. Her lavender perfume filled the area with a sweet, floral fragrance.

He held up his palms. "I know this isn't proper, Melinda, but right now I don't care. We need to talk about marriage—our marriage." His eyes began to adjust to the darkness, though he could barely see her face. The carriage lanterns did little more than cast deep shadows inside.

"You must give me time," she insisted. "I'm not sure what I should do."

"Make the sensible decision. I can give you anything that Simon could offer and more. Jewels, clothes, carriages, whatever you desire. And you know Nell needs us both. Together. She'll be so much happier if the three of us become a family. We don't have to live in the Fifth Avenue house with my parents. We can build our own. Tell me what you want and you shall have it."

"You're very generous, Nick," she murmured.

"I want you to be happy. And Nell too." He held her hand and she didn't pull away. "Will you accept my proposal?"

She slowly shook her head. "I need a little time, Nick." Her voice was barely a whisper.

"Yes, of course. But don't keep me waiting too long." Slowly he wrapped an arm around her and pulled her close. Gently he turned her chin toward him and leaned down to kiss her on the lips with an intensity he didn't know he had. She felt surprisingly good in his arms, so warm and soft, and her lips so sweet . . . But then she pulled back and turned her head.

"I'll leave now." As much as he longed to stay, he needed to go before he lost his resolve.

As he jumped from the carriage, he heard her murmur, "Thank you, Nick." But there was no joy in her tone. Only, what? Tension? Utter confusion? Resignation? But underneath, perhaps a touch of wonder? Hope?

He considered it, all the way home to Summerhill, and hoped they might share another brief word before the night was over. But by the time he returned the horse and gig to the stable, Nick discovered Melinda had already gone to her bedroom.

If she placed Nell's welfare above her own, she'd accept his offer. He couldn't imagine she'd marry him for love, but he prayed that giving Nell a family would be enough for them both.

That was clearly the Lord's will.

Wasn't it?

MELINDA STAYED AWAKE for most of the night weighing the advantages and disadvantages of marrying or becoming a spinster, and a poor one at that. She chided herself for resenting the fact that she'd been given what she prayed for—a marriage proposal, from two entirely suitable gentlemen, no less—and yet she could find no peace in it.

She fell into a light sleep and awoke early, still tired from a restless night. The evening's unexpected proposals came rushing back to her mind. She wanted to avoid Nick until she'd sorted out how she felt and made a decision. At least one thing was clear after the night apart. No matter what she decided about Nick, she needed to decline Simon's offer as soon as possible. She could never force herself to spend the rest of her life as his wife. Even social disgrace and oblivion trumped marriage to a man who disdained children. He wasn't altogether disagreeable, as Phinneas Dalton had been; she hoped he found someone soon who would appreciate him for his good points—and perhaps shared his mundane interests.

Denise arranged Melinda's hair and helped her dress in a pale yellow frock with small tucks in the bodice and lace on the sleeves and skirt. She glanced around the room still feeling at loose ends. It wouldn't help to pace across her bedroom carpet all morning and brood about her decision. No, not in the least. She'd get on with her day and hopefully speak to Glynna.

Once downstairs she met the Van Tassels in the foyer surrounded by luggage.

"Are you off on a trip?" she asked Jasper, who accepted his bowler and walking stick from the butler. Eddie, the footman, carried his truck and valise through the front door toward the waiting carriage.

"Yes, my mother needs some legal work done in New York, so I'll be gone for a few weeks. I hate to leave Newport for the heat of the city, but I'm afraid this can't wait."

"Do have a pleasant trip," Melinda said as she made her way to the breakfast room, her spirits lifting at Jasper's unexpected departure. And it appeared the conniving man had not yet heard of either Simon's or Nick's proposals.

"Good morning," Glynna said, looking up from her plate.

Melinda took a seat across the table, glad to find Glynna alone. It was too early for the Brysons to gather for breakfast, so they had the room to themselves. They talked about the gloomy weather while they ate their soft-boiled eggs, toast, and oatmeal. Melinda kept watch for Nick and his father. She avoided Frederick as much as possible since every time she attempted a conversation he either ignored her or scowled.

She glanced at Glynna. Melinda knew she needed a confidant, and no one was as trustworthy as Glynna, not even her dear friend Louisa Davenport. She couldn't sit here calmly and pretend something monumental hadn't happened last night. Now was the best opportunity to divulge the details. Quickly she summarized her two marriage proposals and ended with a drawn-out sigh. "Mr. Preston and I have little in common. But much worse, he barely tolerates children. So I'm afraid I must consider Nick."

Glynna's face lit up with delight. "What do you mean 'afraid'? He'll make a most devoted husband. And marrying Nick will also benefit Nell. She'll have two parents once again, just as your sister wished."

"Yes, that's true." But there were disadvantages as well and she couldn't ignore them.

Glynna reached across the table and touched Melinda's hands. "Cora hoped you'd marry Nick."

Taken aback, Melinda peered at her. "Whatever do you mean? That's certainly an odd notion. You don't really think she wanted me to marry him, do you?" The idea struck her as preposterous.

"I do, indeed. A few years ago she told me she hoped you and Nick would marry someday. I believe that's why she left you co-guardians. It makes perfect sense."

Melinda didn't speak for several moments. "Well, perhaps." She recalled her sister once or twice mentioned that Nick needed a cheerful wife and she needed a no-nonsense husband. Cora certainly wasn't above meddling. Melinda had dismissed his sister's opinion as ridiculous, but her change in fortune definitely limited her options. "I know marriage to Nick would make Nell's life easier."

"And yours as well."

Melinda sighed. "Yes, mine too. I must marry soon and settle down—for a variety of reasons." She fought the urge to tell Glynna of her financial difficulties, but she couldn't let anyone know, not even this kindhearted woman. Losing—no, spending—one's fortune, without attention to the future, was humiliating.

"I realize Nick will make someone a steady, dependable husband. But I'm just not sure we're right for each other. And I always dreamed of a marriage forged from love, not . . . convenience."

"I don't believe love is as far off as you believe. Your personalities compliment each other. He's serious and reliable. And every time you're in the room, he smiles." She hesitated a moment. "Nick might help you to—"

"Grow up," Melinda said with a rueful grin. "I admit it. I do like to avoid life's responsibilities." Except for the welcome obligation of caring for Nell.

Glynna smiled. "I wasn't going to put it quite that way."

"That's all right. I realize in some ways I'm immature. I shall think over Nick's proposal and pray about it. And would you pray too?"

"Of course." Glynna finished the last sip of her coffee. "I'm going to Calvary Church to pick up some clothing and books and household items they're donating to the mission. Would you care to come?"

"That's kind of you." Melinda stirred sugar and cream into her second cup of coffee. Glynna was everything she wasn't—self-sacrificing and content, even joyful with her lot in life. She'd never marry someone for reasons as crass as social position and financial security. "I'd like to come to the church with you, Glynna." That would keep her away from Summerhill and Nick, at least for a short while. And maybe some distance would do her some good.

Melinda attended Trinity Church when she vacationed in Newport and had never even heard of Calvary Church. Probably most of its members were townspeople. The local Newporters and the cottagers seldom, if ever, mixed.

They spent the morning with the pastor's wife and the head of the Missionary Society choosing lightweight clothes, pots and pans, and an assortment of theology tomes. Melinda later decided to add in a bunch of her own Fannie Cole dime novels that were as exciting as they were uplifting.

Mrs. Perkins handed Glynna a lovely silk shawl. "This was my mother's most cherished possession. Her employer gave it to her when she didn't want it anymore. My mother was the housekeeper over at Ocean Crest for years." She gazed at the shawl lovingly. "I'd like you to have it, Mrs. Farnsworth. I hope when you wear it you'll remember the ladies at Calvary Church are praying for you and your school."

"Thank you so much," Glynna said with tears in her eyes. "But I can't take something you so treasure."

Mrs. Perkins waved her hand. "I have no need for a fancy shawl. It's yours as a gift. Please take it and not another word."

Glynna hugged the woman. "Every time I wear it, I shall think of all you fine ladies and say a prayer."

Melinda folded the garment carefully, a bit overcome by Mrs. Perkin's generosity. Would she give up her own, most treasured possession? She'd never even considered it.

As soon as Glynna had finished her business at church, they returned to Summerhill and Melinda sat down to write a respectful letter to Mr. Preston declining his marriage proposal. As soon as the footman set off with it for his cottage, she felt an overwhelming rush of relief.

Now she could turn her attention to Nick.

And find something of her own to add to Glynna's collection . . .

TWELVE

❧

That morning Nick couldn't concentrate on work. His mind strayed back to Melinda—and how she apparently couldn't make up her mind about whom to marry. He thought his chances were good since she couldn't possibly love that stamp collector, could she? But even her precarious finances didn't persuade her to readily accept his proposal. Nick frowned. Apparently she didn't harbor sufficient feelings for him, let alone love. Actually, he didn't expect love. Well, he'd done his part—what he thought the Lord had prompted. The rest was up to her.

He heard soft footfalls on the library carpet. When he glanced toward the doorway, he found Melinda coming toward him, a tentative smile on her face. He began to rise, but she motioned him to stay seated. She lowered onto a leather chair near him, avoiding the empty place on the sofa by his side.

"I'm so sorry about last night. I was overwhelmed and confused. I'd like to thank you again for proposing. I'm truly humbled and touched."

Nick nodded.

"I thought about Simon for a long time last night." The corners of her mouth turned down.

Perspiration seeped through his skin and dampened his shirt. "And?"

"He doesn't appreciate children and he'd never love Nell. Of course he'd see to her physical needs, but I doubt he'd give her enough affection. When Cora and Parker named us as coguardians, they trusted us to consider such things."

He waited for her to get to the heart of the matter.

"It wouldn't be fair to Nell to marry a man who didn't much care for her. So I've decided to refuse his offer of marriage."

His heart pumped faster as she spoke. Would she now refuse him just as Alma Noble had?

She smiled cautiously. "And I accept your offer of marriage. I shall do my very best to be a good wife."

"Excellent. I'm really pleased." His voice sounded so formal, probably due to his confounded awkwardness when it came to romantic matters. The significance of their commitment nearly stole his breath, robbing him of words.

He wanted to reach over and squeeze her hand, but from the serious, almost troubled, look in her eyes, he didn't think she'd appreciate it. He wanted to envelop her in his arms and press her lips with a long, deep kiss like they'd shared last night. But he didn't dare. Her subdued manner was so unlike the usually exuberant Melinda, he knew she'd only accepted out of necessity. He studied her face and found little joy.

But he had no right to feel offense. He'd only proposed out of duty to Nell and sympathy for Melinda's circumstances. Yet he felt let down. Maybe their fondness for each other would eventually grow into something more. *Lord, don't let this be a marriage in name only even if it's starting out that way. I didn't misinterpret Your direction, did I?* He wouldn't allow himself to think that was even a possibility. It was too late to question his decision.

Nick cleared his throat. "Shall we set a date?" he asked with as much as emotion as he'd demonstrate setting up a business meeting.

But he couldn't help himself; she was so uncommonly restrained it made him feel guarded.

"Yes, let's do. The sooner, the better." She sent him a faint smile, but sadly it looked forced.

He hated to admit that he'd hoped for, and even expected, a more enthusiastic response from such a warm-hearted woman. Disappointment washed through him. "Would you like to have the wedding in Newport or would you prefer New York?"

"Newport would be fine. Something small and intimate, I think."

They set a date in two weeks time. "Please excuse me, Nick. I have a lot of preparations to make." She spun out of the library, leaving him a little bewildered and quite dispirited.

They'd made a pact; they'd both have to dig deep to make it work. Only the Lord could help them. And only He could make this *arrangement* so much more. Nick would not second-guess His direction.

An hour later after he'd regained his equilibrium, he searched for his father, dreading the inevitable confrontation. Unfortunately he found Frederick heading down the hallway, anger cutting across his face. Nick suppressed a groan and braced himself.

"Florrie told me your news. She learned it from your intended. Didn't have the nerve to tell me yourself, did you?" his father scoffed. "Let's go to the office to talk."

"I was looking for you, Father. I wasn't trying to hide my engagement." Nick's shoulders tensed.

Frederick gave a loud sniff. The parlor maid seemed to melt silently into the wall as they passed her. These days his father walked with a stiff gait that slowed him down. They entered the office and settled in the chairs near the back-to-back desks he and Jasper used.

"I warned you against Melinda Hollister. She'll spend your money and break your heart." Frederick leaned forward. "If you marry that woman, I'll have to seriously consider installing Jasper as president of Bryson Steamship Company by the end of the summer. What do you think of that?"

Anger rose within Nick and threatened to explode in a torrent of words he'd immediately regret. "You'd be making a big mistake."

Nick bit his tongue rather than spewing suspicions he harbored. "I just don't trust him." About Jasper wanting to adopt Nell so he'd have access to her trust fund—why else would he truly want her? He'd not spent a single hour with the child this summer. He was certain Jasper would run Bryson Steamship Company into dry dock if he were put in charge.

But he couldn't say all that. Not to Frederick.

As Nick observed his father, he saw a tired old man with waning insight and fading wisdom.

Frederick's eyes narrowed. "Jasper is a good businessman. Just not as aggressive as you are. But you'd never see *him* marrying someone as unsuitable as Melinda. You're exactly like Parker."

Nick felt heat firing through his cheeks. He was nothing like his easygoing, generous brother. He wished he were more like him, in some ways. Obviously his father didn't notice or care.

Nick stood. "Melinda and I will marry in two weeks."

Frederick shook his head in disgust. The anger in the old man's eyes pierced. "Do as you wish, but be prepared to take the consequences."

Nick nodded and left the room. He'd proposed and he'd stick to his offer, no matter what happened.

MELINDA MADE A list of preparations for the wedding and then she and Nick went to Nell's room to give her their news.

"Uncle Nick and I are going to be married soon," Melinda said. Sitting up in bed with her rag doll and picture book, Nell clapped her dimpled hands and shouted with glee, though Melinda doubted she quite understood the meaning of marriage. Then Nell stretched out her arms, and Nick and Melinda leaned forward for a hug. Her embrace was remarkably ardent, considering she was still fragile from sickness.

"I'm so happy," Nell said, her eyes brimming with joy.

"The three of us will live together in New York," Melinda explained as she leaned closer to her niece. Nell was feeling better every day just as Dr. Dean had predicted. The bloom was gradually returning to her cheeks; they were already pink and soon they'd deepen to rose.

Melinda gave Nick a sideways glance and noted the grim press of his mouth. Her spirits spiraled downward and all her enthusiasm fizzled. Obviously this engagement wasn't making him happy. Or if it was, he certainly didn't know how to show it.

Then a sudden realization struck her like a slap in the face. He'd never said he loved her. She'd so hoped he harbored at least some affection. If he didn't, why had he proposed? She certainly didn't want a man who didn't care for her. If she wasn't suddenly so poor and so desperate, she'd turn Nick down right this very instant. But she didn't have an acceptable alternative. Clayton Underwood wouldn't stay faithful for five minutes and she'd have to move to Texas; Simon was pleasant, but bland . . . and his mere tolerance of children was most unsettling. And Phinneas Dalton—why, she'd never seriously considered him. Even Nick, who didn't demonstrate any affection toward her, was infinitely preferable to any of the others. Melinda sighed.

After her visit with Nell, Melinda telephoned Mama.

"This is splendid news," her mother said. "You'll make a beautiful bride, my dear. If you'd like, I shall send you my wedding gown. Cora wore it when she married Parker. Would you like to carry on the tradition?"

"Yes, thank you, Mama." Melinda would've preferred a gown

of her own, but she knew this was important to her mother. Nor could they really afford another. Tradition would be a convenient excuse.

"You'll have no more financial worries," Mama said. "Nicholas will provide everything you've ever wanted."

"All I want is his love," Melinda blurted, amazed and immediately sorry she'd admitted a truth that sounded so preposterous.

Mama paused. "Love will come in time, if you let it. It's far better to let love grow, rather than watch it fade away."

"Yes, you're right of course, but . . . Well, never mind. I am indeed fortunate. Nick is a good man."

If she confessed her reservations, she'd just upset Mama, who shouldered more than her fair share of worries. And besides, the telephone wasn't designed as an instrument for baring one's soul. Happily, Mama agreed to come to the wedding even though she remained in mourning and had to oversee the move to a smaller house. When they hung up, Melinda returned to the veranda, feeling restless and burdened with all the tasks that lay ahead. The only good part was that if she kept busy, she wouldn't have time to worry about the actual marriage.

Nick soon joined her and leaned against the railing, his back to the sea. He cleared his throat. "So have you made all the wedding plans yet?" He half smiled.

She stood beside him and let the breeze brush against her face. "No, but I've been thinking. We'll have a small, tasteful ceremony if that's all right with you."

"Whatever you want." He nodded politely.

She'd always dreamed of a large, lavish wedding with a dozen bridesmaids, an ivory satin gown from Worth, and an adoring groom. She stopped her train of thought. Truly she didn't care anymore about an exquisite, one-of-a-kind gown from the Parisian couturier. Mama's gown would do. And she didn't care about the number of bridal attendants. But she did care about the groom.

Much more than she wished. She so wanted him to gaze at her with love in his eyes and fondness in his voice. If he'd only lean over and kiss her, she thought she might actually swoon. She needed some sign of his affection. *Please, Lord . . .*

But he stood still and stiff, his eyes staring absently at the hanging basket of impatiens, apparently lost in thought. If the set of his granite jaw meant anything, those thoughts weren't joyous ones. Melinda tilted her head.

Had his stolen kiss, in the carriage last night, meant nothing? If it took every bit of her energy, she'd capture his interest and charm him into loving her. But practical matters came first.

"Nick, there's something I ought to tell you, though it's rather embarrassing. My mother can't afford an elaborate ceremony or reception. I'm so sorry, but we'll have to keep it quite simple."

"If you want a big wedding, you shall have it. I insist on paying for everything. There's no need to spare any expense."

It was unorthodox for the groom to take care of the cost; in fact, it was the height of bad taste.

"Thank you," she said, truly grateful. "But that would be a terrible breach of etiquette. But don't worry, I'll figure something out." The cost of the wedding must be borne by the bride's family without exception, and the reception could never be held at the home of the groom or his family. But she and her mother didn't own a Newport cottage and she had no idea where they could hold a wedding breakfast. Perhaps one of her friends might offer a suggestion.

"Whatever you wish is fine with me. Now if you'll excuse me, Melinda, I must get back to my work. If you need help, please feel free to ask me." He sent her a dry smile. "Or better yet, ask Florrie."

She watched him stride across the veranda floor and vanish into Summerhill without a backward glance. Biting her lip to hold back tears, she closed her eyes and wished for a groom with an adoring heart as she'd always dreamed. Nick was so generous, but not in the least bit demonstrative.

She withdrew to her bedroom, donned her straw hat with the silk lilacs encircling the brim, and strolled over to Honeysuckle Lodge in search of Louisa. Her friend met her in their morning room.

"Shall we take a stroll?" Louisa asked with a quick glance toward her mother, who perched primly beside her on the settee. Mrs. Davenport liked to dominate a conversation with tedious gossip about people they either didn't know or care about.

"A stroll would be delightful," Melinda agreed.

As soon as they approached the back lawn, Louisa leaned closer and lowered her voice. "You're bursting to tell me something. I can always read your mind."

Melinda laughed at her friend's hyperbole. "Yes, I do have news. I'm going to marry Nick Bryson."

Louisa enveloped her in a tight hug. "That's wonderful! I'm so happy for you. Nicholas will make a worthy husband, even if he is a bit serious. I'm sure you'll liven him up."

"I believe we'll be quite happy." Or least content from doing the right thing for Nell. Right? What if she was making the biggest mistake of her life?

"When and where will the wedding take place? Do tell me all the details."

Melinda took a deep breath, refusing to succumb to fears for the future. "We don't wish to wait, so we'll be married in Newport in two weeks. I need to rent a room in a restaurant or hall for the wedding breakfast. Do you have any ideas?"

"I most certainly do. You'll hold your reception right here at Honeysuckle Lodge. Mama wouldn't allow you to go anywhere else. Let's go speak to her now before she leaves for the beach."

THAT EVENING, AFTER supper, Nick led her into the rose garden by the side of the back lawn. He swallowed hard as he slid his hand into his pocket and brought forth a small velvet box.

"I hope you like this." He removed a diamond solitaire ring and awkwardly slipped it on her finger. The hopeful look in his eyes made her smile.

"It's beautiful, Nick." She examined the large, round stone. In the early evening light, it sparkled with the brightness of fire. "Thank you."

He bent over and kissed her with warm, eager lips, and her heart surged with joy. But as she responded with equal passion, he broke away and quickly regained his composure. Taking her hand, he asked, "Shall we go back to the cottage? It's getting dark." He looked troubled, as if he feared strong emotion.

A bit disappointed, Melinda nodded. "Of course. We have to dress for the dance tonight."

Would her marriage be like this—warm one minute, but chilly the next?

SHE HAD NO time to ponder this troubling thought as the next two weeks flew by in a whirlwind of planning, details, and mounting excitement. Each and every day Melinda slowly regained her high spirits. She'd prove herself a model wife and then Nick would shower her with all his love. With the Lord's blessing they'd grow closer as her mother promised, like so many other couples had. This might not be a marriage between soul mates, but she'd try her best to bring Nick happiness. When she wasn't busy with alterations to the bridal gown Mama had sent by post, and choosing flowers and refreshments with the Davenports, she prayed the same basic prayer again and again.

I'm doing the right thing, Lord, aren't I? I want to marry the man You have chosen for me, but if You don't tell me otherwise, I shall marry Nick and assume he's that man. Stop me if this isn't Your holy will.

She felt better knowing that God held this marriage in His

capable hands. Surely He'd make something good come of it or stop the wedding before it took place.

With help from Florrie, Glynna, Louisa, and her mother, Melinda finalized all the wedding arrangements in record time. She'd easily incorporated everyone's suggestions, yet managed to keep the cost reasonable. Mrs. Davenport insisted on providing the flowers from her hothouse and garden. And she also gave the breakfast as a wedding gift. She probably heard about their financial misfortune, but of course she never spoke of it.

MAMA ARRIVED TWO days before the ceremony at the same time as Nick's mother, a quiet woman with a regal bearing and little taste for society. Both were dressed in black mourning, but they put aside their grief for the celebration of a new marriage. While Mr. Bryson scowled every time he saw her, Melinda felt his wife's approval in her sad smile and attempt at welcoming her into the Bryson family.

Dear Mama couldn't contain her triumph, despite her continuing sorrow at Cora's passing. She thought marrying another daughter to another Bryson son was quite a feather in her cap. As Mama removed the jacket of her black traveling suit and tossed it on the bed for the maid to hang up later, she leveled a steady gaze at Melinda.

"Word has gotten out about our financial misfortune, though now that you're to be married, it's not such interesting gossip. I wonder if Nicholas has heard. He probably wouldn't have proposed to you if he had. No man wants to marry a woman whose family has lost their fortune. And status."

Melinda shook her head. "I don't know if he's heard. Do you think I ought to tell him? I've been so involved with wedding plans I haven't given our finances much thought." At least she'd intimated their circumstances by telling him they could not afford more than a small wedding . . .

Mama's eyes widened with alarm. "Absolutely not. It's too late for him to call off the wedding, but we must not take the chance."

"But is that really fair?"

Mama expelled a dramatic sigh and rolled her eyes toward the high ceiling. "You must grow up and be practical, Melinda. You're thinking like a child, not an adult."

"Yes, I suppose so," she answered, not convinced that withholding the complete truth was a sign of maturity.

Mama never allowed emotion to cloud her vision and judgment. Melinda just wished Nick loved her so she could trust him enough to confide her monetary troubles. Right now she needed to weigh every word she spoke. But she didn't want him to know she was marrying him foremost for security and secondly for Nell's sake. It seemed so cold and calculating. She sighed quietly as she opened the window higher to let in the sounds of the sea and the cool air. She hoped and prayed they'd soon fall deeply in love. But right now where were those blissful feelings she so craved?

How sad she couldn't confide her misgivings to Mama. But her mother only wanted to share in the excitement of the grand event.

Soon after, they wandered down to the morning room where wedding presents were spread out on a long table for all to admire. A silver tea service, oriental vases and ginger jars, an ormolu clock, a watercolor by Monet in delicate pastels. Several gifts of expensive jewelry from family members rested in the library safe. Mama examined each piece, her smile growing more and more smug. "Quite impressive," she murmured.

Glynna gazed at the presents. "An embarrassment of riches" was written all over her face, though she said nothing. Melinda introduced Glynna to her mother, but after a polite greeting, Mama ignored her. Glynna wore a plain white shirtwaist and tan skirt, no fancier than a shop girl's outfit. That was enough for Mama to disregard her as a poor relation of the Brysons' and unworthy of additional attention. Mama's superior attitude, despite their financial ruin, brought heat to Melinda's cheeks. She hoped Glynna could brush it off without feeling snubbed. She'd seen her take similar snobbery in stride this summer. But the idea of her own mother being the source was horrifying.

Mama and Mrs. Bryson wandered off, leaving Melinda and Glynna alone.

"We have so much more than we'll ever need," Melinda said quickly, surveying the crowded table. "I can't imagine using half these things."

Glynna nodded.

"I would like you to have this vase, Glynna." Melinda held up the squat piece of porcelain painted in garish colors. "I know it's truly ugly, but it should fetch a pretty penny. Sell it and put the money toward your school."

"Oh I couldn't." But Glynna's shining eyes confessed she felt tempted.

"You most certainly could. And you must. Of course we'll have to wait until after the wedding so no one will notice the vase is gone."

Glynna gripped Melinda's hands. "I can't thank you enough, though—"

"You can't turn down a gift, especially for a worthy cause."

Nodding slowly, Glynna said, "Yes, you're right. But I feel like a pauper begging for food."

"Nonsense. You're doing this for others, not yourself."

"It's my pride that makes me hesitate."

Melinda smiled. "We all have our struggles." Hers was a love for things, such as all the exquisite objets d'art cluttering the table, minus the vase. She'd enjoyed collecting anything and everything through the years, though large hats with flowers and plumes were really her downfall. And on a much grander scale—jewelry. She treasured the blue diamond necklace her grandmother had given her.

When they finished surveying the gifts, they started for the door. Melinda swallowed hard, rethinking her impulsive gesture. She'd just handed over an antique vase worth a small fortune and not really as ugly as she pretended. But her rare generosity flooded her with a joy she wasn't used to.

"Good day, ladies. May I speak to you for a moment, Melinda?" Jasper blocked the doorway. Beneath his bristly reddish-gold mustache she saw his thin-lipped mouth pulling downward.

"Of course." She braced herself and waited. "And welcome back, Jasper. Did your trip to New York go well?"

"Yes, it went fine, thank you." As Glynna left, Jasper stepped forward and closed the double doors behind him. He didn't even glance at the gift-laden table.

"I hear you and Nick are to be married. That came as quite a surprise, I must say. Florrie and I wish you all the best." He twitched a smile and then paused as if he didn't know the best way to continue. "I don't know if Nick ever mentioned that Florrie and I wish to adopt little Nell and free you and Nick of your parental responsibilities."

Her jaw dropped down. She paused before responding. "Thank you, Jasper, for your—concern—and generosity. But neither of us would ever consider relinquishing custody." How could he even ask? She couldn't imagine it was out of the goodness of his heart.

He flashed a sour smile and shrugged. "I understand, but I do think you're being foolish. There really is little need for you to go to such trouble simply to give the girl two parents and one home. Not when we're available."

"We are not entering this marriage only to provide Nell one household," she said with as much stately dignity as she could muster.

"So I've heard." He opened his mouth as if he wanted to say more, but then the door opened and Stephen Farnsworth came inside.

Seeing he was interrupting, he said, "Pardon me. I've obviously interrupted."

"No. We're done. For now." Turning on the heel of his shiny black shoes, Jasper whispered, "We must speak again before your wedding. There's something I wish to tell you. It's quite important." And then he strutted from the room.

BUT SHE WAS too busy to carve out time for Jasper. Hours later during the rehearsal dinner, Melinda leaned toward Nick and told him of Jasper's offer.

Nick's nostrils flared. "He just won't give up." He paused for a few seconds and then added grudgingly, "I suppose he means well."

"I can tell you don't really believe that."

He pinched a rueful expression, not quite a smile. "You're right, I don't. Jasper has never been among my favorite relations."

"Why is that?" she asked. She laid her fork on her plate and hoped he'd answer. Was it all right to show curiosity about the family she'd soon join, or was she just plain intrusive?

"Because I don't trust him." He didn't elaborate and Melinda suspected she'd annoy him if she pressed for a more specific answer.

That was the problem with Nick. He confided so little in her. With anybody, really. How could she discover the real man beneath the reserved exterior?

THIRTEEN

❧

T he next morning Nick arose early, galloped his favorite filly down Ocean Drive, and then ate a hearty breakfast. The hours ticked by slowly until eleven o'clock. From his bedroom window he glimpsed the brougham and landau pulling up in front of the cottage. Soon the wedding party would depart for the church.

He stuck his boutonnière in the flower-hole of his frock coat and pulled down his pearl gray waistcoat. His patent-leather button boots shone like glass and his silk top hat and kid gloves were also brand new. Glancing in the mirror he thought he looked presentable except for his glacial expression. He ought to look happier, but he couldn't grin like a fool when he felt so burdened.

He'd mired himself in a mess of his own making. What annoyed him most was the fact that no one had forced him to propose to a young woman he found attractive, but didn't quite love. He cared about her well-being, of course, but it was her charm that drew him in. Unfortunately charm wasn't nearly enough to nourish and sustain a marriage. But perhaps her response to Nell's illness signaled she had grown up. He prayed this was so.

Not long ago he'd envisioned a mature helpmate, someone he could depend upon to listen and understand the pressures he was under. A picture of Alma Noble filled his mind. The pain he'd carried all these years seemed mild now, more like a dull toothache than a stab wound. And that meant he was finally recovering.

If he married Melinda with Alma still holding first place in his heart, then he'd commit a terrible injustice. *Lord, please erase all thoughts of Alma. Please give me hope that my marriage to Melinda is Your will for both of us.* If God had wished for him to marry Alma, she would've fallen in love with him. And she hadn't.

"What's the matter with you, Nicholas? Having second thoughts?" His father snickered from the doorway. He came inside the room and stood unsteadily by the unlit fireplace. "It's not too late to back out of this preposterous marriage."

Nick felt heat creep up his neck and face. He hoped it didn't show. "No, I really want to marry Melinda and I shall in a very short time." His voice sounded pathetically weak.

"You're making a colossal mistake, one you'll regret soon enough."

He might, but he'd never admit that to his father. "No, Father, I believe marrying Melinda is the right thing to do. She's is a kind-hearted woman, and she's a wonderful mother to Nell."

"She's a Hollister," the old man spat.

"You must forgive her grandfather. That ancient grudge is poisoning you. Your brother died years ago."

"That doesn't take the Hollister out of the girl."

"In less than an hour, that girl will become a Bryson."

Frederick reddened and his eyes narrowed. "Did I ever tell you how her grandfather killed my brother? It was his shoddy boots, Hollister-made boots—"

"Yes, Father, you did." Nick held in his exasperation—and fear—that his father's memory was deteriorating faster than he'd imagined.

"If you'll excuse me, I should go before I'm late for my wedding," Nick said with a sigh.

"Before you run off and marry that girl, I want you to understand something. This marriage of yours persuades me to let Jasper take over the business. I'm serious, Nicholas. You're defying me and I won't have it."

The man had threatened to turn the company over to Jasper before, but had apparently forgotten or changed his mind. This vacillation couldn't go on much longer. Frederick was increasingly becoming dangerous to Bryson Steamship.

His father ranted on about disappointment and disobedience, but Nick barely heard him. Blood rushed to his ears. He'd worked so hard for the opportunity to lead Bryson Steamship Company and now the old man was snatching it away out of pique. Nick's gaze hardened as he stared his father down. He knew the old man wouldn't relent, but he couldn't back out of the wedding at this stage even if he wanted to—which he didn't. He was trusting the Lord and he wouldn't question His guidance.

Why would his father turn over his business to Jasper, who knew nothing about ships? Jasper understood facts and figures, but from the paltry profit they'd made lately, he didn't understand much about those either. Though his father was at fault as well.

"Do what you wish to do, Father. I'm going to marry Melinda."

"Even if it means giving up the presidency of Bryson Steamship Company?"

Nick hesitated for a split second. "Yes, although I can't understand why you'd turn over the family business to a man who has no experience in management."

"He's a hard worker."

Shaking his head, Nick let out the truth. "Only since you started to hint he might have a chance at the number one spot. That's when he began taking a real interest in the business. Not before."

His father sputtered and his eyes betrayed his confusion. Another stab of apprehension, along with unexpected sadness, punctured Nick's heart. But he couldn't dwell on his father's mental health today when he had so much else on his mind.

"Now see here, boy—" Frederick continued.

"I am no boy, Father. And I will not listen to any more of your poisonous words on my wedding day." Nick stormed out of the room, resisting the urge to slam the door behind him.

MELINDA FIDGETED IN the center of her bedroom while Mama fussed with the white silk organza gown embroidered with seed pearls, and then fingered the Chantilly lace veil attached to a wreath of orange blossoms, the traditional headpiece of brides. Denise handed her a cascading bouquet of white stephanotis and blue hydrangeas tied with silk ribbons.

As soon as the maid departed, Mama blotted a tear. "You look so lovely, my dear. Just stunning. I do hope Nicholas appreciates you."

Melinda managed a cheery laugh, but she wondered as well. Nick seemed quite immune to her allure. Perhaps she wasn't quite as alluring as she supposed. Or maybe he regretted his chivalrous, but rash, decision to marry her. Still, he'd had two weeks to back out of the engagement and he hadn't. Maybe he was afraid to hurt her feelings or reputation, especially after the invitations had been engraved and delivered to the hundred or so cottagers. But somehow she couldn't picture him afraid of anything.

"I shall be the best wife I possibly can. If he doesn't love me now, I'm certain he will after a while." She wasn't at all sure, but she refused to be gloomy on her wedding day. "Come, Mama. It's time to go."

She met her giggling attendants in the foyer—Louisa Davenport, Glynna, and Nell, her little flower girl. Glynna, the matron of honor, wore rose, while Louisa dressed in pale pink chiffon with a rose sash. Dressed in a cream-colored lawn dress with a pale pink satin sash and matching ribbons in her curled hair, Nell resembled an angel. Even Mama in her plum silk frock looked moderately festive. A mother of the bride, though still in mourning, could wear shades of purple to her child's wedding in place of black crepe. Tears of joy, and undoubtedly relief, flowed down Mama's cheeks.

They gathered their skirts and carefully descended the staircase. A carriage waited to take them to the church, and later it would transport them next door to Honeysuckle Lodge. Everyone chattered on the ride to Trinity Church, but Melinda sat quietly, trying to steady her nerves. When they arrived, Jasper met them in the narthex. She heard organ music coming from the sanctuary and knew it was time. Her hands shook as Jasper offered his arm to walk her down the aisle. If she only had a brother or male relative, she could've turned down Jasper's offer to give her away, but her mother insisted she accept.

The guests rose. Melinda and Jasper started down the white carpet strewn with rose petals and slowly made their way to the front where Nick and the minister waited. Nick took a few steps forward. Her heart fluttered as Mendelssohn's "Wedding March" played, but Nick's cool expression dampened her excitement. Maybe he was just as nervous as she was. He didn't look the least bit happy—or in love.

The ceremony proceeded in a blur of soft candlelight, joyful organ music, and the scent of jasmine and roses. She and Nick exchanged vows, he slipped a simple gold band on her finger, kissed her on the cheek, and then together they walked back down the aisle as husband and wife. It happened so quickly she barely comprehended what had happened. As they stood in the receiving line, the guests congratulated Nick and extended best wishes to her. She thought her plaster smile might crack in pieces.

Later they drove in a flower-strewn open carriage to Honeysuckle Lodge.

"It was a lovely ceremony," Melinda said after several minutes of silence.

"Yes, indeed." Nick took her hand in his, but he gazed at the scenery, obviously distracted. Was he contemplating the gravity of what they'd just promised? To love, honor, cherish each other? The seriousness weighed heavily on her heart. He surely must feel it as well. She glanced at Nick, needing a reassuring word. But he stared again into the countryside, lost in his own thoughts.

Once they arrived at Honeysuckle Lodge, they took their places at the head table in the dining room and feasted on oysters, caviar, filet mignon, truffles, roast duck, and foie gras. Fine wines flowed freely. But Melinda had little appetite and barely nibbled on any of the ten courses that followed one after the other. Nick ate a little of everything without commenting on the taste. He didn't seem to enjoy any of it.

When the meal finally ended, they cut the wedding cake, a dark, rich fruitcake decorated with scrolls, orange blossoms, and roses made of white icing. The servers boxed small pieces to send home with the guests. It was a lovely ceremony and reception, though simple by Newport's standards.

Nick's face didn't soften during the entire ordeal and he seldom looked her way. Hope for the future squeezed from her heart, drop by drop. She blinked back tears as she responded automatically to the guests' good wishes and praise for the lovely reception. But she wouldn't let her disappointment ruin her wedding day.

She leaned toward him. "I shall try to bring you joy, Nick. Please give me a chance." They both understood their marriage wasn't based on romance, but still they need not live as polite strangers.

His grimace warmed to a small smile. "We both want this marriage to work—for Nell's sake especially."

"Yes, and for our sake as well," she dared to add.

Before he could reply Nell rushed over and flung her arms around their shoulders. "I'm so happy," she cried. "Grandmother said to say best wishes."

Melinda pushed back her gilded chair and placed the little girl on her lap, not caring that Nell crushed her beaded and embroidered gown. "I'm so glad, sweetie. It's splendid to see you smile. And wonderful that you're well again."

Any sacrifice was worth Nell's happiness. Nick must think so too since he was grinning at their niece. Melinda felt her spirits lighten. The remaining hour of the reception passed in a daze of chatter and laughter. Slowly the guests' infectious good cheer ignited a spark of renewed hope within her, and her mood lifted. The crowd thinned by two o'clock. Relieved the festivities would soon end she wandered out to the veranda for a breath of fresh air. So much had happened in such a short time she needed a few moments by herself to consider her new life and an uncertain future.

The ocean sparkled with a layer of silvery spangles. A mild breeze blew across the grass in warm, gentle puffs. It was a clear, perfect afternoon. Birds chirped in the trees edging the lawn and seagulls skimmed the sea and the sky.

At the creek of footsteps on the floorboards, Melinda glanced over her shoulder. Jasper. She flicked a cordial smile and hoped he'd go away.

"A beautiful wedding, Melinda." Jasper stepped so close his breath fell on her neck. "I must congratulate you for catching Nick. I thought you might be forced to marry that Texan or maybe the steel magnate with a passion for stamps."

Her heart thudded. "Whatever do you mean—forced to marry?"

"Oh, I'm not impugning your virtue, Miranda. I'm merely saying you surely must have felt Nell needed a stepfather. You're hardly equipped to bring up a child on your own. You need the guidance of a sensible man."

So he probably hadn't learned of her financial misfortune, though she was surprised he hadn't heard in New York.

"Nick was terrified you might marry the first man who proposed to you out of desperation and then take Nell away. So he asked you instead. Very gallant, but rather impulsive, don't you think?" He plucked at his thick, reddish mustache and looked down at her with malicious amusement in his amber eyes. "I tried to warn you yesterday, but you were too busy to listen. I tried to get your attention several times last night, but you ignored me."

Jasper was right. She hadn't made time for him. But it was his words about Nick that rolled through her mind now, in maddening repetition. *Terrified. Desperation. Gallant. Impulsive.*

"I'd hoped you'd see the wisdom of calling off the wedding. But now it's too late. You'll have to live with your mistake."

Melinda's legs buckled and she dropped into a white rocker. A searing pain stabbed at her heart. So Nick had married her only to insure no one would take his place with Nell. This marriage was a complete sham. Always the optimist, she'd held out a glimmer of hope that Nick felt some affection for her. She wouldn't let Jasper sneer at her distress. She sniffed back a sob and formed her lips into a small, determined smile. "We're married and that's all that matters. Many strong marriages have begun with far less in their favor."

Jasper shrugged and sighed as if she were too immature or just too shallow to understand.

"One more thing," he said, but stopped when a few well-wishers joined them.

He disappeared into the cottage, a smug look plastered across his face. Melinda didn't know how long she sat on the chair, trying to compose herself. She wanted to confess to her guests that they should leave and take their gifts with them. She wanted to run into the ballroom and shout to anyone left that the wedding had been a dreadful mistake. They both had ulterior motives and shouldn't have wed. She was just a foolish woman who trusted in the hope of happily ever after.

Of course many marriages were built upon such shaky ground and no one gave it a second thought. But she'd always wanted and expected so much more, and she'd deluded herself that she might actually get more.

"Nicholas is searching for you." Glynna stepped onto the veranda. "Do come inside and say good-bye to your guests." She squinted through her gold-rimmed spectacles. "Oh, dear me, you look sad. And on your wedding day. What's the matter? Perhaps I can help." Glynna sat down beside Melinda and took her hands. In her satin gown, Glynna looked younger and softer than usual.

Melinda kept her voice low. "Nick doesn't love me. I never thought he really felt any grand passion, but I assumed it didn't matter since the marriage suited us both. But now that I know for certain he only married me to keep Nell close, I feel dreadful."

Glynna's brows knit in a frown. "Who told you that?"

"Jasper."

"He's very unkind. And I believe he's wrong."

Melinda shook his head. "In my heart I know he was speaking the truth."

Letting out a frustrated sigh, Glynna reached for her trembling hands. "If you both try, you'll grow to love each other deeply. I'm sure of it."

Melinda rose. "I'm not at all convinced."

"Remember love is more than warm, sentimental feelings. It's about commitment and putting your spouse before yourself. Remember the First Corinthian verses: 'Charity suffereth long, and is kind; charity envieth not; charity vaunteth not itself, is not puffed up, Doth not behave itself unseemly, seeketh not her own, is not easily provoked, thinketh no evil; Rejoiceth not in iniquity, but rejoiceth in the truth; Beareth all things, believeth all things, hopeth all things, endureth all things.' Melinda, let the Lord's Word guide you and you'll be fine."

She nodded. "I appreciate your encouragement."

"Read the Book and follow its precepts. Base your marriage on God's love for you. See how He loves us unconditionally and guides us in our daily lives. And love Nick the same way. He'll return your feelings."

Melinda nodded. "You always give me wise advice."

Her head ached from holding back unshed tears, but somehow she'd carry on as if nothing had spoiled her wedding day. With God's help she'd try hard to appreciate her new husband. Yet could she even look at Nick again without wondering if their love for Nell was enough to bind them together, forever?

"It's something for me to pray about. If you don't mind, let's go inside now."

After most of the guests left, she and Nick withdrew to their separate bedrooms to change into their traveling clothes. Half an hour later in a shower of rice and good wishes, they rode off in a carriage pulled by a pair of white horses. They said little before they reached the pier where Frederick Bryson's steam yacht *Olivia* was moored. Named after Nick's mother, Frederick had loaned them the vessel—grudgingly, she presumed, and undoubtedly at his wife's insistence. They boarded the luxurious vessel with the waiting crew and set sail for Martha's Vineyard and Nantucket where they planned to stop and tour.

Tired from the stress of the wedding, Melinda leaned over the ship's railing and watched the Rhode Island shoreline slowly fade into the distance. High waves slapped against the hull of the sleek boat. Sea spray rose and hissed, but not high enough to reach her. She removed her plumed hat before a strong gust blew it away and let her hair pull loose from its coif. Nick's arm coiled around her shoulder and she instinctively edged away.

"Is there anything wrong, Melinda?" he asked.

Should she confront him now or wait? Or just forget Jasper's pronouncement? No, she couldn't disregard his hurtful words and feign happiness. She turned sideways and her hair whipped around her cheeks and neck. She tried to curve her mouth upward and reassure him all was well, but it wasn't. And she couldn't pretend.

"It's something Jasper said today. He claimed you only married me so I wouldn't wed someone else and take Nell away. Is that true?" The words slipped out in a rush, but the brittle edge in her voice horrified her. She sounded so distraught—and petulant, but she just had to learn the truth.

Would he take her in his arms and kiss away her doubts? That might convince her he truly cared. Melinda sucked in another lung full of salty air and waited for him to squeeze her in a hug and press his mouth against hers. She could forgive him if he only showed her true affection.

AT A LOSS for words, he gaped like a simpleton. He wanted nothing more than to crush her in his arms and dry the tears brimming in her eyes, but she'd stepped away when he'd tried to nestle her in an embrace. Her face drooped with such awful misery that he wished he could hit his brother-in-law.

"Jasper's a troublemaker. You should know that by now. He's always trying to cause dissention."

"You're not answering my question, Nick."

He sighed. "Naturally Nell is part of it. Our union was the best solution for her. It did enter my mind that Simon Preston might bury you in Pittsburgh or the cowboy might propose and take you out West. I feared I'd never see her again." When her face sagged, he added, "Or you either."

She pinched a grimace. He hadn't said the words she wished to hear. Or in the right order. He'd never learned the fine art of flattering women and he'd probably never learn tact. He didn't

184 CARA LYNN JAMES

think it'd matter so much once they were married, but from the displeased look on Melinda's face, it mattered a lot.

But Nell was only part of the reason he wanted to marry her. There was their financial ruin and the potential social shunning. He sighed. He'd made a terrible mess of things. "It's getting a little breezy. Would you like to go inside the lounge?" he asked. "We could talk more there."

She shook her head, and thick strands of blond hair whipped around her face. She looked like a wild woman with eyes alive with pain. "I'd like to stay out here awhile longer. But don't let me keep you." The wind muffled her words as she glanced over the rail to the choppy Rhode Island Sound. But he read her meaning loud and clear.

He bowed and left, relieved—and at the same time tormented—over her dismissal.

WHITECAPS POUNDED THE yacht and sent up a spray that splashed her with cold water. She stepped back, dried her face with a linen handkerchief, and tried to pat the dampness from the bodice of her new mauve frock especially made for her honeymoon. Glancing up, she noted the sky thickening with clouds and quickly darkening. The horizon soon blended into the gray water.

After several minutes passed, large drops of rain pelted her. And then the deck suddenly tilted and threw her off balance. She grabbed for the railing and missed. Slamming into a wooden deck chair she gasped as a sharp pain rammed her side and stole her breath away. She rubbed the spot right above her waist, but the smarting continued. Melinda righted herself. Widening her stance, she stumbled toward the cabin as the deck rolled port to starboard. The whistle of the wind grew louder and the air chillier. Several sailors reefed the flapping sails in the face of the approaching storm, and soon the steam engines took over and started to rumble.

She found the main lounge and dropped into a blue plush chair nearest the door. The spacious salon was as ornate as any drawing room she'd seen in Newport or Fifth Avenue. Chairs and sofas were grouped together beneath a ceiling painted with an azure blue sky and puffy clouds. She took no pleasure in the beauty of the decoration.

A steward who had his sea legs offered her a cup of tea and a pastry, but she declined. The way her stomach churned she felt she might never eat again. She closed her eyes and prayed the room would stop tipping from side to side. All her attention focused on settling her stomach. Perhaps she ought to go below and lie down. But did she have a stateroom of her own or must she share the chamber—and the bed—with her husband? It only made sense that they'd be in the same cabin . . . Her stomach flipped over, and her luncheon threatened to rise into her throat. She put her damp handkerchief over her mouth and fortunately, nothing happened.

Nick entered the area, looking fit and seaworthy. "Are you seasick, Melinda?" At least his eyes reflected concern.

She nodded. "I don't feel so well. Maybe I should rest."

"Of course. Would you like something to eat or does the thought of food make you ill?"

"Ill, most definitely ill."

"We're heading toward Martha's Vineyard. It might take us awhile to arrive, but at least we'll get out of the storm. The weather is deteriorating fast."

"I'm quite prone to seasickness. I believe I shall go to our cabin."

Slipping her arm through his, Melinda fought against the roll of the boat while it plunged into the roiling sea. Through the windows she glimpsed the surf rise above the railing and splash onto the deck. Slowly they made their way to the stateroom. Melinda leaned into the sleeve of Nick's dark blue jacket and liked the warmth of the soft wool against the silk of her blouse. He guided her every step as they staggered down the passageways.

"We're not going to capsize, are we?" she asked.

"Of course not. We'll be fine."

Once inside the stateroom, Melinda kicked off her shoes, dropped onto the large bed, and nestled into the brocaded spread. She curled up like a ball, not caring how she looked.

"I'll send for your maid to help you, um, undress. And I'll get you some ginger tea for your nausea. Don't worry, you'll feel better soon," he said as he headed for the door.

Melinda hoped she could sleep until the seas—and her stomach—calmed. But each lurch of the boat tossed her insides.

Denise helped her into a white lace peignoir, a gown purchased for her wedding night. But there would be no passion this evening. She yearned to feel better; that was all that mattered. Carefully she slid beneath the silky sheets.

A short time later Nick arrived with a cup of hot ginger tea with only a few drops spilled in the saucer. She instinctively pulled the covers up to her neck and blushed; he'd seen a portion of her wedding peignoir. But to sip the tea she had to lower the bedding again. She let the sheet fall only as far as necessary, freed her arms, and accepted the hand-painted china cup. When she tasted the brew, she tried hard to suppress a wince. Nick had gone to a lot of trouble to bring it from the galley.

"You don't like it, do you?" he asked as he carefully lowered himself onto the bed.

"No, it's too spicy. But thank you all the same. I'm sure it will help." If she managed to down more than a sip or two.

But before she finished more than half a cup, her stomach rebelled and her lunch spurted upward. She grabbed a napkin Nick had brought and slapped it against her mouth. She saw both Nick and Denise glance around the cabin—no doubt for a basin, but not finding one. Melinda pushed herself out of bed.

"Show me the head," she said.

Nick took her by her clammy hand, led her to a small restroom on the far side of the large stateroom, and mercifully left her alone to retch. She heaved until her stomach emptied. She rinsed out her mouth and splashed water on her face as the boat rolled and then pitched. The engines grumbled. Slowly she stepped back into the bedroom. Nick's arm caught hers and she warmed with gratitude. He helped her across the soft carpet, back into the bed, and then tucked her in as gently as he would a baby.

"Melinda, why didn't you tell me you suffered from seasickness? We didn't have to take a cruise."

She groaned. "I was marrying into a family of steamship owners. I'd hoped the sun would shine and the sea would stay calm. I knew you enjoyed sailing and I thought I'd be fine, especially since this is such a large boat. I didn't expect a storm."

He took her hand and she let his heat travel up her arm. Weak and exhausted, she didn't fight his fond gesture. Closing her eyes, she basked in the relief of a settling stomach. If she could only sleep, the constant motion wouldn't bother her.

"I'll leave you now," she heard Nick say, but his voice seemed far away. "If you need me, just send Denise to fetch me. She'll stay with you until I return."

"All right." Melinda opened her eyes and half smiled. Nick brushed her cheek with a gentle kiss and disappeared. She hoped that was all the affection he expected tonight.

When she awoke it seemed as if a lifetime had passed. The steam yacht barely rolled anymore. The roar of the engines had ceased and the wind had died to a whisper. They must be anchored at a sheltered spot out of the storm's path. She couldn't see her hand in front of her, let alone the outline of the furniture. But she heard Nick's faint breathing from beside her in the bed. Was he awake? She dare not turn over and find out. What if he was waiting in ambush for her to declare her recovery? This was their wedding night, and she felt sure he'd want to taste of its promises.

Before now Melinda hadn't really considered that aspect of

marriage. With all the distractions of wedding preparations, she'd swept such questions to the back of her mind and concentrated on the details of the ceremony. But with the festivities over, the marriage was about to begin. A cold sweat sent rivulets of apprehension down her back.

She'd feel better in the morning when the sun shone once again. She tried to fall asleep. But the sound of his breathing kept her awake and alert.

FOURTEEN

❧

From the change in her breathing, Nick thought Melinda had awakened. The last time he'd lit the kerosene lamp and glanced at his pocket watch lying on his end table, he'd read two thirty in the morning. It must be well past three by now. He remained awake in case Melinda needed something and on the off chance she'd feel better and—well, to be blunt, invite him to come closer. She stirred. He heard the slight rustle of sheets. He held his breath in his throat. Would she turn over and extend a hand or move closer to him? He waited. But she didn't move a muscle.

Apparently her seasickness left her too shaky for anything other than sleep. Disappointment seeped through his chest, poisoning his optimism for their future. Then he reminded himself this was merely one night and she was genuinely ill. They'd celebrate their wedding night tomorrow.

He kept repeating the word *tomorrow* silently in his head, until at last he dozed off.

HE FELT A little better in the morning, but too little sleep left him restless and on edge. Quietly he rolled out of bed and dressed, not wanting to awaken her—nor make her feel uncomfortable. He sat in a chair in the corner, reading yesterday's paper, until she stirred.

"How are you feeling?"

She jumped, as if she'd forgotten he was in the room, and peeked over at him. "I'm better, thank you, but not quite well." She sat up in bed, her long blond hair flowing down her back and spreading out on the pillow. He noted she was still dreadfully pale.

He nodded. "Shall I have breakfast delivered to you, or would you prefer to come to the dining room?"

"I'll get up in a while, but not just yet."

He left her to sleep awhile longer and then to dress. An hour later she appeared in the dining room. Looking distracted, she sipped a cup of coffee and refused anything to eat. Her face was etched with misery and he didn't know what to do to help her recover and regain her good humor. He offered her ginger tea, biscuits, a game of checkers, and several magazines. She turned down every suggestion with a wan smile. At a loss, he felt his frustration rise. They spent a long, awkward morning in the main salon and filled the silence with sporadic small talk. They finally gave up and succumbed to reading.

He hesitated, not sure how to delicately say what he'd mulled over all morning. "Melinda, I'm wondering if you'd prefer to return to Summerhill or go onto Martha's Vineyard. I hate to keep you onboard the *Olivia* if you'd rather be on land."

She perked up. "Let's go back to Newport, if you don't mind. I'm terribly sorry to ruin our honeymoon, but I'm certainly not much of a sailor, especially on the open ocean. I hope you understand." He heard more relief in her voice than regret.

They had so little in common and so little to say to each other. He didn't want to continue like this for another week as they'd planned, on board or on shore. And obviously neither did she.

"No, that's fine," he agreed quickly. "I have more work to do before I negotiate with Blue Star again." *If* he still had a job. He felt sure they both knew returning home was merely a ploy to end their wedding trip. He felt a flood of relief at ending the uncomfortable start to their marriage. Maybe they could find their footing again at Summerhill.

BY THE TIME they arrived in Newport toward the end of the afternoon, his spirit had lifted. His father had forgotten he'd ousted him from the company, so his position was secure, at least for now. And with Nell to fill the gaps in their conversation, life might seem more normal here than on the yacht. Eyebrows raised in surprise when they returned, but Melinda smoothly admitted how foolish she'd been not to warn him of her tendency toward seasickness. Both their mothers had departed Summerhill earlier that morning, but everyone who remained nodded their understanding and sympathized.

"Are you going to travel somewhere by train, perhaps?" Florrie asked at dinner, never one to leave anything unexplained or unexplored.

"We haven't discussed it, but I'd love a trip to New Hampshire in the fall. The New England foliage is spectacular. What do you think, Nick?" Melinda asked during the fish course.

"Autumn is perfect for a honeymoon. Your idea sounds grand." By that time they'd know each other better and the strain would undoubtedly ease. And with any luck he'd have purchased the Blue Star line, so he'd be under less pressure.

During the early evening he and Melinda took the three girls down to Summerhill's small stretch of beach where they all collected shells. Melinda seemed better, but she still said little and looked lost in her private thoughts. He'd never seen her so quiet— and so unhappy. Was it his fault? How could he make her smile again? Perhaps she regretted marrying him.

After dinner Melinda turned down an invitation to a concert, citing exhaustion. But when he insisted on staying at home as well, she twitched a grimace—for only a second, but long enough for him to see she didn't relish his company. Well, he thought angrily, she'd gotten what she needed—a husband to pay the bills, provide security, and keep her at the pinnacle of society. But obviously that wasn't enough to bring her happiness. *Sorry to be such a disappointment!*

"Do go ahead, Nick. I wouldn't want you to miss the music on my account."

He bowed stiffly. "As you wish."

Throughout the performance of the orchestra and opera singer brought from New York just for this occasion, he brooded over Melinda's attitude. He'd give her plenty of time and space to adjust to their marriage before he'd make a move toward marital union. He shifted uncomfortably in his chair; he knew he should have feelings of love before embarking on such a meaningful and intimate act. But they'd shared that kiss . . . He'd caught a glimpse of what it might be, to hold her in his arms, and memories of her in her wedding night finery burned in his memory. Wasn't it a man's right? A woman's duty?

No, that felt all wrong, even just thinking it. But he couldn't help himself.

She'd come around eventually. Wouldn't she?

When he returned to Summerhill around midnight, he found Melinda fast asleep in their bed. He bent over and kissed her lightly on her cool cheek. For a moment he thought she might awaken and smile at him, ending this odd impasse. And maybe welcome him into their bed.

But she continued to sleep as if he'd never even entered the room.

THE NEXT MORNING Melinda found herself alone in the bedroom she now shared with Nick. Strangely, her heart felt deserted and empty. When she trooped downstairs to breakfast, she spotted him already at work in his office.

"Come in," he said with a tight, distant smile.

Her mood plummeted. Was this how their marriage would be—polite and superficial? "I'm about to have breakfast. Would you care to join me?" she asked in a warmer tone.

"I already ate, thank you." He put down his fountain pen. "If you have a moment, I'd like to discuss finances with you."

Finances? She sat across the oak desk from him, her hands folded in her lap. "Yes?" She'd never liked to talk about money, especially early in the morning. But she decided to comply.

"I've set up accounts for you at all the shops on Bellevue Avenue and at the finest dressmakers. I'm sure you'll need more costumes and all the pretty little things ladies want."

"Thank you," Melinda murmured, surprised at his generosity, yet annoyed by his condescension and professional manner. She was his spouse, not his secretary, though she certainly wasn't giving herself to him as a wife should.

"How much do you need per month?"

Melinda shrugged. "My goodness, I have no idea. I'm ashamed to admit it, but I've never kept track of my expenditures." Embarrassment rushed to her cheeks in a blast of heat.

He nodded, as if he suspected as much. "There's no need for you to count pennies or give me an accounting of what you buy. Just tell me first if you want an extremely expensive piece of jewelry or"—he gave a sardonic grin—"if you'd like something large like a new cottage." Many cottagers were still building luxurious mansions up and down Bellevue Avenue and along the Ocean Drive. These newer ones were far larger and more ostentatious than Summerhill—more like banks or museums than homes. And dreadfully expensive to build and furnish.

"I'm sure I don't need a cottage—though perhaps a small one might be nice." She returned his smile.

"I assumed you'd like one, so I contacted an architect. He'll show us the plans soon. We can build on the Bellevue Avenue lot as soon as we decide what we'd like."

She didn't know whether to hug Nick or reprimand him for presuming to know her so well. It had been so long since she had felt the freedom to indulge as she pleased . . . But was her love of the finer things that apparent? She'd hoped she'd changed and grown over the summer. She certainly didn't want him to view her in such an unflattering light, but a home by the sea . . . who could resist that?

Was this cottage his way of showing his unspoken affection? Perhaps it was his way of reaching out to her . . . "That's splendid, Nick. I'd love to spend my—our—summers in a Newport cottage of our own. Thank you," she said softly.

"You're welcome." He looked pleased.

She took a step closer, ready to kiss his forehead and possibly his lips. But instead of beckoning her, he frowned. "Now, I must get back to work. A steamship line can't run well without conscientious management." He returned to his papers.

"Are you dismissing me?" she asked with a decided edge to her voice.

Nick bristled. "Not at all, but I do have to work."

She wouldn't bring up the barriers that lay between them, at least not now when he had to concentrate on business. "All right. I'll see you at luncheon, won't I?"

"We'll see," he murmured, already lost in the detailed paperwork before him.

He had to eat sometime, but obviously he didn't wish to lunch with her. The knot in her stomach tightened. Melinda paused at the door. "Nick, I have a question for you that's off the subject of cottages."

"Yes. What is it?"

"This isn't terribly important, but I am curious. Does Nell have much of an inheritance or is she mainly dependent upon us financially? Jasper sent me so little money over the winter and spring for her support, I began to wonder." Why her sister and brother-in-law named Jasper as a trustee for Nell's estate was beyond comprehension, unless they assumed an accountant would be a logical choice. Or he cajoled them.

Nick's mouth drooped and he stared at her blankly. "Parker and Cora left her a fortune."

"Oh? I wonder why Jasper didn't send me more." Melinda shrugged. "I suppose a little girl barely four years old doesn't need much, but I do enjoy buying her pretty things."

Nick's brow furrowed. "I'll look into it. In the meantime, buy her whatever you wish."

MELINDA'S QUESTION NAGGED at Nick until he saw Jasper strutting into the office with his ledgers later in the morning.

"Do you have a moment?" Nick asked as Jasper took a seat across the back-to-back desks. "I have a question for you."

A frown flashed across his brother-in-law's ruddy face. "Not really, I have a lot to do in order to get you the documents you want for the Blue Star project."

"It's important."

"Yes?"

"When you get a chance, I'd like to find out where Nell stands financially. And we need to set a monthly allowance so Melinda and I can make a few purchases."

Jasper grimaced. "Naturally. But all the records are in New York. Can you wait until September?"

"Of course, but can't you ask your secretary to send them to Newport?" Irritation peppered Nick's voice.

"No, they're in my safe at home. I'm the only one with the combination and I won't give it to anyone."

Nick understood that.

Jasper glanced toward the front door. "Just use your own funds and I'll make sure you're reimbursed as soon as I return to New York."

Nick's father poked his head through the half-open door. "It's good to see you two working together." He glanced around the office looking puzzled. "Where's Parker? I suppose he's out sailing on such a beautiful day."

Nick's heart clutched. "Parker is—"

His father put up a veined hand. "Yes, yes, I know he's gone. I meant to say—well, never mind." He stepped back and closed the door.

"He's getting much worse," Jasper muttered. "He shouldn't be in charge of Bryson Steamship anymore."

For once Nick had to agree with Jasper. "It's past time for me to take over."

Jasper snorted. "Not so fast. I'm certainly as qualified as you."

Nick leaned across the desk and lowered his voice. "That's debatable. And until my father mentioned retirement, you seldom came to the office. I worked more hours in a day than you worked in a week."

"Nonsense." Jasper glared.

"It's a fact. If my father's mind were sound, he'd never consider you for the presidency. I'm sorry to speak so bluntly, but that's the truth."

Jasper jumped up, his amber eyes ablaze. "I must be going."

"I won't keep you." With a weary sigh, Nick got down to work again, wishing Jasper would stick with his accounting and give up any thoughts of running the company.

THAT AFTERNOON MELINDA, Glynna, and Louisa wandered through the Bellevue Avenue shops. Glynna lingered behind, showing little interest in the trinkets and fripperies for sale. She purchased thread and a new thimble, items most ladies didn't need since their maids cared for all the sewing and mending. But missionaries did most of their own work.

As they examined Tiffany's selection of fine jewelry, Melinda noticed Glynna held back. Undoubtedly she could find better use of her funds. She must be so bored by this excursion and maybe even a bit disgusted by the cottagers' shopping habits. Louisa chose a ruby and diamond necklace without inquiring about the price. It was vulgar to ask, and no society lady wished to appear crude.

"Here's an exquisite sapphire broach that exactly matches your eyes," Louisa said. "You must have it, Melinda."

She hesitated. Over the last several weeks she'd gotten used to economizing, at least somewhat. And much to her surprise, she discovered she didn't crave a lot of jewelry anymore. She'd always thought wanting was the same as needing, but indeed, it wasn't. She felt quite virtuous resisting the impulse to purchase everything that caught her fancy. Maybe she was turning into a frugal woman after all—not that she needed to.

"Well, aren't you going to buy the broach? It's too exquisite to pass up." Louisa sounded peeved. She glanced in one of the small mirrors on the counter and adjusted her plumed hat, the same shade of gray-green as her dress.

Melinda shrugged as she examined the sparkling piece. "No, I don't believe so."

"What is the matter with you, Melinda Bryson? I'm sure your husband would want you to indulge yourself every once in a while." Louisa jammed her hands on her hips with mock exasperation.

Melinda shrugged as she meandered toward the door. Nick had freed her to buy what she wished, but she strongly suspected he considered her spoiled and acquisitive. She refused to prove him right. She might never gain his respect—and affection—if she continued with her old habits.

Louisa leveled a skeptical gaze and leaned closer so none of the other shoppers would overhear. "Did Nicholas give you a meager allowance?" she asked with sympathy.

"No, he did not. Quite the contrary, in fact." *Although he did mention wanting to be consulted before large purchases, such as jewelry . . .*

"All right," Louisa said with a noisy sigh, "but I'm afraid marriage has made you too sensible—and mature."

Melinda threw back her head and laughed. "Do stop, Louisa. I haven't changed. Well, perhaps a little, but not as much as I should."

Louisa sighed. "I can't understand why you'd wish to change at all."

Melinda knew Glynna's subtle influence had awakened her to the needs of others, but she also knew Louisa wouldn't understand. The trio wandered down the Travers block of Bellevue Avenue and stopped at a tea shop. They munched on tea cakes frosted with pink icing and then headed back to their cottages to dress for the next activity of the day.

"Would you like to go to Bailey's Beach with me?" Melinda asked Glynna as they entered the foyer. "I'm taking the girls and their nursery maid."

"Yes, that sounds like fun. I've always liked swimming in the ocean."

Half an hour later the group rode to Bailey's Beach, the most exclusive stretch of sand and surf on the entire east coast, but certainly one of the worst beaches due to an abundance of seaweed. Crammed into the open carriage, the six of them sang songs Nanny and Peggy had taught them.

"Don't sing, Auntie Mindy," Nell said. "You don't sound very good."

Melinda bent over releasing a gale of laughter. "You are so right, sweetheart. I have a horrid voice. But I do like to sing, even if only the Lord enjoys my efforts. At least I hope He does." Melinda turned back to Nell. "I promise to sing so softly you won't hear even one note."

As they sang, Melinda mouthed the words and the girls giggled and shrieked.

They arrived at the beach and changed into their bathing costumes in one of the wooden bath houses that was surprisingly plain for cottagers accustomed to luxury. Peggy and the girls sat close by, but far enough away to afford Melinda and Glynna some privacy.

"Glynna, aren't you going to miss all of this? Except for the seaweed, of course."

"Yes, I probably shall. But I'm not really comfortable living among the privileged set. It suits me that the Lord wants me back in Africa."

"Are you sure?" Melinda asked.

Glynna laughed merrily. "Yes, I'm quite sure."

"Do you mind that God calls you to give up so many material things? I know I'd mind." She could imagine curtailing her spending, but never giving up shopping altogether.

Glynna shook her head. "It's easy for me because I've never wanted more than I truly need."

Melinda smiled ruefully. "I'm afraid I can't say the same. But I'd like to contribute to others in my own small way. The Lord will show me how, won't He?"

"Oh yes, you can count on it," Glynna said with an amused smile turning up the corners of her lips.

Melinda recited, "'For unto whomsoever much is given, of him shall be much required: and to whom men have committed much, of him they will ask the more.' It's a verse I memorized as a child for Sunday school. But I haven't thought of it for a long time. It never seemed to apply to me. Yet of course it does. I'm ashamed I've never considered giving back. But the Lord is waking me up." Through Glynna.

"That's wonderful, Melinda, because the need is great."

Melinda nodded. She raked her fingers through the sand.

"But it's the strangest thing. My frugal husband is tempting me to indulge myself. He gave me a large allowance and he also wants to build a cottage." She twisted her mouth in a dry smile. "A cottage on Bellevue Avenue is dreadfully extravagant. I don't understand why he's trying to spoil me."

"Because he cares for you." Glynna laughed as Melinda shook her head. "Nick knows you enjoy beautiful—and expensive—things, so he's giving you what he thinks will make you happy."

Melinda threw back her head and laughed. "How ironic. I'm trying to shed myself of my love for earthly treasures, and he's trying to tempt me with more."

"Then you must explain that to him."

Melinda cocked her head and grinned. "I will, but first I'd like that lovely cottage he promised."

Shaking her head, Glynna gave her a mock slap to the wrist. "You're impossible, Melinda. I can see I must pray harder for you."

"Yes, please do. Truly, I don't want to fall back into my bad habits. I haven't weakened completely. And I know the Lord will give me the grace to sacrifice when I need to."

And maybe, just maybe, a husband in more than name only.

FIFTEEN

❧

Nick was still smarting from his father's renewed threat when Melinda strode into the office. Warm pleasure surged through him. But right after, a cold wave of caution. "Can I help you with something?" He sounded more formal—and colder—than he wanted. Why did he have such a difficult time expressing warmth? He was always stiff as a wooden soldier.

Melinda's cheery smile faded. "I was just wondering if you'd like to take a walk or a buggy ride with the children and me?"

"I'm sorry. I'm too busy to spare even a few minutes, let alone an hour or two."

She put up a hand to halt his excuses. "Of course. I understand perfectly." Her voice was mild and he didn't detect any sarcasm. But her mouth arced down with apparent disappointment. She turned to leave.

He couldn't let her go without clarifying. "Please forgive me, Melinda. Come back and I'll explain."

She paused and then glided toward his desk. Standing like a servant awaiting an order, she looked calm, almost wary. So unlike Melinda. Had he done that to her? He closed the office door and asked her to sit across the desk in the only other chair in the room other than his own.

"I'm not trying to avoid you. My father has put me under a lot of pressure to buy Blue Star. But according to him it's too expensive. I have to negotiate the price, an impossible task, really. I've telephoned the company's representatives and set up another appointment to meet with them. Right now I'm compiling information to make a case for paying the minimum, but I can't see a way to do so without cheating them."

"I'm sorry he's so unreasonable."

"If I fail, he'll turn over the management of Bryson Steamship Company to Jasper and leave me without a job. I would never work under Jasper."

Melinda tilted her head and frowned. "Why would your father do such a thing?"

Nick shrugged. "I don't really understand it myself."

"That's a horrible betrayal. What kind of father would betray his son?"

"The kind of father who's not quite himself anymore." That must be obvious to everyone who spent more than five minutes with Frederick. "He's always been difficult, but he's become unreasonable lately."

Melinda nodded. "So you must now devote all your time and energy to the business."

He felt the lines of his face tightening. "How do you think a husband provides for his wife and family? By slacking off? That's not how it works."

She reached over and tenderly touched his hand. "I am not complaining. I know you have heavy burdens running a company while your father makes ridiculous demands and threats. I've provoked you and I'm sorry. I didn't mean to. Since we're a new couple and a new family, I thought perhaps you and Nell and I could spend a little time getting to know each other better." Her voice softened to almost a whisper. "You're my husband and yet I hardly know you."

He tried to swallow the lump swelling in his throat. "You're right." He placed his fountain pen on the desk blotter and he rose. "I do need a short break. I've been working hard all day and I'm tired. If your invitation is still open, I accept. A walk or a buggy ride, your choice."

Melinda grinned and the wave of warmth returned. He was allowing his emotions to take charge instead of his head. Stress and overwork must be taking their toll on him. Or was it something else entirely?

"LET'S ALLOW THE girls to pick either a walk or a buggy ride," she suggested.

They found the trio upstairs in the playroom with Nanny Wells and Peggy.

Janet, the six-year-old, chose a carriage ride and the others readily agreed. They soon left wearing their favorite afternoon dresses topped with starched pinafores and big bows in their hair. Nick drove the buggy with Melinda beside him and the girls snug in the back seat. The roans trotted along at a sedate pace as the sun cast a golden glow over the afternoon. A gentle breeze stirred the silk ribbons streaming from the back of Melinda's straw hat and brushed against her tight collar. She spread her mint green skirt across her legs and raised her parasol to shade her eyes.

The pair of horses *clip-clopped* against the winding dirt road that hugged the coastline, while a formation of white gulls rose majestically into the deep blue sky. The girls' voices hummed with the same soft sound as the sea washing against the rocks. Melinda relaxed.

Nick pulled over to the side of the road. "Shall we get out and look around?"

The girls jumped down from the open carriage followed by Melinda and Nick. Julie scrambled over the jagged boulders while Melinda took Nell's hand and then Nick's. Slowly they picked their way across the rocks and stopped several yards from the edge. The surf slapped against the stone and exploded into a shower of diamonds. Cooler here than in the buggy, Melinda enjoyed the feel of the light breeze caressing her face and blowing through the thin sleeves of her blouse.

As the girls chattered and then scrambled about, Melinda concentrated on Nick, so close they almost touched. Tentatively, he took her hand as they walked and then, after a while, looped his arm around her waist. She glanced up at him and smiled hesitantly. Perhaps his fondness for her was growing stronger.

Nick Bryson was worth captivating. Even though she married for the wrong reasons, she couldn't abide a marriage marred with tension and without love. But standing here on the rocks she felt they had a real chance of finding happiness together—if only he'd open his heart.

THAT EVENING, WHILE he and Melinda danced the waltz, a march, and later a polka, Nick felt better than he had in weeks. The dance at the rococo mansion of Grassy Knoll was packed with cottagers ready to enjoy the orchestra, fine champagne, and delicious food served all evening in the supper room. Ten to one, he'd rather be at home on the veranda, but he and Melinda seemed to be enjoying something new between them: hope.

He stopped by the card room where he met several members of the older generation who found more than a few dances tiring, and then he strolled into the game room. Jasper bent over the billiard table calculating a shot with their old college friend George Westbrook, who was now married to Miranda Reid, a dedicated charity worker they knew from childhood. George's long, usually mournful face looked almost exuberant—an expression Nick had rarely seen on him before.

He pounded Nick on the back. "It's grand to see you again, old friend. My wife and I are only in Newport for the week, but we're enjoying ourselves immensely."

"Good to see you too, George."

They chatted about family and friends before George took another shot and sunk the ball.

"I'm teaching at a preparatory school in Connecticut now, and Miranda is expecting a little one in April." His dark eyes sparkled. "I heard you married Melinda Hollister. She's a stunner. You're a lucky man. And I certainly am as well."

"Yes, I'm fortunate," Nick agreed.

George leaned closer. "May I speak to you privately as soon as I finish this game?"

"Of course," Nick answered, his curiosity piqued.

Nick wandered off for another glass of champagne and then a dance with Florrie. Twenty minutes later George led him into the deserted picture gallery off the foyer. They passed a host of servants with silver trays filled with drinks for the guests. Even at the end of the darkened gallery, Nick heard a Straus waltz playing in the background.

"What is it, George? You've really got me wondering."

George pulled on the point of his goatee. "It's Jasper. I hate to gossip, but I overheard something you should know."

"Go ahead." Nick tensed; he knew George wouldn't pass along false information.

George frowned. "I was walking by the sitting room earlier and overheard a terrible row between Albert Underwood, Clayton's father, and your brother-in-law."

"Really? How strange," Nick said.

"Mr. Underwood actually threatened to expose Jasper as a deadbeat. Apparently Jasper owes him a large sum of money, and he hasn't paid up. He didn't mention any details and I didn't stop to eavesdrop, but the man sounded angry."

"I understand Mr. Underwood loans cash at a substantial interest rate," Nick said, surprised by George's revelation.

George nodded. "I've heard that too. Do you suppose Jasper is in some sort of financial mess?"

A twist of anxiety unsettled Nick's composure. "I don't know. He's never said anything to me, but then again, he wouldn't. We don't share the closest of relationships, even if we are in the same household."

"Well, don't worry, Nick. I won't mention this to anyone."

"Thank you. I know I can trust you."

They talked some more, then the loose-limbed George ambled toward the ballroom. Nick followed with a detour to the punch bowl. He spotted Melinda laughing with a group of ladies seated on delicate antique chairs set against the wall. Perhaps she'd like some supper. They were soon seated by themselves at a small round table in the corner of the grand dining room obviously designed to impress. Gilded and mirrored, every square inch of the space was overly decorated. As they ate delicacies drenched in cream sauce, he told her what he'd just heard.

"I'm shocked. Surely Mr. Westbrook must have misunderstood. Why would Jasper need money? He and Florrie aren't spendthrifts. They don't own a fifty-room mansion or a string of polo ponies."

Nick shrugged. "He's trying to sell his yacht, but it's really not a large one. And my father pays the rent for Summerhill. It doesn't make sense to me either. But Jasper did want to adopt Nell, and I fear not from the goodness of his heart."

Melinda looked askance. "I don't know about Jasper, but I'm quite sure that Florrie wouldn't ask to adopt Nell for the money."

Nick grimaced as he leveled a disdainful gaze. "You're a bit too trusting, Melinda." Then he smiled as if he found that endearing.

"I'm fond of my sister, but she's not overly thoughtful or altruistic. And Jasper is the most self-serving man I've ever met. I'd wager adopting Nell is his idea. And he talked Florrie into it while she was distracted in her studio."

"That's quite an indictment," Melinda murmured, taken aback by his vehemence.

"It's an accurate assessment," he insisted. "I should look into this."

Melinda tried to hide a smile in her napkin. She hesitated to judge anyone, but she did agree with Nick. "Are you sure you wouldn't be overstepping?"

Nick groaned. "You think I have no business interfering."

Melinda laughed. "Exactly."

He nodded. "I suppose I am. But Jasper's up to something, and I'm going to find out what it is. Believe me, whatever he's planning isn't in Nell's best interest—or ours either."

She set her fork on the scalloped edge of the dinner plate. "I didn't realize you and Jasper are such adversaries. You don't think he's out to harm you in some way, do you?"

From the genuine concern in her eyes, he felt he could trust her. "Maybe not physically, but he certainly wants the presidency of Bryson Steamship Company."

"That's a complete outrage. You're a Bryson and he's not. Your father's behavior is horrid. But, Nick, you must forgive him. He's not himself—not that he's ever been particularly kind. But I don't believe he's deliberately setting out to hurt you. It's the dementia."

He almost smiled at the emotion in her voice. Her unequivocal support came as a welcome surprise. Nick's gaze met Melinda's and their eyes locked. Startled, he realized he needed her not just as a companion and mother to Nell, but as a confident and a wife to share everything, including his heart. Especially his heart. His unexpected vulnerability came as an unwelcome blow.

He didn't trust himself to speak. But for once neither did

Melinda. She sat across the table watching him and smiling, as if she understood he'd come a step closer to her.

"If you've finished your supper, maybe we could go outside for a while," he said as his heart raced.

He wanted to touch his lips to hers and press her so close they would meld together. Just to smell the fragrance of her hair and the lavender perfume she wore set his senses aflame. Surely she wouldn't object to slipping away to the veranda. They were married so no one could possibly object to them kissing beneath the stars and the glow of the moonlight.

As Melinda tilted her head and flashed a coy smile, Nick felt a warm prickle on the back of his neck.

And then Florrie and Jasper appeared along with their hosts, Mr. and Mrs. Carstairs. His hope for time alone with Melinda crashed—for the moment.

"I would enjoy dancing with your husband, if you don't mind, Melinda," Beatrice Carstairs said. "And why don't you dance with your brother-in-law? We don't want husbands and wives dancing together all evening."

Melinda nodded with a forced smile. "Of course."

DANCING THE POLKA with the clumsiest man in Newport was not at all fun. Melinda tried not to yelp when Jasper stepped on the toes of her satin shoes. She stumbled, but his iron-tight grip kept her from falling flat on her face. They continued galloping around the polished floor until she was breathless. The dancers pounded on slippery hardwood as loudly as a stampede of wild horses. She barely heard the music or the background chatter of several hundred guests as they swirled around the room at breakneck speed.

When the music stopped, Jasper leaned closer so she could hear. "Would you like a glass of champagne?" His face looked as red as his hair and he breathed hard from the exertion.

After Nick had shared what he had, she hesitated. But she couldn't let Jasper know. "Yes, please. It's quite hot in here."

He retrieved two flutes of champagne from a passing waiter and led her into the relative quiet of the foyer. Melinda fanned herself to cool off, though a breeze from the open front door stirred the air. She accepted the glass and took a sip. Aside from a few couples who strolled by and nodded, they were alone.

Jasper frowned as she glanced around the vestibule. She searched for something to say but came up with little. "Thank you for the opportunity to cool off. Shall we return to the ballroom now?"

But he made no move to escort her back. "Before we do, I thought you might tell me how you are adjusting to your new role as wife to Nicholas."

What an odd question, especially from a man with only his own interests at heart. What was he up to?

"Everything is fine. Thank you for inquiring." That was hardly the whole truth, but he need never know. Still, she felt more hopeful about her marriage after her talk with Nick this evening.

Jasper shrugged. "With you cutting your honeymoon so short, many wondered."

"Yes, well, there was my sea sickness to contend with," she said, hating that she could feel the blush moving up her neck and cheeks. By the leer in his eyes, he was wondering if they had even consummated their union. "As I told you, we intend to take another excursion this fall."

"Right," he said with a patronizing nod. "Tell me, are you enjoying your position as Mrs. Nicholas Bryson? Is it as advantageous as you expected?"

She recoiled at his tone. "Advantageous? I—I'm not sure what you mean." She sipped her champagne to better hide her bewilderment. She tried to sidestep him to move toward the ballroom, but he blocked her progress.

"You're a wealthy woman now," he continued.

Her chest tightened and the foyer suddenly seemed stifling hot. "Well, yes, of course. Everyone knows the Brysons are prosperous businessmen. That's not exactly a secret."

A sneer turned up the corner of Jasper's mouth. "You're right. But it was a secret that the Hollister fortune practically vanished in a few short years. Everyone knows that now. Your mother selling her Fifth Avenue mansion made your reversal readily apparent."

Melinda drew in a sharp breath. Her legs wobbled and threatened to fold. A part of her had hoped they'd escaped the circles of gossip.

"Of course it doesn't matter anymore now that you've married Nick." The nasty gleam in his eye reinforced his words.

"Are you insinuating I married him for his money?"

Jasper snickered. "No, my dear, I am applauding you for your success."

She couldn't believe Jasper's impertinence. Most everyone married to improve their situation, but there was more to her decision than that. Wasn't there?

Yes. She wanted security for herself and Nell, not cold hard cash to fritter away on her own pleasures. *Oh Lord, I pray my motives were as unselfish as I thought.* Obviously Jasper had labeled her a fortune hunter.

"Jasper, what exactly are you trying to say?" She wasn't sure she could conceal her anger much longer.

"I'm merely wondering if you knew why Nick married *you.*"

She drew out an impatient sigh. "Yes, I do. Don't you remember telling me on my wedding day that Nick married me because of Nell? He didn't want me to marry someone and move far away." The memory still stung, though she understood his reasoning since she'd been equally self-serving.

"I do recall. But we were interrupted and I was never able to finish what I wished to tell you."

Melinda swallowed hard. "If you're so determined to continue, then please do so. Let's finish this conversation at once so I can return to the ballroom." And Nick. Her heart battered against the silk bodice of her gown.

He was enjoying her discomfort. He led her over to the grand staircase far enough away from anyone passing through the foyer. "Nick knew you and your mother were nearly destitute, so he married you out of pity. He felt sorry for your plight and realized no one else in our set would marry a woman without money."

"He knew?" she murmured in a choked-up voice. Her legs buckled. She stepped to the side and braced herself against the far wall, bumping into the gilded frame of Mrs. Carstairs's life-size portrait.

"Yes, indeed. He realized you'd have little chance of marrying a man of breeding and fortune. As far as society was concerned, you'd vanish from the face of the earth. And that would hurt Nell and her opportunities for a good marriage in the future." One of his eyes narrowed. "I feel you had a duty to confess before your wedding, but apparently you thought otherwise. But I take it Nick didn't mention it either."

"He married me out of pity? I don't believe that."

"I assume his primary reason was Nell, though pity had a lot to do with it. He proposed before your shameful situation became well known and fodder for gossip."

"Why are you telling me this, Jasper?" she asked.

"It's always best to face realities up front. Most women enter marriage with ridiculous fantasies of what it might be in the future—best to know, now, so you can make the most of things. Nick felt sorry for you. There's no love involved."

Cora always said Jasper caused trouble among the family and reveled in upsetting everyone. But his sheer meanness astounded her. And he was probably angry she wouldn't allow him to take Nell away from her. Did he still hope to destroy her union with

Nick and swoop in for custody . . . and renewed access to Nell's trust fund? Could he be so evil?

He bowed. "If you'll excuse me, Melinda, I'll be going. Don't take my words too hard. Many marriages are based on mutual advantage. Why should yours be any different?"

Because she wanted Nick to love and cherish her. As Jasper strutted away, painful thoughts ricocheted through her mind. She didn't want a husband motivated by pity as if she were some poor, pathetic creature who needed rescuing.

Melinda wanted to believe he was sowing seeds of distrust between her and Nick, but Nick had never once claimed he loved her. So that must be her answer. She'd counted on their mild affection blossoming into love. A foolish romantic, she'd expected her charm would win her real love, when obviously charm wasn't nearly enough.

Consider the source, Melinda. You can't trust Jasper. Nick just needs more time. We both do.

But a very big part of her wondered if it was impossible to ever forge the kind of love she craved. She sniffed back tears. She wanted to flee to Summerhill, away from the noise of happy revelers, but she couldn't conjure up a plausible excuse to leave.

She sat in a secluded corner of the ballroom to clear her mind. Eventually she forced herself back to the dance floor, pretending gaiety, into the small hours of the morning when Nick and the Van Tassels finally, blessedly, decided to return home. Once at Summerhill Nick followed Melinda into their bedroom, looking uncertain. She retreated into her dressing room to change her clothes with the help of her maid. When she returned he was sitting on the edge of the bed, waiting for her. She gave him a faint smile and slipped into bed without saying a word.

"Is something the matter?" he asked. "You look upset."

"Actually, yes, but I'm afraid I don't have the energy to speak of it right now."

"Would you like me to sleep on the chaise?" he asked softly, pinning her with a hopeful gaze.

Melinda bit her lip. She refused to provoke an argument at two in the morning. This would hold until tomorrow. "Do as you wish, Nick. But I'm exhausted and going right to sleep." She almost added "I'm sorry," but she refused to apologize. As much as she hadn't been entirely truthful with him, neither had he been with her.

His face crumbled with disappointment and maybe a hint of anger. "Don't worry. I won't touch you, Melinda. And I won't bother you again."

The chill in his voice sent shivers coiling around her spine. She rolled over and pretended not to hear him yanking blankets out of the armoire, angrily fluffing a pillow, and plopping it down on the chaise. A part of her wanted to sit up, confess all that had happened, all that she had been holding back.

But she was so dreadfully weary. Could she even form the right words?

And even if she did, what good would it do?

Regardless of the reasons that led them to it, now they were both trapped in a loveless marriage.

Forever.

SIXTEEN

❦

What is the matter with her? Nick wondered as he slid under the blanket on the cold, stiff chaise. He thought they were drawing together last night. They'd sensed hope for their relationship, both of them—he was certain of it. But by the time the ball was over, she seemed distant, preoccupied, and sullen.

Maybe Melinda was mercurial, with moods that swung like a pendulum. Or had something happened to cause her coolness?

He shifted away from her and turned toward the far wall. But even the darkness couldn't put him to sleep. Behind him, he heard her sniff. She was crying—trying to hide it, but definitely crying.

Lord, I ask You to please help me with this. I have a wife who doesn't want to be a real one. I have no idea how to handle this problem. But I'm afraid I can't go on like this indefinitely. Taking time getting to really know each other is one thing, but her sudden withdrawal and hostility is quite another.

Sighing, he flung his legs over the edge of the chaise, groped for his dressing gown on the chair by the fireplace, and padded over to the bed. Gently he sat down on the edge and felt her freeze. "Melinda, I hear you crying. Won't you please tell me what has upset you so?"

"Not tonight, Nick. Please."

He shook in frustration. He couldn't be the only one in this relationship committed to trying. Without another word, he rose and went to the door that connected to his old bedroom. He'd not wanted the household staff to gossip, spreading the news that the newlyweds were not sharing a bedroom. But he had no choice; he had to get some sleep. And right now, being in the same room with his wife would most definitely be an obstacle.

MELINDA WOKE UP to a dreary day with fog brushing against the screens. With it came a damp chill laced with brine she could almost taste. She glanced out the window to a world of swirling gray. Unable to see the lawn only one story below, she felt hemmed in by the gloom. In the distance she heard the moan of a foghorn and the ever-present rush of the sea.

She flung a wrapper around her shoulders, but it couldn't keep the cold from penetrating her bones. Slamming the window shut, she rang for her maid and asked her to bring her a cup of tea.

"Yes, ma'am," Denise said with a small curtsy. Her eyes flicked over the obviously unused side of the bed. She turned up the gaslight and slipped away quietly. Five minutes later she returned with the tea, sugar, and cream on a tray. And one cup. Melinda thanked her and sent her to make ready her first outfit of the day, a simple ecru morning dress.

Nick came through the adjoining bedroom door looking worse for the wear.

"It looks like you didn't sleep well," she said without thinking. His face looked rough with whisker stubble and his hair was disheveled. He hadn't yet dressed.

"No, I hardly slept at all." He stared her in the eye and she flinched. "We need to talk. Now, if you don't mind."

Melinda deposited her teacup on the end table, then sat on the edge of the bed and waited. A shadow of apprehension slid across her heart. Was he angry she wouldn't confide in him? Or disturbed she hadn't embraced him as a proper wife should?

He stood on the far side of the bed. The distance between them seemed far wider than just the width of the mattress.

"Melinda, when we were in the supper room last night, I thought we were coming closer together. But then when we returned, you clearly didn't want me here. That was painfully obvious."

She glanced down at her hands and noticed how she was kneading her fingers. She stopped their nervous twitch and gripped them on her lap. "I'm sorry."

"I'd like to know why you suddenly changed toward me. Did something happen to upset you? If I angered you, I'd like to know what I did wrong."

Nodding, Melinda rose and walked the few steps to the window. She had to respond, though she wanted to laugh it off and claim he was mistaken, or claim exhaustion. But she couldn't tell such a blatant lie. Nor would that solve the problem that lay between them.

"All right, I'll tell you the truth." She tried to steady herself by taking a big gulp of air. "I believed you married me because of Nell. I understand that. But then last night I learned you also married me . . . out of pity. Because my mother and I were nearly bankrupt. You proposed so I wouldn't move away or lose my social position. And Nell wouldn't either. When I mulled it over, I knew you looked at me as a poor, pitiable woman in need of saving, not a woman you hoped to one day love and desire as a true wife and companion."

Nick stared at her, his eyes wide with surprise. But he didn't say one word to defend himself.

"I felt deeply humiliated. And I still do."

She wouldn't tell him she'd awakened to the first stirrings of love, but now her hopes were completely dashed. Tears welled in the back of her eyes, and her head began to throb.

Nick's voice cracked. "Who told you all this? Was it Jasper?"

"Yes."

"Jasper is a meddlesome scoundrel. He ought to mind his own business. I'd wager he told you this so you'd leave me and he'd come forward to adopt Nell. He'd benefit from breaking up our marriage."

"But is it true you knew about my financial disaster before you proposed to me?" Her lower lip trembled.

Nick crossed his hands over his chest. "It's true. Jasper mentioned that your mother sold your home because your family money was gone. But he never should've told you that I knew. It was cruel."

She battled to keep her voice from rising. "You should have told me yourself."

He let out a grunt of exasperation. "I didn't wish to embarrass you. It never occurred to me you might make it an issue."

It was important and one of the primary reasons he'd married her. How could holding back this secret not be important? Not that she had been any more truthful . . .

"I apologize for not confessing, but I didn't wish to distress you," he said.

Melinda shook her head and drew out a sigh. "You should have been honest. Or were you afraid I wouldn't marry you once I understood you only wanted Nell? Did you think I'd marry Simon Preston and leave for Pittsburgh on the next train?"

Nick flinched and she knew she was right. Her anger flared, and its fire burned through her heart, leaving the smoldering ashes of ache behind. They both had so many selfish reasons to marry. And none involved love.

"If we can't be honest, then our marriage has no chance of happiness," she said, struggling not to cry.

He grimaced, piercing her with his steel-gray stare. "Melinda, you could have told me the truth before we married."

His words gripped her conscience. She was so busy casting stones she hadn't stopped to give weight to her own guilt. "Yes, I could have," she murmured, her voice hardly above a whisper.

But she hadn't told him because she feared he'd lose interest in her, just as any man would. She couldn't afford to pay the price of truth, so she'd withheld it. A few tears escaped her eyes and straggled down her cheeks. "I'm sorry, Nick. I was only thinking of myself."

He stood perfectly still. His face showed no more emotion than a marble bust, but she felt sure he was battling to hide his contempt. She'd blamed him when she was equally at fault. She'd acted like a hypocrite. Slowly Melinda lifted her gaze to Nick, but he'd already headed for the door. Her spirits slipped toward despair.

She lifted her Bible off the end table and dropped into the chair by the window. If God's Word didn't console her, nothing would. But she couldn't summon the strength to open it. She just held it, cradled to her chest, and wept.

NICK RETURNED TO his bedroom, shaved, and dressed in a light tan summer suit. This morning after church he'd distract himself from his marital problems by playing with the girls or taking them for a swim or a buggy ride. Tomorrow he'd attempt to discover the truth about his brother-in-law's financial trouble.

Hopefully George Westbrook misunderstood the argument he'd overheard. But if it was true it would confirm his suspicions about Jasper's need for money. And also his sudden interest in impressing Frederick with his newfound work ethic and his determination to gain control of Nell's inheritance.

In the foyer he ran into Stephen Farnsworth. "Good morning," Nick said.

"Good morning," Stephen returned. "Have you had anything to eat yet? I was just on my way to the breakfast room. I think we still have time before church."

"Indeed." Some oatmeal might help his roiling stomach. "I'll join you."

Together they entered the deserted room. The smell of freshly brewed coffee and hot muffins made his mouth water. They slid into chairs set around the long polished table and waited for breakfast to be served, chatting idly. The fog outside the window still rolled in from the sea like giant puffs of smoke, but the breakfast room had a fire crackling in the hearth, warding off the chill. After drinking half a cup of the steaming brew and munching on a blueberry muffin, Nick started on a generous serving of oatmeal with cinnamon sugar.

After the maid left, Stephen turned to him. "What's the matter, Nick? You're acting as if you lost your last friend." Stephen's round brown eyes gazed at him with nothing but concern.

"Actually things could be much better. Are you sure you want to hear my tale of woe this early in the day?"

Stephen wiped the corners of his mouth with a linen napkin and leaned across the table. "Yes, I do. Sometimes it helps to share your concerns with someone else. Even Glynna says I'm a good listener."

Nick couldn't help but grin at the eager and earnest missionary, so well suited to his calling. One of his few close friends, they seldom met these days, but they exchanged letters several times a year. Stephen was one of the few people he trusted enough to confide in.

"The problem is with Melinda and me." He spilled his story without hesitation and then cocked a brow. "You're an old married man. Any suggestions?"

Stephen nodded. "Have more patience. Melinda has gone through a terrible ordeal lately—losing her sister, even losing her home and the Hollister fortune."

Nick grimaced. "And marrying me just to keep afloat."

"You don't know that. You're judging her rather harshly, I think. Look, you both held back things you should have shared," Stephen said. "But what's done is past. Now you must try to make your marriage work. You and Melinda can be happy together. Pray the Lord will show you the way."

"I am," Nick admitted. But the Lord seemed stubbornly silent when it came to Melinda.

"Tell her you love her," Stephen said softly.

Nick gave him a sharp look, but didn't reply. What he felt for Melinda wasn't exactly love. He liked her, even considered her a friend. Before the wedding, he'd prayed it would be love by now, but he'd also believed that physical intimacy would have helped them bridge into something deeper. He'd assumed so much . . . His emotions were all mixed together and indistinguishable, one from another. Affection, anger, betrayal, compassion, guilt, frustration, attraction, passion. Unrequited passion. But not love. Not really.

"You two need to forgive each other."

Nick nodded. "I shall think all this over. And pray."

Glynna joined them and Nick drank more coffee as they chatted. Within the hour, Melinda arrived and they all left for the late church service. He watched her and noted she looked as out of sorts as he felt. She'd obviously shed more than a few tears since he'd left her.

A fine couple we're turning out to be. He dutifully sat beside her, sang the hymns, and attempted to follow the minister's sermon, but his mind wandered and he spent his time praying for answers.

When they returned to Summerhill, he intended to ask Melinda to join him for a walk, but Florrie met him on the veranda before he found the chance.

"May I have a few words with you?" she asked, gently but firmly leading him into the small morning room off the foyer. The others moved on, noting her desire to speak to her brother alone. Melinda didn't glance back.

"What is it?" he asked, irritated. Florrie's eyebrows arched in a worried frown.

She sighed wearily. "Jasper seems troubled lately. I'm wondering if he's having some problem with you or Father. Or perhaps it's the business."

"I presume he's told you Father plans to retire soon and leave the presidency of Bryson Steamship Company to either Jasper or me."

She tucked her chin, and her eyebrows knit together. "No, he hasn't mentioned that. Oh, Nicholas, what is wrong with Father? How could he even consider leaving the family business to Jasper when he has a son?"

Nick shrugged. "You know Father enjoys watching people compete against each other."

"I do, indeed." She sighed and touched his sleeve. "You must feel slighted by Father's decision. And Jasper really ought to bow out like a gentleman. But I doubt he will. I'm sorry I can't step in, Nick. If I ask him to, he'll question my loyalty."

Nick shook his head. "Don't involve yourself with this. Ultimately, it's a wild card, given Father's state of mind. There's little any of us can do."

She sighed heavily. "You're right. I'll keep busy with my art. And the children, of course." Florrie pressed her lips in a thin, sad line. "I hesitate to draw you into my troubles, but if you'd try to discover if there's something else that's upsetting Jasper, I'd be truly grateful."

"You don't believe it's simply this?" he asked, arching a brow. "Has he said something? Or have you overheard something?"

"No. It's little more than a wife's intuition . . ." She paused for several seconds, looked down at her hands, and frowned. "Actually, there's one more thing." She drew a letter out of her pocket and showed it to Nick. "Jasper left this on his chest-of-drawers—by mistake, I assume—so I read it. Perhaps I shouldn't have, but I did."

"What does it say?"

"It's from an attorney who claims Jasper owes a certain New York gambling house many thousands of dollars. They extended him credit, but his losses are enormous, and now they demand repayment. Oh, Nick, what am I to do?"

Nick patted her hand. "I shall try to find out what I can," he said.

As they parted, he wondered to what lengths Jasper would go to obtain the funds.

FIRST THING THE next morning Nick accepted a chocolate brown derby from his valet and hurried downstairs. He disliked altering his usual work routine, but finding out if Jasper was in financial straits took priority.

Once at the Casino he chatted with his old college friends and business acquaintances while they bowled two games together. Quietly he talked to a trusted fraternity brother known to everybody in society as well as more than a few gambling establishments.

"Jasper Van Tassel is over his head in debt," was all Nick needed to know to verify his fears. But his friend added, "He owes Albert Underwood for a loan, and he lost tens of thousands of dollars at Canfields last spring. Bacarrat, I heard."

Nick thanked him and returned home, suffering from acute indigestion. What would this do to Florrie? And it could easily affect the reputation of Bryson Steamship Company as well. Even if he were so inclined, he didn't have enough extra money to help Jasper with his debts. If he told his father, Frederick would no doubt fire Jasper. But where would that leave his sister and the girls? Or he could let Jasper solve his own problem.

He'd pray about this before he'd make such a crucial decision.

Seventeen

❦

Melinda drank another cup of tea and skipped breakfast. She took a walk around the rose garden off on the side lawn and wandered back to the veranda just as the sun broke through the clouds and began to dry the dew. Glynna waved as she strolled toward her, a ream of paper in hand. She wore a black skirt and white tight-collared shirtwaist, but at least the lace at the bodice softened its schoolmarm look. They met on the pebbled path that edged Summerhill's back lawn.

"Good morning, Melinda. I do hope your morning is more productive than mine."

Melinda hid a smile. She never worried about productivity. But Glynna had so many details to work out concerning their voyage and future life away from the comforts of America she couldn't afford to waste time.

Glaring at her papers through her rather thick spectacles, Glynna asked, "Would you mind helping me with my speech? It'll take only a few minutes, but I need someone to listen to my presentation."

"I'd be delighted. And don't be nervous. You'll do splendidly."

Glynna laughed, but it sounded more like a snort. "I have no confidence in my ability to speak before a crowd, even a small one. I'll sputter like a complete fool."

Melinda dimly remembered that her friend was to give a speech at Florrie's reception for the missionaries.

"I've been practicing in my room for days, but I still can't get through an entire sentence without stumbling or losing my concentration."

"If you're that nervous, perhaps you shouldn't put yourself through such an ordeal."

Glynna nodded, still frowning. "I agree, but Stephen asked me to say a few words and I promised I would. I can't let him down."

"Then maybe you should just say a few words and not try to learn pages of information." She nodded toward the stack of papers in her friend's hand.

Glynna chuckled as they lowered to a wooden bench beneath a leafy tree. "A few words to Stephen means a full-blown sermon. I'm afraid the Lord hasn't equipped me to preach even a short one." She lifted her lips in a small, wry smile. "It's my awful pride standing in my way again. I hate to sound like a bumbler and subject myself to ridicule. I'd like to show my competent side and not display my inadequacies."

"I understand perfectly." Like Melinda, Glynna didn't want to be pitied or ridiculed.

"But to be a good missionary and to raise money for the school, I need to ignore my fear and my pride. God's calling is so strong in my heart, but I find it nearly impossible to convey that to others. My enthusiasm is locked inside."

Melinda nodded. "But sometimes we have to do what's difficult and struggle against our nature."

"Exactly. I know I have to trust the Lord to equip me for my mission. Even speaking in public. But it's so difficult at times."

Melinda squeezed Glynna's hand. "I'll pray you'll have courage and a silver tongue. And please pray for me—that I'll want to fight harder against my nature. I tend to be too acquisitive."

"I shall continue to pray for both of us," Glynna said.

Melinda glanced across the wide lawn and spotted Louisa Davenport striding toward them. She wore a buttercup yellow frock with small white stripes on the skirt. Her straw hat with daisies and gauzy bows tilted at a becoming angle.

"Good morning, ladies," Louisa said. "I hope you're both ready for some fun. I'm going shopping and I hope you'll accompany me. Mama wants a certain vase from that darling new antique shop for her birthday. She shall have it unless someone has already bought it first."

"Perhaps later," Melinda answered. "I'm about to listen to Glynna recite her speech for the reception tomorrow."

Glynna shook her head. "No, you go shopping. I need to practice a bit more anyway. Perhaps you can help me later today."

Melinda hesitated. "Well, all right, if you're sure. Let's meet at five o'clock."

Glynna nodded.

"I shall only take a minute, Louisa," Melinda said.

Melinda hurried upstairs to her bedroom. With her maid's assistance she changed into a pale apricot frock with tiny tucks in the bodice and rows of ecru lace at the hem and cuffs. They found the coordinating hat, parasol, and reticule.

Melinda soon joined Louisa on the back lawn. They left Glynna pacing up and down the pebbled path quietly reciting her speech and strolled toward Louisa's carriage house and stable where a coachman awaited them. The open landau was already hitched to a pair of grays, and the coachman helped the two ladies board the shiny black carriage. Melinda slid into the leather seat across from Louisa, ready to forget her troubles for a while—though her marital condition weighed like a boulder on her heart.

"Are you coming to the reception for the Farnsworths?" she asked Louisa as the carriage jerked forward.

"Naturally. I never pass up a party, especially one for a worthy cause. But to tell you the truth, I do hope they're not long-winded.

I'll sit through a sermon on Sunday morning because—well, because Mama insists—but I have difficulty paying attention after the first few minutes."

Melinda smiled. At times she had the same problem, but she usually benefitted from a strong biblical message. "I truly admire the Farnsworths. They're so dedicated to spreading God's Word."

"I marvel at them too. But I could never give up everything to convert a bunch of foreigners and risk my own life and limb."

"Nor could I," Melinda admitted.

"And they've given up so much for others." Louisa sighed. "I can't imagine sacrificing everything."

When they arrived at the small antique shop on Bellevue Avenue, they headed straight toward the section with exquisite china and pottery.

Louisa pointed to a blue and white porcelain vase. "That's the one Mama admires. Isn't it simply beautiful?"

"Yes, it's lovely," Melinda agreed, not paying strict attention.

The antique dealer added with a bow, "It's a Meissen vase from Germany made around 1735." He continued to praise its attributes while Melinda examined a Chinese ginger jar that caught her fancy.

"That jar is exquisite, ma'am," the shopkeeper said as he took Louisa's vase to the counter to wrap.

Melinda put up her palm and smiled. "Yes, indeed. But I'm not here to shop today. I'll return another time." She had to push the words out of her mouth, but she needed to curb her impulse to buy indiscriminately.

She didn't want covetousness to control her and she certainly didn't wish Nick to consider her a spendthrift. That was the last thing they needed right now—another obstacle between them.

AFTER TEA ON the veranda, Melinda listened to Glynna recite her speech. "Well done," Melinda said, clapping. "You'll do very well."

Glynna's smile curved with pleasure at the compliment. She placed her papers on the end table beside her wicker chair. "I meant to ask you something earlier, but then your friend Louisa joined us. May I ask you a personal question?"

"Of course," Melinda said, hoping Glynna wouldn't ask anything *too* personal.

"I've noticed a strain between you and Nick. Is everything all right?"

Melinda glanced down and sighed. "No, not really. As I told you, we were both willing to sacrifice our freedom for Nell's sake."

"And do you regret your selflessness?" Glynna asked as she leaned toward Melinda and grasped her hand.

Melinda shook her head. "No, that was our unspoken agreement. But something else I learned bothers me." She gulped in a deep breath and then let it slowly escape. "Nick discovered my mother and I had lost most of our fortune. He knew I had to marry someone soon or I'd be cut from society. He pitied me so he proposed before the news got out." Melinda closed her eyes for a few moments. "I wanted a husband to love me, not feel sorry for me. It's so humiliating."

Glynna squeezed her hand. "Pity is a dreadful reason to marry, but you must remember he did rescue you from a crisis. Think of what would have happened if he turned away from you when he learned the truth."

"I know, I know," Melinda moaned. Placing her elbows on her knees, she let her head rest in her hands for several seconds before she faced Glynna.

Glynna nodded. "Nick saved you from obscurity. And Nell, from social shunning. That's what you wanted, wasn't it? Perhaps it didn't come together just exactly as you would've liked, but God blessed you. He answered your prayers."

"I've just never looked at it that way before. I've been so wrapped up in the hurt, the embarrassment—"

A gust of light wind blew Glynna's papers. She and Melinda both scrambled to snatch them before they flew off. Once safely in hand, Glynna settled back on her chair. "I don't wish to lecture you, but only to remind you that you ought to show Nick some gratitude. He did you a big favor regardless of his motives."

"I know," Melinda agreed. She leaned back against the porch railing. "But there's also the matter of—you know—*loving him.*" She blushed at the intimate subject no proper woman mentioned, but it was driving such a deep wedge between her and Nick, she needed some advice. "I mean I don't want marital intimacy—until he truly loves me. Oh, Glynna, he hasn't once said he loves me. So I guess he doesn't. And that really hurts."

"Hmm." Glynna drew her brows together in a thoughtful frown. "I understand. But, Melinda, if you didn't want a marital relationship with Nick—a *true* marital relationship—you shouldn't have married him."

"Perhaps not, but I didn't think much about all those physical things at the time."

Glynna threw back her head and laughed, breaking the tension. "You didn't expect to be chaste, did you?"

Heat rose to Melinda's hairline. "Well, no, but I didn't think much of anything through. All I considered was the beautiful wedding ceremony. And how it would resolve so many of our problems . . ."

That's not quite true, she chided herself. She had thought about Nick's broad shoulders and strong, hard muscles bulging beneath the crispest of white shirts. She'd been heavily aware of his intimate presence in their bed, and even when he'd slept in the next room he'd felt . . . *close.* But she couldn't even consider making love to a man who didn't love her. She wanted so much more than he was willing to give.

Glynna pursed her lips in a wry grin. "I'm sure Nick thought well beyond the wedding ceremony. And so must you. You married him and you have a duty to become his wife in every sense. Think about it. He'll become more and more estranged if you don't."

"Yes, I know. And we're bound together for life."

"Thank him for rescuing you. Without him you might have been forced to marry Clayton Underwood or Simon Preston. Yes, I've heard all the gossip when I pay calls with Florrie."

Melinda couldn't help but giggle and shake her head. "How true. Nick did save me from a terrible fate."

Glynna nodded. "Just remember that."

"I shall." She tilted her head and twitched a dry smile. "And I don't want to be only his friend either, at least not forever. I shall try to make every effort to charm him so he won't have a choice but to fall in love with me."

Glynna shook her head. "No, you don't understand. He's already impressed with your beauty and your appeal. He wants more from you."

Melinda felt tears spring to her eyes. How could her dear friend say such a mean thing? "You make me sound so dreadfully . . . shallow."

Touching her hands, Glynna sighed. "You misunderstand me. I certainly don't believe you're shallow, but I'm trying to show you a way to win his heart. He wants a wife like his former sweetheart, Alma Noble."

Taken aback, Melinda frowned. "I thought Nick was over Alma."

"Oh yes. But he might hold her up as the ideal in womanhood."

Melinda sighed, remembering Nan's description of a *tedious bluestocking*. Was that what she had to become to win Nick's heart? Bury herself in books and learn all sorts of fancy, indulgent vocabulary? Become more dull and sober and straitlaced?

Glynna giggled over her expression. "Alma was a pleasant looking girl with a reserved manner and kind heart. If you're worried she might have been prettier than you, don't fret. You know you're a great beauty—"

"But beauty isn't what Nick wants most, is it?" Melinda finished.

"I'm sure he appreciates your appearance, but no, I believe for him looks aren't enough to win his heart."

With a heavy spirit, Melinda rose. "Then what is?"

"Nick appreciates your joy and your zest for living, but he wants you to appreciate him as well. Love him for his stability and serious nature, not in spite of it. He's a bit of a stick-in-the-mud, I'll admit. The positive side of that is he won't jeopardize his fortune on foolishness or impulsive ventures as some men would."

As Melinda's own father had. She shuddered at the memory of those dark days, then and now.

"Nick will always be your rock. You and Nell can depend upon him. Those are qualities to be admired."

"Thank you for your advice, Glynna. I have a lot to ponder."

And she needed to talk to Nick. But that evening, after they returned from dinner at Broadleaf, she found all her words deserted her. She, who chattered like a magpie when nerves overcame her, couldn't form the sounds in her throat to properly say what she'd planned. She sat on the edge of the bed in her nightgown and robe brushing her hair.

From across the room Nick kept stealing glances at her as if he found her nightly chore fascinating. Or maybe he didn't know what to say either. She never knew what he was thinking. It was with some surprise that he'd shown up in their room at all, after how she'd spurned him.

She cleared the lump from her throat. "I need to thank you, Nick." Her voice hardly rose above a scratchy whisper.

"Whatever for?" His dark eyebrows shot up and she noticed a wary look in his eyes.

"I should've thanked you for proposing to me when you heard

about my plight. But I was so upset you married me because you felt sorry for me, I just couldn't. I'm sorry I didn't show any gratitude." The words snagged in her gullet and emerged haltingly. Her apology sounded hollow. She'd wanted her thoughts to pour out with passion, but they didn't come even close to sounding heartfelt. "And I want to be a wife to you. In the full sense of the word." She could feel a hot blush climbing up her face. "I just have so much in my mind and heart that seems to be getting in the way."

He strode across the room and sat beside her, but too far away to lean over and kiss her or take her into his arms. Yet she could smell the fresh scent of soap mixed with his spicy men's cologne. Her pulse quickened. He still wore his black trousers and white shirt now unbuttoned at the collar, but he'd removed his silk waistcoat and white tie.

"I want you, Melinda, more than you can imagine—but not until you truly want me. I'm afraid you'll be intimate out of wifely duty. Nothing more. We should wait until you're really ready. I want this to bring us together, not drive us a part."

She stared at him, bewildered. "All right. We'll get to know each other better." She didn't know whether to cry or feel relief at his unexpected response.

But what if they never felt that much love?

EIGHTEEN

❦

Florrie roped Jasper into attending the afternoon reception for the Farnsworths and he didn't like it one bit. He'd forgotten about it and hadn't noticed the flurry of preparations. Footmen and maids scurried about under the supervision of Mrs. Finnegan and Mr. Grimes, setting up tables on the back veranda, fussing with linen tablecloths and china and silverware. And flowers. Lots of flowers decked the long serving tables and the small round tables that dotted the lawn near the veranda. Florrie fluttered around for a while before she apparently realized she was superfluous and disappeared to her studio, confident the staff would take care of everything as they always did. But Melinda stayed to help out, adjusting floral arrangements and offering suggestions to the army of servants.

Late in the afternoon the guests began to arrive and Florrie reappeared along with the Farnsworths and Nick. Jasper mingled just as Florrie expected him to, ate some of the chef's paté de foie gras and delicious cream cake, and called the dessert the highlight of the event. If he could manage to slip away to the Casino or at least to the Summerhill library, he'd relax. He didn't want to listen to Glynna and Stephen beg for money to finance their African mission school. Of course all of these especially invited cottagers could well afford to contribute to the poverty-stricken natives in whatever destitute country the Farnsworths were heading off to in the fall. Most of the guests would donate substantially to the mission fund and feel quite righteous and self-satisfied.

But not him. He had more pressing matters to attend to.

He glanced toward the French doors leading to the conservatory, his easiest means of escape. Then out of the corner of his eye he spotted Clayton Underwood. He was lounging against the porch rail, sipping something hot from a china cup much too delicate for his big hand. Underwood wore a wide-brimmed, high-crowned Stetson and a ridiculous pair of high-heeled, pointed-toed boots. Too bad Melinda hadn't married him and stayed out of the Bryson family.

That Philadelphia debutante, Jeannette Long, hung on his arm, gazing up at him and batting her eyelashes like a strumpet. Clayton looked his way and raised his eyebrows in a greeting. More an acknowledgment than a greeting. Surveying the crowd, Jasper didn't see Albert Underwood, Clayton's father, until the man was too close to avoid. Jasper's muscles tensed as fear spurted through him. He halted on the pebbled path edging the side of the lawn and turned to face Albert.

"Welcome to Summerhill. Glorious weather, isn't it?" Jasper asked. His face dripped perspiration, but he didn't dare wipe it.

"Yes, it's a fine day. But I didn't come here to chitchat." He glared down at Jasper. "Look here, Van Tassel. I want my twenty-five thousand back, plus the interest. I've been more than patient."

"Yes, you have, and I appreciate it," Jasper said, hating how his voice cracked. "I'll pay you every last cent as soon as I take over Bryson Steamship. It's not public knowledge, you understand, but Mr. Frederick Bryson has said clearly that he expects me to assume the presidency of the company. It's just a matter of—"

Albert shook his head. "That's poppycock, and you know it."

"No, it's quite true," Jasper insisted.

"You have one week. If you don't repay, I'll have a little talk with Frederick and see if he'd like to help you out. That would keep your name and the reputation of his company unsullied."

That would get him *fired*. "I'll have your money. Don't you worry, Mr. Underwood."

"See that you do," Albert said. He leaned close. "Because I'm not a forgiving man."

NINETEEN

❧

Melinda and Louisa poured tea, coffee, and chocolate at the veranda table until Nick came by. Melinda asked with a smile, "Would you like another cup?"

Nick shook his head. "Stephen is about to speak. Shall we go listen?"

"Why don't you, Melinda?" Louisa volunteered. "I'll stay here in case someone wants more to drink. You know how I feel about sermons during the week." A rueful grin raised the side of her mouth.

"All right. Thank you."

They followed the crowd to a grove of shade trees on the side lawn. As the Farnsworths walked toward the spot where they'd give their talk, Melinda and Nick took their seats among the rows of cottagers.

Stephen gave a short but dynamic report about the desperate conditions in Africa and the mission of the school they envisioned. As soon as applause for his speech died down, Glynna glided toward the podium. *Lord, please settle her nerves and don't let her falter*, Melinda prayed. Glynna appeared self-possessed with her head held high, shoulders squared, and a small gleam in her eyes. Melinda feared her friend's shaky legs would collapse before she arrived at the stand, but thankfully they held her upright. Lovely in a light gray frock and straw hat trimmed with a pewter band and streamers, Glynna looked at the crowd and smiled shyly. *Lord, please give her Your words to speak and the courage she needs to say them.* Glenna cleared her throat and held her audience with her sparkling eyes. Her hand barely shook as she began to talk in her sweet but surprisingly strong voice.

"I'm not used to speaking in public or soliciting funds, and I'd prefer to stand by my husband to support him. However, he thought that as a woman, I might have an important and unique perspective about our mission work. We're starting a school in southern Africa to help people who have very few teachers available to them. They're God's beloved children, just as we are. And He's asking us to extend to them what we take for granted." Glynna paused as she glanced down at her notes.

Her face relaxed. She continued on, her voice strengthening with the passion of her task. And ten minutes later when she finished, she smiled and said quietly, "Thank you so very much for listening so attentively. May God bless you." Glynna stepped over to Stephen, and the audience clapped with enthusiasm. They swarmed around the couple, buzzing like busy bees.

"They won everyone over," Melinda whispered to Nick. "I'm sure they'll receive the funds they need for the school."

"They did a fine job," he said.

"Let me speak to Glynna for just a moment." Melinda found her friend and when the crowd around her thinned, she approached. "I'm so proud of you," Melinda whispered. "You were splendid. And what's even better—you showed courage and conquered your fears."

Glynna hugged her. "Thank you. I'll admit I was terrified at first. But the Lord helped me, you know. I didn't find strength on my own."

Melinda nodded. *Just as He is helping me.* She returned to Nick's side, feeling giddy with encouragement. *Is that You, Lord? This is right, isn't it?* They walked arm in arm, away from the crowd, toward the other side of the lawn.

"Nick, have you contributed to the Farnsworths' cause yet?"

"Yes, of course. I've supported them since they first became missionaries."

She leaned a little closer. "Good. Glynna and Stephen deserve all the assistance we can give them."

He squeezed her hand. "They're two of my favorite people and completely dedicated to the Lord." He cast a sideways glance. "They're quite different from many of our friends."

Melinda chuckled. "Yes, indeed." She leaned into his side and whispered, "I suppose you're referring to ladies like Louisa Davenport."

"Perhaps," he admitted, "though I'd rather not name anyone in particular."

"I can't argue with you. Louisa is a dear, but certainly not self-less like Glynna. And I'm sorry to say I'm not so different from Louisa. I try to be a good Christian, but I can't imagine giving up everything. It's such a sacrifice. Being with the Farnsworths this summer has really made me think."

"Melinda, I'd like to speak to you privately—about us. Why don't we walk over to the rose garden?"

Her heart tripped. What was this about? "Yes, let's do that." Perhaps they could begin to draw closer and set their marriage on the right course.

BUT AS THEY made their way to the enclosed garden, Nick heard footsteps following close behind them. He glanced over her shoulder at his father's sour face and his mood plummeted. Why had he come at such an inopportune time? And Jasper followed right at his heels like a panting puppy.

Frederick's hard glance swept over Melinda and then landed on him. "I've arranged for you to meet with Blue Star tomorrow morning at ten o'clock," he said without preamble.

Nick raised a brow. The last thing he needed was his father meddling in the deal. "Why did you change the time, Father? What's wrong with meeting next week as planned? Moving it up will make us seem too anxious. They'll come in with higher expectations than ever."

Frederick dropped onto a stone bench, apparently tired. "What's that? You told me nothing about a meeting next week. And you should have consulted me in the first place before you set up the appointment."

The muscles in Nick's stomach knotted. "I did tell you. In fact we discussed all the details yesterday."

Frederick's thin face reddened. "You think you did, but I don't recall. So your memory must be faulty."

"It's not, but let's not argue about it. I'll be ready to leave within the hour." He wouldn't need too many clothes since he had a full wardrobe in New York.

"Good." His father snapped a nod. "I expect you to telephone me each day. You're to tell me every last detail of your talks. I'd like to go myself, but I don't believe I'm up for the trip."

"Trust me, Father," Nick asked, grimacing. He didn't need his father to supervise him. In fact, he hadn't needed his advice for the last several years, though he tried to accept it with good grace.

"Trust has nothing to do with it. I like to direct what's going on in my company. I expect you to stay in New York until the deal is completed, even if it takes a month or more. Don't return without Blue Star signed, sealed, and delivered."

Nick couldn't fathom staying away for anywhere near that long, especially without Melinda and Nell. If he were stuck there beyond a week, perhaps he'd invite them to join him, though Newport was far more pleasant during the summer than the hot and humid city.

"Father, you're allowing me to increase our offer from the last time, but I'm afraid it won't be nearly enough. Let me go a little higher, if necessary."

"No."

Nick sighed. "In the end we'll have to pay more than we'd really like to because the company is worth more and they know it. Blue Star has no intention of giving away their fleet. Let's be reasonable."

Frederick grunted his contempt. "You expect me to make it easy for you, don't you, boy? Well, you'd better learn to negotiate if you want to take over for me. You'd give them their asking price without batting an eye. What kind of a negotiator does that make you?" Frederick pointed his finger at him. "I'll tell you. No sort of negotiator at all. Certainly not the man who can run Bryson Steamship."

Nick pulled in a deep breath and held it until he controlled his impulse to defend himself. "I only want to pay a fair price."

"You aren't to pay one penny more of my hard-earned money than I authorized. Do you hear me?" Frederick wagged his finger. "I won't turn my company over to a weakling, even if you are my son. Show me you have what it takes." He'd obviously forgotten his threat to turn the business over to Jasper, though he'd remember soon enough.

Let's see who has what it takes, lay on the tip of Nick's tongue, but he gulped down the words, unwilling to toss away his last opportunity to succeed because of a bout of temper. He glanced at Jasper and wanted to wipe that gloating smile off his face.

"I am not a weakling, Father, and you know it." Nick steadied his voice and patted Melinda's hand, which rested in the crook of his arm. "Please excuse us. Good day."

A few years earlier Frederick Bryson never would have risked losing a company he sorely wanted by bidding too low. But the once clever businessman had lost his nerve and common sense. For one short moment Nick felt sorry for him. But his father would run Bryson Steamship right into the ground if Nick didn't gain control soon. And Jasper, if given a chance, would bankrupt it.

Nick exhaled a pent-up breath. He'd purchase the Blue Star Line for an equitable price even if he had to remain in New York until Christmas. He glanced down at Melinda as his father and Jasper departed. "Forgive me, leaving you at this time. If I had a choice . . ."

"But you don't," she said. "I understand, Nick. You need to see this deal done. One way or another. I'll be waiting, regardless of what happens."

He smiled down at her, liking the sound of those words. To him, they held promise—far more than even her vows had on their wedding day.

WITHIN THE HOUR Melinda walked beside Nick down the staircase. His luggage was already piled near the front door waiting to be loaded. "I wish you didn't have to go now," she said, trying to sound cheerful. "We don't have much time before the carriage comes around, but may I have a word with you before you leave?"

Nick nodded and led her into the sitting room. As soon as he closed the door, he wrapped his arms around her waist.

"Nick, I want to apologize for my attitude. I've been harsh with you because I felt sure you only married me to keep Nell. And maybe out of pity for my situation as well. But I've begun to understand you do have feelings for me—as I have for you." She gazed up at him, hoping for confirmation.

He squeezed her so they were practically one person. Bending over, his lips found hers, and they melted together in the most tender kiss she could ever wish for. Her heart fluttered and her breath came in shallow gasps. Nick deepened his kiss and she leaned against him for more. Hope for their future happiness seemed truly possible.

Then the *clip-clop* of horses' hooves on crushed stone sounded in a remote corner of her mind. Nick gently lifted his head, though he didn't pull away. "I'm afraid it's time to go. I'll miss you, Melinda."

"I'll miss you too, Nick."

Soon after, Nick rode off. Melinda watched his carriage disappear onto the Ocean Drive. Dejected, she wandered back to the reception, but the party was over and everyone had gone home. She went up to the nursery to play with the girls until teatime and distract herself from fresh pangs of loneliness. She'd pray for Nick's success and quick return.

THE NEXT MORNING Melinda met the architect Nick had hired to design a cottage for their ocean-front lot on Bellevue Avenue. Even though they didn't know where the Blue Star deal would leave them—in or out with Bryson Steamship—Nick had wanted her to carry on as if all would be well.

Hargrove Pennington was one of the best in the business; he'd designed many of Newport's showiest of showplaces. And after a brief pass through his portfolio, she knew his reputation was well deserved.

She glanced at the sketches and pointed to a shingled cottage design, twenty years out of style but homey in its appeal. "I like this one very much." And then a grand and glorious chateau caught her eye. It could easily rival anything she'd seen in Paris or the French countryside. "These are all remarkable, Mr. Pennington. I'm so impressed with your work. I'm partial to French, but then again this Italian villa is beautiful and quite authentic. And I also love the Tudor." She smiled ruefully. "I shall have a difficult time making a decision."

"Thank you, Mrs. Bryson. Which one do you especially favor?" Mr. Pennington asked leaning over the sketches.

"I'm not sure yet. My tastes are eclectic. I'll need to look these drawings over more carefully." For several minutes Melinda compared the exterior sketches of English manor houses, Renaissance palazzos, Spanish haciendas, and an American combination of all mansion styles that was the only frightful design in the whole group. Then she glanced through drawings of floor plans, noting the entertainment and family spaces, guest rooms, servant quarters, and the kitchen areas.

She'd rapidly advanced from a woman in need of a husband to a wealthy society matron authorized to choose the summer home of her dreams. Her change in status nearly overwhelmed her. But did the Lord truly approve of her spending so freely on herself and her family? She'd pray about it, but already a pinch of conscience diminished her enthusiasm—if only a bit.

"I believe I'm leaning toward the chateau." Disregarding her doubts about cost, she gestured toward the mansion with classical dimensions, long Palladian windows, a grand sweeping staircase, and a ballroom for four hundred and fifty people. "This one is certainly unique, but if you don't mind, Mr. Pennington, I'd like to really study these sketches. When my husband returns we'll make a decision."

The architect bowed. "As you wish, Mrs. Bryson. Please take your time. Building a cottage is a large undertaking worthy of much consideration."

"Yes, indeed," she said. "Then perhaps we can meet again the week after next and discuss more of the details." If Nick returned to Summerhill by then.

She asked Mr. Pennington several more questions before the

butler showed him out. Melinda turned back to the drawings and wondered if these cottages were a bit too grand. Maybe they should chose something more simple. Perhaps she could reduce the scale of the cottage, eliminate a few bedrooms or reduce the size of the ballroom. The architect had even included a playroom for Nell, though maybe, in the future, they'd have another baby or two to use it . . .

She looked up when Glynna peeked into the dining room.

"Looking over house plans, I see. Did Mr. Pennington create a palace or a castle for you?"

Melinda smiled. "Castles are too drafty, but he did design a miniature palace. I'm just not so sure the Lord means for me to become a queen."

Glynna laughed as she glanced through the pile of sketches. "Your architect certainly has a gift for design."

"Every one of these cottages appeals to me, but they're all too extravagant. I'm thinking of limiting the square footage."

"Good for you. Consider how much space you'll actually need to live comfortably and settle for that."

"Yes, I shall," Melinda said. "Nick is certainly spoiling me by building a summer home."

Glynna leaned forward. "I believe this is his way of expressing love. Men aren't always articulate when it comes to romantic words. I believe he's one of those husbands who has trouble saying what's in his heart."

"Yes, perhaps—but I think he might be changing. Nick does tend to *show* his affection instead of admitting it aloud."

Glynna nodded as she handed the sketches back to Melinda. "He's not very comfortable with small talk and sentimentality."

Melinda smiled. "I have noticed that. You understand him much better than I do, Glynna, even though he's my husband. I misunderstood him. Now I'm sorry I kept him away when I should've embraced him. We were going to talk about our marriage when

Mr. Bryson interrupted us. He sent Nick to New York before we were able to open our hearts to each other." She sighed. "Now we have to wait until he returns."

MELINDA READ THE girls a story and then helped them change into their favorite costumes made from fabric remnants left over from Florrie's gowns. Nanny Wells, who was quite the seamstress, designed and sewed on the Singer machine Florrie had purchased for her. The girls loved the matching frocks made for their favorite dolls. And they squealed with delight whenever she arrived with new costumes that transformed them from ordinary girls in pinafores into princesses and other fairytale characters.

Melinda and Peggy dressed the girls in chiffon gowns trimmed with bits of Alençon lace and sent them off to their pretend ball across the playroom floor.

Peggy picked up a few stray toys and placed them in the wooden toy box. "I've been meaning to talk to you, Mrs. Bryson, and Mrs. Van Tassel, too, when I see her. I've already spoken to Nanny Wells." She took a deep breath and grinned. "I'm going to get married soon."

"And who is the lucky groom?" Melinda asked. "Is it the footman?"

"Yes, indeed." Peggy giggled. "Eddie's the tall, handsome one with curly dark hair and the bluest eyes you've ever seen."

"Best wishes, of course." Melinda couldn't muster any enthusiasm for Peggy's choice of a husband. She could only picture him polishing silver candlesticks and washing the crystal chandeliers with a lazy indolence reflected in sly, narrow eyes. His exaggerated politeness veered toward mockery. That kind of attitude certainly couldn't lead to anything good. Poor Peggy.

"We've been seeing each other for several months now." Peggy glowed with happiness that Melinda hoped was warranted.

"When will your wedding take place?"

"In two weeks, ma'am. That's why I'm giving you my notice now."

"Your notice? You mean you're not staying?"

Peggy's smile stretched wider. "Eddie says I don't need to work anymore. He's come into an inheritance from his aunt, so we'll be set money-wise."

"He's going to give his notice too?" Melinda asked.

"Oh, yes, ma'am. I'll be staying on until just before the wedding. We're leaving for St. Louis directly after the ceremony. He's planning to open a dry goods store and be his own boss."

"We shall miss you." Explaining her nebulous and unfounded reservations to a woman in love was futile. But Melinda's instincts screamed that her maid ought not to marry Spriggs. If she mentioned her concerns, Peggy certainly wouldn't appreciate her candor. Even though it would hurt for a while, Melinda hoped something telling might intervene to prevent the marriage, if Spriggs wasn't as sterling a man as Peggy thought.

Melinda hid her niggling concerns beneath a small smile she hoped didn't look too grim. Truly, she'd rather see Peggy a spinster than married to a shifty-eyed lout. Melinda examined Peggy's hopeful face, shining eyes, and blissful smile. Maybe she should have a more charitable attitude toward a fellow she really didn't know.

"I'm so sorry to give such short notice, but if you'd like I can send over some dependable girls from my neighborhood for you and Nanny Wells to interview. And Mrs. Van Tassel too."

"Yes, please do. Are you from Newport?" Melinda asked.

"Yes, ma'am. I'm from the Fifth Ward." The Irish section, not far from Thames Street and the waterfront. Peggy spoke without an accent, so Melinda suspected her parents or possibly grandparents originally emigrated from Ireland.

"Would you like a reference?" Melinda offered.

"I appreciate that, ma'am—just in case I decide to go back to work someday."

"I'll do that right now," Melinda said. She returned to her bedroom and quickly wrote a glowing recommendation and sealed it in an envelope.

If one of the girls Peggy sent over for interviews was half as good with children as she was, then Melinda knew she'd be satisfied. But she couldn't help wishing Peggy would stay and send Eddie to seek his fortune, alone.

TWENTY

❧

Nick and the pudgy Mr. Stanhope toured the *SS City of York*, the flagship of the Blue Star, the largest and most magnificent ocean liner Nick had ever seen. He felt hope rising like a bubble in his chest. Acquiring the Blue Star fleet would not only save Bryson Steamship Company from falling behind the competition; it would thrust them to the front of the pack.

He'd envisioned running a company with the finest fleet on the Atlantic for several years now, even when his father had promised eventual management to Parker as oldest son. Nick had resented Frederick's choice, but not enough to object since his brother always included him on all future plans for the company. What a team they would've made—if only Parker hadn't died. He'd have loved this sleek, powerful vessel too.

Nick had been aboard other Blue Star ships during his stay in England, so he knew the rest of the fleet was equally as well designed and built as this ship. While he was enjoying the tour of the *York* immensely, he itched to get down to business, to conclude the deal and return to Summerhill. Right on the verge of accomplishing a giant step forward in business, he could taste success.

And a future without his father or Jasper at the helm. Then he could concentrate on his family while he ran a company that would truly thrive once again.

Mr. Stanhope continued his tour, commenting as they strolled down the deck. "She was built two years ago at the Harland and Wolff shipyard in Belfast. She's one of the biggest ever constructed: seven hundred feet long and seventy-five feet at the beam."

Nick nodded. He knew all the statistics of this impressive vessel—two funnels, four masts, twin propellers, a speed of sixteen knots, and accommodations for over three thousand people, including the crew. Would he ever be able to conclude negotiations and take over control?

"She cost over one million pounds to build." Mr. Stanhope narrowed an eye at Nick.

He nodded as they entered the grand salon with mirrors, gilding, and all the luxury of Europe's great palaces. For the six ships he hoped to purchase, his father had authorized an inadequate amount of money. He understood why the British company wanted far more. In fact, they'd be highly insulted by Frederick's offer. Nick's hopes faded, but he certainly wouldn't give up before he even started. Failure wasn't an option.

The representative glanced sideways at Nick. "We received another offer yesterday, and a generous one at that." From the pleased look on the man's face, Nick tended to believe him, though of course he might be exaggerating or even lying. But he certainly couldn't rely on that possibility.

"Then perhaps it's time to get down to business," Nick suggested, more than ready to discuss specifics. "We have much to settle."

Mr. Stanhope hesitated. "Will Mr. Van Tassel be joining us as we sit down to negotiate?"

"My brother-in-law? I don't understand."

"A few weeks ago Mr. Van Tassel stopped by our offices to

introduce himself as the future president of Bryson Steamship. He said we'd be dealing with him shortly."

Nick took a slow breath. "Mr. Van Tassel seems to be misinformed." Unless Frederick had promised Jasper the position but hadn't wished to tell anyone else yet. Nick felt the heat of betrayal rise through his body and settle in his face. "I am fully authorized to negotiate on behalf of the company, Mr. Stanhope. Shall we begin?"

Two and half hours later they were at an impasse. Mr. Stanhope insisted upon five hundred thousand dollars more than Frederick Bryson would pay. "That's as low as I can go, Bryson, with the other offer on the table."

Nick had only one choice—to make up the difference with his personal funds. Funds set aside for the cottage he'd promised Melinda.

"Shall we meet again tomorrow?" Mr. Stanhope asked.

"Yes, indeed. I shall present my final offer."

THE NEXT MORNING Melinda, Glynna, and Peggy took the three little girls to Bailey's Beach to play in the sand and surf. Melinda and Glynna lounged under a cabana in their black alpaca bathing costumes. Despite the wool fabric and long black stockings, a cool breeze kept them comfortable.

Melinda glanced at Glynna seated beside her on the soft sand. "I never got a chance to ask if the fund-raising for the school was successful. The cottagers seemed quite interested when you and Stephen spoke."

Glynna sighed. "To be honest, we didn't receive as much as we hoped for."

"No? I'm shocked. There's no scarcity of funds in this colony."

Glynna raked her fingers through the sand. "I have no reason to complain, because they were generous. But I'm afraid we still need more to build the size school that's so desperately needed."

"Then I shall ask Nick to contribute."

"Please don't. He's donated more than anyone else."

"Surely Florrie will have some helpful ideas. Perhaps she knows more people who might help."

Glynna shook her head. "No, I can't ask her. She's already done so much for us. Her reception really did raise quite a large amount of money. Truly, Melinda, I know the Lord will provide, but right now I'm not sure how that will happen. We're leaving next week, so I know He'll act quickly." Beneath her cheerful and confident smile Melinda suspected she felt a pinch of worry. Or more likely, she'd seen enough surprises from the Lord to know He always came through, though sometimes in unexpected ways.

"Of course He'll provide." But like Glynna, Melinda wondered how the Lord would accomplish this. He'd no doubt act through His people. She hoped they were listening.

And then an idea entered her mind—one she wanted to dismiss as silly. But the thought stuck like a barnacle to a boat. She had a valuable item that she could sell. Was she the one the Lord expected to help? She wanted to beg Him to find someone else—preferably someone who could contribute several thousand dollars they'd never miss. Surely the Lord didn't want her to sacrifice something she cherished. Or would He?

"What's the matter, Melinda?" Glynna tilted her head and peered at her.

If she admitted her plan—or the Lord's plan—Glynna would convince her she'd find some other means to fund the school. She'd never allow her to sacrifice something she treasured. And Melinda feared she'd weaken and convince herself that the Lord had some other way in mind.

"Nothing is wrong," Melinda said without conviction. She looped strands of loose hair behind her ears. So much for ridding herself of selfishness. She'd struggled to curb her appetite for possessions, and she believed she'd overcome, but obviously her flesh was still weak. Maybe she'd battle with covetousness for the rest of her life. It wasn't an encouraging thought, yet she knew deep down the Lord would stand beside her as she fought.

No, she wouldn't tell Glynna about her plan until she actually accomplished it.

WHEN THEY RETURNED home a few hours later, she found crusty old Mr. Bryson on the veranda with Jasper. For someone who wanted control of the company, Jasper didn't spend nearly as many hours working as Nick, though she had seen him in the office from time to time of late—probably to impress Nick's father with his industriousness.

"Please excuse me, Mr. Bryson," Melinda said with an apologetic smile. She knew he'd scowl when he glanced up from the chessboard. He did. "I'd like to get my blue diamond necklace from the safe and, of course, I don't have the combination."

Mr. Bryson raised one eyebrow.

"Can't you see you're interrupting?" Jasper said from across the small table.

Melinda gritted her teeth, then relaxed her mouth. It never paid to argue, especially with someone like her brother-in-law. "I am truly sorry."

"In case you've lost track of time, you have no need for jewels at this hour. I shall get them for you later this afternoon." Frederick turned back to his game, dismissing her.

"All right," she said sweetly. "Whenever it's convenient."

Melinda retrieved a Fannie Cole dime novel from her bedroom and returned to the piazza, taking a seat at the other end but directly in Mr. Bryson's sight. He couldn't forget her request if she stayed near. She hoped he wouldn't, anyway. An hour ticked by, giving time for her to reconsider her generosity toward the Farnsworths.

Lord, let me hold fast. Don't allow me to act spoiled and selfish.

But another half hour passed before Mr. Bryson and Jasper arose.

"Oh, are you still here?" Jasper asked, scrunching up his nose.

"She is, indeed." Mr. Bryson drew out a long, exasperated sigh. "Come with me, Melinda. I'll get the necklace now before luncheon."

"Thank you," she said politely.

She followed him into the library where he opened a safe hidden behind a small oil painting. He handed over the glittering necklace.

"Take good care of that. It looks like it might be worth a fortune."

"Yes, it is." At least she hoped it was as valuable as her mother and grandmother had led her to believe.

He cocked his head and narrowed his eyes to slits. "Are you sure you want to wear such valuable jewelry? You should have a replica made of paste and put the genuine one in a bank vault."

"Sound advice, sir. I'll consider it." But she knew in a few hours the necklace would no longer belong to her. A pinch of regret caused her to hesitate. What was she thinking? Why this sudden burst of altruism? She'd never worried about others before—at least to this extreme.

She knew she needed to hurry to her jewelers before she changed her mind and disappointed herself. Mr. Bryson's face displayed skepticism, as if he knew what she was up to and thoroughly disapproved. Never one to keep his opinions to himself, she feared he was gearing up to question her further.

Melinda hastened to the door. Looking over her shoulder she said, "Thank you, Mr. Bryson." And then left to the sound of his *harrumph*.

The drive to the Bellevue Avenue shops seemed to drag on forever, and her doubts increased with each mile. But when the carriage halted in front of the jewelry store, she inhaled a steadying breath and marched inside while her maid waited for her. She completed the transaction within twenty minutes, concentrating on the generous amount offered instead of how sentimental tears were welling in her eyes. They offered to make a less expensive copy of the necklace, but she declined, knowing she'd never wear it for fear someone in her set might purchase the original.

The jeweler had promised anonymity and she hoped he'd keep his word. Check in hand instead of the signature brown and beige box she usually carried out of the store, Melinda headed toward the bank. Her heart felt surprisingly light. She deposited the check in her account and wrote out another one to the Farnsworths.

Relinquishing the heirloom diamond necklace wasn't easy, but it wasn't nearly as heart wrenching as she'd anticipated.

BACK AT SUMMERHILL she found Glynna and Stephen strolling around the grounds, arm in arm. When she handed them the check, Glynna's jaw dropped open and tears glistened.

Melinda grinned at her reaction.

Glynna opened her arms wide and hugged her tight. "Thank you so very much. It is exactly what we needed to complete the school. How did you know?" Her voice shook with emotion. "And where did you get the money?"

"Well, I certainly didn't steal it," Melinda said with a sly smile. "And don't worry—I didn't ask Nick."

For a moment Glynna looked puzzled. "Tell me you didn't sell your beautiful blue diamond necklace?"

She hesitated just long enough to confirm it. "Oh, Melinda. You shouldn't have given up your grandmother's heirloom. Had I known, I would've stopped you."

Melinda almost let out a sob of joy, mixed with just a twinge of sadness. Sacrifice wasn't completely without cost, at least a small one, in this case. "I'm thrilled that I did. Your school needs the funds far more than I need a pretty bauble."

Glynna accepted that, but Melinda knew her friend didn't wish to minimize the gift and her sacrifice. It felt so wonderful to help, she found herself thinking of other things she could sell. "This was one of the only unselfish acts I've ever done in my entire life. And I'm so grateful God gave me the courage to follow through." She'd been so afraid she'd fight Him all the way to town, but instead she'd felt a sense of peace. His peace.

Stephen squeezed her hand, placed the check in his coat pocket, and disappeared into the cottage while Melinda and Glynna scrambled over the rocks to watch the tide roll in.

"I can't thank you enough." Glynna sniffed as she clutched Melinda's hand.

"Actually, I owed you that and more. You've helped me this summer, Glynna. You made me realize I needed to live my faith, not just talk about it. I'll always be thankful to you." Melinda lifted a rueful twist of her mouth. "And in other ways too."

NICK SETTLED INTO his home office in New York. The house he shared with his parents on Fifth Avenue loomed dark and lonely with a mere handful of servants left behind while the others summered in Newport. Stifling humidity seeped through the open windows without even a pleasant breeze.

He telephoned Summerhill and waited for Mr. Grimes to locate his father. Drumming his fingers on the polished mahogany desk, Nick wanted to get this discussion over with before he enjoyed a long talk with Melinda.

The line crackled. "Nick? It's Stephen. Mr. Grimes asked me to take your telephone call since he couldn't locate your father. He's gone outside to continue searching."

"Good day, Stephen. How are you and Glynna? And how are Melinda and Nell?"

"We're all fine. Glynna and Melinda are taking a walk right now. I know she misses you."

Nick's heart warmed. "I hope to speak to her as soon as I talk to my father."

"Melinda gave Glynna and me the most wonderful surprise this afternoon."

"Oh, what was that?" Nick asked.

"She sold her blue diamond necklace to help the mission school. I was shocked. Did you know about it?"

Nick took a breath. "No. It comes as a surprise to me, but I'm glad she helped." He struggled to keep his voice steady. Unfamiliar feelings welled in his chest, but he kept them in check. "She's a remarkable woman."

"Indeed, she is. And I'm sure selling an heirloom was quite a sacrifice. Glynna and I were both touched by her generosity."

"I am as well." But maybe he shouldn't have been so stunned. Melinda had prayed about overcoming her weakness toward purchasing every little thing that caught her eye. He'd doubted she could conquer years of greed—and bluntly, that's what it was— yet she had trusted the Lord to give her the strength she needed. "I'm very proud of her."

They talked a few more minutes before Stephen said, "Your father just came into the office. I'll put him on the line."

Nick gripped the receiver, stealing himself for the confrontation that lay ahead.

"Hello, Nicholas," Frederick said into the telephone. He sounded gruff, as usual. "How are you this evening? Have you concluded the negotiations yet?"

His throat dry, Nick forced out his words. "No, but I hope to tomorrow."

"Oh? What's wrong?" Nick pictured his father's jaw jutting forward and his eyes scrunched up.

"They lowered their asking price quite a bit, but not enough to accept our offer. We're about half a million dollars apart. And there's another offer on the table. I strongly suggest we meet their price. It's reasonable."

"I don't care if it's reasonable or not! I shall not pay one cent more." Nick held the receiver away from his ear and winced at the anger pouring through the telephone.

"Are you prepared to lose the Blue Star Line?" Nick asked calmly, unwilling to match his father's temper, though he was sorely tempted.

"You need to put some pressure on them, make them understand this is our final offer. Take it or leave it."

"They'll leave it, Father," Nick said in an even voice.

"We can do without their ships, then. I'll not give in to highway robbery."

Nick suppressed a grunt while tension mounted in his chest. "We *cannot* do without their liners. We must purchase them or have our own built immediately. And that will take too long. We're behind the times and if we don't keep pace with our competitors, they'll soon force us out of business. Cunard, White Star, and Inman—"

"I don't care what they do," his father shouted, then lowered his voice to a menacing hiss. "You listen to me, Nicholas. If you don't return home with Blue Star, then I shall fire you. You'll not just lose the possibility of the presidency, you'll lose your very job."

"You just said we could do without Blue Star."

"And then you changed my mind. Prove it to me you can land the deal, boy. Or be on your way."

Nick inhaled sharply. "You don't mean that, Father."

"I do indeed. Now see to it they come around."

"Of course I shall try again. I'll use my own money if I have to," Nick muttered.

Frederick guffawed. "You must want those ships badly to use your own capital. That just goes to show what a poor businessman you really are."

Nick's teeth clenched. "You're not thinking logically, Father."

"I'm perfectly lucid, though apparently you aren't. Spend your money if you wish; I shall not use a penny more of mine. I must be going. Good morning to you, Nicholas."

"It's evening, Father." Nick blew out a sigh. He felt drained from his father's threats. If he had to, he'd start his own business from scratch. Yet he'd have to begin at the very bottom. And without enough capital, he couldn't really launch a new company with any hope of success. No, the best way would be to add the funds to finalize this deal, regardless of what his father thought about it.

He could accept whatever happened, if he knew he'd offered all he could.

Frederick hung up the telephone before Nick could ask to speak to Melinda, but that was just as well since he needed to settle down before they spoke. He shouldn't vent his anger on his wife. Yet he craved hearing her voice, usually so full of good cheer and optimism.

He also needed to ask her to delay their plans to build a cottage. He dreaded the disappointment he'd cause her. But he had no other choice but to use his—make that *their*—money to purchase the Blue Star liners. He'd sleep on it and pray about it until he received an answer. Right before his meeting tomorrow he'd telephone her. He hoped that her selling her cherished necklace was indicative of a new, far-sighted Melinda who could join him in this new dream.

JASPER WANDERED OUT to the piazza and found old Frederick red-faced and sputtering to himself. It might be better to disappear while the man fumed, but as he turned to leave, Frederick spoke up.

"Sit down, Jasper. I've got some news from Nicholas. My son is so set on making the Blue Star deal work he's volunteered to use his own money to make up the difference. What do you think of that?"

The old man's white eyebrows jerked upward and Jasper couldn't tell if his father-in-law was truly angry or testing him. From the hard gleam in his eye he might be mocking him. Impossible to tell. "I suppose that's good, Mr. Bryson."

"Yes siree, that's splendid. It shows how dedicated he is to the business." Frederick slapped the hard railing for emphasis. "At first I thought him a fool, but the more I thought about it the more it dawned on me his first priority is Bryson Steamship Company. Just like mine."

Jasper nodded and did his best to appear the supportive executive, even as his hope for the presidency—and paying off his debts—sank to the pit of his acid filled stomach.

MELINDA AND GLYNNA sauntered down the path toward Summerhill as the sun began its slow descent to the sea.

When they entered the cottage, Melinda was waylaid by Stephen, a smile spreading across his face. "Your husband telephoned, Melinda. I'm sure he'd appreciate a return call from you."

She rushed to the office, contacted the operator, and waited impatiently for Nick to answer.

"Good evening, Bryson residence," said a servant.

"This is Mrs. Bryson. I'd like to speak to my husband if he's at home."

The footman replied, "I'm afraid Mr. Bryson has just left for the evening. He's having dinner with friends. May I take a message, ma'am?"

"No message. Just tell him I telephoned. Thank you."

Disappointed, she sauntered off to the nursery playroom to read bedtime stories to her three nieces.

THE NEXT MORNING she and Glynna helped the maids pack the clothing and books donated by the Calvary ladies. They filled several barrels to be shipped to the new mission school.

"Shall we stop by the nursery and visit the girls for a while?" Glynna asked when they'd completed their chore.

"Yes, I like that idea. I'd love for Nell to help me finish the

albums of her mother and me as girls. She seems to enjoy looking through the photographs. And so do I. Maybe it will help her
remember Cora better."

But when they entered the playroom, Melinda only spotted
Nanny Wells, Janet, and Julie dressing their dolls. Normally the
girls were all together like a three-leaf clover. Nell loved to play
with her cousins and had grown quite close to Julie.

"Nanny, where's Nell? We were hoping to see her for a while.
I thought she might be missing her Uncle Nick and in need of some
extra attention," Melinda said.

Nanny Wells nodded as she carefully tucked the baby dolls
into the pram. "Indeed, she is. Nell didn't want to go to the park
with her cousins and me, so I left her here with Peggy."

"Where are they now?" Melinda asked, glancing around the
room.

Nanny Wells wore a frown. "We've just returned; a coachman
said they'd gone for a carriage ride. Peggy left me a note promising
to return by nine thirty." She glanced at the mantle clock. "They
ought to be back by now." Nanny handed Melinda the slip of paper
with Peggy's brief message.

While Melinda waited for her niece's return, she read fairy
tales to Janet and Julie. But when the clock bonged ten, a twinge of
anxiety unsettled her. Where were they? Perhaps something had
delayed their return. But what?

Nanny Wells placed a reassuring hand on Melinda's arm. "I
wouldn't fret, ma'am. Peggy is very responsible and she adores
Nell. They're both fine, I'm sure."

"Of course they are. I tend to worry unnecessarily." Melinda
laughed ruefully. "I'm a new and insecure mother, I suppose."

But by eleven, when Nell and Peggy still didn't appear, Melinda
felt the first flames of fear scorch her nerves. "I'm afraid I can't sit
calmly and wait." She started for the door of the nursery. "I shall
ask if anyone knows where they've gone."

Hurrying down the staircase, she struggled to keep her apprehension in check. Once outside, she jogged toward the stable, not caring if anyone saw her. So what if someone noticed her unladylike behavior. This was an emergency—or at least it might be. Of course someone would know something pertinent, and then she'd feel foolish to have given in to panic. But her heart raced until it almost hurt. She halted in front of the stable until she calmed her breathing. She hated the constriction of a tightly laced corset that made her gasp for air. A stable boy appeared and tipped his cap. Her nose twitched from the stink of horses and horse manure. She heard neighs from inside along with the grooms' voices.

"Ask all the men to come outside please," Melinda directed. She didn't wish to get any closer to the stench than necessary.

A short time later the boy appeared with several men, coachmen, stable boys, grooms.

"Do you need a carriage, Mrs. Bryson?" a uniformed coachman asked.

"No thank you, but I do need information. Do any of you happen to know where Peggy and my niece Nell drove off to a few hours ago? They're late returning from their drive and I'm becoming somewhat concerned."

"I hitched up the gig for Peggy," said a groom, "but she didn't say where she planned to go."

"Did they drive off alone?" Melinda struggled to keep composed.

"Yes, ma'am," the groom confirmed. "Would you like me to look for them?"

Melinda nodded. "That's an excellent idea. I'd appreciate a report as soon as you finish."

None of the others had any helpful information, so Melinda thanked the men and returned to the house. No doubt she was an alarmist. At least she hoped so.

Lord, please bring them home safely and quickly. I'm growing afraid for their welfare. And please calm my heart.

Could they have gotten into some sort of carriage accident? That was always possible, though the weather was clear of fog, and traffic around the rural Ocean Drive was usually light. Or possibly they drove into town while Peggy did an errand and got waylaid.

Inside the cottage, Melinda questioned all the servants about Peggy's whereabouts, but no one knew anything. But then Mr. Grimes piped up.

"Eddie Spriggs isn't here either, ma'am. I don't have any idea where he might have gone. He didn't tell any of the other footmen, but I wouldn't be shocked if he went off for a ride with the nursemaid. Ever since he gave notice, he's felt no compunction at disappearing." The butler grimaced. "It would be just like him to sneak out without permission."

"The groom said Peggy and Nell left by themselves—although I suppose Spriggs might have met them at the end of the driveway."

The normally sedate Mr. Grimes sputtered between gritted teeth. "I should've followed my instincts and fired him the first day I saw him . . . Well, it's not important. Now."

"It might be."

"Yes, of course. I thought he might be—dishonest."

"Oh?" She knew butlers kept strict account of silver and took responsibility for the dining room, pantry, and wine cellar. Knickknacks and priceless display items found in the rest of the cottage came under the purview of the housekeeper. But certainly if Mrs. Finnegan had discovered anything suspicious about one of the footmen, she would've spoken to Mr. Grimes at once. "Did something go missing?"

He frowned. "Yes, for a short time. Let me fetch Mrs. Finnegan. She can explain."

"Yes, let's do that right now." Melinda paced the long hallway between the foyer and the back of the cottage while the butler found the housekeeper.

Mrs. Finnegan soon bustled into the foyer, looking energetic despite her age and girth. She straightened her doily cap that listed to the right side above her crooked white bun. "What can I be helping you with, Mrs. Bryson? Or is it you who wants to see me, Mr. Grimes? Me maids have been behaving, haven't they now? I've given them a good talkin' to about too much girlish silliness when they're supposed to be workin'."

Melinda explained the situation and waited for the housekeeper's response.

"Yes, I remember that well. You see, Mrs. Bryson, Nora, one of the parlor maids, noticed a small piece of bric-a-brac was missing in the drawing room. 'Twas early one evening awhile back. I started asking questions, I did, but not one of me maids claimed to know a thing. But that isn't surprising, now is it? If we have a thief among us, he or she isn't about to confess."

"So you never discovered the culprit?" Melinda asked.

Mrs. Finnegan shook her head. "No, ma'am, I'm afraid not. But the odd thing is the next mornin' Nora found the little figurine in its rightful place. How could that have happened I ask? She admitted she must have made a mistake, but she seemed mystified. She said she was sure that piece had disappeared earlier."

"It's quite odd," Melinda agreed.

"I've never heard of any thief returning something he stole. I thought Nora must be daft," Mr. Grimes added.

Mrs. Finnegan shrugged her thick shoulders. "Normally she's a sharp little thing, not like some of the flighty girls. But anyone can make a mistake, can't they now?"

They all agreed. Mrs. Grimes said, "But then I got to thinking. Spriggs often did the heavy cleaning in the drawing room, so I questioned him. He denied stealing anything, but he didn't convince me he was telling the truth."

"I'd like to speak to him when he returns," Melinda said.

"Yes, ma'am." Mr. Grimes nodded, looking troubled. He glanced toward the deserted driveway, his mouth pinched.

Melinda's fear grew as the minutes ticked by. She wandered around Summerhill and asked everyone she encountered if they'd recently seen either Nell or Peggy or Eddie. No one knew where they'd gone or when they'd return. So she strode around the grounds and prayed for the pair. *Lord, please bring them home right away. I needn't worry because I know You'll take care of them. But I'm afraid.*

By eleven thirty she felt the acid of panic corroding her stomach. She paced back and forth across her bedroom carpet, pausing to glance toward the stable in the hope of seeing the horse and buggy drive down the lane with Nell and Peggy on board. Anxiety swelled in her chest until she thought she might burst open. She had to do something to discover Nell and Peggy's whereabouts. She wished she could telephone Nick in New York, but he probably was meeting with the Blue Star people. If she left a message asking him to return her telephone call, she knew she'd alarm him. It might be better to gather some information first before she tried to contact him. He couldn't do anything in New York except fret.

But she couldn't wait patiently for Nell and Peggy to return. She headed downstairs to find Florrie in her art studio. "Nell and Peggy are late coming home from a carriage drive and I'm sick with worry."

"Oh dear. Is there something I can do to help?" Florrie put down her paintbrush.

Melinda nodded. "Do you by chance have Peggy's address on file? She once told me she came from Newport. She's moving soon. Perhaps they went to visit her family and lost track of time."

"Yes, of course," Florrie said. "It's in my top desk drawer in my sitting room. Just ask my maid to help you find it. Oh, and Mrs. Finnegan has it as well."

"Thank you," Melinda murmured.

She found Florrie's maid, Rose, fussing with the gown her mistress would wear to the ball this evening. It looked gossamer sheer with its thin overskirt, but all the ball gowns actually were heavier than they appeared.

The young woman glanced up. "May I help you, ma'am?" She asked with a curtsy.

"Yes. Mrs. Van Tassel said I could find Peggy's address in her desk."

"Peggy Nolan, the nursemaid?"

"Yes, I believe that's her name."

Melinda located the information in a book found in the drawer of Florrie's delicate, cream-colored and gilded desk. "I see her parents live on Simmons Street. Do you know where that is, Rose? I know it's the Fifth Ward, but haven't been there before."

"Yes, Mrs. Bryson. It's not far from King's Park. Go down Wellington Avenue, turn right on Marchant a block before Thames Street, and then left on Simmons. My own family lives close by."

"Oh? And do you know Peggy well?"

"Yes, quite well." Rose hung the gown in Florrie's large wardrobe.

Melinda's pulse quickened. "Would you have any idea where she might have gone with my niece?"

Rose shook her head. "I'm sorry, ma'am, but I can't even fathom a guess. She's planning to marry Eddie Spriggs, that I know, and nothing anyone said would stop her." The maid gasped and slapped her hand over her mouth. "I didn't mean to say anything bad about Eddie. I'm sure he's a nice enough fellow, once you get to know him."

Melinda merely nodded. She didn't have time to delve into Spriggs's personality faults. "You don't expect they'd run off and elope, do you?"

"No, ma'am. Peggy's parents are planning a small wedding party for them in two weeks. She's looking forward to it, so I don't think anyone, even Eddie, could persuade her to elope. And she'd never run off and disappoint her family after all the plans they'd made together."

Then perhaps it was merely a coincidence Peggy and Nell were gone at the same time as Eddie. Melinda sighed heavily. None of this made any sense.

Melinda copied the Nolans' address on a piece of Florrie's stationery and left to grab her reticule and hat from her room. On her way downstairs she met Glynna on the landing.

"Where are you going in such a rush?" her friend asked.

"I'm off to question Peggy's parents. Maybe they know where she is or why she's late." Lowering her voice to nearly a whisper, Melinda confided, "I'm so afraid she and Nell may have been in an accident or run into some sort of trouble."

Glynna wrapped her arm around her shoulder. "Don't worry. The good Lord is watching over them."

"I pray you're right. Would you and Stephen like to come with me to pay a visit to the Nolans?"

"I'd be glad to. Stephen is meeting with one of the pastors in town and won't be back until after luncheon. But I'll come. I won't have you go alone."

Grateful for the company, Melinda led the way to the stable where she found the coachman and groom she'd spoken to earlier driving up. The coachman jumped down from the gig and tipped his top hat.

"Good day. I'm sorry to report we saw neither hide nor hair of Peggy, Spriggs, or little Nell. We searched around the Ocean Drive and everywhere else we could think of. I'm sorry to disappoint you, ma'am. Have you thought of contacting the police? They might be able to help."

"I shall if I don't find them soon. Right now I'd like to take the gig."

"Wouldn't you rather I drive you, ma'am?"

"No, I'll drive myself." She and Glynna boarded the small, two-person carriage pulled by the lone horse. "We shall return within an hour or so."

Melinda took the reins and spurred the gray to a trot. They followed a familiar route toward Thames Street and the Newport harbor. She had no trouble finding the road. The small, clapboard houses, squeezed together on tiny lots, had a few adults rocking on front porches while children played hopscotch on the sidewalks. Quickly locating the Nolan house, Melinda and Glynna descended from the small carriage and climbed the steps to the porch.

A middle-aged man with a pipe clenched between his teeth sauntered across the veranda. The floorboards creaked with each step. Head tilted and eyes wide, he looked curious. "Can I help you, ma'am? Would you be lost?"

Melinda shook her head. "Are you Mr. Nolan, Peggy's father? I'm Mrs. Bryson of Summerhill. Peggy takes care of my nieces."

"How do you do, ma'am." A tiny lady who strongly resembled Peggy, except for the deep lines of age in her face, came forward from the shadows and joined the man. "Peggy Nolan is our daughter. Nothing's wrong, is there?" Alarm registered in the woman's clear blue eyes and in her thick, musical brogue.

Melinda explained the situation as the older woman waved her and Glynna onto the porch.

When Melinda finished, Mr. Nolan scratched his thick thatch of carrot red hair. "We haven't seen Peggy since last week on her afternoon off," he said.

Melinda sighed, but knew she couldn't give up before asking every possible question that crossed her mind. "Can you think of any place she might go with Nell? A friend's home perhaps? Someplace she wanted to see before she and Eddie get married and move away?"

Mrs. Nolan shook her head. "All Peggy's friends live in the neighborhood and sure as I'm standing on this porch, she wouldn't have visited them without stopping by to see us first. And I know she'd not take the little girl along."

Melinda nodded. She hated to bring up Spriggs, but she couldn't avoid mentioning him. "What about her fiancé, Eddie? Is there any chance they might have gone off together or possibly eloped?"

"Heavens no," Mrs. Nolan said. "She's not one to do anything impulsive. Peggy is a thoughtful, dutiful girl."

"Then I find all this difficult to understand," Melinda murmured.

Glynna asked, "Can you not think of any place we might continue to search for them? Someplace from her childhood, that she might wish to share with Nell? Perhaps they took an ill-traveled road and broke a wheel or the horse came up lame."

"No, not a one," Mr. Nolan said with a sad shake of his head.

"Thank you for your help," Melinda said hollowly as she started for the steps. "If Peggy doesn't return in a few hours, I shall send word to you and contact the police."

Mrs. Nolan gasped, but then nodded. "Yes, that would be best. But she's such a good girl. She'd never do anything to harm the child or put her in any kind of jeopardy. She's told me again and again how fond she is of Nell. Don't you be worrying about them. They'll turn up shortly, and with a perfectly understandable explanation."

Melinda nodded. "I know. That's why this is so puzzling. Perhaps I'm blowing this all out of proportion. Maybe they've returned home as we speak. I do hope so."

Melinda and Glynna boarded the buggy. Dejected, Melinda struggled to hide hot tears ready to stream down her cheeks. If only Nick were here; she needed his love and support, especially now. She grasped the reins when the sound of boots clattering down steps caught her attention.

"Mrs. Bryson, beggin' your pardon, but I believe I might've thought of something useful."

Melinda's heart suddenly thumped painfully. "What is that?"

Mr. Nolan leaned closer to the carriage. "My Peggy has no connections outside of Newport, but that man she's hoping to marry comes from Jamestown. Maybe his family could be of help if you can find them."

"Thank you. I'll look into it."

If Eddie and Peggy had taken Nell as far as Jamestown, there could be only one reason.

They'd kidnapped her.

TWENTY-ONE

❧

Once they got back to Summerhill, Melinda and Glynna drove straight up to the house and rushed up the veranda steps and into the foyer.

"Have they returned yet, Mr. Grimes?" Melinda asked.

The droop of the butler's jaw gave the answer before he even spoke. "I'm sorry, none of them have come back. Oh yes, Mr. Bryson telephoned from New York earlier."

Melinda nodded. "I shall try to get in touch with him."

"He said he'd be in a meeting for most of the day so he'd be hard to reach."

"Then I'll speak to his father first."

With Glynna beside her, Melinda headed out to the back veranda where she found Jasper seated beside Frederick. The rockers on his wicker chair ground into the wooden floor as he thrust back and forth. His jaw clenched.

Frederick's steely eyes focused on Melinda and she flinched. "Jasper just told me Nell is missing—possibly taken by the nursemaid and footman. Why wasn't I informed earlier?"

Melinda breathed deeply. "I was about to tell you. I didn't want to alarm you unnecessarily, but now so much time has passed . . ." She sniffed back hot tears, unwilling to break down in front of the bitter old man.

Frederick grunted. "All right. Don't start whimpering! So did you call in the police?"

Melinda shook her head. "No, not yet. But I shall, right away." Perhaps if she'd telephoned immediately, Nell would already be safe at home and the mystery solved.

Frederick shook his head. "The police are bumblers, so I'm glad you didn't call them. And we don't want the publicity. I shall hire detectives to find her."

"Yes, of course. I suppose that would be best," Melinda said, grateful he had a valid suggestion.

He nodded, obviously accepting her gratitude as his due.

"I'll make the call, Frederick," Jasper volunteered.

"Telephone Buckley and Smith. They're locals, but I've heard they're very good."

Jasper rose. "Right away, sir."

"Did you inform Nicholas yet?" the old man asked, turning his attention back to Melinda.

"No. I'd hoped Nell would be home by now. And I thought Nick needed to concentrate on the negotiations."

"He does. We shall resolve this ourselves," Mr. Bryson said.

Melinda nodded reluctantly, unsure it was the wisest course of action. She didn't wish to disrupt Nick's meeting, but he had a right to know about Nell. He'd want to know. "All right. I'll wait a short while."

Melinda's gaze shifted from Nick's father to Glynna to Stephen, but no one gave even a faint smile of reassurance. Worry etched deeply into their faces.

Glynna rose and followed Melinda out into the hallway. Keeping her voice low, she asked, "What do you plan to do?"

Melinda leaned back against the wall and shook her head.

"Dear me, I don't have the foggiest notion. I'm certainly not a detective. But I shall pray there's a good explanation and that the Lord will bring Nell home soon."

Glynna grasped Melinda's hands. "I'm praying for her as well. Don't worry. I feel sure He will take good care of Nell."

"Yes, I know. I do trust Him. But it's so hard to wait!"

Glynna abruptly sank down into one of the hall chairs. "Please excuse me. I'm feeling so tired, I think I must go and take a nap."

"You do look utterly exhausted," Melinda said, fully turning to her friend for the first time. "Are you ill?"

Her friend smiled shyly. "Not at all. Stephen and I just learned we're expecting a baby. I would've told you our good news earlier, but with Nell missing, the timing seemed all wrong."

Melinda bent down and folded her arms around Glynna in a hug. "Congratulations! That's wonderful news. I'm so happy for you."

"Thank you." Glynna rose and started for the foyer. "If you need me, don't hesitate to wake me up."

Supporting her friend's arm, Melinda helped her up the stairs, saw her to her room, and then went on to the nursery. "Nanny, perhaps you could help me go through Nell's bedroom and see if anything is missing."

Nanny nodded and together they searched the wardrobe and chest of drawers. Melinda rifled through stacks of nightgowns, ribboned and ruffled like her own and fragrant with floral sachet. Were several gone, along with socks and undergarments? Or merely with the laundress?

Nanny twisted toward Melinda, a frown deepening the lines around her mouth. "Some of her dresses and pinafores are gone. The wash was completed just yesterday. Apparently Peggy planned to take Nell on some sort of trip. But that's odd. She never mentioned it to me. I didn't see her pack. They must have had a change of plans at the last minute, but I wonder why." Nanny wiped her eyes with a linen handkerchief. "Pardon me, ma'am. I can't help myself."

"Dear me, I certainly do understand." Melinda inhaled a fortifying breath. "Is there anything you can remember that might be important?"

"No, except that footman who's sweet on her stopped by for a minute or so right before I took Janet and Julie outside. I had to shoo him away. He can be an awful pest."

"But Peggy loves him, doesn't she?"

Nanny shrugged. "So she says. I don't know what she sees in him. She must be in love with love. She couldn't possibly love the actual man."

Melinda gave a small smile. "But if they went off together why would they take Nell along?"

Nanny rested her hands on her hips. "There's no reason I can think of. Peggy is such a kind, good-hearted girl. Never one to court trouble. It's so hard to believe she'd purposely cause us so much worry."

Melinda nodded. "She's always treated Nell with such affection. I believe I'll check Peggy's bedroom to see if she left some hint of her whereabouts."

Starting for the door Melinda choked back tears swelling in her aching head. She tried to swallow the lump blocking her throat before she lost all control of her emotions. Maybe if she concentrated on finding clues to their strange disappearance she'd regain her composure. It wouldn't help Nell if she spent the day sobbing in her bedroom. She needed to think logically and not succumb to her grief.

If Nick were here he'd take charge and know exactly what to do. He'd solve the puzzle and locate their niece in a hurry. No matter how distressed he felt, he'd stay calm and steady. And then he'd act fearlessly and without hesitation. *Oh Lord, please send Nick home. I'm not doing well at all without him.*

She checked Peggy's tiny bedroom in the maids' quarters on the third floor and found most of her clothing missing, at least enough for several days. None of her uniforms or street clothes remained, though a few personal items were tucked neatly in the chest of drawers. A half-knitted winter scarf, a prayer book, and a few romance dime novels. And on the chest stood a framed photograph of her standing between her parents on their front porch. Surely she wouldn't have left this picture behind. *Peggy must be planning to return to Summerhill.* There'd be no way she'd kidnap Nell and expect to return for the rest of her personal belongings.

Melinda's spirits lifted. Of course Peggy hadn't kidnapped her beloved Nell. There was some logical explanation for their disappearance. Clattering down the steep third-floor stairs, Melinda bumped into a footman coming up.

"Excuse me, ma'am," the young man said. "I have a note for you. It was pushed under the front door and Mr. Grimes just found it." He presented a letter addressed to her on a silver salver.

Hand shaking, she took the envelope. "Thank you." She hurried to her sitting room where she could read in private. Once inside, she grabbed her letter opener and slit open the crease, stabbing her finger. No blood oozed out so she ignored the pain.

Mr. or Mrs. Bryson,

I have Nell. If you want her back safe and sound leave $50,000 in the Gull Rock tunnel on the Cliff Walk. Have it there by midnight tonight. No police or you'll never see the girl again.

Melinda's legs wobbled like tree limbs in a hurricane. She dropped into the upholstered chair by the window and sank into the thick cushions. But even their softness couldn't comfort her as she reread the message written in a bold, sloppy script. Large, black lettering looked too masculine for a woman's hand.

Eddie Spriggs penned this hideous ransom note. She hated to think that sweet Peggy Nolan was his accomplice, though she had to be involved. This would break her parents' hearts. How could the nursemaid be so callous and cruel? If guilty, she'd be sent to prison for kidnapping. Melinda shuddered at Peggy's fate, though she quickly blocked out any sympathy mounting in her heart for the young woman.

Though Melinda doubted Peggy would harm Nell, she feared Eddie Spriggs might. Certainly the note hinted at that horrid possibility.

Melinda rushed down to the office and tried to contact Nick by telephone. Impatiently she waited for him to pick up, and finally he answered. "Oh, Nick, I'm so glad you're home."

"Melinda, I've missed you. I'm home right now, but I have a meeting with Blue Star later. They want more money than my father will authorize. I can give them some of it from my personal account, but the rest will have to come from the fund I set aside for the cottage. What do you think—"

"Nick, I have something dreadful to tell you." But the connection broke up and he continued as if he hadn't heard a word.

Tears streamed down Melinda's face. "Nick, please stop talking about business. I have some awful news." She took a deep, ragged breath and explained Nell's disappearance and read the ransom demand as unemotionally and coherently as possible, struggling to keep her tears in check and her voice from choking. *I need you!* she screamed silently.

"I'll come home today," he stated. "I'll leave right away."

She knew he wouldn't listen to any objections, but she needed to try. *Lord, give me courage.* "Nick, if you need to stay, then stay. I'll find a way to cope. Your father is hiring detectives and surely they have the best chance at finding Nell."

"Do you know when they'll start to search for her?" he asked.

She sighed. "No, I don't have any of the particulars, but I assume they'll begin soon."

"Melinda, we can't rely on my father to follow through."

"Jasper telephoned the detectives himself."

"That's good, but I still need to come home and help find Nell."

"I understand." She choked down a sob. "And of course I want you here with me—so very much. But what will you do here? Pace alongside me as we await word? Promise you'll finish your negotiations tonight and then return home." Her voice trembled and tears ran down her cheeks.

Nick paused. "I'm sorry. I can't promise that. Don't worry about the ransom. I shall take care of it. I'll figure something out."

"I can deliver the money if you tell me how to get it. And please don't say I can't because I'm perfectly capable of delivering a bundle of cash."

"You're a brave woman, Melinda, but I don't want you to make another move without me. It might be dangerous."

Her voice grew soft. "Remember, Nell is my niece too. I want to help get her back."

"I understand, but let me handle this. I'll take care of the money."

He was determined to keep her out of harm's way. Melinda knew she couldn't convince Nick that she needed to take an active role. "All right." Arguing wouldn't do anyone any good. But she'd find another way to help.

"Let's hang up so I can make some calls. Keep praying, Melinda. We'll get Nell back soon."

"Yes," she said through her strangling tears. "Good-bye, Nick."

She set the receiver down. If only Nick were here! She could bear this ordeal if they struggled through it hand in hand, able to seek each other's comfort and to give comfort as well. But Nick was gone—she needed to clear her mind from paralyzing fear and think through this mystery.

Lord, please guide me as I search for Nell. Let me find her quickly and unharmed.

Hearing unfamiliar voices in the foyer, she hastened to see if the detectives had arrived. Three men in their early thirties dressed in sack suits with derbys in hand listened to Jasper. Melinda joined them, thankful the investigation would soon be underway.

"You should start with Clayton Underwood. He's the most likely suspect on my list," Jasper said, nodding firmly. "Those Underwoods are a most unsavory sort."

"Jasper, whatever would make you think Clayton is involved?" Melinda asked.

Her brother-in-law's jaw jutted. "He might very well seek revenge against you for marrying Nicholas."

Taken aback, Melinda shook her head. "Nonsense. Clayton isn't vindictive. Besides, he has a fiancée in his life, so I'm quite sure I'm not on his mind." She looked at the detectives. "Someone sent me a ransom note. I believe it must be from our footman, Eddie Spriggs. He's the most likely suspect."

Melinda handed the note to the short, squat detective with a walrus mustache who looked older than the others and acted in charge. Jasper read it over the detective's shoulder and blanched. With his gaze fastened the handwriting, he finally introduced the men to her in an offhand way.

"Oh my, ransom money. This is more serious than I realized," Jasper murmured.

"Of course it's serious, Jasper," Melinda said. "Did you think someone was playing an innocent joke on us?"

He ignored her. "I don't think Eddie Spriggs would dare do such a terrible thing. He's too cowardly. Definitely begin with Mr. Underwood."

Melinda persisted. "Jasper, Clayton has no reason to ask for money. He has plenty of his own."

"Perhaps he doesn't. He might gamble or some such thing."

"No, I doubt that. Detectives, I believe you'll waste your time with Clayton Underwood, but naturally you must decide where to begin."

Jasper added, "You might see about Nell's young nursemaid, Peggy Nolan. She's the most likely culprit aside from Underwood."

"We'll find her," the olive-skinned detective assured them with a firm nod. "Who delivered the note to Summerhill?"

The butler stepped forward. "A young boy, but he ran off before I had time to question him."

"Go after him," Jasper advised, "though I suspect he could be any one of the boys who hang out around Thames Street."

The lead detective led the others to the door. "We'll report to you just as soon as we learn something useful."

As soon as they left, Melinda headed for the stairs.

"Have you told Nicholas about the ransom demand?" Jasper asked.

"Of course," she answered as she climbed the steps.

When she arrived at her bedroom, she remembered what Peggy's father had said about Eddie Spriggs. He came from Jamestown, a small town on Conanicut Island between Newport and the Rhode Island mainland. Perhaps she should check out Eddie's family, see if they'd heard from the couple. The small tourist town of Jamestown lay only a short ferry ride away across Narragansett Bay; she could get there fast.

If only she'd thought of this sooner, the detectives could've looked into Spriggs' background first. Though Jasper thought it was more logical to start with Clayton. No matter, she'd search for clues herself.

With Glynna in a fragile condition, Melinda decided to go alone. She thought about asking her maid to accompany her, but Denise served Glynna too, so it would be unfair to take her away when she might be needed.

Although ladies seldom travelled alone, she'd ignore the rule just this one time. Only a short jaunt to Jamestown, and she'd be home in no time. She located Mrs. Finnegan in the housekeeper's office.

"So it's Eddie Spriggs you're after. I do hope you find him, ma'am. He's a sly one."

"I wish I'd thought to tell the detectives he comes from Jamestown. But perhaps I'll do some of the investigating for them and find information on Spriggs."

Mrs. Finnegan searched through the files she kept for the entire staff and found the address. "It's Bay Shores Hotel on Canonicus Avenue. He lists it as his last place of employment and residence."

Melinda wrote the information down on a scrap of paper. Just in case something delayed her, Melinda left word of her plans with Mrs. Finnegan.

"Beggin' your pardon, ma'am, I know it's not my business to be buttin' into yours, yet I worry if you might be walkin' into a nest of vipers. This could be a mite risky."

"Do you believe Eddie Spriggs is truly dangerous?" A mocking smile didn't make a man dangerous.

"Dangerous? If only I knew. But better to be safe than sorry, Mrs. Bryson. Do take care."

Melinda sent the housekeeper a patently false smile reflecting all the reassurance she didn't feel. "I shall be most careful. I don't truly expect to encounter him in Jamestown. But I'm hoping someone will give me some sort of clue." Not that she'd recognize a clue, even presented to her on a silver salver.

Anxiety flashed in the housekeeper's eyes. She bit down on her lip, but then said, "You ought to be leaving the detecting to the detectives, ma'am. But if you can't wait for them to come, do be on your guard."

Melinda headed for the door. "Don't fret, Mrs. Finnegan. I shall be as wily as a Pinkerton man."

The housekeeper's eyebrows arched and she looked skeptical. "I'll say a prayer for you, and of course for the little scamp. A long and fervent one on my knees. God bless you." Mrs. Finnegan shook her head and ambled off more slowly than usual.

Melinda donned a plain gored skirt of black serge, matching jacket, a high-necked shirtwaist, and a simple straw hat. There was no point in standing out from the crowd. She quickly left Summerhill, reticule and parasol in hand. Fear for Nell's safety swallowed up all other thoughts. Yet she refused to dwell on the horrors that might've befallen the child. The good Lord would help her find her niece.

Lord, please give me Your hope and Your tranquility. Protect Nell. By the time the carriage arrived at the pier, she felt a gentle wave of comfort that could only come from the Lord. "Thank You," she murmured, ready to proceed with her task.

With five ferry crossings per day, one was bound to leave soon. Then she noticed a large ferry chugging through the waters of the bay toward Newport. Melinda's heart raced. She'd arrive in Jamestown before she knew it. She soon boarded the large boat and left for Conanicut Island.

This was the first time Melinda could remember going anywhere by herself. Normally her mother, a friend, or her maid accompanied her, but now she was alone. And she felt quite alone. She ignored everyone who glanced her way, leaned against the railing, and watched for the town of Jamestown to come into view.

TWENTY-TWO

❧

Jasper paced in front of the office desks as he waited for the telephone operator to connect him with Nicholas in New York. An eternity later Nick came on the line.

"Yes, hello, Jasper. Any news about Nell? Have the detectives come?" Nick's voice sounded strained, but he expected as much.

"Yes, the detectives are on the job, and no, we don't have any information about Nell yet. I'll get directly to the point of my call. Melinda is falling apart. The kidnapping is more than she can bear alone. You must return to Summerhill immediately and take care of her. It's your duty."

Nick paused. "I'll return as soon as I possibly can. And I'm well aware of my duties."

"I just thought you might be more concerned with business than with your niece."

"That's insulting, Jasper."

"Sorry. I didn't mean anything by it. But I know how distracting such things can be. If you'd like, I can take your place in New York and finish up things. It would be no trouble."

"No need. I'll manage on my own." Nick's voice dripped with sarcasm.

"For goodness sake, don't snap at me. I'm merely trying to help you."

"Until I get to Newport, please try to reassure Melinda everything will be all right."

"Of course I shall. We're family, aren't we? But do hurry home. Your place is with your wife."

JASPER'S WORDS ECHOED in Nick's ears as he telephoned the Blue Star offices. "Mr. Stanhope, this is Nicholas Bryson. A family emergency has come up, so I regret I'll be unable to meet with you later today. I need to return to Newport immediately."

"I'm sorry, sir. I hope it isn't anything serious." Mr. Stanhope paused and when Nick didn't explain, he continued. "Now about our negotiations. Do you have an answer for me? Are you ready to make the purchase?"

Yes, he was more than ready. He didn't care one bit about a Newport cottage, but Melinda might. He wouldn't agree to turn over the funds until Melinda agreed to give up the cottage for the foreseeable future. He'd promised her a summer home and he wouldn't disappoint her. No matter what it cost him.

Nick cleared the lump from his throat. "I must check with someone first. I was about to ask when I became distracted by the emergency."

"Of course, Mr. Bryson. I understand. And I'm so sorry for your family crisis. But you understand another company is eager to purchase Blue Star . . ."

Nick's gut clenched. "Yes, but I hope the line will still be available when my problem is resolved. I want Blue Star very much. But at the moment my family comes first. I hope you'll understand. If you'll excuse me, Mr. Stanhope, I must leave for Rhode Island. Good day."

Nick rushed to the bank to withdraw the ransom money and then headed to the railway terminal. He arrived early in the afternoon, bought a ticket for first class, and settled into a seat beside a businessman on his way to New Haven. After a few minutes of polite small talk, Nick closed his eyes and prayed for Nell and Melinda and the success of the detectives.

Hour after hour, the train rumbled over the tracks as restlessness and anxiety burned through his stomach.

And Nick kept praying.

THE COASTLINE OF Jamestown loomed ahead. Tall clapboard hotels built across the street from the piers pushed into the bright blue sky. As soon as the ferry was tied up at its mooring, Melinda strode off and glanced around, unsure of where to go or how to proceed. She searched her reticule for the name of the hotel she'd written down, but no amount of rummaging brought forth the slip of paper. Exasperated, she stamped her foot on the dock.

What am I to do now, Lord? I've gone and lost the name!

She stared out at the water, looking about the bay. The name Bay Shore Hotel popped into her mind, like an answer from above.

Thank You, Lord. With her confidence renewed, she headed toward the row of hotels.

She lifted her chin and marched into Bay Shore's lobby, refusing to falter, despite the doubts creeping through her head. What if she couldn't locate Nell? What if she had to return to Summerhill without even a hint to her niece's whereabouts? Tears swelled in her eyes, but she blinked them back and swallowed her rising panic. Stopping at the front desk of the scarcely furnished lobby, she forced a pleasant smile. A skinny young clerk looked annoyed at the interruption.

"Good day. Perhaps you can help me. I'm looking for a man called Eddie Spriggs. Do you happen to know him or his family? He was employed here awhile ago."

The man's mouth thinned as he put down his pen. "I don't know anyone named Spriggs except for a chambermaid. Or maybe her last name is Briggs. I'm not sure. I'm sorry I can't help." He glanced down at his ledger. "If that's all, I need to return to my work."

"Would you mind checking on the maid? This is terribly important." Should she tip him for his inconvenience? Or was this part of his job?

Before she had to decide, a girl no more than sixteen or seventeen dressed in a chambermaid's black uniform came forward. "I'm Lina Spriggs, the one he's talking about. Eddie is my cousin. He works for one of them rich families in Newport. He's a footman, I think." Her lip twisted. "What's he done?"

Melinda didn't know whether to cheer she'd found her first lead or cringe at the girl's suspicions of her cousin. "I don't know if he's done anything, but I'd like to speak to him—or his friend Peggy Nolan."

The chambermaid shook her head. "I don't know any Peggy Nolan." Her eyes narrowed. "Why did you come here looking for Eddie?"

"He listed the Bay Shore Hotel as his permanent address on his job form."

She leaned against her broom. "I don't think he actually has a permanent home. He did work here once awhile ago."

"Perhaps his parents know his whereabouts," Melinda said, hoping desperately this conversation was leading somewhere besides in circles.

The girl snorted. "I doubt that. They've both been dead for the past five years. He's got a brother, but I don't know where he lives or works. Somewhere in town, I guess. He's not a friendly sort."

The tightness in Melinda's chest constricted until she could barely breath. "It's crucial that I find Eddie Spriggs." She reached for her reticule. If she had to pay this maid for information, she'd do so gladly.

The girl hesitated for a moment and then touched Melinda's hand to stop her. "No need to pay me. I don't mind telling you what I know." But Melinda slipped her a dollar. The girl shoved it into her pocket and mumbled her thanks. "Just this morning I saw someone who looked like Eddie go into one of them rental places down the way. It's called Larkspur Cottage, I think. It's fairly large, but certainly no mansion. When you leave here, go left and you'll find it set back from the road."

"Thank you." Melinda stepped closer. "So you didn't stop to talk to your cousin?" She kept her voice even, trying hard to hide her rising excitement.

The girl shook her head. "No, ma'am, me and Eddie aren't what you'd call good friends. And I can't even be sure it was him."

"Thank you again for the information. I appreciate your time."

The girl shrugged and moved on with her mop and pail.

Melinda hurried outside into the golden light of late afternoon and headed toward Larkspur Cottage. She passed several shingled houses with open porches and gables, each surrounded by a well-kept lawn. She judged these were vacation homes for middle-class families who enjoyed the shore. After trudging several blocks, she noticed the house with the sign Larkspur Cottage beside the front door. She took a steadying breath and pressed her hand against the bodice of her shirtwaist to calm her pounding heart. *Please, Lord, let Nell be here and safe.*

Would she be walking into a trap if she went straight to the door? Unable to decide the right course of action, Melinda paused. She'd come all this way; she couldn't just freeze like a statue and do nothing. Steeling herself, she strode down the flagstone walkway that cut across the grass and climbed the steps to the porch.

She peered into the front window, framed with white lace curtains, and spotted Nell curled up on the sofa next to Peggy. Nell! With a book in hand, Peggy appeared to be reading. Melinda hurriedly stepped out of sight, puzzled by the happy, domestic scene. But whatever the explanation, at least Nell seemed out of harm's way. *Thank You, Lord*, Melinda prayed silently. Her body trembled with relief, though the nightmare wouldn't end until Nell was in her arms again.

Without hesitation Melinda rang the doorbell. She only waited a few seconds before Peggy opened the door. Her face flashed a bright smile. "Good day, Mrs. Bryson. It's grand to see you! Nell's been waiting patiently. Do come in, ma'am."

Peggy stepped aside and let Melinda enter into the front hallway. As soon as she glimpsed Nell in the small parlor, Melinda rushed over and enveloped her niece in her arms. "I'm so, so happy to see you, sweetie. Thank God you're all right." The little girl looked well cared for and wore her favorite violet gingham dress with a purple bow in her hair.

Nell pressed close. "I've missed you. Why did you take so long to get here?"

"I don't understand." Melinda glanced at Peggy, who'd followed her into the parlor. "I arrived as quickly as I could."

Nell gave a small pout. "But Peggy said you'd come sooner. I've been waiting and waiting."

"What is she talking about?" Melinda asked. "Did you expect me?"

Peggy stood by the arch leading into the parlor. It was a clean, airy room painted cream with white trim. "We thought you'd arrive by noon. That's what Eddie told us. But that's all right that you're late. We've had a splendid time playing together, haven't we Nell? Would you like a cup of tea, ma'am?"

Melinda shook her head. "No, thank you. Peggy, I'm totally confused."

Peggy cocked her head. "Why is that, ma'am?"

Melinda rose and lifted her chin, facing Peggy eye to eye. "Please explain why you're in Jamestown and not at Summerhill."

Peggy tilted her head, obviously bewildered. "Of course, but beggin' your pardon, Mrs. Bryson, but are you feeling all right? You sent us here."

Melinda's eyes widened as she jumped to her feet. "I most certainly did not. Mr. Bryson and I have been worried sick about Nell ever since you kidnapped her. "

Peggy's hand flew to her mouth. "*Kidnapped her?* No, ma'am, we certainly didn't *take* her. We were following your orders." Peggy's face paled with panic. "You told Eddie we were to bring Nell to Larkspur Cottage and you'd join us directly. He said you wanted a few days of peace and quiet before Mr. Bryson returned from New York. You needed a little getaway."

Melinda paced in front of the fireplace. "I told him no such thing. In fact, I never even saw Eddie this morning."

"But he said you made a spur-of-the-moment decision to come to Jamestown and we had to leave Summerhill immediately so as not to miss the next ferry." Looking crestfallen, Peggy stared at Melinda. "Isn't that right, ma'am?"

"Not in the least. You and Eddie sneaked Nell out of Summerhill and took her here without telling anyone. I've been out of my mind with worry."

"Then why did Eddie say he was following your orders?" Peggy's voice rose with growing comprehension.

"Obviously he lied to you, Peggy. I'm sorry to have to tell you this, but he demanded ransom money for Nell's safe return."

Peggy collapsed into the nearest armchair. "No, that can't be right. You must have misunderstood. My Eddie would never kidnap Nell and lie to me about it. We're going to be married soon and start our life together in St. Louis."

"He's going to finish his life in a Rhode Island prison if I have anything to say about it."

"No, you must be mistaken, ma'am." Peggy buried her head in her hands, and her shoulders shook from a violent sob. "I'm so sorry," she murmured. "I didn't know. Oh my goodness, you must've been frantic."

Melinda sighed and then touched her arm. "It'll be all right, Peggy."

"No. Nothing will ever be right again." Peggy burst into tears and Melinda felt at a loss to console her. She patted her on the shoulder, but she knew that wouldn't help. Peggy's dream was shattered like a broken mirror and there was no way to mend it.

"There, there," Melinda said. And then she felt a jolt to her heart. "Peggy, where is Eddie now?" They had to escape before the kidnapper appeared.

Peggy looked up, startled, dried her cheeks with her hand-kerchief, and blew her nose. "Please excuse me. I don't mean to carry on so. Eddie has gone to the grocers to buy some food. He said you rented this cottage, but no cook or maid came with it."

"We need to leave, right now." Melinda glanced around the room. "Forget the things you brought with you. We can replace everything. Come . . . before he returns." She shuddered to think how Spriggs would react if he knew she'd caught on to him or found his hideaway.

"Are you sure you're right about Eddie?" Peggy's desperate eyes begged for a retraction.

Melinda wished she could admit she was uncertain about Spriggs. But she'd made no mistake. "I'm so sorry, Peggy. This must be quite a blow to you."

Peggy nodded and dabbed at her wet eyes. "Should I hire a carriage to take us to the ferry?" she asked, rising from the chair. Her face was ghostlike and her legs seemed to wobble. "Oh dear, the cottage hasn't got a telephone."

"Well, we can walk then. It won't take more than five or ten minutes," Melinda suggested. The urge to escape became so strong she could barely think of how to accomplish it. "But if he's on his way back here he might see us heading for the pier. I wonder if there are any alternate roads."

"Perhaps, but I don't know of any." Once more Peggy heaved a sob, but then she gathered her wits and stumbled toward the front door to join Melinda and Nell.

"We have to hurry," Melinda said as she opened the door. "There's no time to waste."

"Well, look who's here!" a rough, masculine voice broke in. "Clever of you to track us down." Eddie Spriggs stomped into the room, pulled a gun out of his pocket, and pointed it directly at Melinda.

She gasped as she stepped in front of Nell. The child clung to her skirt and whimpered. For a few moments Melinda thought she might faint. But she had to protect Nell from the brute that menaced them.

"What a surprise seeing you, Mrs. Bryson. And not a pleasant one." He gestured with his weapon and hard gaze. "All of you go sit on the settee."

"Eddie—" Peggy began.

"All three of you!"

Shaking, they did as they were told.

"So how did you find me?" He gave Melinda a harsh stare that sent chills down Melinda's spine. "Who knows you're here?" He dropped his bag of groceries and moved to the front window to peer out the window.

Peggy practically crumbled as she buried her head in her hands and wept. She would be no help. But her tears just made Nell cry harder. "We'll be fine, sweetheart," Melinda whispered. "Don't worry."

"Who knows you're here?" Eddie repeated in a shout, making them all jump.

"Listen to me, Eddie Spriggs," Melinda returned. "You'll pay a high price for your crime. Don't think you can get away with kidnapping."

"We'll see if I don't." With one hand Eddie closed the Venetian blinds in all the parlor windows, throwing the room into darkness. "You didn't answer my question! Who knows you're here? How'd you find me?"

Melinda tried to settle her heartbeat, but it proved futile. It beat as loudly as the banjo clock on the wall. *He might leave us behind if he believes reinforcements are on the way* . . . "Mrs. Finnegan had your Jamestown address. Someone told me at the hotel that they'd seen you here." Summoning her strength, she rose. "Now you tell me, how did you get into this cottage? Who owns it?" Her words might have been demanding, but her voice squeaked. *So much for the attempt at reestablishing authority, Melinda* . . .

Eddie shrugged. "I have no idea. My brother is the caretaker and has the key while the owners are away. He let me borrow it."

"How could you be so cruel as to kidnap my niece?" She glared at the footman, dressed in common laborer's clothing. The pain of her heart slamming against her ribcage made her think she might pass out. *Help me, Lord. Protect Nell and me. And Peggy too.*

His malicious laugh sent shivers down her back. "Sometimes a man has to make some hard choices in order to score some hard cash." He leaned back against a side table while keeping his gun pointed at the three on the settee. "Sit *down*, Mrs. Bryson."

She did as he asked, since he looked like he might strike her if she didn't. "But fifty thousand dollars in ransom, Spriggs. Surely you don't need so much."

He stayed silent for several seconds and then said quietly, "I'll put it to good use when me and Peggy leave here."

Peggy raised her chin defiantly. "I'll not go anywhere with you, Eddie Spriggs. You're a criminal of the worst kind—taking a child and then lying to me about it. And I'm supposed to be the woman you love."

"I do love you, Peggy—"

"Well, listen up, Eddie, you don't love anybody but yourself.

You won't get away with this." And then Peggy once again dissolved into tears.

The veins in Eddie's neck pulsed with anger. He rose and walked over to her. "Peggy, listen—"

"No! Never again!"

He clamped his lips shut and turned his fierce gaze upon Melinda. He leaned lower, menacing her. "You tell me who knows you're here. Right now."

"My husband," Melinda lied, looking into his eyes. "Detectives. You'll never escape. Your best chance, Eddie, is to—"

"Shut up," he seethed, standing straight again. "You're a poor liar, Mrs. Bryson." He shook his head. "And a fool woman, coming out here all alone. Lucky for me that you don't have the brains to match your beauty." He reached out and touched the underside of her chin. She wrenched away, pulling Nell closer. Peggy sobbed anew.

"I can't listen to any more female hysterics," he said. "Get up, all of you." He gestured with his gun toward the kitchen. "Get going."

They followed his command with Peggy in the lead, still whimpering. Nell clung to Melinda's skirt.

"Open that door, Peggy," he directed.

She obeyed and then looked at him, puzzled.

"Down to the cellar, the lot of you."

Melinda gasped when she saw steep steps leading into a black hole. Who knew what lived down there besides mold and mildew. Spiders, mice, rats. She shook with dread and her legs threatened to buckle. Spriggs prodded her in the back with the cold, hard muzzle of his gun. She hastened down the stairs as she continued to grip Nell's hand.

When she reached the dirt floor at the bottom, she heard another gruff, male voice with Eddie. She glanced upward. The talk stopped and a tall, well-built man who resembled Eddie clattered down the steps. Without speaking or even glancing in their direction, he looked around the cellar and strode over to the opposite wall. He retrieved coils of rope; Melinda knew what Eddie had in mind.

Eddie pounded down the stairs. "Give me that," he said to the man who she assumed was his brother. "Help me tie them up."

"No, Spriggs, let us go," Melinda said with more bravado than she felt. "The police will come and arrest you—"

"Shut up, lady," the strange man yelled as he lashed her hands together behind her back and tied her to an old rickety chair.

She watched them bind Nell and then Peggy. Fury mounted in her chest, but when Eddie stuffed a rag in her mouth and tied it around her head, she knew she'd never be able to call out. Tears of rage spilled down her face as the two men climbed upstairs and slammed the door.

Wrapped in darkness, Melinda understood her only recourse was to pray.

TWENTY-THREE

❧

Nick picked at his light supper in the dining car before the train pulled into Wickford, Rhode Island. After a short trip to Wickford Landing, they boarded a steamer to Newport and arrived an hour and a half later, right past sunset. Nick hired a driver and returned to Summerhill. Would Melinda and Nell greet him at door?

Instead Florrie met her brother in the foyer and threw her arms around him, sniffing back tears. "Welcome back."

"Is Nell home yet?" he asked, knowing the answer.

Florrie shook her head and sighed. "I'm so sorry, Nick, she's not here. I can't imagine what's going on. The detectives are out looking for her."

"Where is Melinda?"

"I suspect still in Jamestown."

"Jamestown?"

"Or maybe she's on her way home. I thought it imprudent of her to search by herself, but understood why she had to do something. I'm sure this was all just a dreadful misunderstanding."

"Why did she go to Jamestown?" he asked, barely able to keep from shouting.

"Mrs. Finnegan said she wanted to locate Eddie Spriggs's family. She thought they might know his whereabouts."

Nick closed his eyes and shook his head. "That was so rash."

Nick excused himself and asked Mr. Grimes, the butler, to find Mrs. Finnegan. *Lord, help me find both Melinda and Nell. Quickly.* This was in God's hands, not his own. The housekeeper soon chugged into the front hall, straightening her cap.

"It's a blessing you're back, sir. I haven't heard anything from your missus, though I expected to hours ago. Staying the night in Jamestown would be the most prudent thing to do, now wouldn't it, sir? But I must admit I've been a bit fretful these past hours."

He nodded. "So have I, Mrs. Finnegan. Perhaps you'd give me the address where she went?"

"I remember it's the Bay Shore Hotel. No doubt she's there now with the little one all snug in their bed." But Mrs. Finnegan didn't sound at all confident. "I'm praying for them both."

"Thank you," Nick said before climbing upstairs to their bedroom. He stared out the window as he changed, trying to think of the best way to handle the ransom and locate Melinda and Nell. Were they together now or was Nell still with her kidnapper, and Melinda out alone, still searching? Thoughts of their possible fate gripped him until he realized wallowing in grief would only paralyze him. With great effort he cleared the fears from his mind and formed a plan.

Without telephone service between Newport and Jamestown, he'd have to go in person. But first he'd check on the detectives' progress. He found his father playing chess with Jasper in the library. When he asked about the detectives, Jasper looked up.

"Everything is under control. I feel confident they'll find her soon."

Not quite so sure, Nick nodded anyway. "Let's hope so."

Frederick glanced at Nick. "I'm sorry about Nell. But you should've stayed in New York. There's nothing you can do here." His eyes narrowed. "Did you buy Blue Star?"

Nick braced himself and shook his head. "No, not yet. Nell was more important than closing the deal." When he'd telephoned Melinda earlier, he'd fully intended to ask her to postpone their cottage so he could invest his savings in the purchase of the steamship line. But Nell's kidnapping had erased all thoughts of business.

Frederick banged his fist against the table. "I gave you a job and you failed. I regret to say I'm obliged to turn over my company to Jasper. At first I thought you were foolish to put your own money into the deal, but then I reconsidered. Now I realize I was right in the first place. So I've made up my mind. No more wavering between the two of you. He'll begin tomorrow."

Jasper's face lit up like a bonfire. "That's a great honor, Mr. Bryson. I'm humbled and grateful."

"You're making the biggest mistake of your life, Father. Jasper should put his own house in order before he tackles Bryson Steamship."

Jumping up, Jasper turned a fiery look toward Nick. "How dare you!"

"I don't have time right now to explain all he's been doing, but I certainly shall after I find Nell." Nick headed for the door and heard his father's voice.

"What's he jabbering about, Jasper? Is there something I need to know?"

"Definitely not, Mr. Bryson. Perhaps we should finish our game."

Nick strode through the dimly lit house and then ran across the darkened lawn to the stable where he waited for his gig. Nick climbed onboard the two-wheeled, one-horse carriage, flicked the reins, and galloped toward the harbor. The stores on Thames Street had closed several hours earlier, but the bars were lively with plenty of music and imbibers. A few sailors stumbled down the sidewalk singing tunes off-key.

Nick drove onto the wharf where his father kept the *Olivia*.

Nick quickly roused the crew into action. Before long they cast off and set sail into the inky blue waters between Goat Island and Fort Adams. Once they passed Rose Island, the lights of the Jamestown shoreline came into view and grew brighter as they drew closer.

Nick could barely contain his impatience to get started on his search. He'd find Melinda and Nell tonight, no matter what it took. Dread kept scraping across his heart, and he clung to Mrs. Finnegan's hope that the pair might be snuggled happily in a hotel bed. *Oh Lord, let it be so.* He paced along the deck, willing the ship to go faster as it sliced through the black water. With less than three hours before midnight, he had to find Melinda and Nell in a hurry.

As soon as they pulled into the dock and secured the lines, he shoved a knife in the back of his waistband, grabbed a lantern from a hook, stepped off the steam yacht, and strode down the pier toward Canonicus Avenue where he saw the row of tall, clapboard hotels that catered to summer tourists. He walked across the empty street and entered the lobby of the Bay Shore, Jamestown's most exclusive hotel. A sleepy desk clerk greeted him with a "May I help you, sir?"

"Yes. My wife came to Jamestown today and may be staying here. Would you mind checking? Her name is Mrs. Nicholas Bryson."

The clerk studied the ledger and then shook his head. "I don't see her name. But please allow me to ask the staff if anyone has seen or heard of her."

"Thank you. And please see if anyone has seen a man named Eddie Spriggs today. He's originally from Jamestown, but he works in Newport now."

"Yes, of course, sir."

Nick paced the lobby while the clerk vanished for what seemed like an endless amount of time. When he reappeared, Nick knew from his frown he had little to tell.

"No one has seen Eddie Spriggs, but a lady came in this

morning inquiring about him. A young blonde? She didn't give her name."

A spark of hope rekindled. "I believe she may be my wife. Did anyone give her any information?"

"Yes, sir. Our morning desk clerk told me one of the maids thought she saw Spriggs go into Larkspur Cottage early today. I'm afraid that's all he knew."

"Do you know if the cottage is occupied or is it a rental?"

"It's a rental, sir. The owners usually rent by the week or the month during the summer."

Nick nodded. "Thank you. You've been most helpful. Can you point me in the direction of Larkspur Cottage?"

The clerk gave him directions and Nick took off at a fast pace. Questions rumbled through his mind. If Melinda chose to remain in Jamestown overnight, why was she staying at a rental instead of a hotel? It didn't make sense. And was Nell with her? Were they safe from Spriggs and Peggy? Or had Melinda run into the trio at the rental cottage? What if . . . He couldn't bear to imagine what might have happened if Spriggs had caught her snooping around.

He hurried by a few more hotels, strode another two blocks, and then approached a group of smaller cottages set back from the road on wide, well-kept lawns. Few were bathed in the glow of gaslight. He calculated it must be well after nine o'clock, probably closer to ten, and he suspected most of the inhabitants were already in bed. If he found his wife and niece soon, he'd wake them up, and with luck, they'd return by midnight to catch the kidnapper trying to collect his ransom at the Gull Rock Tunnel. He increased his pace to a jog.

If he found them soon, he'd have enough time to return to Newport and leave the ransom in the tunnel. If he couldn't find them, then he'd have to leave, pay the money, and hope to catch Spriggs. But what if the kidnapper held them captive?

Nick slowed down. The sign by the road said Larkspur Cottage.

His heart raced and he drew in a long breath. *Lord, show me what to do.* The bungalow stood in darkness and Nick saw little more than its outline against the black sky. Branches from a tall, heavy-limbed tree obscured most of the porch, and the leaves shook in the light breeze.

Stepping to the side of the flagstone walk, he strode softly across the grass toward the front door. He heard the hum of crickets and the wash of the sea from across the road, but no human sounds. When he glanced through the parlor window, he couldn't see a thing. Should he knock on the door and pray Melinda would answer? Something held him back. If Spriggs was keeping her captive, he shouldn't give away his presence. Trying not to make the planks creak, Nick padded to the back onto the lawn. Quietly he circled the house, glancing in every window, seeing nothing. In the darkness of the backyard he stood by the cellar doors and wondered what to do.

Then Nick took a step and his shoe struck a hoe lying across the dark yard. He tripped and slammed to the ground. As he reached out to balance himself, his hand hit the cellar window. The sound fractured the silence of the night and he winced. *Well, if they didn't know I was here, they do now . . .*

STARTLED, MELINDA AWOKE from her dazed sleep and yanked her head upright. What was that noise? Was her imagination playing a trick? How late was it? Had Eddie gone to collect his ransom and returned? Certainly Spriggs wouldn't leave them all here to die.

She heard what sounded like footsteps outside the tiny cellar window, stealthy ones, and realized that it had been the sound of splintering glass that had awakened her. She spotted a shadow in the broken window, round like a head. Someone was peering inside, but she couldn't distinguish facial features. She grunted through the rag binding her mouth, trying to shout, "Help! Come free us!" But just as in a nightmare, her words emerged muffled and unintelligible. *Please, God, help us.*

Suddenly Peggy screamed against her cloth with an animal ferocity, followed by little yelps from Nell. All together they sounded like a pack of muzzled, howling wolves, loud and desperate. Didn't the shadow at the window hear them? Didn't he care?

She heard the rattle of cellar doors and then footsteps fading away—followed by a loud crash from the front of the house. Had someone forced the door open?

The three of them stopped shouting as a lantern light cast an eerie glow on the long legs of a man now coming down the stairs. Who was it? Eddie—or *Nick?* It couldn't be . . . could it? As he reached the bottom and lifted the lantern, she moaned.

"Melinda?" Nick called tentatively. "Nell?"

"Yes, yes," she tried to scream.

He rushed forward, untied the knotted rag, pulled it from her mouth, and then loosened the lines that bound her hands so tightly. "Oh, Nick."

"Shh, I'm going to get you out of here." He immediately moved to Peggy and Nell. "Where are the men who did this?" he whispered.

"Gone. Back at any moment," she said, her voice cracking. *We have to get out of here! Fast!*

But then Nick was there, engulfing her with one powerful arm, holding Nell in his other. Kissing her. Kissing her head, her cheek. A low sound escaped him as he squeezed her in his tight embrace. She reached up and touched Nell's cheek. "It's all right, sweetheart. We're all right," she said.

"Thank you, Nick," she murmured. *And thank You, Lord.*

With his arm still around her shoulders, he rushed them all up the stairs and out onto the lawn.

"Who did this?" he growled.

"Eddie Spriggs," Melinda said, blinking back tears. "He kidnapped Nell. He told Peggy I'd join them for a short holiday. She didn't know anything about his plan."

"Where is he now?" Nick asked, turning toward Peggy.

"Probably on his way back to Newport. But it's possible he's still in Jamestown. If he is he won't let us get away."

"Don't worry about Spriggs. I'll take care of him. Let's see if we can catch him in Newport," Nick said, already leading them toward the harbor, Nell in his arms. "I sailed over in the *Olivia*. It's docked close by."

Melinda followed after Nick as fast as her shorter stride and tight corset would allow. Along the pier, lit with periodic gas lamps, she glimpsed the steam yacht rolling gently at its mooring. If only they could get to it before Eddie found them. But was he here in Jamestown or in Newport or somewhere in between? She looked around nervously. Nick was strong, but he'd be outmanned if Eddie returned with his brother.

Alert for every sight or sound that might warn of trouble, Melinda's nerves stood on end. But when they finally came to the *Olivia*, she and Peggy hastened on board, with Nick and Nell right behind. They headed for the salon and dropped into soft couches loaded with pillows. Nick handed Melinda their little girl, and Melinda cuddled her and allowed more tears to flow.

He turned to a steward. "Tea, and something to eat for these ladies."

"Right away, sir."

A whistle blew and sailors called, back and forth, releasing lines. The hum of the steam engine gained speed and she could hear the wash of gentle waves outside as they moved again toward home.

Safe at last, Melinda's tears of relief turned to a nearly heartbursting love for Nick and Nell. And for the Lord who provided for their rescue.

"Nick, I prayed you'd come for us, but I assumed you'd have to leave the rescue to the detectives."

He shook his head and for a moment he looked offended. "I understand why you might think so." He kissed the top of her head. "You two are too important to leave your fate in the hands of detectives."

She fought back tears. "Thank you." Melinda let the warmth of his affection surround her. "Nick, in all the excitement I forgot to ask you if you finally bought the steamship line."

A corner of his mouth twisted. "No, not yet."

Melinda narrowed her eyes. "I thought you were close to an agreement."

"Close, but we haven't quite finished."

"But will you return to New York?"

He nodded. "I hope to."

She reared back and assessed the sad look of his face. "What aren't you telling me, Nick? You're holding something back and I want to know what it is."

He sighed. "All right." He half smiled. "I can't resist you, my dearest." He shifted around. "Someone else is interested in the company and may buy it out from under us."

"Then why didn't you agree on a price before you left today?"

He hesitated. "Because I wanted your permission to use all our cottage money toward the purchase. It'll take every last cent I set aside."

Melinda squeezed his hands and looked him directly in the eye. "Nick, that's your savings, not mine. You certainly don't need my permission to spend your own money. Did you think I was so selfish I'd say no?"

"Actually, I thought you'd say yes. You've changed so much this summer, I felt sure you'd agree to postpone our plans for the good of the company. I hated to ask you, but I was going to anyway because I knew you'd understand the position I was in. We need those ships."

"Then why didn't you ask me?"

"I started to when we talked earlier, but the telephone connection was bad and the news about the ransom took priority. You and Nell are so much more important to me than anyone or anything else."

"Oh, Nick." Melinda threw her arms around his chest and hugged him. Tears streamed down her cheeks. "I love you so much. But I'm so sorry about the company."

"That's all right. Since you're gracious enough to postpone our cottage, I'll telephone the Blue Star representatives first thing tomorrow morning. Lord willing, we'll buy the line and finally be done with it," Nick said with a heavy sigh. "I need to go to the bridge for a while." He leaned down and tenderly kissed Melinda on her forehead and then on the lips. "I'll be on the lookout for Spriggs while we make the crossing. Try to rest, all right?"

"I shall," she promised. She glanced toward Peggy, whose eyes were closed. Nell was fast asleep at the end of the long settee. It wasn't all that late; it was only that they'd endured such dreadful things this day . . .

Melinda leaned back and let her head rest upon the rounded top of the sofa. She shut her tired eyes as Nick turned down the brass kerosene lamps to a faint glow.

But then he was back, beside her, on his knees. "I love you with all my heart," he said. "When I thought you might be in danger, I realized just how much you mean to me. I need you, Melinda—in every possible way. Please forgive me for not telling you sooner."

Melinda smiled. "I love you too, Nick. More than I can ever express in words."

He kissed her tenderly and then left the salon, but the echo of his words remained in her heart and the glow seeped into every pore of her body. She'd waited for this for so long. And even if it took such a horrible event as Nell's kidnapping, at least something wonderful came from it.

This time a voyage on the *Olivia* would signify the true beginning to their marriage.

NICK LEANED OVER Melinda and Nell, shaking them awake. "We're here," he said softly.

"Any sign of—" Melinda began.

But he shook his head grimly. No one wanted to catch Spriggs more than he, tonight. But the man hadn't been sailing back to Jamestown—they would've seen him. Chances were great he was somewhere in Newport.

They disembarked and headed back to Summerhill in the carriage Nick had left behind. When they arrived, he led them inside and rushed them all upstairs, past the weeping Mrs. Finnegan and grinning Mr. Grimes. With the help of Nanny Wells, they tucked Nell into her bed, and then he and Melinda departed the nursery.

"Stay with her, won't you?" Melinda asked Nanny Wells.

"By her side, the night through," promised the woman.

The hallway gaslight flickered dimly and they looked into each other's eyes. "You too, Melinda. Go to our bed. I'll be back as soon as I can." He bent and kissed her cheek tenderly, then heard the grandfather clock chime eleven. He turned toward the stairs.

"Nick, where are you going?" she asked, following him, wringing her hands. "Please, stay here with me."

He hesitated because he didn't want her to worry. She'd been through so much already. And he found it nearly impossible to resist her pleading gaze. "I'm going to see if Spriggs comes for the ransom." He gave her a rueful smile. "There'd be no way for me to sleep while he's still on the loose."

Hands on hips, her eyes widened. "Why don't you tell the police to pick him up at the tunnel? I promise you'll be happier if you stay at home with me."

His tempting little vixen brought a smile to his face. "I'd much rather stay, but it would be better if we caught Spriggs trying to pick up the money. And I also have a hunch . . ." He'd said more than he should have.

"A hunch about what?" she asked, touching his arm.

"I'll tell you later. I promise." He stepped away. "I really have to leave now."

She gave a playful pout. "All right. But if you're going, I'm coming along." She raised her hands as she passed him on the stairs, leading the way now. "Please don't argue," she said over her shoulder, "because it won't do any good."

"It—it could be dangerous," he sputtered. "You should stay here to rest and recover from your ordeal."

She gave a snort. "Accompanying you will be no more perilous than being captured by Eddie Spriggs."

"Nell will want you here if she awakens."

"Nanny Wells will see to her until I return."

Nick raised a brow. "Haven't you had enough adventure for one day?" he asked, eyeing the door.

"Indeed, I have. But if I can't convince you to stay, then I shall come along. And don't think you can stop me."

Nick let out a deep breath. He knew when he'd lost. "Let me check to see if the detectives are here."

Together they made their way to the library where they found his father, Jasper, and Florrie. He briefly explained the rescue.

"I'm so relieved," Florrie murmured, her hand against her chest.

"Good for you, boy," Frederick said, "I'm so very proud of you."

A sudden change of tune, but Nick had come to understand his unexpected moods and comments were all part of his dementia. "Thank you, Father. Have the detectives returned? I'd like to speak to them."

Jasper shook his head. "No, they're still out looking. We'll tell them the good news as soon as they come back."

Nick and Melinda hurried out the door.

"Where are you going?" Jasper asked, coming after them.

"To make sure Spriggs is caught," Nick answered.

"That could be dangerous," he said, stepping in front of them. "You just get your wife back safe and sound and now you'll lead her back into danger? Leave this to the professionals."

Nick stepped closer to his brother-in-law and stared down at him. "Leave my wife's well being to me. Understand?"

He pulled her around Jasper and they stopped by his office to telephone the police. After a long round of questions and answers, he and Melinda boarded the gig. She leaned into his side. "You don't truly believe this will be dangerous, do you? He had a gun, earlier."

"When Spriggs finds out he can't have the ransom and that you and Nell are safe, he'll run. He's brash, but he's not stupid. Fortunately, the police will be there to apprehend him. With luck, *after* I find out if there was someone else behind this mess."

He reveled in the warmth of her hand wrapped around his arm and her body leaning close to his. He felt an overwhelming urge to turn the carriage around before they'd even come to the end of the driveway, thinking of whisking her upstairs to their room and unpinning her silky hair . . . But he spurred the horse on, anxious to conclude this nightmare and begin his overdue honeymoon with his affairs properly set in order.

They had to hurry if they were to reach the tunnel before midnight. The ride toward Bellevue Avenue seemed endless as they drove across the town. They flew past mansions blazing with light and carriages rolling through open gates. For once he wished they were on their way to one of the dances or musicales instead of enduring this. He parked the gig on a side street nearest the entrance of the Gull Rock Tunnel on the Cliff Walk. Nick helped Melinda climb down from the carriage. He lit his lantern; Melinda grabbed his hand and moved closer, as if comforted by the warm glow. They walked in silence, broken only by the surge of the unseen waves. The sky loomed as black as mourning crepe as clouds blocked the stars and the moon. A cool wind blew off the ocean and moaned like a distant Banshee.

The tunnel loomed ahead. Nick placed the canvas bag at the opening and slowly made his way into the dark depths, searching the deep shadows. Melinda followed close behind.

She asked, "Do you think Spriggs might be hiding?" Nick took her hand and pulled her into the dankness of the long passageway.

"Hush," he whispered. "He might be near by. If we catch him in the act of picking up the bag, we'll have that much more evidence against him."

"But where are the police?"

"They'll be here shortly."

"I do hope so," she muttered.

He led her to the middle of the tunnel and leaned against the cold, stone wall. "There's something more to this, something we're missing. And I need to know what it is."

She nodded. "Tell me your suspicions. Please."

"Later. Right now we should stay quiet. I don't want to alert him we're here."

Eyes wide, she nodded again and he snuffed out the lantern light.

It had to be nearly midnight. If someone were going to appear, he'd come soon. And they'd discover if Spriggs had acted alone.

Melinda squeezed his hand and nestled closer as the minutes ticked past. He couldn't really judge how much time had elapsed, but it seemed like an eternity.

Then he heard footsteps outside the mouth of the tunnel. Every muscle in his body tensed. He strained to see if Spriggs came into view, but he could only see a shadow bending down to the bag.

Squinting, he identified the outline of the tall man. Quietly he stepped closer, untangling his fingers from Melinda's grip.

"Stay here," he whispered, "it's safer."

But as he eased his way forward he heard the swish of her skirt right behind.

He watched the hazy figure lift the bag and step away into the shadows obviously prepared to run. In three long strides Nick closed the gap between them. He grasped the back of Eddie's jacket. As Eddie broke loose and spun around, the bag slipped from his hands.

In the split second that Spriggs was distracted, Nick grabbed him.

"Be careful, Nick! He's got a gun!" Melinda screamed just as Nick noticed Eddie's hand slide toward his pocket.

With a quick thrust of his arm, Nick knocked the gun out of Eddie's grip. It flew toward the rocks and disappeared into a crevice. Nick pummeled Spriggs with his fisted hands. They both slammed against the ground and rolled toward the rocks, pounding each other as Spriggs yelled obscenities. Breathing heavily, Nick pulled the footman to his feet.

"Did someone pay you to kidnap Nell? Who was it?" Nick yelled, tightening his grip.

"It was all Mr. Van Tassel's idea, not mine. Blame him, not me."

"And I suppose he insisted you ask for a ransom," Melinda said.

When Spriggs hesitated, Nick knew the money was purely the footman's idea. "Well, you're not getting a cent of my money."

"That's what you think." Spriggs twisted his arms out of Nick's grip and shoved him hard.

Nick tilted backward but regained his balance before he fell onto the rocks. As Eddie lunged back up the hill for the bag, Nick tackled him. The two traded punches, falling to the ground, rolling over and over again, growing closer and closer to the edge of the walk.

MELINDA WATCHED IN horror as they edged closer to where the rocks met the sea, fifteen feet below. "Stop, both of you!" she cried. "Nick! Be careful!"

But they weren't listening. A second later the pair tumbled off and disappeared into the sea. Melinda heard Spriggs scream as she stumbled over the jagged boulders to the edge. A stampede of footsteps caught her attention and she glanced back toward the sound. Several uniformed policemen swarmed down the Cliff Walk and then over the rocks.

"We'll fetch them," one of the policemen shouted to Melinda. Two others ran to the edge of the boulders and jumped in.

Melinda stood by the edge shaking, barely able to see the men flailing in the water. But she heard screams and the crash of waves. A stiffening breeze whipped her skirt around her legs and whistled in her ears. Endless minutes seemed to tick by until Nick emerged from the sea, sputtering water. Hoisting himself on the rocks, he paused for several seconds to catch his breath, then stumbled over to Melinda.

She folded him into her arms, ignoring his cold, wet clothes. They clung together, shivering. Tears streamed down her face. What if he'd fallen to his death?

Then she spotted two policemen pushing Spriggs onto the rough boulders. He coughed hard as he was tossed to safety.

A policeman standing nearby said, "We'll haul him off to jail."

"He admitted my brother-in-law, Jasper Van Tassel, hired him to kidnap my niece."

"Do you believe him, sir?" the man asked, apparently surprised.

"I'm afraid so." Nick related the story and the policeman nodded.

"Two of our men will follow you to Summerhill, Mr. Bryson."

Once they started down the dark path toward the road where they'd parked their carriage, Melinda murmured, "Why would Jasper do such a despicable thing?"

Nick shrugged. "We'll find out. But I suppose it was desperation. He thought his only way out was to take control of Bryson Steamship. He probably thought I would bungle the deal or leave it behind in my rush to take care of Nell—which might very well have happened."

Melinda shivered. "I dislike Jasper. But I never thought him capable of such a horror. What a terrible blow this will be for Florrie and the girls."

"Yes. For our whole family, really." Nick walked beside her with the canvas bag tucked securely under his arm.

On the way home, Melinda nestled next to Nick, appreciating the warmth of his arm around her shoulders. She stared up into the velvety sky and the thousands of stars. Stars. *Blue Star.*

"Nick, I want to thank you again for putting me ahead of the most important business deal of your career. It means so much."

He leaned over and kissed her. Knowing there were more kisses to come, she enjoyed the tingle that swirled through her. "I'm grateful too, Melinda. You were willing to sacrifice your cottage for Bryson Steamship."

Melinda laughed. "I'm happy to help."

"I should've put you and Nell in first place long before today." He squeezed her hand. "I think I had to learn how precious you two truly are. I shall always put you first in my life, Melinda, to truly cleave with you, as God asks. I'm sorry it took me so long to acknowledge I love you."

"Mmm, you don't know how long I waited to hear it," she said, reliving his beautiful declaration.

He smiled a sheepish grin. "I shall try to be more verbal in the future. And tell you how much I love you over and over again."

Melinda laughed. "I love you too, Nick, with all my heart. And from now on we shall both cleave tight, just as the Lord intended."

THE CARRIAGE TURNED down Summerhill's driveway. They disembarked in front of the cottage and strolled inside, arm in arm.

He asked the policemen to give him a few minutes to prepare his family. "I'll call if we run into any trouble with Jasper."

"We'll be right here, sir."

He and Melinda reluctantly climbed the stairs, feeling the weight of what was to come.

"Did you have to fish the kidnapper from the sea?" Stephen asked with a smile when he saw him.

Nick handed the butler his bowler. "In a way." He glanced at Jasper and then to his sister, so sorry he had to be the one to tell her.

Florrie was wringing her hands. "Nicholas, tell me the truth. Was Jasper involved in some way?" She grabbed hold of the staircase banister.

Jasper bristled. "Of course I wasn't. How could you think that?" He reached for Florrie's hand, but she brushed him off. His ruddy complexion deepened to a hot pink color.

"I want to know," she said in a scratchy voice. "Tell me."

Nick wrapped his arm around his sister's shoulder and eyed his brother-in-law. "Florrie, I'm afraid Jasper paid Eddie Spriggs to kidnap Nell. When we caught him, he implicated Jasper."

"I don't understand." But from the look in her eyes he knew she believed him.

Nick continued. "Jasper knew Nell's kidnapping would distract me and I'd come running home before I finished the Blue Star deal. And he was right. That would anger Father so much he'd turn the presidency over to Jasper. Father did just that."

"Jasper, why are you suddenly so ambitious?" Florrie asked, staring at her husband. "You never particularly cared for business until recently."

Nick explained. "He owes a fortune to creditors. From bad investments and gambling debts. He wanted to control Bryson Steamship Company so he'd have a free hand with the finances."

Florrie nodded slowly, then turned to Jasper, her eyes ablaze. "And that's why you wanted us to adopt Nell. You wanted full control of her trust fund money." She buried her face in her hands and sobbed into Nick's chest.

"Now see here," Jasper objected without his usual bluster.

"You're fired," Frederick bellowed. "I shall see to it you spend many years in jail. It'll cause a scandal, but it will be your scandal, not ours."

"The police are outside," Nick said, moving to the door. "They want to talk to you, Jasper."

In moments, Jasper was led outside.

Florrie sighed heavily as the door closed behind him. "This will be hard on the girls and on me. But we'll manage to weather the disgrace somehow."

Melinda touched her arm. "We'll help in any way we can."

"Thank you. Now I think I'll go upstairs to bed," Florrie said. Shoulders hunched, she slowly climbed the stairs.

Nick helped her to her room and then came right back down to the group. His father, folded into a chair by the wall, looked shrunken and ten years older.

"This is a terrible blow." He glanced up, his eyes glazed. "You must take over the company, Nicholas. I don't have the energy or the will to continue any longer. It's been getting harder and harder lately. And now this. I shall rely on you to make Bryson Steamship prosper."

"Yes, Father, I'd be honored to take over. And don't worry; I'll see us through."

His father rose and shuffled off toward the library. "I believe I shall have a drink before I retire. Would anyone care to join me?"

They all declined.

"We should retire too," Stephen said, glancing at Glynna.

Glynna nodded. "I quite agree. It's been a very long day."

After they disappeared up the stairs, Nick turned to Melinda and encircled her with his arms. "Come closer, Mrs. Bryson. Shall we start our married life with a kiss?"

Before she had a chance to accept, he drew her close, lifted her chin, and gazed into her wide eyes. Bending over he tenderly eased his mouth to her warm lips. He tasted the sweetness of her mouth and wished for so much more. All the events of the day faded away. But moments later she stepped back, a smile still clinging to her mouth.

"That was wonderful," she murmured. "But there's no point in lingering in the foyer when we have a bed upstairs," she said with a welcoming smile.

"Now that's the best suggestion I've heard in a long time." He took her small, smooth hand in his and led her up the steps. "I love you so much, Melinda."

As they ascended, she leaned into him and said quietly, "I love you too, Nick. And I'd like to show you just how much."

ACKNOWLEDGMENTS

❧

A novel is a collaboration of so many people, not just the work of the author. I'd like to thank all the Thomas Nelson staff for giving me so much support and encouragement. They're true professionals with the personal touch. I'd particularly like to thank my editors, Natalie Hanemann and Lisa T. Bergren, who helped turn a story into a real novel. Their talent and dedication is amazing. My appreciate also goes to my wonderful agent, Karen Solem.

A very special thanks to Lorraine ZuWallack, RN, for patiently answering countless medical questions about turn-of-the-century diseases and treatments. We've been close friends for nearly fifty years and I hope we'll continue to be for the rest of our lives!

Thank you to Sherry Chancellor, a Pensacola, Florida, attorney and fellow writer, who answered all my legal questions. Her expertise helped me narrow down my plot possibilities until I found the right one for this book.

As always, my Seeker sisters kept me motivated and laughing. I'd feel so isolated without you ladies! Thank you for brainstorming when I ran out of ideas. Your brilliant ideas could fill dozens of books and I imagine they probably will.

Thank you to my husband, Jim, for your ongoing support and encouragement. I'd never have time to write without your help.

Last but not least, I'd like to thank my writer friends, Fran McNabb and Janet Jones Bann, who cheer me on every step of the way.

READING GROUP GUIDE

1. When Melinda was a teenager, her father lost his fortune. Even though he regained it, she was deeply affected by the experience. How do you think that traumatic event influenced her future? Do you think that justifies her plan to marry for reasons other than love?

2. Should Melinda have confessed her financial situation to Nick before they married? Or do you think it was none of Nick's concern? Unlike Melinda, would you be willing to take the chance of losing your fiancé?

3. Should Melinda have been more understanding of Nick's workaholic tendencies, or should she have understood he was under a lot of pressure from his father? Why didn't Nick automatically put Melinda and Nell first in his life?

4. If Glynna hadn't influenced Melinda to curb her materialism, do you think she would've done so on her own? In what ways did following 'the Book' make a difference in Melinda's attitude?

5. Melinda and Nick had different ways of expressing love. Do you think men and women often tend to show their love for each other differently, or do you think it just depends on the individual?

6. Why was it so hard for Melinda to sacrifice her possessions for the greater good of someone else? How did Glynna convince her to become a more selfless person?

7. Do you think Melinda and Nick should have married for Nell's sake even though they weren't in love? Do you think people ever marry or stay together for the children's welfare in the twenty-first century? Is it a good idea?

8. Why did Nick find it so difficult to tell Melinda he loved her?

9. With society exerting such powerful pressure on all the characters, do you think Melinda and Jasper could have solved their problems without resorting to such extreme measures? How?

10. In what ways did money or the lack of it influence the behavior of both the servants and the cottagers?

11. Do you think Nick should have confronted his father earlier? Why didn't he?